## Praise for Sarah L[...]

"In *These Tangled Threads*, author Sarah Loudin Thomas delves into the history of the famous Biltmore House and the industries once supported there of weaving, woodworking, and more. The history is fascinating, but the characters and the challenges they face are what make this story one to remember."

Ann H. Gabhart, bestselling author
of *In the Shadow of the River*

"This book [*These Tangled Threads*] is my new favorite! So many great stories woven together to create an even greater story, one we all can relate to, and the Vanderbilt stories are done beautifully with respect and authenticity."

Cathy Barnhardt, Biltmore Floral Displays Manager,
Retired

"Sarah Loudin Thomas never disappoints! *The Finder of Forgotten Things* brings together a rich cast of characters, each at war with conflicting desires and ultimately destined to decide whether, even in the worst events, redemption waits to be discovered."

Lisa Wingate, *New York Times* bestselling author
of *The Book of Lost Friends*

"Thomas returns with an uplifting novel that strikes all the high points of redemptive love and coming of age within a historical murder mystery."

*Booklist* starred review of *When Silence Sings*

"Complex characters wrestle with justice, mercy, inequality, honesty, and the fact that they are all prodigals still searching for the way home. Sarah Loudin Thomas delivers a stunning tale . . . underlined with a moral imperative to love one's neighbor that still hits home today."

"Sarah Loudin Thomas introduces a multifaceted cast in this strong historical."

"Wonderful, simply wonderful. A story of love, healing, and forgiveness sure to grip the heart of every reader."

"Splendid. *Miracle in a Dry Season* is genuine and heartfelt with just a touch of the Divine. It's a story of forgiveness and reckoning and realizing that love does cover a multitude of sins. Thomas will be a go-to author."

"Nobody brings Appalachian stories to life better than Sarah Loudin Thomas. From the first word to the last, *The Finder of Forgotten Things* delivers an emotional page-turner that will stick with readers long after they close the book."

# THESE
# TANGLED
# THREADS

# THESE
# TANGLED
# THREADS

A NOVEL *of* BILTMORE

## SARAH LOUDIN THOMAS

BETHANYHOUSE
a division of Baker Publishing Group
Minneapolis, Minnesota

Published by Bethany House Publishers
Minneapolis, Minnesota
BethanyHouse.com

Bethany House Publishers is a division of
Baker Publishing Group, Grand Rapids, Michigan

Printed in the United States of America

Library of Congress Cataloging-in-Publication Data
Names: Thomas, Sarah Loudin, author.
Title: These tangled threads : a novel of Biltmore / Sarah Loudin Thomas.
Description: Minneapolis : Bethany House, a division of Baker Publishing Group, 2024.
Identifiers: LCCN 2023051045 | ISBN 9780764242014 (paperback) | ISBN 9780764242861 (casebound) | ISBN 9781493445295 (ebook)
Subjects: LCGFT: Christian fiction. | Novels.
Classification: LCC PS3620.H64226 T44 2024 | DDC 813/.6—dc23/eng/20231031
LC record available at https://lccn.loc.gov/2023051045

Unless otherwise indicated, Scripture quotations are from the King James Version of the Bible.

Scripture quotations labeled NIV are from THE HOLY BIBLE, NEW INTERNATIONAL VERSION®, NIV® Copyright © 1973, 1978, 1984, 2011 by Biblica, Inc.® Used by permission. All rights reserved worldwide.

Cover design by Kathleen Lynch/Black Kat Design

Author is represented by Books & Such Literary Agency.

Baker Publishing Group publications use paper produced from sustainable forestry practices and postconsumer waste whenever possible.

24  25  26  27  28  29  30       7  6  5  4  3  2  1

*For Becka, Mariah, Megan, Scott, Sean,*

and for all the kids like them who are trying
to make the best of an impossible situation
and often succeeding.

The gem cannot be polished without friction,
nor man perfected without trials.

*—Dutch proverb inscribed*
*on a fireplace stone, Grove Park Inn*

# *Prologue*

·······························

# ARTHUR

**ELKINS, WEST VIRGINIA**
**1897**

Arthur stilled his hands the moment the slim, mustached man stepped into the sunlit room and asked to see Reverend Swope. He felt his breathing slow as the man's dark eyes swept the simple space. Arthur had the sense their visitor planned to describe what he saw in detail later. When that warm, interested gaze landed on him, Arthur quivered like a rabbit in the shadows. He tucked his newly braced foot further under his chair.

The man moved closer, his steps unhurried. He picked up the deer Arthur had finished carving the day before and held it to the light. Arthur clutched the block in his hand more tightly. It would soon be a fawn to pair with its mother.

The man turned the small figure over and over before looking at Arthur once again. "This is fine work. Are you the artist?" Arthur cleared his throat but only nodded, gripping the penknife so tightly his fingers felt numb. "How old are you?"

Arthur wet his lips. "I'll be nine soon enough, sir."

The man's eyes crinkled. "Impressive."

A door opened, and Reverend Swope stepped into the room. "Mr. Vanderbilt. What a pleasure to have you visit us today."

The man—Mr. Vanderbilt—turned to greet Arthur's guardian. "Thank you for meeting with me on such short notice. As I mentioned in my letter, I have an exciting opportunity I'd like to discuss with you."

Reverend Swope, always cheerful, grinned even wider. "Indeed, indeed. Only too happy!" He looked over Mr. Vanderbilt's shoulder and winked at Arthur. "No time like the present."

As the door closed softly behind the two men, Arthur realized Mr. Vanderbilt had not returned his carving.

1

# LORNA

"It must be——" Ellen Harshaw closed her eyes and kissed her fingertips, her shoulders dropping as she exhaled and flung her hand wide—"*exquisite*. Yes, that's the only word for it. Edith has carried your homespun fabrics to the height of fashion, and this gift for Cornelia . . ." She trailed off, shaking her head. "I trust you can create something exceptional. Perhaps like you did for her twenty-first birthday party?"

Lorna tucked her hands behind her back and forced a smile. "Absolutely. I'll begin sketching out the design immediately."

Mrs. Harshaw gave Lorna a sidelong look. "And don't tell anyone. I'm sure the engagement won't be announced for *ages*. But I have it on excellent authority that there will be a wedding within the year. Even as early as next spring." She simpered. "I'd name the groom, but that would be telling, wouldn't it?" She stood and tugged her gloves into place. "I absolutely must take advantage of what I've been hearing to have the most unique gift for the newlyweds. And for heaven's sake, not a *plaid*." She wrinkled her nose. "Plaids are so common."

Lorna nodded. Of course, plaids weren't the least bit common if you really understood what the patterns meant or how challenging they were to weave. But Lorna supposed Mrs. Harshaw wanted something showier that would make her gift stand out among what was sure to be an ostentatious display of silver, crystal, and even jewels at the society wedding of the year if not the decade.

Lorna had met Cornelia, Biltmore Estate's heiress, on several occasions. When they were both youngsters, Tarheel Nell, as the locals called her, was often a visitor to Biltmore Estate Industries, where Lorna had first learned to weave. She'd even spoken to her on her birthday two years earlier when Lorna had mistakenly counted herself lucky to supply those blasted curtains that were coming back to haunt her now.

Of course, Lorna didn't really know Cornelia, who was three years her junior and a thousand miles her social superior. No matter that she had laughed and played with the village children once upon a time. Now Mrs. Harshaw seemed confident that she was about to become engaged at the age of twenty-three. Her father wouldn't be there to walk her down the aisle, which was a sadness Lorna understood. Keenly.

"Can you give me a hint?" Mrs. Harshaw cooed, interrupting Lorna's thoughts.

"A hint?" Lorna blinked. "Oh. As to the design?" She shook off her reverie and gave her customer a wide-eyed look. "I might let you have a peek once I'm further along. But for now, you'll just have to trust that I will create a design unlike any you've seen before."

"Wonderful!" Mrs. Harshaw stood and tucked her bag

under her arm. "And remember, the cost is of no consequence." She tossed her head and laughed. "Use gold thread if you like! Just be certain the end result is utterly unique." She leaned close and lowered her voice. "It should be fit for *royalty*."

Lorna walked the older woman out to her waiting driver and waved her off with a confident smile. She watched the car disappear down the mountain. When she returned to her desk, Mr. Tompkins, her supervisor, stood there, tapping his toe. "Can you deliver on that promise you just made?"

Lorna swallowed, her mouth suddenly dry. "Of course I can," she said lightly.

He pinched his lips. "Really? Because it's been quite some time since you produced anything even close to what that woman will be expecting." He narrowed his eyes and stabbed the desk with his finger. "And if you fail, I feel confident your time here will be at an end. I know some people go so far as to credit your early designs with helping to save the company, but it's been nearly two years since your last release."

Lorna hoped he didn't see her flinch. Mr. Tompkins had been hinting for months that the administrative work she handled could be done by someone younger and less skilled just as well for less money. She suspected the only reason she was still employed was because Mr. Seely had a soft spot for her. And because she was always willing to step in and help with weaving and training to keep production on schedule. There were rumors that the business was, once again, flagging as it had been when Mrs. Vanderbilt sold it in 1917.

She lifted her chin and looked down her nose at Mr. Tompkins. "Prepare to be astonished," she said. He harrumphed and left the room.

Lorna slumped into her chair and resisted the urge to bury her face in her hands. She had just promised the impossible.

She hadn't had an original idea for a fabric design in years. Once upon a time—when she was first starting out—she'd had a few ideas that shone. When she first learned about open work, she'd pulled off a handful of patterns that were applauded. But they'd ultimately been deemed too complicated and phased out of production. As the years rolled by and her focus turned to training others, she'd rarely even tried to come up with something original. There was just so much to do . . .

Now the fabulous designs she'd "borrowed" from Gentry were long gone. Technical skill wouldn't be enough this time around. How would she ever deliver on this impossible task? She suspected that more than her own employment depended on her coming through. Mrs. Harshaw could spur sales among other ladies in her set and boost their business overall. If Biltmore Industries failed, it would affect nearly one hundred workers.

For a moment, Lorna felt nostalgic for the "old days" when the business had been supported by the Vanderbilts and the focus had been on training unschooled Appalachian youth in viable trades. Once, eight looms had seemed like an overabundance. Now the weaving house was lined with dozens of looms, many of them operated by men. Lorna sometimes wondered if she should give up and move on. But no. She could still contribute. She could still be part of ensuring that Biltmore Industries was around for a long time to come.

For the first time in years, she thought about Gentry and wondered where the girl with the wild imagination and natural instinct for design might be.

· . ˙ ˙ · · . . · ·

Lorna strolled through the dappled shade at the weekly market on the lawn of the Cathedral of All Souls in Biltmore

Village. She wasn't paying much attention to the wares for sale. She'd just needed to get away from her office, away from the weaving room. If only she could get out of her own head as easily.

"Miss Blankenship!" Lorna turned and slowed her pace. A young woman caught up to her. "Miss Blankenship, I thought that was you." The girl tried to calm her breathing and laid a hand on Lorna's arm. "I hope this isn't too much of an imposition, but I wanted to show you something."

"Not at all," Lorna said, slipping her mask of professionalism back into place. The girl looked familiar, but she couldn't place her. "I'd be delighted to see your wares."

"Oh, it's not mine," the girl said with a blush as she steered Lorna toward a table tucked against the wall of the church. "It's just that I know you're the best weaver in all of Asheville, maybe in all of North Carolina"—Lorna allowed a faint smile at the praise—"and I knew you'd be interested." The girl faltered. "Well, I thought you would be. Of course, my eye isn't as good as yours, but this cloth . . ." She finally let her words spin out.

"What's your name?" Lorna asked.

"I'm Bernice Collins. I've been working in the weaving room for about six months." She ducked her head. "I haven't worked with you directly but I know who you are."

"I'm glad you're taking your training seriously enough to examine the work of others," Lorna said, patting her hand. "Now, show me what you've found." She tried to mask her weariness. The last thing she wanted to do was examine some inferior homespun produced in who knew what backwoods holler. While the traditional fabric had certainly started on small homesteads, where women did everything from shearing the sheep to spinning the thread to weaving the rough cloth, what they made at Biltmore Industries was finer and of a much higher quality. She'd make short work of this and then slip inside the church where she might find a moment's privacy and stillness.

"See?" Bernice lifted a shawl from a table that mostly offered squash, eggs, and some coarse knitted items. She held the garment out as if it were an offering. Lorna blinked. Then she stretched out her own hand to take the fabric. It was soft—luxurious even—and the pattern was perfect. The finely rendered plaid in the colors of autumn showed crisp definition while still blending and flowing together in a way that gave it a softness and subtlety she'd rarely seen before. For just a moment, despite the heat and humidity of the August day, she felt the bite of an autumn morning and smelled the earthy, tobacco scent of fallen leaves.

If Mrs. Harshaw could see this, she just might change her mind about plaid.

Lorna turned to the woman standing behind the table. "Did you make this?"

"Why do ye need to know?" she said with a scowl. "If ye like it well enough, buy it."

Lorna pulled out her purse, and the woman stuck out a gnarled hand. Fishing out some coins, Lorna eyed the woman. "What if I wanted more like this? Do you have others?"

"Could be. But I ain't got 'em today."

Lorna extended her hand but didn't release the coins. "Perhaps I could visit the weaver to buy other cloth directly."

"Oh, aye, and leave me out of it." The woman snatched Lorna's money. "I'm not the one makin' the cloth, but if you want more, you'll have to talk to me."

Lorna felt frustration bubble. If the weaver, clearly highly skilled, had other designs, perhaps she—or he for that matter—could be persuaded to share a unique design with Lorna. Otherwise, she was going to be hard-pressed to satisfy Mrs. Harshaw. She thought quickly. "Tell the weaver I'd like the finest piece of cloth she has." The woman's expression suggested her guess that the weaver was a woman had been correct.

"Might need a few coins to persuade her to part with her finest," the woman said in a wheedling voice.

Lorna tamped down her irritation. She fished out another coin and handed it over. "When can you bring it to me?"

The woman snorted. "Don't come to town but for market. I'll be back next week with yer pretty piece."

"Very well," Lorna snapped. She could wait a week if it meant saving her reputation. "I'll look forward to seeing what she sends." The woman grunted and turned to another customer.

Bernice tugged on Lorna's sleeve. She'd forgotten about the girl. "It really is very fine, isn't it?" she asked. "Will you try to make something like it?"

Lorna smiled mechanically and pushed the shawl into the bottom of her basket. It would never do for word to get around that she was getting her ideas from other weavers. "I suppose it might provide inspiration," she said with an airy wave. "But my drafts are all my own."

Bernice smiled and nodded with a movement bordering on a curtsy before she scurried back to the Biltmore Industries table with its tea towels and carved bowls. Lorna stared after her, not really seeing the market or the people. She'd just uttered the biggest lie of her life. A lie that grew bigger every day she wove one of the patterns she called her own. Because the truth was, none of them were.

2

# GENTRY

BILTMORE VILLAGE
ASHEVILLE, NORTH CAROLINA
DECEMBER 1915

Gentry watched, mesmerized, as the thread flew between Lorna's fingers. Was she guiding it, or was it unfurling from her fingertips the way a spider spins a web? It was as if the filament were part of who and what she was.

Gentry thrilled to see the fabric coming to life on the older girl's loom. The colors shimmered as though they had a story to tell. And in wanting to learn that story, Gentry forgot for a moment how much she didn't want to be in this place. She hadn't wanted to come to Asheville. Hadn't wanted to leave the farm and the sheep, although she was happy enough to be shut of Grandad and the way his anger hovered near even when all seemed well.

Eleanor Vance and Charlotte Yale had welcomed her at the train station the first week of December. When Grandad saw the pair picking their way carefully through a skift of snow on the station platform, he shoved her toward the ladies in their long skirts and shabby hats. "Do what these here women tell you," he commanded. Miss Vance smiled, but Miss Yale watched Grandad like a hawk. Gentry stepped closer to the sharp-eyed woman, who moved as if to come between her and her grandfather. What appeared to be a simple act of solidarity made the tight band she'd long felt stretching from her shoulders to her neck ease a little. "You hear me girl?" Gentry nodded once, quick, clutching her mother's dulcimer tighter lest someone try to take it. Miss Yale set a hand on her shoulder, and the band eased another inch.

"We'll take good care of your girl," Miss Vance said, her eyes dancing.

Grandad grunted and swung back onto the train. Gentry watched him move past the windows until she saw him take a seat. He didn't look at her. Didn't wave. Didn't do anything but stare straight ahead.

"Well," said Miss Vance, her bright tone fading.

Miss Yale squeezed Gentry's shoulder. "Well, indeed." And for the first time in ages, Gentry felt the tension in her shoulders unwind completely.

On the way to the boardinghouse, they told her their best weaver would be instructing her. "Lorna is a young woman of eighteen," Miss Yale said. "And she's already our star. You will do well to follow in her footsteps."

Now Gentry stood watching Lorna demonstrate the process of weaving. It hadn't been terribly interesting until she'd taken a seat at the loom and began sending the shuttle flying between the threads—what had she called them? The warp and weft. She couldn't remember which was which. It was fast and noisy, the speed and clatter making Gentry's hands and feet tingle to try this dance herself. Although younger than Lorna at fourteen, she was confident she could outdo the missish girl seated at the loom. What she was doing certainly didn't look any harder than playing the dulcimer, and Gentry could do that with her eyes closed.

She was about to demand a turn when Lorna slowed, then stopped the percussion of her work altogether. The sudden silence left an empty space in Gentry's mind where music lived.

"The cloth is coming along very well," Lorna said. "It's a shame to stop now, but this is a good place to give you some instruction."

"It doesn't look that hard," Gentry said, eager to take Lorna's seat.

Lorna chuckled. "That's because I'm good at it. You can be good at it, too, but there's a lot more to it than you think. It takes ages to dress a loom, which is what you'll begin with before you weave. A properly dressed loom is what makes beautiful cloth. Setting a perfect warp—that's the threads attached to the loom—is what allows the weft—the threads you weave back and forth—to make something beautiful. If your foundation is off, the whole fabric will be flawed."

Gentry felt that if she didn't get to do something more than stand and stare, she might explode. How much of this did she have to listen to? Couldn't she just weave something?

"Do you understand?" Lorna asked.

Gentry nodded. "Can I try that?" She pointed at the wooden thing wound with thread in Lorna's hand.

Lorna sighed. "I prefer for my students to start at the beginning, but if you'll be careful and follow my instructions explicitly, I suppose you can add a few rows."

Gentry wiggled in her eagerness as Lorna stood and let her slide onto the stool.

"Do you see these long wooden slats at your feet?" Lorna gestured toward the bottom of the loom. Gentry hadn't even noticed anything down there. "Those are the treadles. You press on them with your feet to create varying sheds in the cloth."

Gentry wanted to rub her hands together. She got to use her feet and her hands. Like dancing while she played her dulcimer. This was getting better and better.

"And this is the shuttle." Lorna picked up the wooden piece that carried the thread. "You pass it through each shed being certain to snug the thread into place with the beater bar each time. That makes for a tightly woven piece of cloth."

Gentry nodded, only half listening. She took up the shuttle, loving the feel of the smooth, warm wood in her palm. She pressed one of the treadles and reached to send the shuttle through the opening it made.

"Wait! No. Not that one. You must do it in the right order," Lorna scolded. "See, this is what I'm trying to tell you. Weaving is a precise art."

Gentry frowned. "Which one, then?"

Lorna pointed, and Gentry moved her foot, then shot the shuttle through the slightly different opening. Except it didn't glide through like a bird skimming the surface of a pond. It went about halfway and snagged.

Lorna laughed. "Not as easy as it looks, is it?"

Gentry frowned and released the treadle, trapping the shuttle in a web of threads.

"Don't do that," Lorna said, shaking her head. "Press the treadle again, and I'll fish the shuttle out for you."

She did and sent it through easily. "Now press the next treadle to the left." Gentry complied, changing the shed once more. "Okay, try it again. Use your wrist to flick it through so it skims over the threads."

Gentry bit the tip of her tongue and tried again. This time the shuttle made it all the way through the shed.

"Now release the treadle and use the beater bar to snug

21

that thread into place." Gentry did, wondering at how slow this was. "Next, back to the first treadle and do it again."

In that manner, Gentry was finally able to weave a few rows. But only a few. And she hardly seemed to have added anything to the length of fabric before her.

"How were you doing it so fast?" she whined. "This is going to take forever."

"Miss Vance told me you play the dulcimer, right?" Gentry nodded. "Were you able to play it perfectly the first time?"

Gentry shrugged. "I guess not."

"Did you get better the more you played it?"

"Yeah."

"Weaving is like that. The more you do it, the better you get." She bumped Gentry's shoulder and slid back onto the stool. "Watch."

She resumed her rhythmic weaving, the shuttle flying as the treadles clacked up and down and the beater bar swung back and forth. Tired, Gentry sat on the floor to watch. Like a flash of lightning, she remembered sitting at her mother's feet like this under her loom in the loft of the little cabin they shared with Grandad. The fabric had formed a growing roof above her, and the clatter of the loom was a lullaby sending her off to sleep. It was a good memory. She tapped her fingers against her knee in time with the rhythm.

Lorna noticed and grinned at her. "I think you're going to be a natural. It just takes a bit of patience."

"My mother was a weaver." Gentry froze. She hadn't meant to let that slip. She didn't want Lorna to know about her mother. She would likely ask questions Gentry couldn't answer.

"Really? Did she teach you anything about it?"

"She died." The lie fell from her lips so easily. There. Now in place of questions, maybe she'd get a little sympathy.

Lorna stilled. "My mother died. When I was little. Now it's just my father and me."

This was an unexpected turn of events. Gentry took the advantage. "What happened?"

"Something . . . happened inside her head. 'A breakage,' the doctor said. She'd lain down with a headache but never got up again." She pushed her lips into a fake smile. "But Father and I do well together. I daresay he couldn't get along without me now." Her voice softened. "Nor I without him."

Silence fell over them. Then Lorna reached out and took Gentry's hand. "What about your mother?"

The touch felt like an electric shock. When had anyone ever taken her hand? Grandfather never did. Miss Vance and Miss Yale had touched her arm or shoulder to guide her, but no one had clasped her hand in their own in this, what, comforting way? Gentry bet Lorna's father touched her like this all the time.

"She fell off a horse and broke her neck." Again, the lie was out even before she'd thought to form it.

"How awful. I'm so sorry."

Gentry stared at their clasped hands. "I am too," she said, then tugged her hand away.

. . . . . . . . . .

"Do you want to come to see the train arrive or not?" Lorna snapped at Gentry. She'd been extra nice since they talked about losing their mothers, but apparently Gentry had used up that measure of goodwill.

Gentry pooched her lip out. "Of course I do. But I don't see why I must finish setting this stupid loom before I go. We can do it later." She peeked up at Lorna through her lashes, hoping her wheedling would get her out of the odious task. The sett had to do with how many warp threads there were per inch of cloth. And each of those threads

23

had to be threaded through—what were they called again? Dents. Which made no sense since they were slots, not dents. And they were in the reed. And the reed was a piece the width of the loom that moved the threads when you pressed the treadle. Which created the shed for the shuttle to pass through. It was not only tedious but also confusing.

She heaved a sigh. She could stand to do the weaving, slow as it was, but setting the loom was beyond boring. Especially when there was the excitement of visitors arriving by train to spend Christmas at Biltmore House.

Lorna clenched her hands. Gentry was pretty sure her teacher had no idea she was doing it and took a perverse pleasure in disrupting her usual calm. Lorna was altogether too composed for Gentry's taste. She vaguely remembered her mother sobbing and throwing things. And she absolutely remembered her grandfather's simmering anger that would suddenly explode into action. Although she preferred not to dwell on that. Lorna's steady patience and quiet presence left Gentry feeling like her teacher was hiding behind a high wall. It was always a relief when she could get Lorna to snap or lash out. Like now. Although she didn't want to push her so far that she would refuse to let Gentry see the Vanderbilts' guests arriving on the afternoon train.

"Later? Tomorrow is Christmas Eve and then it will be Christmas Day, and I doubt you'll want to do the work then." Lorna flung an arm toward the loom that still lacked more warp threads than Gentry liked to count. Lorna lifted the watch pinned to her blouse and sighed. "You haven't even finished sleying the reed. Do that at least or you won't be going to the train station." She spun on her heel, leaving Gentry with a cross of thread over the fingers of her left hand and far too many dents in the reed still to thread. With a sleying hook of all things. Who came up with these names?

Gentry let her shoulders sag and picked up the hook that she was supposed to use to snag the threads and tug them through each dent in the reed. Dressing a loom was the definition of tedious, and this was only the first step. Maybe she could trick one of the other girls into threading the heddle running behind the reed, which was even worse since the openings were smaller yet.

Frowning in concentration, Gentry forced herself to draw the threads, one by one and in order, through the narrow gaps in the reed, imagining each poke and tug was a jab in Lorna's direction. She'd been surprised to discover that she enjoyed the rhythmic process of weaving fabric once a loom was dressed, yet the endless monotony of preparing it was torture.

Gentry cursed softly when she realized she'd missed a dent. Now she'd have to pull all the threads to shift them over one place. She gnawed her lip and glanced around. Or she could pretend she didn't see it. So what if there was a flaw in the fabric? She hurried through the rest of her task, skipping lunch so she would be finished in time.

Lorna reappeared as Gentry drew the final thread through the heddle. "I'm all done," she announced, moving to block Lorna's view of the loom before she could take note of any mistakes. "Is it time to meet the train?"

Lorna shifted, trying to get a better look at the beater with its threaded reed. "Yes, the others are heading that way. Are you sure that you—?"

"Great! I'll get my coat." Gentry darted toward the cloakroom before Lorna could detain her. Lorna frowned but followed instead of examining the loom.

"Gentry, you really must try harder to focus on the task at hand," she lectured as they went. "The others are almost ready to weave, and you still have much to do."

Gentry grinned and slid her arms into her shabby green

coat with its too short sleeves. "But once I start weaving, I'll race past them in short order."

Lorna sighed. "I know, and I'm not sure that's a good thing. While you excel in creativity, your accuracy is still lacking."

Gentry tossed her mass of unruly curls that were always escaping whatever pins she bothered to secure them with. "The people who buy our fabric don't care. They just want a colorful souvenir of their time in Asheville." She ran for the door. "It doesn't really matter."

"Everything matters," Lorna said with a frown. "And you'd do well to remember that."

But Gentry was already out the door and plunging into the group of apprentices from Biltmore Estate Industries. She didn't have any particular friends among the boys and girls who were learning woodworking and weaving, but losing herself in their midst was better than listening to Lorna natter on.

They made their way through the chill December air, a chattering mass of laughter, toward the train station near the French Broad River. The sun was high, adding its warmth to their holiday high spirits. Gentry heard the train whistle and hopped in place, excited to see who would disembark on their way to the castle at the top of the mountain. She still couldn't quite believe people actually lived in it.

As they neared the station, two sleek motorcars approached. Murmurs made their way through the group, whispering that these were from Biltmore House itself. They might even be carrying the Vanderbilts.

Gentry sobered, remembering that George Vanderbilt had died the previous spring. She felt a pang of sympathy for Cornelia Vanderbilt, who at fifteen was only a year older than she was. It was her first Christmas without a father, and no fancy clothes, automobiles, or big houses could make up for that.

A sharp whistle and the thrum of an approaching train interrupted Gentry's thoughts. She felt a thrill as smoke billowed from the engine, and brakes squealed until the iron beast finally throbbed to a stop at the station.

A tall woman got out of one of the automobiles, her head held high. She waved to the crowd, a gentle smile on her face. A slim girl followed her, a little awkward in her movements. She wore a stylish hat that nonetheless looked wrong for her—like she was hiding beneath it. "That's Tarheel Nell," one of the adults said. "As close to a princess as we'll ever see in these mountains."

Gentry wrinkled her nose. "Why do they call her Tarheel?" she asked a young man standing nearby. She'd seen him before and thought his name was Arthur.

"North Carolina used to produce an awful lot of tar and pitch—sticky stuff. During the American Civil War, North Carolina soldiers were known to 'stick' their ground while others would go slipping off to the rear to avoid the fighting." He gave her a gentle smile. "It's a compliment. Lets folks know we consider her ours here in the Old North State."

Gentry smiled back, finding Arthur's presence a solid rock amid all the excitement. He felt steady, and without giving it too much thought, she stuck close to him as people began disembarking from the train.

Arthur leaned closer. "That's Mrs. Brown. She's Mrs. Vanderbilt's sister. And here comes her son, John. Her husband died in 1900, the same year the boy was born—the same year Cornelia was born."

Gentry watched the cousins greet one another. "Both fatherless," she whispered. "Like me."

If Arthur heard, he didn't comment, and Gentry was grateful for that. She didn't want people to know things about her. It was like giving them a part of who she was, and there was little enough of that to go around. Arthur, though, didn't feel like the sort to use information for his own advantage. And as they watched the Vanderbilts and the Browns climb into their cars to drive away, Gentry let herself feel like maybe, just maybe, she could belong here.

# GENTRY

**BILTMORE HOUSE**
**DECEMBER 25, 1915**

The wagon jolted and jounced as they made their way up the winding road to Biltmore House on Christmas Day. Arthur drove, guiding the team through the winter-bare woods, Lorna seated primly at his side. Gentry bounced in the back with several other girls and might have complained except that Lorna had already threatened to leave her behind. Not only had she skipped a dent in her reed, but she'd also gotten some threads crossed. She'd had to redo them while Lorna stood over her, glowering and complaining that she had better things to do. Which, no doubt, she did. Gentry pointed out that her teacher was free to leave anytime. That hadn't gone over well either.

By working for too many hours on Christmas Eve, Gentry had finally completed setting her warp threads. Lorna had proclaimed her work adequate but even so threatened to leave her at the boardinghouse alone on Christmas Day if she didn't promise to try harder. Gentry had been only too happy to deliver the promise. As if promises meant anything. Her mother had taught her how easy they were to make and break.

And now she held her peace as they neared the gates that led to what she'd heard was an actual castle right here in the mountains. She peered through the wrought iron, trying to glimpse something, but didn't see a thing other than sky and some stunted-looking trees.

Then they were through the gates and turning right. Gentry gasped and fell back against the side of the wagon. It was a castle just like in a fairy tale, only bigger and better. The massive stone structure gleamed in the early afternoon light, chimneys and spires piercing the sky. As they drew closer, she could pick out carvings—faces and figures perched hither and yon. And there, on either side of the massive front doors, were two lions that looked so lifelike, she thought she saw one twitch his whiskers.

"Not too shabby, hey?" Arthur spoke over his shoulder.

Gentry managed to stagger to her feet in the moving wagon, clutching the back of Arthur's seat. Lorna frowned at her, but Gentry didn't care. She just wanted to see more of the dream unfolding before her eyes.

"What's it like inside?" she whispered.

"Don't be thinking you'll get to go in," Lorna scolded. "We're lucky to be invited into the carriage house."

Gentry blinked slowly, trying to take everything in at once. "What's a carriage house?"

The fire in Lorna's eyes banked, and she sighed. "It's where the carriages are kept. Fancy people have houses even for their conveyances. And it's beautiful in its own right." She smiled, giving in to the soft spot Gentry knew she had for her. "There will even be a tree, and of course presents."

Gentry's eyes widened. "Presents? For me?"

Arthur chuckled. "Yes, ma'am. Presents for everyone, along with cookies and cider and all sorts of good things."

Gentry swallowed hard. She'd almost let her stubbornness make her miss this. Just seeing the house was worth all the hours she'd spent dressing her loom. In a burst of feeling she threw her arms around Lorna, squeezing tight. "I'm sorry I was difficult. Thank you, oh thank you for not leaving me behind!"

Lorna flushed and patted Gentry's arm. "Just keep your promise and do your work without so much fuss in the future. I'm glad we're here now." She paused, then added, "Together."

Gentry straightened and clapped her hands before lunging to grab the back of the seat again. "I can't wait to see what my present will be."

They drove through a sort of enclosed porch with a lovely arched ceiling made of shiny tiles. Gentry looked back down just in time to take in a courtyard outside the carriage house. Excited, she tried to jump down from the still-moving wagon. Lorna grabbed her arm, and Arthur drew back on the reins. "Hold on there, girl," Arthur said. "No need to twist an ankle or worse in your hurry."

"Yes, stay with us, Gentry. We will all go in together," Lorna admonished. "And for heaven's sake, try to contain yourself. This is a time to be on your very best behavior."

Gentry shifted from foot to foot and clasped her hands in front of her. She could behave herself. She knew she could. For Lorna, who let her come despite her misbehavior, and for Arthur, who was kind to her for no reason at all.

As their little group walked together toward the carriage house, Gentry even managed to straighten her back and raise her chin so she would look dignified. She saw Lorna smile and shake her head, but she didn't care. She'd show them just how nice she could be.

But as soon as she passed through the doors into the large room with its massive Christmas tree, fragrant swags of greenery, and more candles than she could count, she forgot her manners and let her mouth gape open. She snapped it shut even as she registered the wonderful aromas of gingerbread, spices, and sugar.

A girl who didn't look much older than her nodded at each of them in turn. Gentry managed to nod back, realizing with a jolt that this was Cornelia—Tarheel Nell. She faded back into the crowd and tried to clean the toes of her boots on the backs of her stockings. Lorna had suggested she polish her shoes, but she hadn't found the time. Now, seeing how beautifully Mrs. Vanderbilt and her daughter were dressed, she wished she'd made the effort.

Gentry wormed her way toward the tree so she could see the sparkling ornaments and packages tied with ribbon. Someone pressed a gingerbread cookie into her hand, and she nibbled it as she gazed starry-eyed at the grandeur around her.

"And this is just the carriage house." Gentry jerked and nearly dropped what was left of her cookie as Arthur spoke from behind her.

He smiled. "I don't know about you, but all of this makes me feel a bit out of my depth."

Gentry nodded and crammed the last bite of gingerbread in her mouth. "Why do they let us come here?"

Arthur's eyebrows lifted. "Let us? Well, I supposed they appreciate all the hard work their employees and tenants put in." His eyes crinkled when he smiled. "And I think they just like being generous."

Gentry frowned. She wasn't much used to kindness. Mama had been kind. Right up until she left Gentry to fend for herself—the meanest thing anyone had ever done to her. And Grandad hadn't been kind to anyone ever. While people here in Asheville hadn't been outright mean, they hadn't gone out of their way to be nice either. Gentry brushed some crumbs from the corner of her mouth. Except for Miss Vance and Miss Yale. And Arthur. She glanced up at him, and he smiled down at her. She allowed a smile of her own to bring lightness to her heart. Come to think of it, Lorna was nice, too, even if she was also bossy. Maybe things would be different now. Maybe coming here would turn out all right.

Someone cleared their throat behind her, and Gentry jumped as though she'd been caught doing something wrong. "This is for you." Cornelia stood so close, Gentry could see that her nose was a little too long for her face. It made her look more like an awkward schoolgirl than a princess. Gentry found it comforting that the richest girl in the world might not be completely perfect. "It's a gift," Cornelia said, holding the small parcel out toward Gentry.

"Oh." Gentry took the package, the paper crinkling under her fingers. Arthur nudged her. "Thank you," she said with a jerk. "What is it?" She held the package like it might bite her.

Cornelia smiled, and suddenly she was quite pretty. "Open it and see."

Gentry watched the princess of Biltmore move on to hand out more gifts. Arthur said softly, "Aren't you going to open it?"

She smoothed the paper and admired the satiny ribbon. She was afraid whatever was inside would be a disappointment. Something insulting like a bar of soap, or boring like a pair of mittens. "I think I'll save it for later," she replied, tucking the package in her pocket.

"Suit yourself." Arthur shrugged as Lorna walked by, sipping a cup of cider and laughing with another girl. His eyes tracked her, and Gentry was struck by the notion that he might be taken with Lorna. She snorted.

"What did you say?" he asked.

Gentry opened her mouth to make a rude remark, then changed her mind. She stuck a hand in her pocket and felt the paper crinkle under her touch. Hope surged in her. Maybe it was something wonderful after all. "I said Merry Christmas, Arthur."

He laughed and hugged her from the side with one arm. "Merry Christmas to you, too. Now, if you'll excuse me, I'm going to find a cup of cider." He made a beeline for Lorna even though she wasn't anywhere near the cider table.

Gentry darted behind the massive tree and drew her package from her pocket. Gnawing at her lip, she undid the ribbon and folded the paper back. Inside were two of the loveliest handkerchiefs she had ever seen. The pristine fabric was embroidered with flowers—lily of the valley on one and daffodils on the other. The stitches were perfect, the threads vivid in yellow, green, and white. She could almost smell the flowers, they looked so real. She lifted them to her face and pressed the softness to her cheek. She'd never owned anything so lovely before in her life.

"Do you like them?" The soft voice drew Gentry's attention from her prize. Cornelia stood, head cocked to the side, watching her.

"I love them," whispered Gentry. "Daffodils were my mother's favorite."

"Were? Is she not with you anymore?"

Gentry remembered that this was Cornelia's first Christmas without her father. "She . . . she's dead." The lie was so much easier than explaining that her mother had abandoned her. And now that she was telling it for the second time, it came more readily.

"I'm sorry," Cornelia said.

34

Gentry blinked back tears. "And I'm sorry about your father."

Cornelia ducked her head. "As am I."

And for just a moment, Gentry dared to think that maybe the princess of Biltmore Estate wasn't so very different from her after all.

# 4

# ARTHUR

Arthur stared out the window of the woodworking cottage behind Grove Park Inn. He still missed the workshop at Biltmore Estate, but the view over the Blue Ridge Mountains was almost as good from here. He pulled the carved fawn from his pocket and rubbed it with his thumb as he watched clouds chase their shadows over the ancient peaks. He almost always had the small carving in his pocket—a sort of good luck piece. And stroking the wood, now worn to silk over more than two decades, helped him think.

Although he was almighty tired of thinking.

"Did you hear the latest?" Wendell, one of his best carvers, slapped Arthur on the back.

"If you mean the announcement that Biltmore Industries is now the largest handweaving industry in the world, then yes. I heard." Arthur withdrew his hand from his pocket and ran it through his dark hair.

"I reckon Mrs. Vanderbilt wearing a homespun suit to talk

to the North Carolina General Assembly on the first of the month might've had something to do with it," Wendell said.

"She did cut quite the figure," Arthur allowed.

"And had them politicians eating out her hand. Did you hear how she started her talk?" Wendell was clearly eager to tell, so Arthur refrained from saying that he had. "She said she'd been told a good speech should be like a modern skirt." Wendell could barely contain his glee. "Long enough to cover the subject and short enough to attract attention!'" He guffawed and slapped his thigh.

Arthur laughed with him. "She did North Carolina proud."

Wendell sobered. "But where does that leave us wood-workers?"

"Right where we've always been," Arthur responded with forced cheer. "Working for one of the best companies any-where."

"But the weavers are getting all the glory and have been since Mrs. Vanderbilt sold us off in seventeen," Wendell pro-tested. "Our woodwork's been around longer, and I daresay it's just as popular."

Arthur managed to smile. "Right you are. I'm sure we'll get our due." He pulled out a pocket watch Reverend Swope had given to him on his thirtieth birthday. "Now, aren't you meant to be meeting a production deadline?" He winked at his apprentice. "Don't want to let the weavers show us up."

Wendell grinned and hurried off to his workbench. If Ar-thur remembered correctly, he was finishing up a batch of frames carved with dogwood blossoms—very popular with the tourists who came to Asheville, often for their health. Just as Eleanor Vance and Charlotte Yale had done, bringing Eleanor's mother to the mountains to "take the air." They'd hoped to pursue mission work in far-flung places, but like Arthur, their dreams had given way to the needs of others.

The two missionaries had been biding their time in Asheville when George Vanderbilt brought Reverend Swope here to lead his Cathedral of All Souls. That was the second time Arthur found himself carried to a place he hadn't chosen, and unfortunately it hadn't been the last. Of course, it had ultimately been to his benefit that Reverend Swope helped the two missionaries form a small school teaching boys and girls to build and carve furniture and other items like bowls, frames, and even hearth brushes. Arthur soon became their prize pupil, helping to teach the younger children.

From there he'd made his way to the cabinetry shop at Biltmore House. It was a position he'd never thought to leave. Then, when Mrs. Vanderbilt decided she had no choice but to sell the business to Fred Seely at Grove Park Inn, his talents became part of the deal. A sacrifice he'd been more than willing to make for the sake of a friend he still hoped might be more one day.

He frowned realizing his hand had found its way back into his pocket. He wasn't one to feel sorry for himself or to bemoan his fate, but seeing the focus shift from woodworking to weaving in addition to his frustration with the friend in question was leaving him wrung out. Lorna, of course, was thrilled with the success of her weavers. The weaving rooms were where she spent her days—training, creating new designs, overseeing production, and managing what had undoubtedly become a thriving business. Arthur was delighted to see her success; he just wished the busyness of her job didn't give her an excuse to avoid his advances. He'd done everything short of proposing and only hesitated to do that because he was almost certain she'd refuse him.

"There you are, Arthur!" Lorna appeared as though his thoughts had conjured her. "Did you hear the announcement?" Her brown eyes glowed with a warmth that pierced him.

Arthur didn't have to force a smile this time. Lorna made him smile without trying. "Of course I heard! Congratulations." He clasped her outstretched hands, reveling in her touch as she clutched his arm and leaned into him.

"It's so wonderful." Her cheeks flushed pink. "And Mr. Grove mentioned my recent designs as part of the reason why we've seen such success with our fabrics."

Arthur felt himself begin to hope. Maybe this was the boost she needed to finally look toward her own future happiness. He felt his heart pick up speed. And perhaps that could include him. He'd certainly sacrificed enough for it—though he hoped she'd never know how much.

"I wish Gentry were here to see it," he said. "She was so wildly creative, and even though the two of you struggled sometimes, I have a feeling she would have grown into a skilled weaver." He noticed the light in Lorna's eyes dimming and hurried on. "Under your tutelage, of course. She always needed a firm hand to guide her."

Lorna released him and turned toward a window. "I haven't thought of her in ages," she said, the warmth fading from her voice. "She was too volatile and in too much of a hurry." She straightened her back and spoke without looking at him. "Why in the world would you bring her up today?"

Arthur shrugged, wondering why himself and wishing he hadn't. "I don't know. Something about that last design you did—it reminded me of her."

"That's ridiculous," Lorna snapped, the color leaving her cheeks. She took several steps toward the door and spoke again, her voice gentler this time. "I'm sure she's better off wherever she is." She laughed lightly, although Arthur thought it might have been forced. "I'm sure her passion and her gift for music has taken her in a completely different direction. She's probably wildly happy and living the good life in some far-off locale." Lorna nodded as though agreeing with herself. "Now, I came to invite you to a celebratory tea this afternoon. Mr. Seely will address the managers, and you mustn't miss it. Even Mr. Grove will be there."

"That sounds nice. Thank you for letting me know."

Lorna smiled, some color returning to her face. "You've been my friend for so long now, Arthur. It wouldn't be a celebration without you."

He watched her go, frustration, hope, confusion, and maybe even a spark of anger battling within him. He gritted his teeth, and his fingers found the fawn in his pocket again. He'd just have to nurture the hope and pray that his frustration and anger would wither from lack of attention.

***

A few days later, Arthur blew on his chill fingers in the workshop. He thought about his time working at Biltmore House. Even on the coldest days of winter, he and the other workers could count on warmth from the heat supplied by massive boilers in the subbasement of the castle on the hill. Richard Morris Hunt, the architect, had designed the château to enjoy something called "central heating." Steam-heated air moved all through the house by way of natural convection, adding to the pleasure of crackling fires to keep them all comfortable. Arthur tried not to think about the warmth or Mr. Hunt right now. Neither were subjects to give him much peace.

"Cold enough for ye?" Angus McTeague chafed his own hands and leaned against the doorframe, watching Arthur work. "You always did have a fine way with the details," he added, nodding toward the bowl in Arthur's hand. "Fine enough you might've done more than teach callow youth to make bowls and frames."

Arthur narrowed his eyes at Angus. "I have the feeling you're getting at something."

Angus stepped into the room and made himself comfortable on a stool. "I've been wondering. What sort of man turns down a chance to work with one of the greatest architects in America if not the world?"

Arthur groaned and tucked his numb fingers into his armpits. "Who told you about that?"

"Word has a way of getting around." Angus scratched his grizzled chin. "Can't think what would make a man pass up an opportunity like that. Chance to see the world. Work in fancy houses. Eat good food."

Arthur shrugged and picked his bowl up again. "It didn't suit me."

Now it was Angus's turn to narrow his eyes. "I saw the way you were watching that girl who's over the weaving room. Making eyes at her at church last Sunday. Like a pup eyeing a sausage through a locked gate. Don't suppose that would have anything to do with your decision."

"Angus, why do you care?" Arthur didn't even try to hide his exasperation. "Seems like you've taken up meddling in place of the work you used to do."

Angus held up his hands. For the first time, Arthur really looked at his gnarled fingers and the way they shook—not a lot, but likely enough to make carving difficult. "Your namesake's got ahold of me. Even worse on cold days like this. When a man can't work like he wants, he must find something else to occupy his mind."

"Arthritis? I'm sorry, old friend. I should have noticed."

"It's a point of pride to me that you didn't." He massaged his knuckles. "Thing is, if you get people to talking, they don't notice things like how you can't hold a chisel or a knife anymore." He flexed his fingers and cocked his head. "Anyhow, what I heard is, that Lorna girl wasn't gonna get took on when Mr. Seely bought Biltmore Estate Industries from the widow Vanderbilt. Seems like she wasn't up to snuff.

41

Then"—he winked—"and this is the interesting part, all of a sudden she's moving up from weaver to administrator, and you're turning down a sure thing with Mr. Hunt to run the woodworking shop."

Arthur concentrated on getting the dogwood petal he was carving exactly right. Maybe if he ignored Angus, he'd go away.

"Only one reason I can think of that a man would make a sacrifice like that," Angus said.

Arthur grunted and put down his chisel. "Is that right? Maybe I just wanted to be in charge over here. Could be as simple as that."

"Only reason I bring it up is to say I think you oughta do something about it."

Arthur frowned. "About what?"

Angus chuckled. "That spark in your eye I see every time you look at the lovely Lorna."

A flush brought a wave of heat to Arthur's face. "I've known her for years, and she's never welcomed my attentions. She's friendly toward me, but I don't think she'd ever consider me . . . like that."

"Can't see why not. You're a fine-looking fella. Gainfully employed. Keep your workbench tidy." He squinted at Arthur. "I'm betting you've never done more than wish when it comes to that one."

Arthur shook his head and stared at the floor. "Just saving myself the heartache."

"She'd be lucky to have you," Angus said. "What's holding you back?"

"Two things. First, she really hasn't been the same since the big flood and all the sorrow that brought her. And second . . ." Arthur stuck his right foot out and thumped his leg. "There's this."

"First, that flood was five years ago. And second, you've got a bum leg. So what?"

"It's not a bum leg. It's a clubfoot, and it's ugly as sin."

"Hunh. Clubfoot. That mean you were born with it?"

Arthur nodded, staring at the heavy shoe with its thick sole. He could feel the brace that was hidden by his trouser leg. "Reverend Swope took me to a doctor when I was just a tyke, and the doc did what he could to help. But my foot will never be right. Not really." He tried to laugh. "Guess it's like your hands. I just try to distract folks so they don't notice it too much."

"Still seems to me you've got a lot to offer that girl. And if she knew you gave up a big job so she'd get took on by Mr. Seely, well, that'd count for even more."

"I don't want her to ever know," Arthur said, tucking his foot under his chair. "If she did come to like me, I'd want it to be for . . . well, for me."

Angus nodded. "I can understand that." He stood and ambled toward the door. "Of course, seems to me you're robbing her of the chance to get to decide if she does like you by not asking her to walk out with you on a Sunday afternoon." He grinned. "It's easier to order a slice of pie if somebody hands you a menu."

Arthur shook his head and waved his old friend off. He suspected Angus was right, but in the years he'd known Lorna, he'd seen her look at his leg with pity more than once. He also suspected the only thing worse than going on hoping Lorna might care for him was finding out for sure and for certain that she didn't.

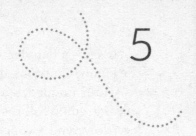

# 5

# LORNA

**Weaverville, North Carolina
September 1923**

Her feet ached, and she'd gotten mud all over her skirt. The streetcar ride to Weaverville hadn't been cheap, and now this walk was taking much longer than she'd anticipated. At first she'd enjoyed the lovely scenery passing from wide bottomlands to steep mountains and narrow valleys. She'd even gotten a look at the Reems Creek Milling Company's gristmill with its huge waterwheel turning beneath a rush of water. She'd enjoyed their cornmeal at Mrs. Brady's table time and again.

It had all felt like quite an adventure. But now she was beginning to worry that she'd miss the last streetcar back to Asheville. And then what would she do?

The woman at the market had not brought her another piece of cloth. Instead, she'd given her instructions for finding the weaver. Initially, Lorna had felt this was excellent news. But as the day wore on, she was less certain.

Her instructions had been to follow Reems Creek from the mill until she came to the Brank Cemetery. From there she was supposed to follow a smaller stream to the left until she came to the third cabin up Pink Fox Cove. She'd seen two cabins and was beginning to wonder if there really was a third. Or had she simply been sent on a wild goose chase?

"Serves me right," she muttered, slipping along a muddy stretch of what was little more than a dirt track. Never mind the cardinal flowers shining with the purest red she'd ever seen. Never mind the cascades of frothy virgin's bower growing along fence lines. She was past finding inspiration in her surroundings. She just wanted to find this weaver and be on her way again.

"Who in the blue blazes are you?"

Lorna froze when she heard the voice above her among the trees. She'd already been feeling thirsty, but now her mouth went so dry she could hardly swallow. Turning slowly, she spotted what she could only describe as the classic picture of a bearded mountain man, pointing a gun at her. Some sort of rifle, although she wasn't certain.

Fisting her free hand in her skirt, she tried to wet her lips. "I'm looking for a weaver. I was told she lives up this way."

"You've got no business being up here."

She reached into her basket and pulled out the shawl. "I need to find the person who made this cloth," she said, surprised that she could get the words out.

"Need? I doubt that. This world's full of needs, and that doesn't sound like much of one." He made a jabbing motion with the gun. "Now be gone."

"But I—" The sound of the explosion made Lorna feel as though her heart had stopped, and for a moment she feared a bullet had done that very thing. But no. The man had missed her. "You shot at me!" she blurted.

"No, ma'am. I shot *around* you. Stay a little longer and you'll understand the difference."

Before she realized she'd decided to do anything, Lorna

hiked her skirts and sprinted back the way she'd come. She darted a look over her shoulder, tripped, and sprawled across the rough path, dropping her basket. The heels of her hands burned where they slammed into rocks and dirt, and her knee throbbed. Nonetheless, she regained her feet, scooped up her basket, and continued her speedy retreat along the nameless stream. It wasn't until she saw the cemetery that had been her first landmark that she finally slowed and took stock of her situation.

Her hands were scraped and bloody with two nails broken. Her skirt was even dirtier than before, and there was a tear where her knee must have bashed into a sharp stone. She braced a hand against her side and panted until she was able to slow her breathing and calm her racing heart.

Well. That had not gone according to plan.

Lorna found a pinecone and used it to brush as much dirt from her clothing as she could. It would seem the woman at the market didn't know what she was talking about. Or maybe she did and these people simply didn't trust an outsider who walked in unannounced. She washed her hands in the creek and patted them dry with a handkerchief, wincing as she brushed the abraded flesh. She lifted the watch pinned at her breast and saw that if she hurried, she could still make the last streetcar.

She rushed back along Reems Creek, trying to ignore the stabbing pain in her knee. "Such a waste," she said to the sky. "Of both time and money."

All right then. She was going to need help if she intended to track down this mysterious weaver. And while she knew exactly who to ask, she was afraid he might say no. She suspected she'd had something to do with his up and leaving Biltmore Industries like he did. She tried to remember the last time she'd done more than nod at him on a Sunday morning. Right. It had been on a chilly March Sunday a year and a half ago. And he'd suspected the truth about her then.

⋯⋯⋯

Lorna thought that the building she was approaching more closely resembled a cozy English cottage than a wood-working shop. She checked the slip of paper she'd written the address on one more time. Yes. This was the place.

She wet her lips as she raised her gloved hand to knock on the door. She pressed her other hand to her stomach to still the fluttering. She'd intentionally avoided Arthur for too long. Seeking him out now, she realized how much she'd missed him.

She dared not examine the why of that too closely.

A young man flung the door open, releasing the smell of fresh lumber and linseed oil. "Can I help ya?"

Lorna took a deep breath, finding the aromas unexpectedly comforting. "I'm looking for Arthur Wescott." She craned her neck to see past him. "I believe this is his shop?"

"Yes, ma'am, but he's occupied at the moment." The man brushed wood shavings from the front of his shirt. "If it's a commission you want, I can take the order." He stuck his hand out. "I'm Donnie."

"Do you get many commissions?" she asked.

"Oh, all the time. Cain't hardly keep up with 'em. Arthur, he likes to talk to clients himself, but I'm okay to get the ball rolling." He mimed rolling a ball from his palm.

"Could he make me a shuttle?" Lorna was surprised by her own audacity. She'd had no notion of asking Arthur to do any such thing.

Donnie furrowed his brow. "A what?"

"For weaving—the wooden shuttle that carries the weft thread between the warp threads." She tried to demonstrate with her hands, but it didn't seem to be helping.

"You'd better come in." Donnie held the door open wider, and she entered a small front room comfortably furnished with mission-style furniture much like they had at Grove Park Inn. "You can sit if you want," he said, waving at one of the chairs before disappearing into the recesses of the cottage.

Lorna perched on the edge of a chair with her hands clasped over tightly pressed knees. She was grateful her gloves hid her injuries from the day before. She brushed a thread from her skirt and noticed her hand was shaking. She wove her fingers together and tried to be still even though her heart and mind were racing.

She heard footsteps approaching, and the sound stirred a memory she couldn't quite place. She looked toward the door just in time to see Arthur appear. His smooth expression burst into a smile. "Lorna? Is that you?" He hurried to her side in that hitching gait she'd forgotten. That was the memory—the sound of one foot hesitating to follow the other. She would never have claimed to associate it with Arthur, but seeing him now, it brought back memories—and shame—that made her clench her hands even tighter.

"Hello, Arthur."

"When Donnie said a pretty woman wanted me to make her a shuttle, I had to come see." He dropped into the chair beside her and braced his hands on his knees. "Generally, I don't tend to every commission—I'd never get anything done if I did—but I'm so glad he fetched me this time." He stopped talking and shook his head, smiling. "My goodness. How are you? You must still be weaving if you need a new shuttle."

Lorna blushed and smoothed her skirt over her knees. She began pleating the fabric between her fingers, then caught herself and reclasped her hands. "I don't really need a shuttle. It's just the only thing I could think of at the moment."

Arthur tilted his head to one side. "Then you've come for another reason?"

"I . . . I need your help."

"Few things would make me happier than being of service to you."

She wanted to believe his words but couldn't imagine that they were true. She'd shut him out. Accused him. And he'd left Biltmore Industries. Left a position he'd worked long and hard to build. Although, looking around, she considered that he might have done well enough in business on his own to have no regrets. "I need to find a weaver."

He laughed. "I'd think you'd trip over them every day." He considered her more seriously. "Or have you left Biltmore Industries, too?"

It stung a little that he didn't know. She'd known exactly where to find him—known precisely what he was doing. "No, no, that's not it." She retrieved the shawl from her bag. "I found this at the market in Biltmore Village."

Arthur whistled long and low. "Well, now that *is* a beaut." He took the cloth and ran it between his fingers. "You say you bought it at the market? Did the seller not tell you who made it?"

"She claimed she didn't know, but I think she was keeping the weaver's identity from me. Then she sent me on a wild goose chase."

"Why would she do that?"

Lorna shrugged one shoulder. "I assumed the weaver is one of those types who live back in the hills somewhere, refusing to have anything to do with society. Perhaps she's backwards or shy. Or maybe the woman who sold me the cloth wasn't supposed to have it." She sighed. "I've thought of all sorts of scenarios, but in the end, I just want to find this weaver."

"Why? And why would you need my help?" Arthur handed the shawl back.

Lorna took it, running her hand over the soft cloth with its rich colors. She just couldn't get enough of how it stirred her imagination. Even now, the simple act of holding it gave her the sense of tasting crisp apples while a cool breeze teased her hair. She knew it was precisely the sort of pattern she needed to impress Mrs. Harshaw. "I tried to go to the place along Reems Creek where the weaver is supposed to live, but I wasn't particularly welcome. I understand you source wood from that area, and I thought you might have some knowledge that would help me." She hoped he wouldn't notice that she hadn't exactly answered his question.

Arthur chuckled. "Folks back in the hills aren't always eager to welcome strangers." He winked. "Even pretty ones."

Lorna was taken aback by the compliment. She hadn't been certain she'd be welcome here, and Arthur was not only welcoming and kind but . . . dared she think he was *pleased* to see her? "Yes, I'm afraid the fellow I encountered made it abundantly clear that he expected me to leave. With haste."

Arthur frowned. "He didn't hurt you, did he?"

"No. He did have a gun, but I don't think he would have actually shot me." She refrained from mentioning that he'd fired his weapon in her general direction.

Arthur made a humming sound. "Probably not, but you never know." He clapped his hands together. "Basil Howes has been drying some cherry for me. I can take you with me when I go to see him on Saturday. He knows everyone along Reems Creek and can surely point us in the right direction."

Lorna blinked in surprise. "I . . . that would be most help-ful."

"Good." He winked again. "I'll pick you up Saturday morning at seven."

"I could meet you—" she began, but he jumped in.

"No need. I go right by Biltmore Village on my way to Weaverville."

She nodded, then something struck her. "How do you know I still live in the village?"

Arthur flushed and shoved his hands in the sagging pockets of his jacket. "I, well, I was just supposing you hadn't moved."

"I haven't," she said slowly.

"Good, good. Saturday then?" He stood, and she knew that was her cue to leave.

"Thank you, Arthur. This means a great deal to me. Maybe even to Biltmore Industries."

He smiled, drawing his shoulders back. "And it means a great deal to me that you would come here for help." He exhaled, his voice dropping. "I've missed you."

She ducked her head. "You're missed as well. It's not the same without you around the shops."

His smile slipped a notch, and she wondered if she'd said something wrong. But then he escorted her outside, and they shook hands as she took her leave. His hand was rough with calluses that caught on her thin gloves. It felt like the hand of someone who could keep her safe. Of course, she'd thought the same thing about her father's hands . . .

"Say," Arthur said, interrupting her thoughts, "wouldn't it be something if the weaver turned out to be Gentry?" He chuckled. "Don't suppose she ever turned back up, did she?"

Lorna felt her head swim. "No. No, she never did." She forced a laugh of her own. "I'm sure she's far away by now. Probably gave up weaving for music. She certainly used it as an excuse to shirk her work when she was here."

Arthur nodded. "Yes, she never did have the patience for all the steps required. But she sure did have a gift for color and design."

Lorna's laugh sounded nervous to her own ears. "Yes, well, the weaver I'm looking for would certainly have to be meticulous, and I'm not sure Gentry would ever have been that."

"I guess not," Arthur agreed. "Well, see you Saturday."

She took her leave, moving slowly until she heard the door click shut behind her. She stood for a moment on the street, one hand pressed to her throat. What if the weaver *was* Gentry? The notion would never have occurred to her. But now that Arthur had planted the seed, fear coiled in her belly. She had to have a new design to save her job. Maybe to save all of Biltmore Industries. But not at the cost of facing Gentry again after all these years.

# 6

# GENTRY

**BILTMORE ESTATE INDUSTRIES**
**JANUARY 1916**

"You think you can just boss people around whenever you want?" Gentry flung the hank of thread she'd been holding at Lorna, turning it into an impossible tangle. The older girl squawked in outrage, although Gentry knew it couldn't possibly have hurt.

"Did you just throw that at me?"

Gentry didn't think that question was worth answering. Instead, she picked up a shuttle and flung it with all her might so that it crashed into the wall behind Lorna, whose mouth formed a perfect O. Her eyes went so wide, Gentry nearly laughed.

"I can't believe you just did that," she said in a monotone. "It's a miracle you didn't injure me."

"If I wanted to *injure* you, I would have," Gentry taunted. "I missed on purpose."

Color rushed back into Lorna's cheeks. "I've had just about enough of—"

"Ladies, sounds like quite the party's going on in here." Arthur swung into the weaving room and smiled easily, as if they were playing badminton instead of being on the verge of tearing each other's hair out. "Anything I can do?"

Lorna stomped her foot. "You can make this *child*"—she said the word with a sneer—"treat her elders with respect and do the work that's been assigned to her."

Gentry curled her hands into fists and huffed air through her nose like a bull ready to charge. "And you can make this *tyrant* treat us like human beings instead of like machines."

"Sounds like you both have a point you'd like to make. I'm thinking throwing things and yelling isn't the way to get that done."

Lorna gasped. "Arthur, who are you accusing of yelling?"

Gentry smirked. "Seems like you raised your voice pretty good, Miss Holier Than Thou."

Lorna took a step toward her, and Gentry dodged behind a loom. Arthur caught Lorna's arm and spoke softly near her ear. Gentry could see the older girl's hair move with his breath. Lorna stilled and seemed to be listening. Then she inhaled deeply, straightened her shoulders, and let the air out long and slow. "Gentry," she began, "I've noticed that you—" she paused and glanced at Arthur as though he'd have the words she was searching for—"that you've fallen behind in your tasks. Is there anything I can do to help?"

Gentry jerked her head back as if Lorna had taken a swing at her. She was used to fire being met with fire. She flung her arm toward the loom with the plain, windowpane-patterned fabric she was meant to be working on. "It's just so *boring*."

Lorna sighed and stepped over to the frame to examine the cloth. "This is a lovely tattersall," she said. "Did you know it's named for a horse auction house in London where the horses' blankets were woven in this pattern? You're weaving history. I know it's slow work, but isn't it satisfying to make something so beautiful?"

Gentry snorted, though she liked the bit about horses. "Beautiful? It's plain. My mother made beautiful fabric. She would have been just as bored as I am with this stupid pattern."

"I'd forgotten your mother was a weaver." Lorna stepped closer, her eyebrows raised in interest. "Why don't you tell me about her and her patterns?"

Gentry felt heat flush her cheeks. She hesitated to share anything about her mother with anyone. Those memories were *hers*.

Arthur tilted his head and examined her. "Did she teach you to weave?"

Gentry ducked her head and gnawed on her bottom lip. "I was too little." Her voice was low. "And then she was gone."

Lorna sighed heavily. "I'd think you'd want to learn to honor her memory."

"What would you know about it?" Gentry jutted her chin in the air. "Maybe if you let me make patterns half so pretty as hers, I'd want to."

"If you remember, I also lost my mother when I was young, so I do know something about it." Lorna heaved a sigh. "Alright then, if you can describe one of your mother's designs, we'll make it." She held both hands up. "Of course, you don't know enough about weaving to even begin to know how to read or write a draft." She frowned. "Which is the design as it's written out on paper." She shook a finger at Gentry. "Which is why you ought to be willing to buckle down and learn."

Gentry spun on her heel and ran from the room. She could hear Lorna calling after her. But she kept going until she'd made it to the boardinghouse and her bedroom. She retrieved yellowed papers from their hiding place and darted back down the stairs to the porch. She burst through the door to find Arthur and Lorna gasping for breath.

"You sure are fast," Arthur panted.

"And you're slow," Gentry countered without thinking. She cringed. Of course Arthur was slow. He had a bad foot. "I'm sorry," she said. "I didn't mean anything by it."

Arthur chuckled. "I *am* slow, and you're not the first to notice." He thumped his leg. "Just the way it is. Now, tell us why you took off like that."

"I came to get my mother's whatcha call it, drafts, so we can choose one to weave." She held the paper in the air.

"You have your mother's designs? Why, that's wonderful." Arthur held his hand out. "May we see them?"

Gentry slapped the sheaf against his palm as though it were a stack of hundred-dollar bills. "Granddad didn't know about them. Mama said they're her legacy and I should always keep them safe."

Arthur thumbed through the pages one by one, taking his time and nodding. "I'm not an expert like Lorna"—he pierced Gentry with a look—"and she is an expert, but these designs look impressive. Unique." He handed them to Lorna.

Nerves hit Gentry then. What if this was a mistake? What if Lorna wasn't impressed? "I saw the cloth my mother made, and it was prettier than anything we make here."

Lorna flipped through the pages slowly. "These are special," she said at last. She held up a finger. "Don't imagine that you'll be able to make these anytime soon, though. You still have a lot to learn."

Arthur grinned and wrapped one arm around Gentry's shoulders. She wasn't fond of being touched, but Arthur made her feel protected and cared for. Like a big brother who was looking out for her. "Lorna is the very best person to teach you how to weave your mother's designs. I know it's hard, but if you'll just be patient and put in the time, she can help you become an amazing weaver." He gave her a gentle squeeze, and she relaxed against him. "I see how creative you are. I've heard your music. You have wonderful gifts, and Lorna can help you make the most of them."

Gentry sighed and felt some of the buzzing and spinning ease from her stomach. She didn't notice it most of the time, but now that the clenched feeling had relaxed, she was glad of it. "I'd like that."

Arthur laughed, and she felt the rumbling in his chest. "Lorna's a bit of a perfectionist," he said with a wink, "but that's what makes her such an incredible weaver. If you let her careful ways rub off on you, maybe she'll let some of your passionate flair rub off on her."

Gentry thought he sounded like he hoped that would be the case but didn't pay that much heed. She turned to Lorna. "And then we can make my mother's patterns?"

"Yes," she said. "But I expect that will take months. Maybe we should go ahead and make one now. I can do the more difficult weaving, and you can help." She looked almost greedy as she spoke.

"I'll pick one tonight," Gentry said, holding her hand out for the drafts.

Lorna hesitated. "It would make more sense for me to hold on to these and choose which one. Since I can read them."

"No," Gentry said. "They're mine. I'll choose."

Lorna looked like she was going to say something more, but Arthur gave her a look, and she handed the pages back. Gentry felt a rush of pleasure as she imagined making something her mother had designed. Something her mother had made. It was almost like getting to see her again.

The next morning, Gentry clutched a single page. She was wrinkling the paper, but she couldn't seem to relax her grip. What if Lorna changed her mind? She'd certainly given her teacher reasons enough to turn her away. She'd returned the other drafts to the hollow behind the top right drawer of the dresser in her room the evening before. She was meant to share the room, but being considered *difficult* had its benefits. The last girl assigned to sleep in the second bed had dragged that bed across the hall to share with two other girls. Mrs. Brady, the matron, just pinched her lips and shook her head.

The weaving room was silent as she stepped inside. There was still a good hour before the rest of the weavers would arrive for their day's work. Gentry stood, examining the paper, wishing she knew how to make sense of it. The lines and numbers meant little to her. But the heart in the lower right-hand corner told her this one was special. Should she have started with one that wasn't marked? She was so lost in thought that she didn't hear Lorna enter the room.

"Gentry? What are you doing here so early?"

Her head snapped up, and she whipped the page behind her back. "I . . . I wanted to . . ."

Lorna came closer. Gentry took a step back. This had seemed like a good idea the day before. She slowly held her hand out, the crumpled paper shaking, much to her shame. "I want to make this one."

Lorna took the slip and tried to flatten it in her hands. Her brow furrowed, and she moved to a table where she smoothed the paper, pinning it down and studying it closely. The minutes ticked by. Gentry shifted from foot to foot. Why was Lorna taking such a long time? Had she picked a bad design?

"Give it back." Gentry held her hand out. "It's mine."

"Of course it is." Lorna gave her a confused look before turning to the paper again. "It's just . . . it's remarkable."

Gentry sidled closer. "It is?"

"Yes. You see how the threads and colors mix here?" She ran a finger along some figures. "And the use of spacers? This will be gorgeous. I've never seen anything like it."

Gentry bent her head near Lorna's, but she couldn't make sense of what she was seeing. "Can I make it?"

A sharp laugh burst from Lorna. "No. You can't. I can, but it will be challenging. I'm not sure there will be much for you to do with this one. Maybe help to sett the warp."

Gentry snatched the page from under Lorna's fingers. "You said I could help with the weaving." She crushed the page in her hand and crossed her arms. "You just don't want me to do it. You want to save it for yourself."

Lorna blinked, then straightened from where she'd bent over the table. "No, Gentry. You simply aren't skilled enough. That's an incredibly complex design."

"*Yet*. I'm not skilled enough yet."

Lorna gave a half smile and shook her head. "I'm the best weaver here and I'm hardly skilled enough. Even if you follow my every instruction and work as diligently as you can, it will still take you a long time to be good enough to weave something like this."

Gentry felt something big welling up inside her. It rose from her belly to her chest, where it expanded and filled every inch of her body. Her breath came in short bursts, and stars appeared in the edges of her vision. "Then no one can make it!" Her voice was so loud, it shocked her. She ripped the page once, then twice, letting the pieces fall to the floor and clamping her hands over her ears. She screamed in frustration. The look on Lorna's face eased some of the pain tearing through her. She'd shocked and horrified her teacher. And causing someone else pain magically eased her own, as if she'd transferred some of the agony she felt every single day on to Lorna. Panting, she dropped her hands.

Lorna just stared, mouth hanging open.

"Guess I won't bother to do any weaving today since you don't think I'll ever be good enough." Lorna continued to gape as Gentry spun on her heel and flounced from the room.

# ARTHUR

**BILTMORE ESTATE INDUSTRIES
MARCH 1921**

After a couple of weeks of dithering, Arthur thought he was finally ready to take Angus's advice regarding "the lovely Lorna." He hurried to catch up to her outside the weaving room. He'd never make himself heard over the clack and clatter inside, plus he'd rather no one witnessed him asking Lorna to dine with him at the Grove Park Inn.

He stumbled and righted himself. While he'd long ago made peace with the misshapen foot he'd been born with, there were days when he longed to be as agile as other fellows who walked, ran, and jumped without thinking twice. Thankfully, the special shoe and brace he wore made the problem easier to manage. Most days. Days when he wasn't shaking with nervousness because he was going to ask someone he'd long admired to spend time with him.

"Lorna," he called, trying not to sound breathless.

She glanced at him over her shoulder, and he saw storm clouds in her eyes. She blew a breath out through her nose and stopped. She wasn't quite tapping her foot, but it seemed like she might start any moment. Maybe he should do this another time.

"What is it?" she said. There was no feeling or warmth in her tone.

Arthur had been half in love with this bright, artistic woman for years—since before the great flood and all that happened as a result. He'd thought her too young to pursue before then, and since that fateful July day five years ago he'd vowed to wait. At first in deference to Lorna's loss, and then because she seemed distant and preoccupied with her work. But in recent months he'd thought he sensed a thawing, an easing of the sorrow she carried. And Angus had convinced him the time was right.

Plus, Reverend Swope had been pressing him to meet his niece. Arthur knew his mentor hoped he would marry and settle down. Not that he was opposed to the idea. As a matter of fact, it was his imminent meeting with Clara Peters that had finally spurred him to act this very day. If Lorna allowed him to court her, he'd be able to deflect his mentor's schemes.

Lorna crossed her arms and began to lightly drum her fingers. She raised her eyebrows. Oh well. In for a penny . . .

"I was hoping you'd join me for dinner at the inn tonight." The words came out in a rush, all at once. The finger-drumming stopped.

"Dinner? What's the occasion?"

He felt heat creep from beneath his collar. "Just a pleasant meal between, uh, friends." He swallowed wrong and coughed. "I, ahem, thought it would be a pleasant diversion."

She gave him a suspicious look. "Did Mr. Seely put you up to this?"

Arthur scrambled to make sense of the question. "No. I mean, why would he?"

She flicked the fingers of one hand in the air. "No reason." She glanced at the watch pinned to her blouse. "I really must be going."

Arthur almost gave up and let her go but instead reached out and grabbed her arm. "And dinner? Shall we say six o'clock?"

She gave her head a shake. "Alright. That sounds nice. I'll meet you in the lobby."

He tried to jump in and tell her that he'd escort her to the inn, but she'd already spun on her heel and was hurrying away. He watched her go as a second person exited the weaving room, releasing a cacophony of sound.

LeeAnn Brady startled when she saw Arthur standing there. "Oh. I thought to catch Miss Blankenship."

"Lorna seemed in a hurry," Arthur said and waved in the direction she'd gone.

LeeAnn twisted her fingers in her skirt. "She dropped this," she said, holding out a folded piece of paper. "I thought it might be important."

Arthur took it. "I'll be seeing her this evening." Just saying those words soothed his spirit. "I'll be happy to give it to her then."

"I suppose that'd be alright," the girl said. "So long as you tell her I'm the one what found it for her."

Arthur bit back a smile. "I'll be sure she knows who to thank," he said.

"And tell her I didn't read it."

"I'll be sure of that, as well." The smile slipped out. She looked at him with narrowed eyes but apparently decided he could be trusted and returned to the whirl of the weaving room.

Arthur moved to slip the paper into his coat pocket, then fumbled and dropped it so that it fell open on the floor at his feet. As he bent to retrieve the note, he couldn't help but see that it was from Fred Seely and began with the words, *It has come to my attention.* He averted his eyes and quickly refolded the page to tuck away in his pocket. He wished he hadn't seen that first line. Something about it felt ominous. And the last thing he wanted to do over dinner with Lorna was to quiz her about work.

⁕⁕⁕⁕⁕

The necktie would *not* cooperate. Arthur's fingers felt fat and clumsy. He shook them out. He was a woodcarver for heaven's sake. He did all sorts of fine carving without a single slip. But this evening he couldn't manage to perform a simple task he'd done a hundred times before. Initially, he'd intended to tie a fashionable Windsor knot. Now he'd settle for the plain old four-in-hand knot, but even that came out lopsided. He finally gave up, hoping Lorna wouldn't notice.

As he walked the short distance from his rented rooms to the hotel, he saw a streetcar stop outside the massive stone edifice. Lorna alighted, pausing to let her gaze travel all the way up to the red-tile roof of the Grove Park Inn. He considered that no matter how many times a person might see the building, it was hard not to pause to drink it in. While it wasn't as grand as Biltmore House, it had a solidity and a rough beauty that Arthur preferred. Made of native granite, Fred Seely had instructed his Italian stonemasons to place stones with their rough faces out, giving the structure a craggy look. It was almost as if the building had always been there, and they simply carved away the side of Sunset Mountain to expose it.

He jogged to catch up to Lorna before she went inside. She smiled when she saw him, but it was an automatic sort of smile—not the kind he'd hoped would light her face. A uniformed doorman welcomed them, and they stepped through the double doors into the towering lobby with its massive stone fireplaces at either end, burning ten-foot logs. A man would only have to duck a little to step inside if he dared. Mr. Seely had quotes printed on the stones, some of which were as big as a man. Arthur smiled as he recalled his favorite: *"Be not simply good—be good for something."* Henry David Thoreau had said that, and Arthur would take the words to heart tonight.

Lorna tilted her head back to take in the immensity of the space—one hundred twenty feet long and eighty feet wide—then caught herself gawking. She tucked a strand of hair under her bell-shaped hat, and this time her smile was one of forced gentility. "Isn't it lovely here?"

"Not half so lovely as you." Arthur cringed. That had sounded more corny than charming. And from the guarded look on Lorna's face, he'd bet she agreed. He cleared his throat. "What I mean to say is, you look very nice."

She tugged at the white gloves she wore with her pale blue, dropped-waist dress. Arthur had never been fond of this style, preferring to see a woman's shape, but it was all the rage, even here in Asheville.

"Thank you," she said and seemed to be waiting for something more.

"Oh. Right this way," Arthur said. He cocked his elbow for her to grasp. "I've reserved a table for us."

They were escorted to a table overlooking the mountains. He'd been timing it and knew the sun would set right around six-thirty, hopefully about the time they were enjoying their delicious entrées.

"Arthur, it was very kind of you to invite me here, but I'm not certain I understand why you asked."

His stomach knotted. That was certainly direct. Well, he could be direct, too. "I like you," he said, and this felt much better than his earlier awkward compliment. "I've enjoyed your company for years, and I hoped—"

A waiter swooped in to take their orders. Arthur was thankful Lorna would be first to order, as he'd barely glanced at the menu. She asked for the filet of sole with lemon butter sauce and cucumbers. "I'll have broiled lamb chops and asparagus salad," he said, choosing the first thing his eyes landed on. The waiter bowed, murmured something about their excellent choices, and flitted away.

Lorna fiddled with her napkin while Arthur tried to pick up where he'd left off. "Remember that Christmas when Gentry first came? I loved seeing how you worked with her—how you handled her impatience and helped her learn to weave. You even helped her with one of her mother's patterns, didn't you?" Lorna looked pale, and her lips formed a narrow line. He felt as though he was losing ground and rushed forward. "Anyway, I've always admired you—your skill and your gift for weaving. You're smart and kind and pretty." He was so thirsty. "And I've been hoping we might be more than friends." There. He wanted to wipe his brow with his napkin but resisted, reaching for his water glass instead.

Lorna removed her gloves and set them beside her plate. "Arthur, I'm grateful for your friendship. You've been an important part of my life for some time now." She sipped her water. "But I think you and I remember Gentry's time here differently." She laughed lightly. "I wasn't at all patient with her, and we never did make her mother's pattern." Her eyes flicked away. "As a matter of fact, she tore up the only pattern she brought to the weaving room. In a fit of pique."

Arthur opened, then closed his mouth. He felt like they'd gotten off track. Maybe he shouldn't have brought up Gentry. "But I remember what a good teacher you were. Still are, I'm sure. And I admire you for it."

She frowned. "I hardly teach anymore. Mr. Tompkins has relegated me to administrative work. And I'm never given sufficient time to come up with new designs." She tossed her head as though shaking off something unpleasant. "Not that that keeps Mr. Tompkins from complaining that I haven't presented him with a new pattern in far too long. And now Mr. Seely——" She stopped abruptly. "At any rate, as flattering as your description of me is, I'm not sure it's accurate."

What could he say to that? Certainly not what he'd been practicing in the mirror all week. He forced a chuckle. "We've sure been through some interesting times together, haven't we?" She smiled, but it was small and pinched.

This time, when the waiter swooped in, Arthur was grateful. They both began eating, though he wasn't sure either of them was enjoying the food. This called for drastic measures. "I'm leaving Biltmore Industries," he blurted.

Lorna's head jerked up, and her fork froze with a morsel of fish halfway to her mouth. "Leaving?"

"Yes." He'd hoped to discuss the possibility with Lorna— not the certainty. But maybe if she knew he wasn't going to be around as much, she would realize that she'd miss him. It was a long shot, but what else could he do? He'd been needing something to tip him into action, and this felt like the right moment. "I'm starting my own shop. Cabinetry, woodworking, custom jobs—that sort of thing."

"But why?" Her fork quivered, and the bite of fish fell to her plate. She set the fork down and clasped her hands. "You've worked so hard as the manager for Mr. Seely."

"Orders have dropped off, and Mr. Seely is focusing on the weaving side of the business." Arthur took a bite of lamb—it really was delicious. He swallowed and patted his lips with his napkin. "I have some ideas about how to grow—how to draw more customers." He cut another bite. "Plus it's time. I've been following the lead of others long enough now. I'm going out on my own."

The hollow place that opened in his chest after Lorna's

failure to respond the way he'd hoped began to fill. He'd sacrificed more than she knew to stay with Biltmore Industries when Mrs. Vanderbilt sold it to Mr. Seely. And it was true that Fred Seely was less and less interested in woodworking. He could do great things, and if his leaving also spurred Lorna to miss him, all the better. And if it didn't, well, then he'd rather not see her every day.

This wasn't how he'd hoped the evening would go, yet for the first time in a long time he felt as if he was setting his own course instead of chasing after a dream that might never come true.

"Look," he said, nodding toward the horizon. Lorna turned, and together they watched the sun slip behind a mountain, golden rays shooting out, turning the clouds gold, then red, then orange before finally fading to a rich purple. "Dinner and a show," he said.

Lorna turned back to her plate and speared a bite of cucumber. "Thank you for inviting me."

He nodded, and they finished their meal largely in silence. They decided against ordering dessert. Arthur walked Lorna back out the grand front doors before he remembered the slip of paper LeeAnn had given him. He'd tucked it in his coat pocket before leaving his room and fished it out now.

"I almost forgot," he said. "LeeAnn from the weaving room said you dropped this today."

She snatched the paper from his hand and crumpled it in her fist. "Now I understand," she said, her words laced with ice. "You read this, didn't you?" She shook the paper at him. "Did you think telling me you're leaving Biltmore Industries would somehow win me over? That I'd tuck my tail and run off with you?"

Heads turned in their direction. Arthur took Lorna's elbow and gently steered her into the shadows. She snatched her arm away. "Well, I'm going to prove to Mr. Seely that someone's been spreading lies. Those designs are *mine*." She pressed a fist to her chest.

Arthur held up both hands. "Lorna, I don't know what you're talking about. I didn't read whatever's on that page."

Even in the darkness and shadow, Arthur could see the sparks in Lorna's eyes. She didn't believe him. "I'm glad you're leaving. And I'm sorry I came out with you." Then she whirled away and practically ran to climb aboard a streetcar.

He watched the car start down the mountain before walking home. He'd imagined making this trip with the whisper of Lorna's kiss on his lips. Instead, he walked away confused, conflicted, and wondering if he might not be better off simply washing his hands of Lorna once and for all.

# 8

# GENTRY

**BILTMORE VILLAGE**
**FEBRUARY 1916**

Gentry stabbed the floor of the weaving room with her broom. Sweeping up was her punishment for working too slowly. It seemed like every time she tried to dress a loom, she'd miss threading a heddle or miscount how many threads made up a sett. Once, she'd even used the wrong thread entirely and had to pull it all and start over. It was infuriating, exhausting, and worst of all, boring.

And now she was relegated to sweeping up the snips of thread other girls like LeeAnn and that flatterer Bernice had cast onto the floor. Girls who wouldn't give her the time of day. They'd all finished their tasks and left without sparing her a glance. Meanwhile, Lorna sat oblivious at her loom, making the shuttle fly like a bird between the perfectly arranged threads. She was making yet another boring plaid, and Gentry tried to tell herself she didn't want to work on something as uninteresting as that anyway. Although perhaps sweeping was worse.

The clatter of Lorna's loom stopped. She stood and stretched her back. "Aren't you finished sweeping yet?" she asked with a pointed look. "I've woven a foot of cloth in the time it's taken you to make a single circuit around the room."

That was an exaggeration. Gentry gripped the broom, imagining what it would feel like to smack Lorna on the backside with the flat of the straw end.

"What are you smiling about?" Lorna asked, taking half a step backward and looking at Gentry from under lowered brows.

Before Gentry could make a smart remark, a figure appeared in the doorway. Arthur took off his hat and smiled at them both, but Gentry saw the way his smile grew when his eyes landed on Lorna. "I thought I'd walk the pair of you to supper," he said.

Lorna turned from Gentry, smoothing her skirt and tugging at her sleeves. "How thoughtful. I know I'd be delighted to accompany you, but I'm not sure Gentry is finished with her work here." She quirked an eyebrow in Gentry's direction.

"Just a minute." Gentry rushed to find the dustpan and made short work of the pile of threads and dirt she'd corralled. She clattered the broom and pan into the narrow cleaning closet and rushed to Arthur's side. "I'm ready."

Arthur laughed. "I see all you need is the inspiration provided by Mrs. Brady's cooking."

"All I need is something to hold my interest." Gentry rolled her eyes. "And just about anything is more interesting than being here." She made a face at Lorna.

"Now, Gentry, you know Lorna's purpose is to teach you a skill that will help you succeed in the world." Arthur placed one of his large, work-roughened hands on her shoulder. Gentry settled under the weight of it.

"If you say so." Arthur let his hand drop, and Gentry

bounced on her toes. "Tell us all the gossip while we walk," she said, darting for the door.

Arthur laughed and, with his hitching gait, walked to the cloakroom where he retrieved Gentry's ugly green coat. She sighed and let him help her into it. Honestly, she hardly felt the cold once she was allowed outside at the end of an overlong workday.

"Hold your horses," he said as he helped Lorna into her coat next. Gentry heaved a sigh. As if either one of them weren't perfectly capable of dressing themselves.

Finally outside in the bracing air, Gentry danced circles around Arthur and Lorna. She'd been in awe of the village when she'd first arrived. Miss Vance told her it was meant to look like an English village with rows of shops and cottages all covered in something called pebbledash, with heavy, dark timbers setting off the pale walls. Gentry didn't know about all that, but she did know it looked like something from a fairy tale. Although, if this were a story, she wished her fairy godmother would hurry up.

She circled back to Arthur and Lorna, who were walking arm in arm like old people. "The gossip, Arthur, what's the gossip from the castle?"

Lorna gave her an exasperated look. "Gossip is shameful, and it's not a castle. It's a château, if you insist on calling it something other than Biltmore House."

Gentry swooped in and clung to Arthur's empty arm. "I don't care. Tell us something interesting."

Arthur chuckled. "Well, one of the kitchen maids left the gate in the hall open, and two of Cornelia's dogs got into the rotisserie kitchen this morning."

Gentry chortled. "The Saint Bernards? Oh, I bet that French cook had something to say about that!"

"Indeed," Arthur laughed. "And I think it's just as well most of the staff didn't understand a word he was saying."

As their laughter faded, Arthur got a serious look. He glanced at Lorna. "There is some other news I thought perhaps I ought to share."

Lorna frowned. "Is it serious?" She tightened her grip on his arm. "I hope no one is sick. Losing Mr. Vanderbilt the way they did was so hard."

"No, not sick, but it does have to do with Mr. Vanderbilt's death."

Gentry released Arthur's arm and scooped up some pebbles to throw in the river as they walked. She nearly hit a duck, taking satisfaction in its squawk and flutter. She didn't even glance toward Lorna since she could imagine the reproving look without doing so. Arthur lowered his voice, but Gentry's ears were good, and she listened carefully.

"There's money trouble," he said. "I've heard Mr. Vanderbilt left less money than first reported." He paused. "And more debt." He glanced toward Gentry, who pretended she wasn't listening at all. "And Biltmore Estate Industries isn't as profitable as hoped."

"What can we do?" Lorna asked.

"I'm not sure there's anything for us to do," Arthur said with a shake of his head. "If the Vanderbilts can't fix the situation, I don't see how we could."

"We could weave fabric so beautiful that everyone—even the fancy people—would want it, and we'd sell it as fast as we could make it." Gentry tossed the rest of her pebbles in a shower that clattered around them. Lorna frowned, but Gentry was used to ignoring people who frowned at her. "And you could make carvings that people even in big cities couldn't resist buying." She dusted her hands. "Just make more money if that's what's needed."

"It's not that simple, Gentry." Lorna's voice carried weariness.

"Now hold on." Arthur stopped and dug a hand in his

overcoat pocket. He pulled out a piece of wood and handed it to Gentry. It was a cunningly carved squirrel, holding a perfect acorn between his paws. "We've been making the nut bowls with grapevines and dogwood, but what about one with oak leaves, acorns, and"—he nodded at the figure—"squirrels."

Gentry laughed in delight. "Who could resist?" she crowed.

Lorna held out her hand, and Gentry reluctantly handed over the sweet carving. "This is delightful, Arthur." She turned it in her hand. "I suppose if we came up with some new designs for fabric, we could perhaps tempt shoppers like Mrs. Vanderbilt's friends and family." She handed the squirrel back to Arthur. "It's worth a try."

They reached the boardinghouse, and Lorna went up the stairs to the porch. Gentry hung back. Arthur turned and waited a moment until Lorna disappeared inside. "You're a good thinker, Gentry. Who knows, your idea might save Biltmore Estate Industries."

Gentry kicked at the bottom step, her boot thunking against the wood. "It's your carving. And her weaving." She pooched her lip out. "It probably won't work anyway."

Arthur pressed the squirrel into her palm. "If it doesn't work, at least we will have tried." He winked. "And I say give credit where credit's due." He tapped her forehead lightly with his finger. "You have quite the mind there, Miss Gentry. Once you learn to harness all that energy jumping around inside you, you'll be a force to be reckoned with." He smiled and headed for the door. "And I'll be proud to tell people I knew you when you were just starting out."

Gentry watched him hitch his way up the steps and disappear inside the light and warmth of the boardinghouse. He didn't live here, but he often took his meals with them, and Gentry was glad of it. He was the only person she'd found whom she really liked here in Asheville.

A tear escaped and slid down her cheek before she could catch it. She dashed it away in disgust. Her grandfather would accuse her of being sentimental, soft. And if there was one thing she'd learned in this world, it was to never let her defenses down. She steeled herself and realized she was clutching Arthur's carving so hard it bit into her hand. She relaxed her fingers and examined the squirrel again in the light from the front window. She smiled. Maybe she could afford to relax around Arthur.

Just a little.

"Today I'm going to let you finish the cloth I've been weaving on the loom at the end of the row." Lorna made the announcement like she was crowning Gentry queen of the weaving room.

Gentry was about to inform Lorna that she didn't want to finish her stupid cloth, but then caught herself. It would be easier than setting up her own loom. And it was certainly better than doing all the mundane cleaning and tidying tasks she had to do when she'd messed something else up. Why not take advantage?

"Why?" she asked, suspicious.

Lorna smiled in a way that was almost mischievous. "Because I'm going to weave some cloth that will save Biltmore Estate Industries." She waved toward the loom with the cloth in progress. "But that piece still needs finishing. It's a plain weave so surely you can manage it."

Gentry frowned at what sounded like an insult. "Of course I can manage it. Even though it's completely *boring*." She laced the last word with scorn so Lorna would know the work was really quite beneath her.

"Good," Lorna said, already beginning to sett an empty loom. Gentry slouched over to the work in progress and began to move the shuttle back and forth, using the beater to snug each thread in place. It kept her interest for about ten passes. Then her gaze strayed to Lorna and the beautiful threads she was working with. They looked much more interesting than the plain gray of the cloth Gentry was making.

Her work slowed to the point that Lorna noticed. "If you don't pick up the pace, I'll be done with the new cloth before you finish the old."

Gentry stilled. Was that a note of teasing in Lorna's voice? Something about it thawed a spot in Gentry's chest. She sucked in her lower lip and began weaving faster. Soon she'd developed a rhythm that reminded her of playing music, and before she knew it she'd completed a wide section of cloth.

Lorna appeared at Gentry's elbow and leaned over the loom. "Very good," she said. "I don't see even one mistake." She laid a hand on Gentry's shoulder, and for once, Gentry didn't shrug it off. "Would you like to come see what I'm doing?"

Gentry looked up in astonishment. "I . . . yes." It was all she could think to say.

Lorna had sett the weft of her loom with threads in undulating shades of blue. She began talking about floats and finger-controlled weaves, waving her hands in the air as she described what she planned. Gentry could hardly make sense of it since she hadn't paid all that much attention to her lessons. But Lorna's enthusiasm was contagious, and she found herself nodding along, eager to see the finished product.

"Is it very hard?" she asked at last.

Lorna paused in her description. "Well, yes. I suppose it is." She smiled but looked kind of sad at the same time. "I've always been able to handle the technical difficulties of weaving. It's the creativity that escapes me."

Gentry frowned. "But this seems awfully creative."

Lorna flushed and turned away. "It's not my design if you must know," she mumbled. She clapped her hands. "Now, you get back to your work and I'll get back to mine."

Gentry sighed and returned to her loom. She still wasn't quite eager, but she was more determined to do a good job than she had been since being sentenced to hard labor at Biltmore Estate Industries.

"When can I see it?" Gentry whined. It had been a full week since Lorna began her secret weaving project.

"When it's finished." Lorna's answer wasn't what Gentry wanted to hear, but she said it with a teasing gleam in her eye that won a smile.

"Have you shown anyone?" Gentry asked.

"Not a soul. You and Arthur will be the first."

"*Whennn*," Gentry threw her head back and dragged the word out.

Lorna laughed. "Actually, it's done." Gentry clapped her hands. "But we have to wait for Arthur. I asked him to stop by before supper so I could show you both."

"Did I hear someone mention my name and supper in the same breath?" Gentry had been so focused on Lorna, she hadn't heard Arthur come into the room.

"Lorna's going to show us the cloth," she crowed. "The one that's going to save Biltmore Estate Industries."

Arthur chuckled. "Pipe down there, Gentry. At this point, we're the only ones who know about that. Let's see this amazing fabric before we announce it to the world."

Gentry rolled her eyes and tried to wait patiently as Lorna disappeared into the workroom she'd commandeered.

"I bet it'll be amazing," she whispered.

"If Lorna made it, you know it will be," Arthur agreed.

Lorna walked to a cutting table with her bundle covered

in linen. She stood at one end of the table and unfurled the cloth. "Ta-da," she said with a look of triumph.

Arthur began to make appreciative noises. He lifted the fabric and whistled. But Gentry just stood there frozen, staring. In her mind, it was winter back home on the mountain. An icy wind made the cabin she shared with Mama and Grandad shudder. Snowflakes sifted through the crack in the door. She caught some on her cold palm and watched the perfect pattern melt away. She could feel the cold, could taste the bite of ice on her tongue, and behind her she thought she heard the crackle of a fire on the hearth.

"Well?" Lorna's voice came from somewhere far away. "Gentry, what do you think?"

"What?" Gentry shook her head slowly, trying to clear it. Her hands were so very cold.

"Are you alright?" Arthur stood at her elbow, peering into her face with worried eyes.

"It's like snow," Gentry said.

"Is it?" Lorna tilted her head and considered the cloth. "I suppose it is. The draft just seemed to lend itself to whites and pale grays with that background of blue. You don't think it's too plain?"

Gentry took a stumbling step closer and reached out to touch the fabric. She was surprised when it was soft and warm. She'd been expecting something icy and brittle. "It's so pretty," she murmured.

"It is striking, Lorna," Arthur said. "And I think the fashionable ladies will be captivated by it. You could almost make a wedding dress out of it."

Lorna beamed. "Yes, you see how the different shades of white and gray play off one another? And then the openwork gives it a lacy effect, almost like tatting." She blew out her breath. "And the threads are the finest I could manage. That's why it took so long to make even this sample piece."

"I remember . . ." Gentry began to speak, then broke off. She felt a sudden chill. As if someone had opened a door on a gusty, winter day. She could almost see the glint of sunlight on ice, hear the crunch of footsteps in snow. Then a warmth passed over her, and she shook off the feeling.

"Yes?" Lorna raised her eyebrows, waiting. "It reminds you of something."

Gentry shook her head and waved a hand in front of her face as if a gnat were buzzing there. "Something. I can't quite remember."

"But you like it?" Lorna pressed.

A tightness rose in Gentry's throat, and tears gathered behind her eyes. "Yes. But it makes me sad, too."

Lorna wrinkled her brow. "Well, that's . . . odd."

Arthur wrapped an arm around Gentry's shoulders. "Lorna, this fabric is going to put Biltmore Estate Industries on the map." He looked down. "And, Gentry, you're an artist who recognizes and is touched by rare beauty." He gave her a squeeze. "I'm lucky to know you both."

Lorna beamed, and Gentry managed to smile. But she still felt sad. And a little bit like the fabric on the table in front of her should be hers and hers alone.

# 9

# LORNA

**WEAVERVILLE, NORTH CAROLINA**
**SEPTEMBER 1923**

Saturday morning came and with it a whole swarm of butterflies in the pit of Lorna's stomach. Why did she have butterflies? She couldn't remember the last time she'd felt so nervous. It was only Arthur coming to escort her into the hills so she wouldn't be shot dead by some mountain man. A bubble of laughter burst from her mouth, and she clapped a hand over her lips. How inappropriate. She was acting like a foolish schoolgirl rather than a woman of twenty-seven who had survived the loss of both parents and a near drowning. Of course, she was also a woman who had taken advantage of one of her students. And now Arthur had planted the notion that that very student might be the elusive weaver she sought.

She startled when someone knocked at the door. Whirling, her heart in her mouth, she took a deep breath before placing her hand on the knob. She exhaled and opened the door to find Arthur standing there, a boyish flush to his cheeks and his hat at a jaunty angle. He gave her a lopsided grin that made her heart somersault. Much to her annoyance.

"Ready to brave the bear in its den?" he asked.

She laughed—a nervous titter. She bit down on her lip and tried to compose herself. She'd already noted that Arthur didn't wear a wedding band. She told herself she was only looking out of curiosity. Any chance at romance had died when she'd failed to accept his advances that night at Grove Park Inn. And then ran off in a fit of pique that now seemed utterly childish.

"Are you armed?" she asked lightly.

Arthur paused, then lifted both of his arms wide. "As you can see, madam. Not one arm, but two."

Lorna laughed. It was a release of tension, fear, anticipation, and she didn't know what all. And it felt good.

An hour later, Lorna's focus was elsewhere entirely as they made their way back up Pink Fox Cove. They were drawing closer to the cabin where the mountain man and his rifle lived. She realized she was carrying the bag with the prize shawl in it across her chest like a shield.

"You think that cloth bag will stop a bullet?" Arthur looked over his shoulder with a twinkle in his eye.

She lowered the bag and tossed her head. "Of course not. But we are approaching the place where someone fired a rifle at me, so you'll have to forgive me if I seem anxious."

"Wasn't a rifle."

Lorna stifled a scream and clutched her bag closer as a man stepped from the depths of the woods onto the path. She flicked her eyes from him to Arthur and back again.

"'Twas a shotgun." He shook his head. "Can't you tell the difference?"

Lorna lifted her chin and stepped closer to Arthur. "It would seem not."

"Basil, is it true that you took a shot at this fine lady?" Arthur finally spoke, and Lorna exhaled, realizing that was what she'd been waiting for.

"Nope. Fired on an empty chamber, and that's a different thing altogether." He stepped forward and offered a hand to Arthur. "Haven't seen you in a month of Sundays." He cast a sideways glance at Lorna, then turned his head to release a stream of tobacco juice. "If I'd known she was yours, I would've been politer."

"Oh, we're not—" Arthur's look stopped Lorna's tongue, and she pressed her lips together, tightening her grip on her bag.

"I know you wouldn't hurt a woman, Basil." Arthur chuckled, much to Lorna's annoyance. "Only give her a story to tell her friends when she gets home. When she said she ran into a mountain man, I wondered if it might be you."

Now Basil chuckled and slapped Arthur on the shoulder. "Come sit a spell," he said and started along a path Lorna hadn't noticed before.

Arthur made a you-first gesture, and Lorna scowled at him before preceding him along the narrow way. She could hear Arthur's soft laugh and was grateful that he couldn't see her own features softening. She didn't much appreciate Basil's attitude toward women, but if she was honest, she didn't mind one bit that he'd assumed she and Arthur were a couple.

They soon emerged onto a grassy hillside, where a small cabin sat as though it were rooted there. Flowers bloomed in pots on the porch, a morning glory twining its way up a porch post. The steps and the packed earth leading to them had been swept clean. A cat curled in a cane chair, cleaning its face.

"But this isn't your house. I found you farther along," Lorna said.

Basil looked at her, then turned to Arthur with raised eyebrows. He lowered his voice. "Is she simple?"

Arthur coughed, but his eyes laughed, and Lorna wanted to kick him in the shin. He cleared his throat. "Lorna, this is where Basil's mother, Mrs. Howes, lives. Sounds like you did, indeed, find Basil's place on up the cove."

Which, Lorna realized, meant this was the third cabin and she'd gone too far on her previous trip. Before she could say as much, the screen door swung open, and a woman in a gingham dress and apron with her hair in a high bun stepped outside. "Basil, it sounds like you brought me some company," she said. "And you know I dearly love company."

"Yes, Ma. It's Arthur, and he's brung a lady with him."

"Brought, son. And I know you speak that way to annoy me or perhaps to entertain our guests." She shook her head and held out a hand. "Come join me, my dear. I don't see so well, but it's a fair guess there's a cat in the chair there at the steps. Shoo her out and have a seat."

Lorna did as she was told, scooping the cat onto the porch, where it landed lightly and began to push its head against her leg, purring. She wasn't fond of cats but decided this wasn't the time to mention it.

Mrs. Howes settled into a rocker, which she set into motion with one foot. Basil and Arthur found seats on the porch steps.

"Arthur, tell me your friend's name," she said, looking into the middle distance. Lorna supposed her eyesight must be very bad indeed.

"This is Lorna, Mrs. Howes. She's a weaver like you."

Lorna's eyes widened, and she shot a look at Arthur. Was this woman the weaver she'd been looking for?

The older woman clapped her hands. "How wonderful!

And call me Elspeth, dear. Now, tell me about your weaving." She leaned forward but still didn't make eye contact. Lorna realized her eyes were cloudy. Was she altogether blind? If so, how could she weave?

"I've been a weaver with Biltmore Industries for more than half of my life. These days I mostly handle the administrative side of the weaving business, ensuring orders are filled and the weavers are properly trained."

Elspeth's cloudy eyes dimmed. "Oh? You don't do the actual weaving?"

"I can, and I do on occasion. It's just . . . well, there's so much to be organized, and orders for our homespun just keep coming. Not to mention that most of the weavers are men now." She laughed lightly and darted a glance at Arthur, who didn't meet her eyes. Did he know her designs had been dismissed again and again? That she'd been pushed into an administrative role because she'd never been able to match those early designs meant to make the weaving business profitable?

She shook off the feeling that Arthur knew more than she might like. "But I was hoping to talk about your weaving," she said. "Do you . . . that is to say, can you still . . . ?" She hadn't thought how to delicately address her question in her rush to shift the focus of the conversation.

"No, my dear, I don't weave any longer." Elspeth patted the air as if to soothe Lorna's discomfort. "My eyes began to dim years ago. I kept working as long as I could, but now even the coarsest thread is too fine for me to work with."

Lorna's heart sank. This couldn't be her weaver then. Unless the shawl she had wasn't new cloth. She drew the fabric from her bag and pressed it into Elspeth's hand. "I'm looking for the weaver who made this." She bit her lip. What could the woman tell without her sight?

Elspeth's fingers curled around the soft cloth, and the

muscles of her face relaxed. She stroked the shawl, then rubbed it between her fingertips as though they could read the pattern of the fine threads. "Ah. Such a lovely piece." She turned her head to the side, and Lorna realized she was using her peripheral vision to get a glimpse of the gorgeous colors. "Lovely," she repeated.

Basil rose and approached his mother. "Ma," he said in a low voice.

"Not now, Basil." She pressed the shawl to her cheek and closed her eyes. "All is well."

"But, Ma—"

"Lorna—like Blackmoore's heroine." She turned her hazy eyes in Lorna's direction. "Are you as stalwart as she?"

"I . . . I don't know. It's been a long time since I read the story."

"It's a good story," Elspeth said. She thrust the shawl out, waiting for Lorna to take it. "I did send this cloth to the market to sell, although I was sorry to part with it. The woman who wove it surely has an exceptional gift. But it was not I."

Lorna took the cloth, glad she needn't bother to hide the disappointment written on her face. "Where did you get it? Can you help me find the weaver?"

"It was a gift from long ago. I'm glad it's found its way to someone who can appreciate it." She folded her gnarled hands in her lap. "Why do you want to find this person? Will you recruit her to weave fabric for the likes of the Vanderbilts?"

Lorna swallowed hard, knowing that was essentially what she hoped to do but sensing that Elspeth wouldn't approve. "I'd like to learn from her," she said at last. "The business is faltering, and we need something new to ensure it continues. Biltmore Industries has grown over the years, and there are a lot of people relying on it for work. I'm hoping this weaver can help me inject new life into our homespun fabrics."

"That sounds like a wise plan," Elspeth agreed. "I hope you find what you're looking for." She smiled. "Now, tell me more about the fabric you make. I understand President Coolidge has admired it."

Lorna tolerated another twenty minutes of small talk before finally announcing it was time she and Arthur returned to Asheville. Elspeth stood and held out her hand for Lorna to take. "It has been a pleasure talking with another weaver, my dear. I'm glad there are women like you carrying on this wonderful tradition." She pressed Lorna's fingers and released her hand. "Come and see me again if you like. My days are quiet, and there is less for me to do than there once was."

Lorna murmured her goodbyes and promised to come again, though she doubted she would. Arthur took her hand, helping her descend the porch steps, then tucked her arm through his as they returned to the path. Basil trailed after them.

Once they reached Reems Creek with its wider path, Basil turned upstream. Then he paused. "There are stories about a weaver." He glanced back toward his mother's cabin. "Supposed to be able to take the leaves and rocks and mountain sunshine and spin 'em into thread for her cloth." He snorted. "Hogwash." He shrugged. "But stories have a way of starting with something true more often than not."

Lorna gripped Arthur's arm. "Where would we find this weaver?"

"Can't say," Basil said. "Just stories. Tall tales if you ask me. But I thought you'd want to know. Ma can be tight-lipped until she gets to know you."

Arthur reached into his pocket and pressed something in the other man's hand. "Thank you, my friend. If you hear anything more about this mystery weaver, I'd be glad to know it."

Basil nodded and trotted up the trail before stepping into the woods and disappearing among the trees like some wild thing.

Lorna looked up at Arthur. "Do you think there really is another weaver?"

Arthur took a slow breath and tilted his head back to watch a skein of geese unfurl across the sky. "Why not?" he said. "Looking at that cloth you have there, I can almost believe it's made from goldenrod and pumpkins with a dash of cinnamon fern thrown in for good measure."

"Birch leaves," murmured Lorna.

"Yes." Arthur snapped his fingers. "With the brown of the trunk to make the gold stand out."

"We have to find her," she said. "She's the one."

Arthur looked straight into her eyes, leaving her feeling breathless and comforted all at once. "Then we will," he said. And she believed him.

⋯⋯⋯

While they hadn't found the weaver, Lorna felt certain they were getting closer. And with Arthur's help, she trusted they would find her soon. Add to that the fact that she had frankly enjoyed spending an early autumn day walking the hills with Arthur, and she realized she was in a cheerful mood for the first time since . . . well, in a long, long time.

"Will you join me on the porch for a simple supper?" she asked. It was forward of her to suggest dining alone with a man at her home, but surely if it was done in the open, no one could accuse them of anything untoward.

"That sounds like a fine idea," Arthur answered, his smile telling her just how fine he thought it was.

She pointed to a small table. "Pull that out and I'll get some food. It won't be fancy." She laughed. "Or even hot, but it's the least I can do to thank you for today."

"That's not necessary," Arthur said. "But I'm glad for the meal and the company."

Lorna went inside, wondering what in the world had possessed her. Was it the feeling that she was finally doing something worthwhile? Was it Arthur reminding her of the days before everything good in her life washed away in a flood? She didn't dare examine herself too closely. She knew all too well that her motives were rarely pure.

In the kitchen she gathered two apples, a wedge of cheese, half a loaf of bread, and a jar of cider she'd been saving for a special occasion. She arranged everything on a tray with some napkins, a knife, two glasses, and carried it outside.

As soon as Arthur saw her, he jumped to his feet. "Let me take that," he said, opening the screen door and relieving her of her burden.

He settled the tray on a low table, and Lorna busied herself with slicing bread and cheese and pouring cider. When she had everything to her liking, she looked up to see Arthur smiling at her.

She flushed. "You must think me silly, fussing over nothing."

"I think you're an artist, and if this is nothing, I'd be glad to trade something for it."

"Well, I have plenty of nothing these days." She settled into a chair with a sigh. "No notion where to find this weaver, no new ideas for designs, and only a smidge of hope that I can—" She stopped abruptly. There was no need to tell Arthur that she was desperate to create a fabric that would not only impress Mrs. Harshaw and the Vanderbilts but would also save her job and maybe everyone else's, as well. She'd painted a noble picture for Mrs. Howes, but her own needs weighed heaviest. And there was such a thing as too much honesty. "Cheese?" she asked, thrusting a plate his way.

He took a piece and ate it in two bites. "You didn't really tell me why it's so important to you to find this weaver. What you said to Mrs. Howes back there makes it sound like this is about more than being taken with a scrap of cloth."

She plucked at some burrs clinging to her hem. If she could trust anyone, it was Arthur. "I'm hoping this weaver can help me with a design good enough for Cornelia Vanderbilt." She sighed and gave in to the urge to confess her struggle. "You called me an artist, yet it seems I'm a bit . . . rusty when it comes to new designs. I've been given a commission that could make all the difference for my future. Perhaps for the future of Biltmore Industries. It's been a long time since we celebrated being the largest handweaving industry in the world." She folded her napkin into ever smaller squares, deciding to tell a partial truth. "There are rumors that business is down. And I'm tired of doing the administrative work. I want to get back into the weaving room—to make beautiful fabric that will delight those who wear it." She shook her head and pressed a finger to her lips. "I seem to let my guard down with you, Arthur. Even though it's been a long time since we've talked."

"It has been a long time," he agreed. "Too long." He looked into her eyes. "There was Cornelia's twenty-first birthday with the sedan chair, and then we talked that next spring, I think." He shook his head. "And I don't guess I've seen much of you since. I've been pretty busy with . . . some difficult circumstances."

Lorna paled, suddenly remembering that last conversation. Arthur had been asking about her earlier designs. Designs that belonged to Gentry. She focused on the memory of Cornelia's birthday party as a diversion. "Oh, that chair." She laughed and made a face. "It was the fabric I used then that made Mrs. Harshaw come to me for a gift for Cornelia."

"That's good to hear." The warmth of Arthur's smile made Lorna feel like the fraud she was. "Sounds like I did you a good turn back then."

Lorna realized that if Arthur knew the truth about her designs—which he'd nearly guessed once—he wouldn't want to sit on her porch, eating her food. He wouldn't want to help her. He certainly wouldn't want to reach across the little table to take her hand the way she had a feeling he might.

She stood, knocking a slice of bread onto the floor. "My goodness, I've just remembered an engagement. I promised—" she floundered for a moment—"LeeAnn. I promised LeeAnn I'd show her how to incorporate spacers on her loom. You remember LeeAnn, don't you?" She made a show of looking at the watch pinned to her blouse. "I really must go, I'm so sorry. Please, take some bread and cheese with you. Or an apple." She snatched up an uncut piece of fruit and handed it to Arthur. "Again, thank you so much for today."

Arthur stood as if in slow motion, the apple held in front of him like some sort of talisman. "No need to apologize. I enjoyed spending the day with you." His eyes softened. "I think I saw the Lorna I used to know today. The one who loved to share her passion for weaving with her students. The one who encouraged me when Biltmore Industries was struggling back in sixteen." He started down the steps slowly as though reluctant to go. "A lot has happened in my life since we last met. I'm betting the same is true for you. Maybe we could . . . meet again? And if you need my help, don't hesitate to ask. I'm always happy to help a friend."

Tears sprang to Lorna's eyes, but she fought them back. Instead, she smiled. "I know that's true Arthur. I've always known I could count on you." She only wished he could say the same about her.

# 10

# ARTHUR

**SOUTH ASHEVILLE**
**APRIL 1921**

Something was missing. Arthur stood back and looked at the front of the little cottage he'd been lucky enough to rent just south of Biltmore Estate. It wasn't precisely what he'd hoped for in the way of a woodworking shop, but it was affordable. With an apartment above where he could live more or less comfortably. Its shortcomings could be improved upon as his business grew.

He felt a stab of panic and stuck his hand in his pocket to grip the carved fawn that was always there. What if the business didn't grow? No. He wouldn't allow discouraging thoughts to creep in. It was too late now. Fred Seely had been understanding when Arthur explained that he was leaving the woodworking shop to open his own business, but he'd seen the look of disappointment. And Mr. Seely hinted at the time and money he'd invested in men and equipment to keep the shop up to date.

Arthur shook his head. No. The writing had been on the

wall. Mr. Seely was no longer focusing on woodworking. His passion was for the homespun cloth Lorna and her weavers produced. Arthur had made the right decision. Not to mention the fact that seeing Lorna had become a sweet torture since their muddled dinner together. He still didn't know what had been written on the note that made her so upset with him. But there were rumors that she wasn't quite the apple of Mr. Seely's eye anymore.

It was easier to simply not see her. To not hear the whispers about her and feel the need to defend her. Because how could he? She didn't trust him enough to tell him what was really bothering her. He'd thought time would heal the grief over the loss of her family. He'd thought she might be ready to look to the future—to a new family. But once again his plans didn't mesh with the world's. And what was left to do but lick his wounds and move on?

He tilted his head and considered the front of the cottage again. What was it? There were some cracked roof tiles, but that was hardly noticeable. The front door gleamed with dark green paint, and the sign proclaiming *Arthur Westcott, Woodworker* was pristine. Yet the place looked somehow . . . lonely.

"Good morning, Arthur," a voice boomed as an open motorcar pulled to a stop behind him. Arthur turned to see Reverend Swope climb out and walk around the automobile to take the hand of a young lady in the passenger seat. "Clara and I have come to see your new enterprise."

"You're most welcome," Arthur said with a tip of his hat and foreboding in his heart.

He had finally met Clara at services the Sunday prior. And he had to confess that something about her tugged at him. She seemed kind, thoughtful, and intelligent. Not to mention pretty, even though something sad clung to her that he couldn't quite identify. He smiled, thinking that perhaps he should just give in and take the time to get to know her better.

The pair joined him in front of the cottage, and Reverend Swope wrapped an arm around his shoulders. "Must be satisfying to see your name on that sign," he said. "I know it does my heart good."

"Yes, sir, I've worked hard to get here." He nodded at the young lady. "Miss Peters. It's good to see you again."

"Uncle Rodney continues to show me around Asheville," she said with a sweet smile. "It's so very kind of him.

"Stuff and nonsense," his mentor blustered. "It's nothing but pleasure for me. Squiring a pretty girl around and telling people she's my relation. What could be nicer?" He turned to take in the shop. "Open for business?"

"As of today," Arthur answered. "Would you like to come inside and see?"

"What do you say, Clara? How about a tour of young Arthur's new shop?"

Arthur felt his stomach flip. Was the shop as ready as he thought? Did he want his mentor and Clara to be the first people to see it with customers' eyes?

Clara smiled and nodded. "I'd like that."

Her simple response put Arthur at ease. If she had gushed her enthusiasm or clapped her hands at the prospect, he would have been suspicious. But her eyes were simply alight with interest and curiosity.

He motioned for the pair to precede him to the door. Clara hesitated and tilted her head to one side. "What is it?" he asked.

"It's a lovely shop. I especially like the color of the door. Only . . ." She frowned.

Arthur leaned in. "Yes? I'm eager to hear what you think."

Her cheeks pinked. "It's probably presumptuous of me to say so, but have you thought about curtains for the windows?

Or perhaps flower boxes out front? Here and here," she said, indicating spots below each window. "It's just that it all looks a bit plain."

Arthur laughed and snapped his fingers. "I was just standing here thinking there was something missing, and I do believe you've put your finger right on it." He grinned and offered her his arm. "And dare I ask that you help me choose the flowers?"

She smiled, making a dimple form in her right cheek. A very charming dimple. "I can't think of anything I'd enjoy more."

Arthur cast a glance at Reverend Swope as he escorted Clara inside. And he was pretty sure he caught a gleam in the old fox's eye. Ah well, sometimes it was wise to let someone else steer your course for a time. He looked down at the gloved hand on his arm. Wise indeed.

Three weeks later, Clara stood on a stool Arthur had finished shaping only the day before and stretched to position a sweep of curtain. He had to admit, the pale green fabric shot through with gold threads softened the space, making it feel cozy and inviting. He was grateful for her help, and as he watched her slim figure outlined against the window, he thought he might be grateful for more than that. He moved closer to admire her work.

"Just a little further," she said, stretching onto her toes. She wobbled, and Arthur put a hand to her waist to steady her. They both froze for a breath, and then he was using both hands to help her down from her perch. He released her reluctantly. How long had it been since he'd done anything more than offer a woman his arm?

"Thank you, Clara. You've worked wonders."

She flushed. "No, you're the one working wonders." She

picked up a simple frame that emphasized the beauty of the curly maple. "Your work isn't as ornate as it was at Biltmore Industries," she said, running her hand over the silken wood. "But I prefer the way you've captured the beauty of the wood itself rather than a design you've forced upon it."

Arthur felt a knot form in his throat. Had anyone understood so plainly what he was doing before? "Thank you," he croaked and cleared his throat. "I only wanted to point to the beauty that's already there. I'm glad you can see that."

She smiled and resettled the frame on a small table with other items for sale. He felt like a shadow had settled across her face even though the light had not changed. "Are you alright?" he asked.

"What? Oh, yes, of course. I was only thinking." She smiled again, but he thought her expression was more sad than glad now. He hoped he hadn't done anything to change her mood.

"How long will you be staying in Asheville?" Arthur asked.

"If my mother has her way, I'll stay here for good." Clara sounded sharp, but she quickly added, "Which would suit me fine. I adore Uncle Rodney, and the mountains are so beautiful." She turned and began rearranging items on a counter.

"There's nothing to call you back to—where is it your family lives now?"

"Iowa," she said. "We moved . . . suddenly. And Mother thought it would be good for me to spend time with Uncle Rodney while she settled in." Clara's hands stilled. "But Uncle Rodney and Aunt Mary have hinted that they would be glad for my companionship. So I'm considering staying here." She turned her luminous hazel eyes on him.

Without pausing to think it through, Arthur stepped forward and placed his hand over hers. "I would certainly be glad for you to stay." He started to withdraw his hand, but she turned hers and twined their fingers together.

"Would you?"

Arthur found he could barely speak. "I . . . yes. Clara . . . would you . . ." He cleared his throat and rubbed the back of his neck with his free hand. "Would you allow me to court you?"

"Yes, Arthur. I would." She smiled and squeezed his hand before turning away. He caught the glint of tears in her eyes and wondered that she would be so emotional. He'd never had that effect on a woman before that he knew of. And, he had to confess, it was a heady sensation.

"Clara, are you part of a large family?"

She turned back toward him, any hint of tears gone. "Not so big—just my brother and I, along with Mother and Father. Sometimes I wish I had sisters so Mother wouldn't focus quite so much on me." That shadow fell again. "She's determined to see me 'settled properly.'"

Arthur's breath caught. "Do you think she would . . . well, that she would approve of my courting you?"

"Oh, I know she would. Uncle Rodney speaks highly of you."

The words should have reassured him, but her tone—dry and perhaps even dismissive—gave him pause. "Are you sure?"

She smiled, and this time her voice was warm as she stepped closer and laid a hand on his arm. "Quite sure."

He grinned—foolishly, he imagined. But she didn't see as she turned to add her feminine touch to another display in the shop. He watched her, thinking that while the memory of Lorna would likely sting for some time, Clara had already done a great deal to soothe the burn.

# 11

# GENTRY

**BILTMORE VILLAGE**
**JUNE 1916**

She'd dreamed of her mother again. Gentry rubbed her eyes and stared at the far wall, where dawn's first light painted the scuffed paper with a flash of gold. Now she remembered. Her mother had been wearing Lorna's lacy fabric in the dream. Except it wasn't Lorna's, it was her mother's. And now Gentry knew the truth. Somehow, Lorna had woven one of her mother's patterns.

It had taken a while, but she'd finally realized what it was about the fabric that was so familiar. She'd seen it before. The memory had finally floated to the surface of her mind. She'd seen her mother kneeling beside a trunk in the room they shared—a beautiful dress pressed to her face as she cried. It had startled Gentry, and she'd begun to cry as well. Mama rushed to her side and let her look at the dress, probably to distract her. It was the same fabric Lorna had made, except the background had been pink instead of blue. Like crocuses poking up through a crust of lacy snow.

Gentry flung a foot out from under the lightweight coverlet, one she'd woven herself. It was hers now because it was flawed. Badly flawed and no one wanted it. But Miss Vance and Miss Yale said it mustn't go to waste, and so Gentry had to give up the beautiful coverlet she'd been given when she first arrived to sleep under this one with its faulty warp.

She'd been trying to do better. Honestly, she had. Trying to be patient and please Lorna. But her teacher had changed since weaving the cloth that everyone raved about. It had indeed boosted sales for the company. Since then, she'd been more and more demanding, as if her own success made her less tolerant of Gentry's failure.

She crossed the room, the naked wood floor rough under her bare feet. She'd been working on a rag rug to soften the cold boards, but like so many things, it lay unfinished in a corner. She pulled the top right drawer of her dresser all the way out and fished out her mother's drafts. She was angry that Lorna had stolen a design, but seeing the fabric and the memory it stirred had given her an idea. What if hidden on these sheets of paper were clues about her mother? They might even hint at where she had gone.

She sat on the floor and spread the pages all around her. Because she'd been making an effort to pay attention to what Lorna taught her, she now had an inkling as to what the notations meant.

She picked up a yellowed sheet with a note in her mother's slanting hand—*Mountain Cucumber*. She squinted at the marks and gradually picked out a sense of what the pattern would look like. Then, like a bolt of lightning, she remembered it.

"This coverlid will be yours one day," Mama said, smoothing it over the fat tick beneath. "And when I'm long gone, you can snug down under it and remember that green was my favorite color. Green like the leaves of a maple in May before the summer's heat and dry spells have toughened them."

Gentry's breath came in little gasps as the memory washed over her. Mama turned the cover back, and they slid beneath it together, finding softness and warmth. Mama wrapped her arms around Gentry, tucking her close. And then she'd hummed a tune . . .

Gentry leapt to her feet and fetched out her dulcimer. She closed her eyes and began culling the notes from her memory. The tune came slowly at first and then faster and stronger until she was playing the song she'd forgotten until this moment.

She didn't know the words, only the mournful tune that made her think of green meadows fading to autumn and then winter's ice. She played and played until she came to the end of the song—or maybe it was the end of herself—and then simply sat in the middle of those scattered pages, tears dampening her checks.

She was swiping at her eyes with a sleeve when she heard a soft tap at the door. It eased open, and Mrs. Brady leaned in. "Gentry, what's that song you're playing?"

"I don't know."

"It sounds like a ballad my granny used to sing back home in Monroe County, West Virginia. I haven't heard anything like it in more years than I can count." She eased into the room. "Would you mind to play it again?"

Gentry turned her face so the matron couldn't see her tears. She closed her eyes and struck up the tune once again. She snuck a look back at Mrs. Brady and saw that she needn't hide her tears. The older woman, who'd hardly had a kind word for her since the day she arrived, was shedding tears of her own.

"So pretty," she whispered when the song was done. "Do you know any more like that?"

Gentry looked at the pages scattered around her. Would

they conjure more music for her? "Maybe," she said. "You say it's a song you heard your granny sing?"

"Sure enough. The old folks would get together and sing the ballads their kin carried over from England way back when." She shook her head. "I'd forgotten all about it."

"Did you ever hear that song anywhere else?" An idea began to form in Gentry's mind.

"No, can't say as I did. Not that I've traveled very far, but I think it was common to the folks up there where Virginia and West Virginia come together."

"I'll try to remember some more," Gentry said, touching another draft, turning it to see if she could make sense of it. Lifting the page, she examined the marks. An image of an indigo blue pattern against a linen warp floated into her mind. And with it came a song. She lifted her dulcimer and began to play.

When she finished, she turned to look at the matron. The older woman had a handkerchief pressed to her eyes.

"Do you know that one, too?" Gentry asked.

Mrs. Brady sniffled. "I do. Oh, the memories you're bringing back to me. It's like I've been carried back to my childhood."

"Do you think . . . ?" Gentry considered how to phrase her question. "Do you think those songs are particular to the place your granny lived?"

The matron took a deep breath and let it out slowly, composing herself. "I don't know for certain, but I haven't heard them since."

Gentry nodded and gathered the pages into a neat stack. "Maybe my mama was from the same place as your granny," she ventured.

"What was her name before she married?"

Gentry flushed. "I don't know. I was little when she . . ."

Mrs. Brady stood and laid a hand on her shoulder. "It's

all right, child. Losing a mother is a hard thing no matter how old you are. If you ever find out her family name, let me know." She smiled as she turned to go. "Who knows, we might even be kin."

Gentry held the drafts close and tried to think. Maybe her mother was from Monroe County in West Virginia. And if she was, maybe that was the place she'd gone back to. A place where, by now, she might even be sorry she'd left her only daughter behind.

She gripped the pen and stared at the blank sheet of paper. Gentry hated writing letters. Truth be told, she simply hated writing. Corralling her thoughts and pinning them down on paper was hard. And then there was the labor of shaping the letters, of spelling, and of putting the periods and commas in the right places. None of it suited her.

She bit the tip of her tongue and steeled herself to get through this.

*Dear Aunt Eulah,*

There, that was a fine start. Eulah was her father's sister. She'd come to see Gentry and Grandad twice a year after Mama left. Once in the spring and again in the fall. She would see that Gentry had shoes and clothes that fit, would cut her hair, and either helped plant the garden or harvest it depending on the season and the signs. She tried to explain all the business about the phases of the moon and which element the signs were in once, but Gentry found it endlessly confusing and Aunt Eulah gave up.

Gentry suspected the visits—always exactly four days and three nights—were made from some sense of duty. Grandad certainly never seemed pleased to see his daughter, his only living child. The first few times she came, Gentry hoped her aunt would take her away. But she lived in Johnson City, Tennessee, where she said she had a life of her own. Even now, Gentry didn't hold out much hope for Aunt Eulah being helpful, yet she had nowhere else to turn. She renewed her grip on the pen and pressed it against the paper once more.

*I am doing okay in Asheville. I miss the sheep back home. I have my dulcimer and can play it in the evenings. I am learning to weave, but I don't much like it.*

She laid the pen down and massaged her hand. Surely that was enough of a beginning. Now she could get to what she really wanted.

*Do you know what my mother's name was before she got married? Do you know where her people come from? I would like to know if you do.*

Gentry hesitated. Should she explain why she wanted to know? Aunt Eulah had never been affectionate with her. Had never said she loved Gentry or tried to talk to her beyond what was needed to complete the tasks she set herself on each visit. She'd sent one letter to Asheville with a dollar bill and a few lines admonishing Gentry to make the most of her opportunity.

Gentry decided not to explain. She signed the letter with her name, sealed it, and carried it to the post office where she used her aunt's dollar—which she still had—to pay for postage. Pocketing her change, she walked back to the boardinghouse feeling that, possibly for the first time ever, she was taking her future into her own hands.

Gentry had nearly given up hope of receiving an answer from her aunt when, two weeks after posting her letter, Mrs. Brady handed her a crinkly envelope with a Johnson City return address. Breath catching in her chest, she flew up the stairs to her room, not caring if she was about to be late for the evening meal.

She ripped the envelope open and let it fall to the floor. Unfolding the thin paper, she could see that there wasn't a whole lot to it.

*Dear Gentry,*

*I have been meaning to write to you. Your grandad is very sick. I did not know it at first. When I went to help with the spring planting, he was laid up in bed, just skin and bones. He must have been that way for a while. I brung him to my house. He does not much like it.*

*I think your mother come from somewhere in West Virginia. I am surprised you do not know her single name because it is Gentry. She did not leave you much else, but I guess she give you that. I would say you should come see your grandad before he dies, but I bet you don't have the money for the train and neither do I.*

*You should try harder to like weaving. It is your best chance at a life. Do not waste it.*

*Eulah, your aunt*

Gentry let her hand drop to her side and stared out the window, unseeing. Grandad was sick. Maybe dying. She tried to care and found she did not. The news that made her heart quiver and her fingers tremble was that she was named after her mother. After her mother's people who were from West Virginia. Most likely Monroe County like Mrs. Brady mentioned.

Now all she had to do was find a way to get there.

# 12

# ARTHUR

**BILTMORE VILLAGE**
**JULY 1921**

A whirlwind romance. Who would've thought?

He'd been walking out with Clara for three months now. He'd taken her to supper—though not at Grove Park Inn—dined at Reverend Swope's, and spent many an evening strolling with her along the French Broad River.

On this evening, he surprised her with tickets to the Majestic Theater, which had only recently begun showing moving pictures. A uniformed usher led them to their green-and-white upholstered seats just beneath the balcony, where they had an excellent view of the ornate decorations and rich, red curtains on either side of a large screen.

Clara snuggled close as the lights dimmed, ready to watch *The Conquering Power* starring Rudolph Valentino. The film was about a rich playboy who loses his fortune and must live with his miserly uncle. He falls in love, yet his uncle is determined to arrange a different, more profitable marriage. Arthur thought it was a bit predictable, but enjoyable. Although that might have had something to do with the feeling that the playboy wasn't the only one who'd fallen in love. Clara didn't seem to like it much, though.

Later, they walked arm in arm along Market Street, the occasional automobile clattering over its brick pavers. Arthur felt tension bubbling from the woman by his side.

"Did you enjoy the moving picture?" he asked.

She was silent for several beats. "I'm glad it worked out in the end, but the uncle was terrible. The scene where he was buried in his gold and died was awful. I can almost believe he deserved it for keeping the lovers apart."

"It's just a story," Arthur said. "And it all worked out in the end."

"Things don't always work out in the end, though, do they?"

Arthur sensed she was talking about more than the film. "No, I suppose not." He stopped in the street and turned to her. "But sometimes they do. Sometimes they work out just right." She turned big, sad eyes on him, and he suddenly wanted to make everything work out right for her. He felt breathless. He felt invincible. He felt like he'd found his family.

"Marry me, Clara. Marry me and prove that happy endings really do exist."

She flinched and looked away. Then she stepped closer, took his hand in hers, and looked him in the eye. "Alright," she said.

His heart soared, and he scooped her into an embrace. Though he wanted to kiss her senseless, he restrained himself since they were on a public street. He let her go, and she gave him a crooked smile. "I'd better let Mother know right away. I'm sure Uncle Rodney will let me use the telephone."

Arthur didn't want to take her home. He wanted to keep walking and talking and dreaming about the home they'd make together—about the family they'd build from scratch. At last, he could do this right, could make up for the mistakes his parents had made. Fleetingly, he thought he should try to send word to them that he was getting married. Yet they'd been gone from his life for so long that he dismissed the notion as quickly as it came. They gave him away. He owed them nothing now.

Clara turned toward the streetcar stop, and he let her lead him in that direction. He'd never been engaged before, so he figured he'd better let Clara and her family guide him in what came next.

What came next was a whirlwind of another kind. It was decided that the young couple would wed right away. Arthur wasn't directly consulted, but he had no complaints. He was eager to start his life as a husband. And hopefully a father ere long. He almost had the feeling that Clara's family didn't want to let him get away, but that was silly. She was the catch, not him.

Two weeks later, he approached his mentor's front door, late for supper with Clara and her parents. He was embarrassed, but a customer had detained him. He hurried inside, apologies on his lips, but the words fell away as soon as he saw Reverend Swope, sitting alone in his parlor and looking grim.

"What—?" Arthur stumbled, regained his footing, then sank into a chair since his legs felt suddenly like jelly. "What's happened? Is Clara alright?"

Rodney, a smiling man ever ready with a comforting word or touch, looked like he was about to unleash God's own wrath. He cleared his throat. "My niece has absconded."

Arthur gaped, unable to make sense of the words. The reverend scooted his chair closer to Arthur. "I'm so sorry," he said. "I feel this is partly my fault. Clara's mother sent her to me to separate her from an inappropriate beau." He took a deep breath. "But it seems the young man followed her here, and they have eloped." He handed Arthur a folded piece of paper. "She left you this."

Arthur heard a buzzing in his ears. Rodney's words were like mosquitoes he couldn't swat away. "I don't understand," he managed.

"No. I wouldn't think so." The reverend laid a steadying hand on Arthur's shoulder. "Take a deep breath." Arthur did. "Again." The buzzing began to fade. "Now, if you're steady enough, I'll leave you to read that."

"I'm steady enough," Arthur croaked.

"Good. Keep breathing. I'll be just through there." He pointed to the dining room door. Arthur nodded, watching this man he'd known and loved most of his life give him privacy for whatever would come next.

He unfolded the note.

*Arthur,*

*I expect you will never be able to forgive me for using you so callously. I wish I had chosen someone less kind, less compassionate for my ruse. But then perhaps that is my punishment. By the time you read this, my one true love and I will be wed. He is a good man, but my family forbade our union due to his lineage being "impure" as Mother put it. I think, knowing you better now, that if I had dared to take you into my confidence, you would have helped me.*

*But I was afraid and so I pretended. I am sorry, and I hope I have not caused you too much pain. You are a good man, too. And I hope you find your own true love—a woman who can make you happy as I could not.*

*Clara*

Arthur crushed the page in his hand, then smoothed it back out, folded it, and tucked it in his pocket. He found the carved fawn and drew it out. He balanced the figure on his knee, appreciating the way the fine weave of the charcoal fabric set off its smooth lines. He supposed the only thing worse than being jilted by his fiancée would be marrying someone who did not love him. He fisted the carving and tilted his head back. At least he hoped it was worse.

Two weeks after Clara eloped, Angus McTeague came to see Arthur on a day when he was alone in the empty shop. "Hear you've had a rough go of it," his old friend said.

"Guess you're referring to me being unlucky in love," Arthur answered. He pushed back from the table where he was working and rubbed his eyes. "Might be marriage just isn't for me."

Angus grunted and lit on a stool. "Or maybe she was the wrong girl. Whatever happened to the lovely Lorna?"

Arthur folded his hands across his belly so his fingers wouldn't go looking for the carved fawn. "I made her angry. Then I left Biltmore Industries to open this shop. We haven't kept in touch, and I can only assume she prefers it that way."

"Assume. Which means you don't know."

"Ah, Angus, what's the point? She made it clear to me she wasn't interested, and now Clara has been plainer yet." He waved a hand at his worktable. "So this is where I plan to put my focus. I'm going to do the best woodwork anyone in Asheville has ever seen. I'll find the finest wood, the best carvers, and the newest designs." He stood and paced the room. "And it will be what I want. It won't matter how I walk or what anyone else expects from me. I'll be doing things on my own terms from here on out." He returned to the worktable, which he thumped for emphasis. "This place is my family from now on."

Angus chuckled and stroked his grizzled beard. "That's the most sensible thing I've heard you say, and I always did think you were more sensible than most." He nodded. "I thought you might be feeling like this, so I've come to give you a hand."

Arthur's eyebrows shot up before he could catch them. He schooled his expression. "Have you?" He tapped his fingers against the table. "I'd be lucky to have a woodworker as skilled as you." He paused. How could he say this? "But, Angus, seems like maybe you . . . uh . . ." He flexed his fingers in the air.

"Oh, I can't much do fine work with a knife or a chisel anymore. No, what I'm offering you is *connections*." He emphasized the last word. "I know a fellow back in the hills who can get you the prettiest wood you ever laid eyes on. He cuts and cures it himself. Does some carving, too, but not like you can." Angus grinned. "And I'm not lookin' for pay. All I want is a chair in a corner where I can do a little work when ole Arthur lets me." He sighed. "A man gets to feeling useless if he doesn't have a job to go to, work to do. I don't blame Mr. Seely for letting me go. I couldn't produce the way he needed." He held up a gnarled hand. "But I can still do some work, and I thought maybe you'd let me."

It was by far the longest speech Arthur had ever heard Angus make. He felt a lump rise in his throat. He'd been so busy feeling sorry for himself, he hadn't even asked how Angus was doing—hadn't kept up with his old friend at all. "I'd be honored to have you, Angus. And you can help me teach Donnie a few things. He's my apprentice. He's sharp, but I can't spend as much time with him as he needs. I'm betting you can show him a few tricks."

"That I can," chortled Angus.

"And this fella you mention who has cured wood"—
Arthur felt enthusiasm rise in him for the first time since
he'd been jilted—"when can we go see him?"

"Soon as you brush the sawdust from your britches,"
Angus said. "Basil Howes ain't hard to run down." The old
man's eyes twinkled. "All you gotta do is turn up on his land
and listen for him to draw the hammer back on that shotgun of his."

# 13

# LORNA

**BILTMORE VILLAGE**
**SEPTEMBER 1923**

"Mr. Tompkins wants to see you."

Lorna's head jerked up. She hadn't seen Bernice approaching. "Pardon?"

Bernice darted a worried look over her shoulder. "Mr. Tompkins. He said you were to come right away, and he didn't look a bit happy about it."

Lorna sighed. She wasn't happy about the request either. She'd been avoiding her supervisor since he'd asked if she could deliver on her promise to provide Mrs. Harshaw with a breathtaking fabric fit for a Vanderbilt. And she feared she was no closer to delivering on that promise.

She held her chin high as she entered Mr. Tompkins's office. "You asked to see me, sir?"

"Have a seat, Miss Blankenship." She sat and tucked her hands under her legs, pinning her skirt in place. She could feel the muscles beneath quivering and willed herself to be still. "I'd like an update on your commission for Mrs. Harshaw. I saw her at church on Sunday and found myself in the position of being uninformed as to your progress." He glared at her over his glasses. "It also came to my attention that you were not in attendance. Were you ill?"

Lorna wet her lips. "I attend irregularly."

Mr. Tompkins made a *tsk-tsk* sound. "That simply will not do. But let us discuss the more pressing matter. What is your progress on the fabric?"

Lorna felt sweat prickle beneath her blouse. She thought back to Elspeth's description of the mountain weaver's fabric. "I'm working on the draft now," she lied. "It's inspired by the mountain vistas that drew Mr. Vanderbilt to this area."

A wrinkle formed between Mr. Tompkins's eyebrows. "Yes. Go on."

"The colors suggest the blues of the Blue Ridge Mountains, and they're accented with silver and white to reflect the low clouds and mists so common to this area."

Now Mr. Tompkins was nodding. "Sounds promising. When can I see the draft?"

"It won't be much longer," Lorna said, trying to inject a note of confidence into her lies.

"It had better not. Weaving the sort of complex design Mrs. Harshaw expects will take time, and while there has yet to be an announcement, Mrs. Harshaw believes there will be a spring wedding." He flipped open a diary positioned equidistant from the edges of his desk. "I shall expect to see a finished draft ready for the loom no later than the fifteenth of October." He tapped the page with a freshly sharpened pencil. "I trust that won't be a problem."

"Not at all," Lorna said in a rush. She stood, clenching her hands behind her back to hide their shaking. "Will that be all?"

Mr. Tompkins made a vague, waving gesture. "Yes, yes. Back to your duties."

Lorna scurried from the office and made her way immediately to the lavatory. She splashed water on her face and gulped air in an effort not to be sick. What was she going to do? Now she not only had to find her mystery weaver, but she also had to persuade her to create a specific design based on her spontaneous description. And she had only a month to do it.

She slowed her breathing and looked at herself in the glass as she tried to regain control. Pieces of hair clung to her damp cheeks, and the finger waves she'd worked so hard to master had fallen out. She sighed and fished some pins from her pocket to fasten her hair back.

Inhaling deeply and releasing the air slowly, she knew what she had to do. She had to go back to Arthur and plead for his help once more. She had no doubt he'd offer it gladly. She only hesitated because she dreaded the day he learned the truth about her. He'd wanted to meet again, to catch up on the months since they'd last met. She shook her head. She had little to tell him, and not much of it was good.

.·´¯`·.....·´

Thankfully, Lorna didn't have to contact Arthur again. The next morning, Donnie was waiting on her front porch as she left for Biltmore Industries. It had been so convenient when the business had been right here in Biltmore Village, but since Mr. Seely purchased it, she had to take the streetcar all the way across town.

"Arthur asked me to bring you this," Donnie said, holding out a folded piece of paper. Lorna accepted it and tucked it in her pocket. "I think he was hoping you'd read it and send him word back," he added.

"Oh. Well. Yes." Lorna fumbled for the paper. "Give me

just a moment." She turned to the side and unfolded the page, hoping her hands wouldn't shake.

*Lorna,*

*I have heard from Basil that he's found more of your weaver's fabric. If you are able, we can go fetch it today. If not, I will go alone and bring it to you. Give your answer to Donnie. I hope you can come.*

*Arthur*

Lorna felt her heart stutter and leap. Foolish heart. She gnawed her lip and considered what to do. The only time she had failed to report to work as scheduled was the week after the flood of 1916. She shuddered at the memory and pushed it away. Darting a glance at Donnie and then back to Arthur's words, she made her decision. She would go. After all, finding the weaver was part of her job.

"Tell Arthur I'll come with him," she blurted.

Donnie looked pleased. "He said if you were willing to go, I should tell you to wait right here and he'll be along as quick as he can."

Lorna nodded. "I just need to send a note with one of the other girls, explaining why I won't be in the weaving room today. But I'll be here when he arrives."

Lorna jotted a note to Mr. Tompkins, assuring him she was hard at work on her commission and needed to stay home where she could give it her full attention. She stepped down to the streetcar stop and caught one of the girls to deliver the missive. As she returned to her own porch to wait for Arthur, worry began to nibble at her conscience. What if this was a dead end? What if she was risking her job for nothing?

She thumped down on the top porch step and hung her

head. Her job was already at risk. She should probably be more concerned about making a fool of herself with Arthur.

"Ready for an adventure?"

Lorna jerked her head up and gaped at the automobile idling in the street. Arthur stood beside it, the passenger door open, a huge grin on his face.

"Where did you get that?"

"A friend," he said with a wink. "No worrying about catching streetcars today!"

"But I've never ridden in one before." Lorna stood and moved toward the roadster as if in a dream.

"I have, and it's a treat!" He took her hand and helped her in, snugging the door shut behind her. She ran her hands over the dark seats and touched the cool glass of the windscreen in front of her. A giggle bubbled up from she knew not where, and she let it out.

Arthur slid behind the wheel and laughed with her. Suddenly, Lorna felt as carefree as a child running barefoot through the grass on a summer day. She clapped her hands. "I believe I am ready for an adventure," she said and leaned over to give Arthur a peck on the cheek. He flushed, did some maneuvering with the car, and they were off. Lorna grabbed the edge of the seat, braced her feet against the floor of the vehicle, and let the wind carry away the last of the caution she'd been clinging to for far too long.

They met Basil in Reems Creek, where he directed them to a house in the community of Weaverville, much to Lorna's surprise. She had assumed they would once again be heading off into the hinterlands to track down some country bumpkin or yokel. Instead, he pointed to a neat cottage with a white picket fence and a cascade of autumn roses perfuming the air.

"Ma says Virgie might have some fabric like that shawl.

I think she knows more about it than she's letting on. Has her reasons, I guess." Basil pushed the squeaking gate open, and they passed into a tidy yard where a rainbow of dahlias bloomed. A sprite of a woman was cutting the flowers and laying them in a wooden trug as if each one were made of glass and gold.

"Basil, what fresh delight is this?" the woman called, holding a hand up to shade her eyes from the sun as it climbed toward the noon hour.

"This is Arthur. He's a wood-carver. And this is Lorna, who's a weaver like Ma. She wants to see that cloth Ma wrote to you about."

The woman clapped her hands like a child. She swooped up her trug in one hand while hitching her skirts with the other. "Follow me," she trilled and led them toward the cottage. Inside, Lorna wanted to clap her own hands. The space was utterly charming with needlepoint cushions in the chintz-covered chairs, antimacassars, and wood laid in the fireplace, ready to lend its warmth on a cool evening. There was even a teapot and a cup suggesting that Virgie had neglected to clear away her breakfast things. And books were everywhere, like a flock of birds that had landed to roost wherever they liked.

"Pardon the mess," Virgie chirped. "I find a bit of clutter comforting. It prevents me from feeling as though I must keep everything just so."

Lorna drifted through the room, which, while cluttered, was quite clean. She suspected the place was more organized than Virgie would admit. She resisted the urge to pick up a vase here or a pinecone there. She thought she could remain contentedly in this room forever.

"Find a place to perch," Virgie said, "while I give my flowers a drink."

Lorna settled on a chair with a finely knitted shawl draped

over its back. Her fingers found their way into the fabric of their own volition, and she sighed with pleasure.

She looked up to see Arthur and Basil clearly feeling less at home. They surveyed the available furniture and finally selected matching wing-back chairs on either side of the fireplace. Basil braced his hands on his knees as though afraid to touch anything.

Virgie bustled back in carrying a tray with sugar cookies on it. "Some might think it too early in the day for sweets, but I say it's never too early." She plopped the tray on an oversized ottoman and then settled in a rocking chair with proportions that seemed fitted exactly to her. She swiped up a cookie and took a bite, looking at her guests expectantly.

Lorna laughed. The sound of it surprised her. It also eased the fear and stress she'd been carrying over this fabric, her job, and her future. She took a cookie and sank back into her chair, a sense of peace wrapping around her like the shawl under her hand.

Basil glanced toward the door with naked longing. "How about Arthur and I take our cookies out to the yard?" he said. "Ma mentioned the windlass on your well's been sticking."

"Good idea," Virgie sang. "You boys go do manly things while we ladies discuss fabric and weaving." Lorna watched Basil lead the way as though he were making a narrow escape. Arthur followed, but as he passed her chair, he patted her shoulder. Tears sprang to her eyes. She blinked them away before anyone could see.

"Men are useful creatures, but I daresay I have done alright without trying to keep one for my own."

A giggle bubbled up in Lorna, and she let it escape. "Considering your charming home and your obvious ability to take care of yourself, I'd tend to agree."

Virgie held up a finger. "Not that I didn't break my share of hearts in my day. But in the end, I couldn't find anyone who was better company than Mr. Wordsworth or Mr. Dickens." She sighed and reached for another cookie. "Or, heaven help me, Jack London." She gave an exaggerated shiver. "So handsome, so virile. I'd almost go to Alaska with him. Such a shame he died so very young."

Lorna could almost forget her reason for coming here. She wished she could forget everything—her promise to Mrs. Harshaw. The fear of losing her position. Biltmore Industries' flagging sales. Her lost family. Her lost opportunity with Arthur. All of it seemed far away while she sat in this cozy room, nibbling sweet cookies with Virgie.

Yet Virgie remembered her purpose even if Lorna did not. "But you didn't come to listen to my meanderings." She dusted the last crumbs from her hands and sprang to her feet. "Wait here, dearest. I gathered the pieces after I received Elspeth's note." She trotted up a staircase, and Lorna waited, eyes closed, as relaxed as she could ever remember being.

Lorna's eyes flew open when a cascade of cloth tumbled into her lap. She'd been on the edge of sleep and for a brief moment thought the fabric in her arms was part of a dream. A tweedy jacket in pale purple gave her the sense she was smelling lilacs while a soft, spring breeze teased her hair. And a plaid skirt in pinks, reds, and oranges was like holding a sunrise at the birth of a new day.

"These are exceptional," she gasped.

Virgie's tinkling laughter filled the room like bells. "Aren't they, though? I ought to wear them every day, but instead I wait until I need cheering and then I put on one of these and recite Lord Byron's poem." A dreamy smile spread over her face as she whispered, "'She walks in beauty . . .'"

"But where did they come from?" Lorna asked.

"It's a sad story," Virgie said, moving to her rocker. She set it into motion and leaned her head back. "Sabine's husband was half French, and he decided to go and fight in the Great

War in 1915. He was killed about a year later, and she lost their farm—couldn't pay the taxes. So she moved here. She said she had family in the area, even though I'd never met any of them. She became a good friend." Her expression clouded. "The cancer took her . . . oh, I guess it's been a year and a half. Just before she died, she told me to open a trunk in her room." She waved at the clothing in Lorna's lap. "And there was the cloth. It was like opening a treasure chest. I asked why she'd never had them made into clothes. She said she'd always thought they were too beautiful to take a pair of scissors to." Virgie laughed softly. "I told her they were too beautiful *not* to take a pair of scissors to. Sabine said that's why she was giving them to me.

"And so I made them into the prettiest clothes I could dream up with my limited imagination." She reached over and scooped up a simple blouse. "You see this?" She held up the indigo fabric. "I can't wear it without feeling as though I'm wearing the sky at dusk just after the sun has set and just before the moon has risen."

"Tell me about Sabine," Lorna said. "Was she the weaver?"

"I don't know." Virgie set her chair in motion again, the soft swish of the rockers against the rug setting a rhythm for their words. "She didn't share much about her past. And I didn't know her all that long before she got sick." Silence reigned for several beats. "She did mention that she had regrets—something about her sister marrying a man I think Sabine may have cared for herself. She said she'd done her sister a bad turn and had never made it right." She shook her head, sad and slow. "I took that skirt to show her about a month after she gave me the fabric—not long before she passed." Virgie waved a hand at the tangle of cloth in Lorna's lap. "She hugged it tight as if it were a babe in her arms." Virgie closed her eyes. "Now, let me get this right. She said"—Lorna leaned forward and held her breath—"the fabric reminded her that weeping may endure for a night, but joy comes in the morning."

Lorna exhaled and stroked the soft fabric of the skirt. "She might have been talking about dying."

Virgie nodded. "That's one way to look at it."

"You said Sabine lost her farm. Where was it?"

Virgie pursed her lips and looked up. "West Virginia," she said at last. "She mentioned being up there near the Shenandoah Valley."

"Do you think she brought this fabric from there?"

"Oh, I know she did. She told me the bolts of cloth were among the few things she managed to bring with her."

Lorna ran her hands over the sunrise of a skirt, examining each square inch. There. What looked like a flaw in the pattern. Or perhaps an intentional signature by her elusive weaver. She pointed it out to Virgie. "Have you ever noticed this?"

"Yes. As a matter of fact, I've found a similar flaw in most of the fabric. I mentioned it to Elspeth, and she said it might be on purpose."

"Did Sabine know anything about it?"

"She died before I thought to ask."

Lorna nodded, feeling both excited and frustrated. "So you think Sabine was the weaver?"

Virgie leaned forward and laid a hand on Lorna's knee. "Maybe." She hesitated. "This seems awfully important to you."

"It is. And I'm sorry if I've been asking too many questions. It's just that I need to find the person who wove these."

"I've got some scraps I could let you have. None big enough to do anything with, but I hated the thought of throwing them away."

Lorna felt hope surge within her. "That would be wonderful—thank you so much."

A few minutes later, as Virgie pressed a bundle of scraps into Lorna's hands, she felt as though they were breadcrumbs that would lead her to her mysterious weaver. The one who would save her job, her reputation, and perhaps even Biltmore Industries.

# 14

# LORNA

**Biltmore Estate Industries
October 1923**

Lorna wasn't at all certain about this, but she was too far along to give up now. She looked at the fabric Virgie had given her. Surely she could make something comparable. She knew her craft inside and out. If Sabine had indeed been the mystery weaver, there would be no tracking her down this side of heaven. And while Lorna wasn't yet convinced that was the case, she thought it would be a good idea to try to come up with her own pattern.

"An honest pattern," she whispered to herself. Goodness knows, it was past time.

The loom was prepared, her shuttle ready. She took a seat and began weaving, slowly at first, then faster and faster as she found the rhythm that had long soothed her spirit. She lost herself in the clatter and clack, her feet moving on the pedals.

She dared not give the cloth inching across her loom too much attention. She felt as though looking directly at it might make it all go wrong. A cramp in her left calf finally made her stop. She stood and stretched, then glanced at her watch, surprised to see nearly five hours had passed. She walked away, turning her back to the loom. Then she turned and approached with brisk steps as though checking on a student's work.

She blinked. She ran a hand across the short span of fabric. Her intent had been to capture a sunrise over the Blue Ridge Mountains.

She had failed.

Instead of gorgeous, exciting colors, she had somehow created a muddy mess. Rather than a subtle transition between warm and cool, bright and muted, it was just . . . confused.

LeeAnn came into the room. "We saved you some lunch since you didn't stop to eat." She glanced at the loom. "Who done that? Guess you'll be giving whoever it is what for."

"It's not up to our standards, is it?"

LeeAnn laughed. "No, ma'am." She leaned closer. "Although it's made well enough. Too bad the colors are such a mess."

"Yes, too bad," Lorna agreed and began to undo her work.

...........

Mr. Tompkins was making this even more difficult.

"I simply cannot allow it," he said. "You're needed here, and you have yet to show me a design for your commission for Mrs. Harshaw, which, may I remind you, is now past due. How could I possibly spare you for five days?"

"But I haven't taken time away in years," Lorna said. "Not since—" she gulped and plunged ahead—"not since the flood."

Mr. Tompkins's ramrod posture bent just a little. "That involved extraordinary circumstances. I trust there hasn't been that sort of tragedy in your life lately that requires time for you to recover."

Lorna felt tears rise in the back of her throat. She coughed and swallowed them down. Her inability to do something as simple as come up with a new design felt almost as terrible as that day in July of 1916. Yet another failure to ruin her life.

She felt a tear slip free. She dashed it away with the back of her hand. She would not give in to emotion, and she would not back down. "I insist. This time is essential if I am to complete Mrs. Harshaw's commission."

Mr. Tompkins's face reddened. He leaned forward, bracing his hands on his desk. Lorna flinched and took a step back. She expected him to yell, but his voice was low and steely.

"I have had quite enough." He enunciated each word perfectly. "I will not waste your time or mine mincing words. Your impertinence and uncooperative attitude are leaving me with no option but to terminate your position with us. I'm putting you on notice as of now." He stabbed the desk with one finger for emphasis. "Once you have completed your commission for Mrs. Julian Harshaw, our association will come to an end."

Lorna felt the floor sway beneath her. Or was she the one swaying? She grabbed the back of a chair so she wouldn't crumple to the floor.

But Mr. Tompkins wasn't done. "I trust that you will neither shirk nor skimp on this final task. And to help ensure that, your final compensation will only be provided to you once the commission is satisfactorily completed." There was a long pause. Lorna thought she should leave but didn't trust her legs to carry her. "Do you understand me?"

Lorna tried to swallow, yet her mouth was bone-dry. She finally squeaked out, "Yes, sir," then turned and fled the office.

Once outside, Lorna couldn't stop shaking. What had

she done? What had Mr. Tompkins done? Fired. She'd been fired. It was a possibility that had simply never crossed her mind. Demoted perhaps. Her pay docked. But fired? And still expected to fulfill her impossible commission.

She stepped aboard a streetcar without thinking and stepped off again in Biltmore Village. Her feet carried her toward her cottage without her telling them to. She looked up as a train chugged into the station just down the street. For a fleeting moment she considered climbing aboard and simply riding it as far as it would go. Forget weaving. Forget Biltmore Industries. None of this was her responsibility. Not really.

Sinking onto a bench tucked between two buildings, she tried to corral her tumbling thoughts. And there it was—a memory of her father not long after Mother died. Both of them had been stiff and reserved for weeks, slowly finding their way without Mother to cheer them. Then Lorna burned her hand on the stove, and Father fetched salve and a soft rag to bandage it. She hadn't shed a tear. Simply sat there gritting her teeth until he'd finished. He looked at her with wonder. Reached out to touch her cheek. "You're so strong," he said, "just like your mother." She'd cried then and he'd held her, and things had been better.

Lorna watched a train leave the station. And just like that, she knew what she must do.

She would not run away. She would not let Mr. Tompkins have the last word. She would not abandon Biltmore Industries. Hadn't she been asking for time off? Well, now she had it. She would purchase a ticket for West Virginia, a terrifying prospect with her employment at an end. She wasn't altogether certain of what she would do once she arrived there, but she had Sabine's old address from Virgie and desperation to drive her.

She'd almost been overcome once before—that day she

lost Father for good. But not today. Today she would fight to keep her head above water. As she sat in the shadows, she let the memory of that day come. She would remember, and she would use that memory to spur her on.

. . . . . . . . . . . . .

It was mid-July 1916 on a quiet Sunday morning when the rain finally stopped after what felt like weeks of pouring skies. The river was swollen more than she'd ever seen before. She and Father were having an early breakfast with their two boarders. Lorna remembered thinking that they had learned to manage pretty well in the absence of her mother.

Father kept peering out the window at the rising water and finally suggested they walk across the village green to Biltmore House. "There's high ground there," he'd said. He smiled and smoothed her hair back. "Not that there's any real danger, but we can see the river from there. I bet it'll be a sight."

In retrospect, Lorna knew he'd been afraid.

At first it was simply a marvel—wading through water where there should have been dry streets and the grass of the green. She'd wondered if the water would ruin the looms even as it poured into the buildings. Struck by the strangeness of it and certain that she was safe with her father, fear came too late.

She hadn't been afraid until the water suddenly surged higher, pushing against them like a living thing. By the time they reached what should have been the center of the green, it was past their waists.

The water roiled. It climbed faster than she thought possible. Others were on the green with them, and they joined hands as they struggled to make it to Biltmore's Lodge Gate. And then Julie—one of their boarders—was swept away. One moment she was there to Lorna's right and the next she was gone. That's when she knew just how desperate their situation was.

．＊＊・・・・．．＊°

Lorna clung to the tree with what little strength remained to her. Turgid water battered her without ceasing. It had been better when Father shielded her—when his arms still braced her own—when she could feel his chest pressing her to the tree.

How long had it been since he was swept from her?

She had no sense of time any longer, the deceptive sun having played hide-and-seek with the clouds all day. Was it evening yet? It certainly wasn't morning.

How many others had been with them? Lorna couldn't remember. She only knew they were all gone now except for her. She tightened her grip on the rough bark of the tree as something in the water scraped roughly past her. She fought the temptation to just relax and let the water carry her wherever it had taken Father.

She heard a splash and turned to see a man clamber into the tree over her head. Lifeguards had tried to reach them earlier—her and Father—but had failed. She gazed upward, trying to understand how this man was going to save her. Or was he as lost as she was?

"Pull me up," she called. Then louder, "Help me!"

The man pushed wet hair back and shook his head. "I have a wife and children. I have to think of them."

Lorna felt tears prick her eyes. "Please!" she begged.

The man cursed and looked all around as though there might be someone else to assist her. He leaned on a smaller limb, pushing it down until it was within reach. Lorna bit her lip and grabbed the branch, her fingers cold and stiff as they closed around her salvation. The stranger began pulling her up out of the water, her leaden skirts resisting. It was too much. The flood stretched greedy fingers up to tug her back down. With a cry she fell, barely managing to grip the tree once again. She pressed her forehead into the rough bark and wrapped her legs around the waterlogged trunk. She focused on the pain where the bark had rubbed the insides of her thighs raw even through the wet, heavy fabric of her skirt.

Lorna closed her eyes and imagined her father's arms were still wrapped tight around her. She prayed for the water to recede, for all of this to be a nightmare that she would soon awaken from, to find herself safe in her own bed tucked beneath the coverlet she'd woven with her own hands. She felt herself slip deeper into the water until it was over her mouth, her nose, her eyes. She opened her mouth and tasted the swirl of muddy water.

"I gotcha."

Lorna jerked, and her eyes flew open. A man tugged her head above water. He wrapped a rope around her, tying her to the tree. "Some men have gone for a flat-bottomed boat," he told her. "That's safer than me trying to pull you out. Hang on. They're coming."

"Father said they needed a flat-bottomed boat," she told him, choking on the water she'd swallowed.

The man didn't answer, just secured her, then swam back to shore, fighting the current the whole way. He crawled out and stood panting above the floodwater. A tall, regal-looking woman hurried to wrap a blanket around his shoulders. She peered across the swirling water to where Lorna now sagged against the rope and held out a hand as if to say *I'm coming*. Lorna could almost imagine it was Mrs. Vanderbilt herself.

Exhausted, Lorna barely noticed the way the rope cut into her. She watched as a boat was pushed into the water and her rescuers came to fetch her. She found she was too weary even to be glad that she might live to see her eighteenth birthday.

Lorna brushed at a tickle on her cheek and found her face to be nearly as wet as it had been the day Arthur dragged her onto a boat and took her to shore. In fact, it had been Mrs. Vanderbilt she'd seen at the bank. The kind widow draped a blanket about her shoulders and then Gentry appeared. Lorna wondered now what the younger girl had been doing there. She thought she remembered Gentry singing to her. Something about a cuckoo telling no lies. Well, she'd told some lies, hadn't she?

She wondered what made Arthur take such a risk. She was pretty sure he cared for her, but enough to risk his life?

She'd been in the water nine hours that day. It had taken weeks for her to recover her health. She supposed she'd never fully recovered from losing her father like that. She wished she'd been stronger then. She vowed she would be strong now.

# 15

# ARTHUR

**SOUTH ASHEVILLE**
**AUGUST 1921**

Angus was turning out to be more useful than Arthur had anticipated. While his work was painfully slow, it was excellent, and he was just the sort of company Arthur needed right now. The sort who offered a quiet, steady presence without offering commentary on his personal life.

"Got a job for ye," Angus said as he clomped into the shop on a morning that carried the promise of a long, hot day with it.

"I thought I was supposed to be giving you work to do," Arthur said.

"And so you do. But this is a special case." Angus's eyes twinkled. "Ever seen a sedan chair?"

"A what?"

"One of those fancy chairs like they use to carry kings and queens around in over in England or France or wherever."

Arthur chuckled. "I guess I have heard of them, but I'm pretty sure I've never actually seen one."

"Well, I'm going to let you in on the biggest secret in Asheville." Angus edged closer and lowered his voice. "The woodworkers up there at Biltmore House are making one that nobody's supposed to know about. But they've run up against some trouble with the poles for carrying the chair. Your old crew sent me to see if you'd come help 'em out."

Arthur ran a hand through his hair. "I've got orders to fill here."

"Won't take long." Angus winked. "And seems like letting folks know you filled a special order for the Vanderbilts won't hurt business down the road."

"I guess not." Arthur grinned. "And who could pass up helping to build a sedan chair of all things?"

"Right-o! I told John we'd run up there before lunch."

"Mighty sure of yourself, aren't you, old man?"

"That I am," Angus agreed. "There's little enough to be sure of these days. Might as well be sure of the one thing I can count on, and that'd be me."

Arthur shook his head. "Let me gather some tools and we'll go." Angus just smiled and settled back to wait.

Being back in the workshop at Biltmore House almost made Arthur wonder why he'd ever left. Especially since his primary reason for moving over to Biltmore Industries with Mr. Seely had been Lorna. He sighed. Water under the bridge. Hopefully being in business for himself was going to be worth all that he'd sacrificed.

"Good to see ya, Arthur." John slapped him on the back. "I suppose Angus has let you in on what we're aiming to do here."

"He said you're making a sedan chair, but for the life of me I can't think why."

John laid a hand across his heart. "It's for Tarheel Nell's

131

birthday doings. There's to be some sort of dress-up party, and our girl plans to make quite an entrance."

"I told ya it's called a masquerade ball," one of the other woodworkers chimed in. "She's dressing up like some important French something or other. She'll arrive at the party sitting inside a real sedan chair, just like the Frenchies used back in the olden days."

"What he said." John jerked a thumb at the other fellow. "Problem is, we need to fix it so four men can carry the thing." He frowned. "And it ain't fancy enough. We need someone who can help us fancy it up, and you were always good at that sort of thing."

"Can I see it?"

"Right this way!" John bowed at the waist and waved Arthur toward an area blocked off by makeshift screens. Behind them he found what looked like an oversized crate with windows in the top half and a bench seat inside. John lifted his cap and scratched his head. "Ain't much to look at yet." He pointed at the sides. "Think you can dress it up?"

"Don't see why not," Arthur said.

"They're gonna paint it real pretty, but it needs some trim or something like that."

"It needs curves, too," Arthur added. "Some softening. And what about the openings?"

"Curtains." John twisted his cap in his hands. "Word is there'll be curtains."

A thought struck Arthur, and he tried to subdue it. He was just there to help his old friends. He shouldn't meddle. "I suppose the curtains will need to be special."

"They oughta be," John agreed. "Ain't nothing too good for our Nell."

"Better call on Lorna Blankenship over at Biltmore Industries. She's the one to turn up the perfect fabric for Cornelia's big day."

"Now, that's a fine idea. The way Mrs. Vanderbilt dotes on that homespun fabric seems like it'd be just the ticket. But none of that plain stuff. It'll need to be fancy."

"Lorna's the one for you, then. There's none better." He'd just meddled. Lorna might not want anything to do with him, but he could still lend her a hand.

He'd always be ready to lend her a hand. She might not realize it, but once a man's risked his life for a woman, he's bound to her forever.

He stepped out of the workshop into a mizzling rain that he found refreshing on this August afternoon. He decided to walk the few miles down Approach Road to Biltmore Village. As he walked, he remembered that terrible July when the rain came in sheets day after day early in the month. They'd finally thought the worst was over. The sun came back out, and he assumed everyone would go on about their business only a little worse for the flooding.

Then the second round of rain came. And dams gave way. And the Swannanoa River running through Biltmore Village crested seventeen feet above flood stage.

Back then Lorna's family lived in a two-story house with a wide front porch near the railroad trestle spanning the river. Arthur had worked with her father. A taciturn man who became even quieter after the death of his wife. He'd been the best cabinetmaker Arthur had ever seen, and he'd learned several tricks from him.

He'd drowned the day the river flooded. As best Arthur had been able to piece the story together, he'd led Lorna and two girls who were boarding with them toward the Lodge Gate at the entrance to Biltmore Estate. It offered higher ground than the house overlooking the river. But they never made it to the high ground. Instead, they clung to a tree until everyone but Lorna had been swept away.

Arthur blew out a heavy breath. There were lifeguards

who were supposed to attempt a rescue, but none of them were willing. He was the one who shamed another fellow into helping him take a flat-bottomed boat out to the tree so they could drag Lorna's nearly lifeless body to safety.

Approaching his shop, he went around back where there was a small portico. He shook off his hat and stepped into the sawdust-infused warmth of his dream come true. Angus sat on a stool, using fine-grit sandpaper to smooth the edges of a chair seat. He nodded but didn't speak, clearly content with his work.

"Angus, do you remember the flood of 1916?"

"Who could forget? Although I reckon there are quite a few who wish they could."

"Where were you then?"

"I worked for Chauncey Beadle down at the nursery." He blew some dust from the chair. "Talk about a mess. That's why I ended up in the carpentry shop. The nursery didn't stand a chance."

"Guess that didn't make it any easier for Mrs. Vanderbilt to keep things going—a loss like that."

"Before the flood, we couldn't sell those plants fast enough. Grew 'em for the gardens up at the big house, too. Old man Olmstead was a pistol. Always knew just what he wanted." Angus shook his head. "Mr. Beadle said they lost eighty-five percent of the stock in the flood." He shrugged. "And that was that. I was dispatched to the woodshop and picked up enough to be sure I'd always keep myself in beans and cornmeal."

He straightened his back, stretched, then settled in his chair in a pose that Arthur recognized as settling in for a good chat. "I was there when you pulled Lorna from the water."

"You were? I don't remember."

"I'd be surprised if you did. You had your hands full. That's when I knew just how sweet you were on that girl."

Arthur made a face. "Anybody would have done it."

"Hardly. Seems like there were a dozen or so 'anybodies' who didn't do it that day. But you, you couldn't stand it another minute."

Arthur felt a strong need to change the direction of their conversation. "Remember how Mrs. Vanderbilt was right there handing out blankets? I heard she did plenty after the fact, too. Lots of folks were facing hard times after that."

"What was the name of that little mite with the dulcimer?" Angus asked. "She was there too, although I suspected she wasn't exactly where she was meant to be that day."

"Gentry. Yes, now that you mention it, she was particularly put out with Lorna." Arthur laughed. "Of course, she was always put out with someone. All fire and no spark, I'm afraid."

"She wanted you to leave Lorna to be washed away."

Arthur shot Angus a look. "I doubt that. She could be bristly, but she'd never wish that. She was just afraid I'd get hurt."

"I heard her holler after you," Angus said, crossing his arms loosely. "Said Lorna had stolen something from her and wasn't worth saving. She was almighty mad. Might not have meant it deep down, but she sure was spittin' bullets right then."

Arthur tried to think back to that day. He remembered seeing Gentry. Remembered her telling him it wasn't safe to go after Lorna. But that was all. "What did she think Lorna had stolen?"

Angus shrugged. "If she said, I don't remember. A letter? A dress? What would one girl steal from another?"

"Who knows? Probably just a misunderstanding." Arthur brushed the conversation off, told himself that Lorna would never steal anything from Gentry. But even as he convinced himself there was nothing to it, he realized he wanted to know what happened to Gentry. What would it take to find her? Mrs. Brady still ran the boardinghouse where Gentry had stayed. He decided he'd start there, and if it seemed too difficult a task, he'd let it go. If not . . . well, maybe he could bring Lorna some closure by reuniting her with her former protégé.

# 16

# GENTRY

**ASHEVILLE, NORTH CAROLINA**
**JULY 1916**

Gentry tipped her face to the weak light of the sky, ignoring the squelch of sodden earth beneath her boots. Such rain! She would be in trouble for missing Sunday services, but when the sun finally appeared, she hadn't been able to resist taking her dulcimer to a high meadow where she could pretend she was still on the farm. Grandad had often been cruel, yet his lack of caring meant he'd paid no mind when she rambled off on her own. Of course, her beloved sheep weren't here, but if she closed her eyes and let her fingers find their way across the strings of her instrument, she could conjure the soft bleats of the flock.

She nibbled a roll she'd filched from the kitchen. Something else she'd likely be in trouble for. But then she'd been dodging Grandad's ire as long as she could remember, and Mrs. Brady couldn't hold a candle to him.

Would they miss her in church? Gentry darted up the hillside to the cover of the trees, her dulcimer tucked under her arm and her boots slipping in the mud. It had been raining forever. Even now the leaden sky was once again darkening as though it might give way again. She knew where to find cover, though, where no one would think to look for her. They'd probably worry. With all the rain and the swollen river, they might even think she'd drowned. She smiled just a little at the thought. Let them fuss. No one took her seriously anyway.

Least of all Lorna. She scowled and picked up a stick just so she could throw it as hard as she knew how. She'd finally figured it out. It must have been the draft she tore up that day. Could Lorna have remembered how it went? She must have because she'd made fabric that should have been Gentry's. When she told Miss Vance that she'd been robbed, the missionary said that if the design was indeed her mother's, she should be pleased to see the idea come to life under Lorna's touch. Then she'd added, "Especially since you have yet to develop the patience to do the work yourself."

That had just been mean, and Gentry let Miss Vance know exactly what she thought of them all. Which had earned her an evening alone in her room with only bread and water for supper. As if that mattered to her.

"Lorna stole from me," she muttered. And she believed it whether anyone else did or not. She didn't remember very much about her mother, but she remembered that dress. And she remembered the day she thought they were leaving together. A day of wind and clouds and darkness much like today. Only something must have happened. Must have gone wrong. And somehow Mama left without her. Maybe headed home to Monroe County, West Virginia.

"It was a mistake," she said to the wet leaves under her feet. "A mistake!" she yelled at the rain-slick branches above her. It felt so good she tilted her head back and howled the words at the pregnant clouds roiling across the sky. "She made a mistake!"

Panting, she moved along a path through the trees that she knew led to an old barn, where she could sit and play the songs her mother's designs drew from her. She hurried, thinking how the music would gush out of her like splashes of cool water on a hot day. It was worth the risk of getting in trouble. And since Lorna was supposed to watch over her as well as instruct her, she would be in trouble, too. That thought brought another smile to Gentry's face.

Of course, Arthur would be cross with her, and she hated to disappoint him. But Arthur always forgave everyone, and more importantly, he would understand why she'd needed time to herself. He was the only one who ever understood her.

.·`·...·`

Hours later, Gentry made her way back toward Biltmore Village and the boardinghouse where she had surely been missed by now. Having spent her passion on the strings of her dulcimer, she felt calmer. Calm enough to hope she might not be in too much trouble. The rain had turned to a misty drizzle, so she carried her instrument wrapped in a feed sack she'd found in the barn.

As she emerged from the woods on the crest of a hill, she abruptly halted, unable to understand what she was seeing. The estate's gatehouse poked up out of a torrent of water stretching out of sight. The great mass seemed almost alive, like a monster intent on consuming everything in its path.

Where was the village? Where was the boardinghouse and the road and . . . the people?

There. She saw a sleek, fancy car—surely one from the estate—parked a little way back from the edge of the water.

139

And just beyond it, people moved about. She crept closer, the roar and hiss of the water making it hard to hear what the people were shouting to one another.

She picked up speed when she saw Arthur among the group. His lopsided way of walking made him stand out. She rushed to his side. Arthur could always be counted on to explain things.

"Arthur," she called, waving her free hand. She had to shout to be heard over the rushing water. "Arthur!"

He spun around, and she saw what looked like relief wash over his face. Yet he didn't move toward her. Instead, he turned back toward the men who were launching a boat into the turbulent flood.

She rushed to his side and grabbed his arm. "What's happening?"

"I'm glad you're safe, Gentry, but Lorna's out there." He pointed toward what should have been the village but was now a confusing mix of treetops, water, and wood.

"What do you mean?" She squinted her eyes to make sense of the scene before them.

"There." He stabbed a finger toward a clump of trees sticking out of the water. "I have to go."

"Wait." She tightened her grip on him. "You aren't going to get on that boat, are you?"

"I must get Lorna. No one else will." He pulled away and limped toward the boat.

Gentry lunged to grab him again. "It's not safe," she cried.

A worried-looking man nodded in agreement. "The girl's right, Arthur. We've lost too many today already. It's foolish to try."

"Yes, we've lost too many," Arthur said, a fierce light in his eyes. "And we aren't going to lose Lorna."

Arthur wrenched his arm from her grip and stepped onto the boat. Gentry clung to her dulcimer, trying to conjure the words to bring him back. "Lorna stole my design," she blurted, but Arthur was already too far away to hear over the roar of the water. "Maybe this is her punishment!" Gentry yelled.

Arthur glanced back and hollered, "Don't worry, I'll save her!"

Gentry backed away from the water lapping at her boots. "Maybe she's not worth saving," she mumbled, turning away so she wouldn't have to see Arthur struggling against the current. She noticed a regal-looking woman watching her, a look of sorrow painted across her face. There was no judgment in the look, only a deep sadness that hurt more than any outright accusation ever could.

Lorna sat there shuddering, a blanket draped around her shoulders by the tall woman who turned out to be Edith Vanderbilt, the one who lived in the castle with her daughter. Gentry stared, not sure what to feel. Lorna had nearly died, and for a moment, Gentry had wished her gone. Not dead necessarily, but out of Gentry's life. And when Arthur risked his own life for Lorna, she'd thought how it wouldn't hurt her feelings if she was swept away before he got there.

That dark thought lingered, whispering about how nice it would be not to have Lorna preaching perfection while stealing her mother's design when no one was looking. How nice it would be if she could just make music and weave bright colors without anyone telling her what to do.

And she was sorry.

Gentry sidled up to Lorna and rested a tentative hand on her shoulder. "Are you okay?"

The older girl turned vacant eyes on Gentry. "What?"

"I asked if you're okay, but I guess that's a silly question."

Lorna didn't say anything, just stared with that look on her face like she couldn't place where she was or who the people around her were.

"Anyhow, I'm glad you're alive," Gentry said. And she was. While Lorna was a pain, she didn't want her to die. Not really.

"Alive." Lorna frowned as though trying to remember what the word meant. "I'm alive." She shook even harder.

Arthur came over, his own sodden blanket slipping and dragging. His limp seemed worse than ever. "Gentry, would you mind putting an arm around Lorna? It's not quite the thing for me to do."

Gentry blinked, then knelt beside her teacher and wrapped an arm around her shoulders. She was surprised at how slight Lorna seemed, not to mention cold. She put both arms around the girl and pressed tight against her. "You're awfully cold," she said.

"Cold. Yes." Lorna turned her face toward Gentry's. They were so close that Gentry could see flecks of gold in Lorna's brown eyes, and she was suddenly as sorry as she'd ever been in her life. "I'll try harder," she promised. "I'll dress my loom perfectly, and I won't complain at all."

Lorna reached up to pat the arms around her. "That's good," she said. Tears began to seep from the corners of her eyes, and she let her forehead fall forward to rest against Gentry's.

A memory of her mother washed over Gentry then. She'd been tucked into bed after one of Grandad's hollering fits. Mama had pressed her forehead to Gentry's and sang,

> "The cuckoo's a fine bird:
> He sings as he flies;
> He brings us good tidings;
> He tells us no lies.
>
> He sucks the sweet flowers
> To make his voice clear;

And when he sings 'Cuckoo!'
The summer is near."

Gentry itched to play the tune on her dulcimer, but she'd tucked it safe under a rock when she realized she wasn't going back to the boardinghouse anytime soon. She hummed the tune instead and rocked gently back and forth the way her mother would have done.

Lorna closed her eyes, and Gentry let her tears mingle with her friend's.

# 17

# ARTHUR

**SOUTH ASHEVILLE**
**AUGUST 1921**

Arthur was both surprised and touched to receive an invitation to be part of the gathering of estate employees on Cornelia's birthday. He rose early to make his way to the house, where some two hundred and fifty workers and their families gathered to celebrate sweet Nell.

They met in the courtyard outside the stables. A handful of musically inclined employees had formed an impromptu band to play dance tunes, making for a lively scene despite the early hour. Cornelia, now an elegant young woman of twenty-one, clapped her hands in time to the music and smiled as though nothing had ever pleased her more. She greeted the workers like old friends, and Arthur supposed many of them were. She'd played with many a staff member's children when she was just a tyke herself.

Arthur remembered the Christmas not so long ago when he'd driven Lorna and Gentry to the staff party. Cornelia had been present that day, as well. Fresh from losing her father, she'd been a gracious hostess. He smiled recalling how Gentry, normally noisy and full of talk, had been struck nearly mute when the girl she called "practically a princess" handed her a Christmas gift. He racked his brain trying to remember what the gift had been.

He mused aloud, "Now, what was it Cornelia gave to Gentry that Christmas?"

"Handkerchiefs."

Arthur blinked and turned toward the familiar voice. "Cornelia gave Gentry embroidered handkerchiefs. I don't think she ever used them, just kept them in a drawer and petted them now and again."

"Lorna. You caught me talking to myself." Arthur felt his ears grow hot.

"I talk to myself all the time," she said with a toss of her head. "It's an excellent way to keep track of what I'm doing while weaving."

"I'm surprised to see you here," he said, then cringed. That sounded terrible. "What I mean to say is, I didn't expect . . . er, since you aren't on staff." He stopped speaking and took a deep breath. "It's good to see you, Lorna."

She laughed. It was so unexpectedly genuine that he felt his heart soar in response. Something he shouldn't let happen. The days of Lorna stirring his heart needed to be left well behind him.

"And it's good to see you, Arthur." She smiled, and her eyes seemed to ask his forgiveness—although for what, he didn't know. "I understand I have you to thank for being asked to make the curtains for tonight's surprise."

He ducked his head. "Yes, I suppose you do. But thanks aren't necessary. I knew John wanted the best, and I knew you were the one to supply it."

"Well, thank you just the same." She looked down and pursed her lips. "I saw John across the way. He said we're welcome to come see the finished—" she looked all around, a twinkle in her eye—"conveyance."

"That would be a treat," Arthur said. He crooked an arm in her direction. "May I escort you?"

"I'd be delighted!"

They made their way to the woodworking shop while talking lightly of the weather, the crowd, and how nice it was to see the estate bustling with activity. Since Mr. Vanderbilt's death, the family had spent more time in Washington, D.C., leaving the estate feeling much too quiet.

"Have you ever attended a masquerade?" Arthur asked.

"Oh, no. I wouldn't begin to know how to dress for one."

"I think you'd make a wonderful Cleopatra," he teased.

She giggled. "And you could be Antony."

They stared at each other for a moment, then burst into laughter. "We had better choose characters that fare better than those two," Arthur said. "Perhaps a sheep and a shepherdess."

"That does sound more like it," Lorna agreed. "I'll be the sheep."

"Are you two here to see the surprise?" John appeared in the workshop doorway. "Come on in. We're taking turns guarding it to make sure none of tonight's guests sneak a look."

Inside, the sedan chair gleamed in a shaft of sunlight. Arthur was proud of how the woodwork had turned out, and the fabric of the curtains seemed to glimmer. "What did you use to make the fabric?"

"It's a basic design. I simply incorporated a metallic thread to make the cloth shine. It also added weight so the curtains drape nicely." Lorna flicked the fabric to demonstrate how it dropped back into place, the folds hanging just so.

"You outdid yourself," Arthur said, fingering the cloth. Lorna's gaze dropped, and she mumbled a reply. "No need to be humble," he said. "You should take pride in such fine work."

"It's absolutely perfect." They turned to see Cornelia step inside, the game bag the staff had given her as a present slung over her shoulder. "I understand you both played an important role in making sure my entrance will not be forgotten anytime soon." She smiled. "Thank you."

Arthur noted the flush on Lorna's cheek that made her look even more charming than usual. Which wasn't something he had any business noticing.

"May I ask what your costume will be?" Lorna asked as though trying to change the subject.

Cornelia grinned. "It's marvelous. I'll be a Renaissance page with a bolero jacket and gorgeous lace underneath." She became more animated as she spoke. "There's a brilliant pink sash that matches the ostrich plume in my velvet cap. It's a stunner."

Lorna looked surprised. "A page? Not a queen with a crown or an exotic costume from the Orient?"

Cornelia made a face. "I've had to wear elaborate dresses too many times. As a page I'll be wearing britches and low-heeled shoes that will let me dance and dance without pinching. We'll have the Garber Davis Orchestra, and this costume means I can dance as much as I like without being encumbered."

"You've thought this through," Arthur said.

John joined them. "Our Nell's a smart one," he said. "And she'll be the prettiest girl in the room no matter what she wears."

Cornelia touched his arm fondly. "You always did stand up for me, John. Now, I'd better get back to the festivities. Again, thank you all for helping make this day so very special."

John grinned, "That's our girl. I believe I'll step out and

kick up my own heels a bit." He winked. "Don't be letting anyone get a peek in here."

They watched John escort Cornelia out. Arthur caught a wistful look on Lorna's face. "She must be missing her father today," she murmured. "It doesn't matter how many years pass; such a loss remains keen."

"As you know all too well," he said.

"Indeed, I do." She turned luminous eyes on him. "Did I ever thank you for saving me that day?"

"It was never necessary. I'm only grateful I was there to do it."

Tears welled. "Sometimes I wonder if I should have just let go. Followed Father wherever he went."

"No." Arthur grasped her arm. "Never say such things. You are . . ." He choked on the word. "You are precious." His voice turned hoarse. "And you would be missed. Very much so."

Two tears spilled, one after the other, plopping onto the back of his hand. "Thank you, Arthur. I didn't say it then, but I'll say it now." She looked up at him. "Thank you for rescuing me."

He found a handkerchief and pressed it into her hand. "You have long been and shall always remain dear to me. I'm grateful for your friendship."

She patted her cheeks with the handkerchief and gave a watery smile. "Thank you for that as well, Arthur. It's good to know I can count on you to be my friend."

"Always." And he meant it, even though his heart ached knowing it would never be more than that.

# 18

# GENTRY

**BILTMORE VILLAGE**
**SEPTEMBER 1916**

Gentry tried to be nice to Lorna. She guessed she was still pretty torn up about her father being drowned and nearly drowning herself. She supposed that was what happened when you liked your family. She tried to imagine how she would feel if she knew her mother was dead instead of just having gone off without her. That would be hard.

"I got that last batch of houndstooth done," she told Lorna.

"Hmm?" Lorna slowed her own weaving to look at Gentry.

"I said I finished the houndstooth fabric. Without your having to tell me to do it."

"Good." Lorna picked up speed again as though she were racing against a clock no one else could see.

Gentry huffed. She needed Lorna's help, but the older girl was always gloomy now. It had taken weeks to clean out the weaving rooms after the floodwater receded—a respite Gentry took full advantage of. But now they were back to work. Each day Lorna came to the weaving room, assigned work to the others, did her own work, and left again. No laughing. No teasing. Shoot, she didn't even fuss anymore. It was like she'd become a machine.

"I've got something to show you," Gentry blurted.

Lorna sighed without even slowing her work this time. "Can it wait?"

"It's quitting time," Gentry pointed out. "We're the only ones left."

Lorna pulled the beater bar one last time and stilled her hands. She glanced around. "So we are." She gave Gentry a puzzled look. "Why haven't you left?"

Gentry threw her hands up in exasperation. "I was waiting for you."

"Oh. That's kind." Lorna stood and did what she needed to tidy her loom until she could pick back up in the morning.

"Can I show you something?" Gentry persisted.

"Fine. Yes. What do you want to show me?"

Gentry grinned and scampered to a table, where she'd tucked some pages in a drawer. "These," she said, withdrawing her mother's drafts with a flourish.

Lorna approached as though her boots were made of lead. She picked up one of the yellowed pages, and for the first time since the flood, her eyes lit. She reached for a second sheet. "Where did you get these?"

"Don't you remember?" Gentry's patience was running thin despite her best intentions. "They're my mother's."

"I thought you just had the one."

"You mean the one you stole?" There, that put some color back in Lorna's cheeks. "There are lots of them."

Lorna's eyes flicked to Gentry and then back to the papers she held. "They are interesting." She heaved a sigh and dropped the draft she was holding. "And I'm sorry I didn't tell you I was weaving one of your mother's designs. But you still aren't skilled enough to weave these."

"Are you?" Gentry asked.

Lorna tilted her head and drew the drafts close again. She bent over them, tracing the lines and patterns with a finger. "They're challenging, but yes, I could do it."

"Do you think someone would pay for the designs?"

Lorna's head jerked up. "Pay? Are you asking if Biltmore Estate Industries would buy them from you?"

"Yes." Gentry felt relief at being understood wash over her.

Lorna shrugged. "Perhaps. They're certainly unique and would add to the collection. Since the first fabric did so well, they'd likely want more."

"Would you take them to Miss Vance and Miss Yale for me? See what they would offer?" Gentry gnawed a broken fingernail. "You know more about what they're worth."

Lorna stood silent for several beats. It felt like an eternity to Gentry. Finally, the older girl nodded her head. "Yes," she said. "I can do that."

Gentry flung her arms around Lorna. "Thank you so much! You have no idea what this means to me." Lorna felt stiff in her arms, but Gentry didn't care. She had a plan to get the money she needed to go find her mother, and that was all that mattered.

⁂

Gentry forced herself not to ask Lorna if she'd sold the drafts yet. She knew her teacher had gone to see Miss Vance and Miss Yale after supper the previous day, but Lorna didn't offer her any news. She tried to do her work—weaving yet another length of plain gray cloth—but she was even slower than usual. Finally, at the end of their lunch break, she saw Lorna pin on her hat and leave in a car headed toward Biltmore House. Could she be meeting with Mrs. Vanderbilt? Did this mean the queen of the castle herself would buy the drafts? Gentry's mind whirled, and her fingers stumbled until at last she asked to be excused due to a headache. Apparently, she looked so miserable the floor manager believed her for once.

In her room Gentry tried to rest with a cool washcloth over her heated brow, but she couldn't lie still. Finally, she picked up her dulcimer, sat on the floor beside her window, and plucked out the softest, saddest tunes she knew. The music worked where nothing else could, and soon she felt her spirit ease.

She was so lost in her music that she didn't hear the footsteps approaching her room. A sharp rap on the doorframe brought her head up. Lorna stood in the doorway, a worried look on her face.

"She didn't want them, did she?" The words burst from Gentry. She shoved her dulcimer away. "Well, maybe I don't want her to have them. How about that?"

"No, no, that's not it." Lorna's fingers worried the buttons on her blouse. "It's just . . ."

"What?" Gentry was on her feet now, impatience buzzing through her so that she simply had to move.

"Maybe it's not as much money as you hoped for." Lorna looked down and straightened her cuffs. "I don't want you to be insulted."

"How much?" Gentry clenched her hands until her nails dug into her palms.

Lorna named an amount that was almost enough to buy a train ticket. Was that an insulting amount? Gentry had no idea. The money she earned weaving mostly went for her room and board, yet she'd also saved a little and that would hopefully be enough to fund her search for her mother.

Of course, Mrs. Vanderbilt was rich. Although . . . Gentry

remembered Arthur saying things had gotten tight for the family after Mr. Vanderbilt died. So maybe it was all they could afford.

"I'll take it," she said.

Lorna locked eyes with Gentry for a brief moment before her gaze skittered away. She dug in the pocket of her skirt and withdrew the money. She paused, looking at the money in her hand. "Are you sure?" she asked as though she were waging some internal battle of her own.

Gentry tossed her head and laughed. "Of course I'm sure. Give it here."

Lorna pressed a bill and some coins into Gentry's hand. Gentry felt her teacher's fingers quiver as she whispered, "Don't do anything foolish with it."

Gentry laughed. "I'm going to do something *smart* with it." She crammed the money into her own pocket and scooped up her dulcimer. She perched on the side of her bed and struck up a lively tune. She glanced at Lorna to see if she would join in the celebration, but the doorway was already empty.

# LORNA

**BILTMORE VILLAGE**
**OCTOBER 1923**

Lorna settled onto the bench seat in the passenger car. She balanced her bag on her knees but quickly realized it was going to be uncomfortable. She looked around. Should she stow it on the floor? Or on the seat beside her? But what if someone else wanted to sit there? Not that she'd welcome a seatmate, but she didn't want to commit a faux pas either.

"I can take that for you."

Lorna jolted and looked up into familiar hazel eyes. "Arthur. What are you doing here?"

He lifted her bag and slid it onto a rack over her head, then settled in the seat beside her. The seat that suddenly felt much narrower.

"That's exactly what I was about to ask you. I'm on my way north to buy wood. Basil has connected me with a fellow who says he has some rare species for me. What about you?"

Emotions warred inside Lorna. She was glad to see Arthur, but how much should she tell him? Being let go still felt too fresh and painful. She settled for the bare-bones version of the truth. "Virgie gave me an address in West Virginia. I'm headed there to see if I can learn anything about my weaver."

Arthur grinned. "I'm headed almost that far. I'll change my ticket and come with you."

Lorna squirmed. She wanted nothing more than to accept his kindness and his company. But she wasn't worthy of him and should politely decline. She knew she should send him away, should save herself the heartache that would surely come if he ever learned the truth about her, but she lost the battle.

"I can't ask you to come with me," she said at last.

Arthur's smile lit the carriage. "You didn't ask," he said and took her hand as naturally as if they'd been holding hands for years. His voice deepened. "You didn't need to."

Tears welled, and Lorna didn't fight them. It was such a relief to give in, to let someone take care of her. "Thank you, Arthur," she whispered. "I don't deserve your help."

He squeezed her fingers. "Yes. You do. You deserve so very much."

She swallowed past a rising lump and smiled at him. If only he knew. But for now, he didn't know, and she would rest in this moment, grateful to receive it and hopeful that it would sustain her when he was gone. As he inevitably would be.

⋯⋯⋱⋅

Lorna jolted awake as the train's brakes screeched. They were approaching the station where they would disembark. Arthur stirred and stretched, as well. Thank goodness he hadn't been watching her sleep. "Is this our stop?" he asked, yawning.

"Yes, we've arrived in Ronceverte."

155

"Now, that's a funny name for a town," he said as he rubbed his eyes.

A nervous laugh bubbled up, and she gulped it back down. "Isn't it, though? I looked it up before I left. Turns out it's French for *greenbrier*."

Arthur grinned. "A troublesome plant. That's one way to fancy up a problem." He clapped his hands. "So, where to from here?"

"The address Virgie gave me says Pickaway." Lorna produced a slip of paper from her bag. "She said it's ten or twelve miles south of town."

As the train thrummed to a full stop, Arthur stood and retrieved her bag. "Well then, let's see if we can hire a wagon. I'm thinking that's too far to walk."

Thirty minutes later, Lorna wished they'd decided to walk no matter how long it took. No one had a wagon they could use, so Arthur had drummed up the use of a roadster that had seen better days. What was left of the top was in tatters, and the passenger door was attached with baling wire. Lorna feared for her life, but Arthur seemed delighted by the opportunity to drive the stuttering motorcar south on a rutted road to Pickaway.

Lorna kept one hand on her hat and gripped the edge of the seat with the other. She wanted to close her eyes but quickly discovered that not seeing was worse than the juddering view through the cracked windscreen.

Thankfully, they soon reached the community of Pickaway, which was little more than a scattering of farms anchored by a school, a church, a blacksmith shop, and a combination store and post office. They stopped at the store to get their bearings and then headed out Hillsdale Road toward the Goodwin family farm.

Arthur brought the automobile to a stop near a barn. Or perhaps the engine simply died. Lorna couldn't tell. The barn leaned toward the road like an old woman peering nearsightedly over someone's shoulder. Lorna felt oddly judged by it. She wanted to hop out and get away from the looming presence but couldn't figure out how to operate the automobile door with its baling wire hinges. Finally, Arthur came around and helped her out.

She stumbled to the ground and hurried around the looming barn. A little red house sat in a tangle of a garden on the far side. All was still.

"Should we knock on the door?" Arthur asked. "And who exactly is it we've come to see?"

"Olive Goodwin. She's a relation of the Goodwins, who ran a weaving mill here in Greenbrier County for years. It's no longer in operation, but Virgie said Olive still teaches people to weave and would likely know about other weavers in the area."

"Doesn't sound like much to go on," Arthur said. He flashed her a smile. "Here's hoping!" He took her hand, and they walked together to the door.

Lorna was so flustered by the fact that Arthur was holding her hand that she barely registered the woman who flung open the door. She looked young—perhaps in her twenties—although the spectacles she wore and the way her hair was pulled back into a high twist aged her.

"If you've come for the cover lid, it's not done yet." She blinked at them from behind round lenses.

"I . . ." Lorna tried to remember what she'd planned to say.

"Are you Olive Goodwin? If so, we've come to ask you about a weaver we think might be living around here. Or maybe did at one time," Arthur explained smoothly and calmly, the pressure of his hand firm and comforting against her own.

"I'm Olive, and I reckon I know every weaver within a hundred miles." The woman smiled and it lit her face, making her look younger. "Come on in. You can talk while I weave."

Arthur gave Lorna a little tug to start her forward, then released her hand once they were inside. She missed his touch instantly. But at the same time, she found she could focus again.

The room was small with a loom taking up more than half the space. The remaining sliver of room offered mismatched chairs that flanked a fireplace, with a little table holding a tumbler and a plate with crumbs on it. Where Virgie's house had been cozy, this one was spartan. Nonetheless, the tension Lorna had carried with her all the way from Asheville began to drain away. She sank into one of the chairs. Arthur took the other. Olive settled at her loom and set her shuttle flying. The familiar rhythm and cozy atmosphere made Lorna's eyelids feel weighted. She began to suspect she was falling under some sort of enchantment.

"Who's this weaver you're searching for?" Olive asked.

Lorna blinked slowly and tried to remember.

"You have some fabric to show Olive, don't you?" Arthur's voice penetrated her haze, and Lorna felt herself come awake again.

"Yes, that's right. I have it right here." She pulled from her bag the shawl she bought at the market as well as the pieces Virgie had given her.

Olive stilled her shuttle and took the cloth. Her face clouded. She ran her fingers over the pattern as though tracing letters only she could read. "Where did you get these?"

"The shawl was a purchase I made at a market in Asheville, North Carolina. The other pieces were given to me by a friend, who got them from a woman named Sabine. She lived somewhere around here, I think."

"Sabine Brooks." Olive whispered the name. "I heard she died."

"Yes, that's what my friend said."

"So you didn't meet her?" Olive turned hopeful eyes on Lorna.

"No, she's been gone a while now."

Olive sighed heavily and shook out the shawl. "She and her sister Vivian were the best weavers I ever saw. And if I weren't opposed to swearing, I'd swear one of them made this."

"Do you think so?" Lorna asked. "I bought it recently, but I suppose it could have been made some time ago."

Olive frowned and examined the piece inch by inch. "It doesn't have a flaw," she mused.

At the words, Lorna felt as though she'd been electrified. "Did Sabine have some sort of mark she included in her designs?"

The other woman flicked a suspicious look at her. "It's one way to keep patterns and designs from being stolen. Not foolproof, certainly. Other weavers can imitate the flaw, but most people don't notice."

Lorna's stomach tensed. "But a skilled weaver could copy a pattern without needing the draft," she said. "Patterns are for sharing anyway."

Olive sniffed. "Common patterns maybe. But this." She held up the shawl. "This is special." She swirled it in the air and settled it around her shoulders. "I'd be willing to bet the secret to my grandma's pumpkin pie that one of the Brooks girls made it, flaw or no."

Lorna's heart nearly stopped. "You're sure?"

"No, but it's likely." She unwound the shawl and handed it over, clearly sad to let it go.

"What do you know about Vivian? Is she still living around here?"

Olive gave an unladylike snort. "She was a wild thing. Ran off and got married when she was fifteen years old. Although she could already weave like a dream. Sabine used to get letters from her now and again. I don't recall from where, though."

"Who did she marry?" Lorna asked.

"Some sheep farmer passing through. I doubt anyone other than Sabine would even remember his name." She got a twinkle in her eye. "I hear he was devilishly handsome."

Lorna felt as if she might cry. "I was so hoping—"

"Wait." Olive held a finger up in the air. "I have one of Sabine's drafts. It's not her fanciest work, but she was kind enough to give it to me before she left for North Carolina." She popped up from her seat at the loom and darted through a doorway. Lorna could hear her rummaging around and muttering. "Aha!" she sang at last. She marched over to Lorna and presented the slip of paper with a flourish. It was yellowed and torn where the page had been folded over and over again.

Lorna took it with a shaking hand. Her mouth was so dry she didn't think she could speak. The fragile paper crackled in her fingers as she opened it and took in the pattern with greedy eyes. Might it be good enough to please Mrs. Harshaw?

Silence reigned in the room that had gone from feeling cozy to suffocating. Finally, Lorna licked her lips, mustering the courage to say something, anything. "It's simple but obviously a lovely design."

"Yes, I've made it so many times, I know it by heart. You're welcome to take that if you think it might be a help."

"Thank you," Lorna said, refolding the paper and slipping it into her bag, along with the shawl. "You've been very kind." The words sounded stiff, but she couldn't think what else to say.

"I doubt that. Seems like all I did was confirm what you already knew." She slid back onto her stool at the loom. "I hope you find whoever made that shawl." One corner of her mouth turned up. "And if it's Vivian, tell her to drop me a line."

"I'll do that," Lorna said refraining from mentioning that if Vivian was who she thought she was then . . . she was dead. She stood and headed for the door. She was outside in the fresh, early autumn air before she remembered that Arthur was with her.

He took her elbow. "I'm thinking that wasn't as helpful as you hoped," he said.

Lost in her own world, she barely registered the words. "No. It wasn't what I expected at all. We may as well see if we can catch the evening train back to Asheville."

They climbed into the ridiculous automobile, and Lorna left Arthur to the joy he clearly took in driving it. She leaned back in the seat, pondering what she had learned. She slipped one hand into her bag and touched the crackling paper with its simple but unique design. It felt hot under her hand, the paper and handwriting exactly like the drafts she had back home, hidden away, so no one would ever know she had them.

# 20

# GENTRY

**BILTMORE VILLAGE**
**SEPTEMBER 1916**

Gentry counted out the coins that would take her from the depot in Biltmore Village to southern West Virginia. She jiggled her purse, noting that there was very little left. For a fleeting moment she considered all the pretty things she could buy with the money. But no. Nothing was more important than finding her mother.

"You aren't traveling alone, are you?" the man behind the counter asked.

Gentry stood up straighter. "What of it?"

"Just seem a mite young to be travelin' on your own." He narrowed his eyes as if she might be doing something underhanded.

"I'm sixteen," she lied. "Plenty old enough to do whatever I like."

The man snorted. "Old enough to do what's foolish more like, but it ain't no business of mine."

"No," Gentry agreed with a sniff. "It isn't."

The man shook his head and waved her off. She stuck her nose in the air, hefted her carpetbag containing her dulcimer and a few items of clothing, and marched to the outside platform to await her future.

She smiled, picturing the look on Mama's face when she found her. Not to mention the look on Mrs. Brady's and Lorna's faces when they discovered she'd left. She felt the tiniest bit sorry to leave Arthur, but maybe she'd write to him. He'd want to know about her adventures. Yes, that was what she would do. Just as soon as she found Mama.

# 21

# ARTHUR

**SOUTH ASHEVILLE**
**FEBRUARY 1922**

Angus was leaning against the door, pipe smoke curling around his ears, when Arthur arrived to open the shop.

"Running late, ain't ye?" he asked.

Arthur grunted. "I'd say you're running early."

"If you paid me, I'd ask fer extry, but since you're a charity case, I'll let it go." Angus hobbled up the steps behind Arthur. "A fine pair we are, all stove up and gimpy."

"Remind me why I keep you around?" Arthur asked with a grin.

"'Cause that Donnie feller you were training up and left ye." Angus settled in his usual chair in the back room with a sigh. "Plus your customers like my yarns almost as much as your furniture."

"Right you are," Arthur agreed. "Got any new tales this morning?"

"Not a tale exactly, but I did hear something that might be of interest."

"Oh? What's that?" Arthur paid little attention as he readied the shop for the day's business.

"That Lorna lass is causing a stir up at the Grove Park Inn." Arthur's head jerked around. He saw a sly smile on Angus's lips much to his dismay. "Thought that might do it."

"Do what?" Arthur said before he could catch the sullen-sounding words.

"Spark ye. Ain't seen a spark since that other one up and left ye."

Arthur threw his hands in the air. "Have you been sent to torment me? Nothing but gossip and bad memories. Can we talk about something else?"

"She's done up some new cloth that's got the fashionable ladies all atwitter." Angus kept speaking as though Arthur hadn't.

Arthur plopped down on his own stool. "Fine, Angus, what is it about this cloth?"

"Can't say as I understand much about fashion and all that, but I guess it's the designs that are extry special. The way she wove 'em sets 'em apart. Word is, Mrs. Vanderbilt is having a dress made that's gonna be all the rage." He drew on his pipe and exhaled slowly. "Whatever that means."

"And you thought this would be of interest to me because?"

"'Cause you're still sweet on the girl. Might be a good time to write her a letter or go see her. While she's flying high, you might say."

Arthur shook his head. "You are a meddlesome fellow."

"Keeps me occupied."

The bell jangled above the front door. "How about you stop meddling and go see if you can charm whoever that is? I've got an order that needs to be delivered today and listening to you isn't getting my work done."

Angus winked and stood from his chair, straightening his

back by degrees. "There," he said. "Takes me a minute to get upright, but I can go all day once I'm up."

Arthur watched the old man head into the showroom, where he immediately struck up a conversation with a matronly woman who was looking for a picture frame for a photo of her first grandchild. Angus could more than handle that order. Arthur, on the other hand, wasn't at all certain that he could handle the idea of trying again with Lorna. He wanted to. Seeing her at Cornelia's birthday party had reminded him of all the reasons he cared for her. She'd been warmer toward him that day, and when she thanked him for saving her from the flood . . . A lump rose in his throat. He wanted her in his life, in whatever way she'd allow. And now he had a reason— an opportunity—to reach out with his congratulations. What did he have to lose? "Other than my pride and self-respect," he mumbled to himself. And those weren't worth much.

He glanced into the showroom to confirm that Angus was well occupied. Then he found a pen and pulled out a piece of the letterhead he'd had printed specially for his business. He should probably just use regular stationery, but he figured reminding Lorna that he was a legitimate businessman wouldn't hurt his chances. He groaned softly. As if he had a chance.

One more peek into the front room and he began writing.

*Dear Lorna,*

*Congratulations on your recent success. I have long found you to be a truly gifted weaver, and I am pleased to see you receiving praise for your skill. I look forward to seeing the cloth you have recently woven. And perhaps I will have an opportunity to see you, as well.*

He tapped his pen against his bottom lip. Was that last line too much? Or not enough? He started to crumple the page, then stopped himself. Again, what did he have to lose?

Before he could change his mind, he added *With affection, Arthur*, quickly folded the page, and slipped it in an envelope. He stood from the table where he'd scrawled the note. As he turned, he yelped upon finding Angus standing just a few feet away.

"Want me to deliver that?" the old man asked.

Arthur looked at the envelope in his hand as though surprised to find it there. "I, uh, I suppose . . . Yes." If he was going to be a fool, he'd own it. "Yes. Please deliver this to Lorna Blankenship at Biltmore Industries."

Angus grinned and saluted him. "Yes, Cap'n. Will there be anything else?"

"You might try to stop meddling," Arthur mumbled, but his friend was already halfway to the door.

. . . . . . . . . . .

No response. Arthur heaved a sigh and tidied his workbench at the end of a successful day. It had been a week since he had sent his note to Lorna and . . . nothing. Would he never learn? Well, he'd had enough of rejection—from Lorna and from Clara. He should continue focusing elsewhere. His business was doing well. Angus had become like family. And he was respected in the community. Shouldn't that be enough?

The bell over the door jangled. He slipped his jacket back on and went to see if he might make one more sale today. But instead of a customer, it was Reverend Swope, who began looking over the wares.

"Rodney. Good to see you. Checking up on me?"

"Not at all," Rodney said with a laugh. "I have an altar guild to do that for me."

Arthur chuckled along with his mentor, but he had a bad feeling. This visit was decidedly unusual.

"Have a seat," Arthur said, waving to a pair of comfortable

167

chairs near the window. Clara said the chairs would be welcoming for guests, and he had to admit she'd been right. "Is everything alright?" he asked, not willing to make small talk with the man who was as close to a father as he'd ever known.

Rodney blew out a breath. "I'm afraid not. You always did have a remarkable sense for what other people were feeling." The reverend removed his glasses and rubbed his eyes. "The problem is, I don't know how you'll feel about this news." He opened his eyes. "Your parents are dead, Arthur."

Arthur stared for a moment. His parents? The people he'd had no contact with since leaving West Virginia with Reverend Swope, what, twenty-four years ago? He finally found his tongue. "I'm sorry to hear that." He wet his lips, wanting to be careful about what he said next. "I suppose I may ultimately feel some loss, but they've been lost to me for so long now, I'll confess this news may not be as hard for me as you're expecting."

"Fever," Rodney continued as if Arthur hadn't spoken. "Took them both. I doubt either of them had particularly strong constitutions."

"No, I suppose their lives didn't get markedly easier after they . . ." Arthur couldn't find the right word for what they'd done with him. "After they *apprenticed* me to the church."

Rodney bowed his head and kneaded his hands. For a moment, Arthur wondered if the reverend was praying. Then he lifted his head suddenly. "The thing is, Arthur, there's a child. A young man, really."

Arthur frowned in confusion. What in the world was he talking about?

"You have a brother who is now without a family."

"I have a . . ." He couldn't finish the thought. "But I had several brothers. And sisters. We were all scattered." He shrugged. "I used to think that it might be nice to find some of them, but the timing never seemed right. Surely we're all old enough to take care of ourselves without the help of . . . of such parents."

Rodney grimaced. "It would seem your mother had a child late in life. Boyd is fifteen years old. And from what I've been told, he has some challenging issues."

Arthur nodded slowly. "Well, what about my other siblings? Are any of them still around to help?"

"Apparently not. Or if they are, they aren't offering. The current rector of Saint Matthews wrote to let me know, thinking that perhaps I would take in another Wescott child."

Arthur felt a stab of, what was it, anger? Fear? Petty jealousy? He couldn't think of any response to all of this.

Rodney leaned forward and looked deeply into Arthur's eyes. "You have been a son to Mary and me. You have been among God's greatest blessings to us." He sat back. "But we are no longer of an age when welcoming a child into our home seems reasonable." He paused. "But if you would like to take him in, you will have our fullest possible support in ensuring this young man has all the advantages he has formerly been deprived of."

"Take him in?" For some reason, Arthur hadn't realized this was an option. "I could take him in?"

Rodney nodded. "Yes, the arrangements could be made quite easily. Persuading the young man to come to Asheville might be the only difficulty. The rector says he goes around with a bad crowd there in Wheeling. It's part of why they hoped he might be able to move elsewhere."

"I'll go fetch him." Arthur was on his feet, calculating what would be required to take him to Wheeling, West Virginia, and back.

"Not so fast, Arthur. You need to think about this carefully. Taking in a teenage boy who's lived the life he has will surely be a challenge. Take some time. Consider all the angles, my boy."

Arthur remembered his own childhood with forgetful, overburdened parents who had little use for the progeny they kept bringing into the world. This boy, his brother, had suffered more years than he had under their care—or lack of it. Arthur had taken refuge in working with wood. Had his brother found something similar? Or would he be little more than a wild creature who had to learn to fend—and fight—for himself?

"It doesn't matter," he said. "He's my brother, and I can't abandon him now that I know he needs me. I'm going to do whatever I can. I have to."

Rodney laid a hand on Arthur's shoulder. "I'm thankful you've decided to take this path. I think it will make a world of difference to Boyd Wescott. And you'll have all the help Mary and I can give you." He smiled. "And God will help you, too, of course. He has a soft spot for orphans. I'll send a telegram asking for details and will let you know when you can make the trip north."

Arthur laughed, his heart light and filled with joy. He was going to fetch his brother. They would be a family. They would belong to each other in a way Arthur had never belonged to another person. He slapped his palms together. "We're going to be quite the pair. The Wescott boys are about to show Asheville something great!"

# 22

# LORNA

Arthur insisted on upgrading their tickets so they could eat in the dining car on the way back to Asheville. Lorna resisted at first but ultimately decided to simply enjoy the gift. "Thank you, Arthur. I'm grateful." The look of pleasure her simple thanks brought to his face lightened her heart, if only for a moment.

They settled at a small table covered with a white cloth as the train chugged toward the setting sun. Lorna unfolded her napkin to make way for the chicken cutlets served with peas and carrots. She began eating mostly because she couldn't think of anything to say.

"Are you terribly disappointed?" Arthur asked at last.

Lorna spent far too much time cutting a bite of chicken and then chewing it. She swallowed and patted her lips with her napkin. "It's been a treat meeting other weavers." She sipped some water. "If nothing else, this search has introduced me to Elspeth, Virgie, and Olive. I hope to stay in touch with them all—to learn from them even."

Arthur cocked his head and considered her. "But are you disappointed?"

Lorna sighed. "Yes. I suppose I am."

"What will you do next?"

Lorna spooned some peas and carrots into her mouth even though her appetite was fast disappearing. She couldn't think how to answer Arthur. She forced the food down. "I might try another design of my own. The draft Olive gave me is simple, but I could dress it up a bit."

"Then not altogether your own," he said. "I suppose there really isn't anything new under the sun."

His words stung a little, though they shouldn't have. "No. Not altogether my own." She smiled, knowing it wasn't reaching her eyes. "But as you say, we all stand on the shoulders of those who came before us."

The waiter approached, and Lorna nodded for him to remove her plate. He traded it out for a small bowl of apple crisp with sugared cream. While it looked delicious, Lorna wasn't certain she could get it down, the smell of cinnamon suddenly cloying and heavy.

"Remember the cloth you made that Gentry said reminded her of snow?" Arthur dug into his own dessert with gusto. "Now, that seems like the sort of thing Mrs. Harshaw would be wanting."

Lorna's stomach heaved, and she pressed her napkin to her lips while she struggled for composure. Thankfully, Arthur didn't seem to notice. "Yes. Just like that."

"I wonder what ever happened to all those drafts Gentry had. The ones that belonged to her mother," he said, scraping the bottom of his bowl.

Lorna lurched to her feet. "I . . . I need some air." She hurried to the end of the car, where she flung the door open and stepped onto the narrow platform leading to the next car. She gulped the night air until her racing heart slowed and she felt a measure of calm. She remembered the cold March day when Arthur had quizzed her about her sunflower fabric reminding him of Gentry. If he were anyone else, she would suspect him of doing this to punish her.

"What is it?" Arthur stood just behind her, his presence a solid mass in a world whirling past them.

The confession bubbled up in Lorna's throat, and she nearly admitted how underhanded and duplicitous she'd been. But a blast from the train's whistle silenced her. She turned to Arthur. The compassion in his eyes nearly undid her. But then she imagined how that look would change if she told him about borrowing—no, *stealing*—Gentry's patterns.

"I think the motion of the train upset my stomach," she said. "I guess I'm not used to eating while hurtling along the tracks." She managed a weak laugh.

Arthur wrapped an arm around her shoulder. She stiffened, then gave up and slumped against him, tears threatening but not quite spilling over. "Poor girl," he said. "And here I thought I was doing you a kindness."

She grasped his lapel. "You are, Arthur. You're the kindest person I've ever known."

He looked down at her, and his arm tightened. His eyes warmed the frozen places in her heart, and she couldn't help but snuggle closer. Then he leaned toward her, and his lips were on hers. The kiss was everything she'd ever wanted, warring with her greatest fear. She ignored the fear. Ignored the knowledge that Arthur didn't really care for the real her. It was the idea he had of her that captured him. But she didn't care anymore. She'd settle for this moment. Here. Now. And let the future bring what it would.

Arthur snored softly in the seat beside her. Lorna shifted, trying to get comfortable. They would be back in Asheville soon, before dawn brightened the sky. She had feigned sleep until she was certain Arthur had drifted off. Since then, she'd sat here as though strapped to some sort of torture device.

She took out the draft Olive gave her. She froze and darted a glance at Arthur each time the paper crinkled. She worried her lower lip with her teeth as she examined the design. It wasn't elaborate, but it would be gorgeous all the same. Simple and elegant, like a great river flowing around rocks worn smooth over time. She pictured it in blues and grays and thought she could smell wet sand and taste metallic water—like wading in a cool stream on a hot day.

It was so like the other drafts—the ones she'd let Gentry think she'd sold to Biltmore Estate Industries. Instead, she'd kept them for herself, had held them in reserve for the day she needed to prove she could be a designer as well as a technical weaver. She hadn't used them for a long time. She knew she hadn't paid Gentry what they were worth. And of course, she'd claimed them as her own. Wrong upon wrong.

Gentry had been gone for, what, seven years now? It felt like a lifetime. All she'd wanted to do was find a weaver and save her own skin. Maybe even save Biltmore Industries. But the harder she tried to do the right thing, the more she seemed to circle back to the wrong thing she'd done to Gentry.

The train began to slow with much puffing and clanking. She quickly refolded the paper and tucked it in her bag. Arthur blinked awake and stretched with a yawn. A warm smile spread upward, lighting his eyes as soon as he saw her face. She felt an answering smile, much to her surprise. How long had it been since she'd felt joy in simply meeting someone else's gaze? Had she ever?

"Seems I slept pretty well in spite of the accommodations," Arthur said. "How about you?"

Lorna glanced at the corner of the draft sticking out of her bag. "I'm surprisingly well rested," she replied. And it was true. Although she hadn't slept a wink, she felt fresher and more awake than she had since that terrible day her father was stolen from her. It was as if she'd been having terrible dreams for years and was now fully awake.

She reached down to push the weaving draft deeper into her bag. She wouldn't use it. She would never weave it, even though she supposed Olive had given it to her with that intent. But she'd taken enough patterns from Vivian, from Gentry, and she would not take this one. No matter what.

As Arthur reached for her hand and wound his fingers through hers, she pushed her guilt down, as well. She'd steered him clear of the truth once before, and she could certainly do it again. There was no need for him to ever know what she'd done.

# 23

# ARTHUR

**WHEELING, WEST VIRGINIA**
**FEBRUARY 1922**

Arthur left for West Virginia within a week of learning he had an orphaned brother. He planned to arrive in time to have a late supper with Boyd and Reverend Greenleaf. Then, after a good night's rest, they would catch an early train back to Asheville.

Arthur stood and made his way toward the exit as the train slowed at the Wheeling station. In his eagerness, he stepped onto the platform even before the train had fully stopped. The misstep caused him to stumble, and he nearly fell, catching himself at the last moment and straining the muscles in his leg. He frowned and rubbed his thigh. That was going to make his limp worse, and he hated to give his brother anything less than his very best.

"Mr. Wescott?" A slender man wearing a collar and small, round spectacles approached, a worried look knitting his brow.

"Yes, that's me. I'm fine. Just in a hurry to see my brother."

Simply saying the words aloud brought a grin to his face. But the look on Reverend Greenleaf's face melted it away.

"Please, come with me," he said. "I'm sure you remember that the church is just two blocks over."

Arthur wanted to pepper the rector with questions but held his tongue. He supposed he'd be getting answers soon enough. The gray stone church with its tall spires looked forbidding in the oncoming darkness. But warm light glinted through its arched windows. He pinned his hopes on that.

The rector held the door open for Arthur, and they were soon ensconced in a small parlor. Reverend Greenleaf settled into an armchair with a world-weary sigh. "I'm so sorry I wasn't able to catch you before you left Asheville."

"Has something happened to Boyd?"

The reverend let his head fall back against the chair. "Everything has happened to your brother over the years. The latest is that he's robbed a local saloon and disappeared."

Of all the things Arthur had imagined, this was so remote that he found himself speechless.

"I believe Reverend Swope may have mentioned that Boyd has had some challenges?"

"Yes, but he didn't elaborate."

"I had thought it best that the young man enumerate his shortcomings to you himself," Reverend Greenleaf said with a heavy sigh. "And he readily agreed." His voice dropped. "That should have been my first indication." He shook his head as though to clear it. "At any rate, it would seem he was simply playing along. Biding his time, you might say. Late this morning, the authorities notified me that after spending much of the night playing cards in a back room, he helped himself to considerable cash and disappeared into the woods."

Arthur stared and blinked. It would seem life with his parents had formed exactly the sort of young man one might expect. His heart ached for Boyd, this brother of his who had to scrabble and fight for what he could get. Who had no one to make sure he didn't need to turn to a life of crime.

He'd managed to forget what that felt like. But it was coming back to him now. "Where?" Arthur asked.

"Where?" Reverend Greenleaf looked perplexed.

"Where's this juke joint, and where did Boyd disappear?"

"Oh. It's across the river, near Martins Ferry."

Arthur nodded. "Pap knew a fella who ran liquor over there. I think I can remember where his place was." He stood and moved to put his coat and hat back on.

"Where are you going?"

"To find my brother," Arthur said, then slipped out into the night.

·······

He'd forgotten how chilly a February evening could be in the northern panhandle of West Virginia. Especially with the Ohio River flowing silently by as though dragging the creeping cold and darkness with it. He'd found the juke joint Boyd robbed but didn't go in. He felt certain the owner wouldn't be interested in simply seeing his funds returned. He'd want blood. And if he couldn't have Boyd's, his brother's would likely do.

Now he stumbled along a washed-out road, its ruts dried and uneven. He almost wished he were given to cursing. Unleashing some foul words seemed the least the situation called for.

Then he saw a glimmer of light.

There, just ahead, closer than he remembered, was a cabin leaning heavily to the rear as though it were about to sit down. He thought the angle of the leaning was new, but otherwise it was much as he remembered from the night Pap dragged him out here to collect payment for something.

While Arthur's memory was fuzzy, he was pretty sure Pap had been persuaded to drink whatever he'd been owed. And then some most likely.

It had not been a pleasant night. Even now, Arthur felt a shiver that had nothing to do with the temperature. He stood beyond the bar of light spilling from a window and watched for a little while. He could see the end of a davenport with a man's booted feet sticking off the end. By their stillness, he assumed the man was asleep. He could also see an armchair with an elbow braced there, the hand cradling a glass of clear liquid. The glass flashed out of sight. When it returned, it was empty. The hand let it fall to the floor.

After another few minutes, there were no other signs of movement or activity. He knew just turning up and knocking on the door was a terrible idea, yet he couldn't think what else to do. The battered porch steps slanted with the house, making them difficult to climb. He finally made it to the porch, which let out a groaning creak that he expected would rouse the occupants better than any knock at the door.

All remained quiet, however. He peered inside and could see the man on the sofa, snoring with his mouth hanging open. Whoever was in the chair remained unseen, but his hand hung loose and relaxed. Arthur gritted his teeth and knocked.

Nary a movement. Nary a sound from inside.

He looked in the window again and found the two men just as he'd seen them before. Heaving a sigh, he tried the knob. The door was unlocked. He eased it open, slipped inside, and shut the door before what little heat there was from a dying fire could escape.

He cleared his throat, eyes on the grizzled man sprawled on the sofa. He flinched in his sleep, and his hand twitched where it lay across his belly. Arthur moved closer to the men so he could see the one in the chair. The sight poleaxed him.

It was like looking in a mirror that had erased the last twenty years. And added quite a shiner to the right eye. He knew without a doubt this was his brother.

The floor creaked as he approached the chair where the young man slept, his hair a mess and his features twisted like he was having a nightmare.

"Boyd." He spoke the name softly, then a little louder, "Boyd." He stirred but didn't wake. Arthur placed a gentle hand on his arm and gave it a shake. "Hey, Boyd."

The unbruised eye—hazel like his own—blinked. The eye with the shiner opened only a slit. A light dawned but was quickly replaced by confusion. Then, like the strike of a snake, the boy was out of the chair and crouched near the hearth holding a stick of firewood. "Who are you?" he growled.

"I'm your brother."

The younger man's brow furrowed. "My brothers all up and left. You ain't none of them."

"I'm the brother Mam and Pap gave away to the church." He crouched down to be at eye level with his brother. "We've never met."

"You sure enough look like me, 'cept old."

Arthur grinned. "Yeah. My name's Arthur. I've come to take you out of here—that is, if you want to go."

Boyd slowly unwound his coiled posture and sat on the edge of the hearth, his big hands hanging between his knees. Arthur recognized the pose from their father. "Guess you might know I'm in a spot of trouble then." He nodded at the man still sawing logs on the sofa. "Percy there took me in, but only 'cause I brung the liquor. When he wakes up, he won't have much use for me no more."

"I've got use for you."

Boyd snorted. "I doubt that. Ain't never been much loyalty amongst the Westcotts."

"Still, I have two tickets to Asheville in the morning, and you're welcome to use one."

Boyd tilted his head. "Might take you up on that."

"It could be problematic if you were to bring any ill-gotten goods with you," Arthur said.

"Ill-gotten. Shoot, what other kind is there? Ain't gonna be a problem, though, since I got rolled for what I took already. Why I'm holed up here."

Arthur checked his pocket watch. Just after midnight. "I'm thinking it might be a good idea for us to head back into Wheeling and see if we can find a room for the night. Or what's left of it. I'm not sure this is a good place to stay."

Boyd heaved a world-weary sigh. "Ain't much for walkin', but I'll allow as to how you're right."

"Alright then." Arthur stood and motioned his brother toward the door. "No time to waste."

Boyd sighed again and hove to his feet. It was only as he started across the room that Arthur realized his right foot turned in so that he walked partly on the side of his foot. He wore too large a boot, strapped onto his right leg. It hit the inside of his left boot, which was worn thin.

"You have a clubfoot," he observed.

Boyd whipped around, murder in his eyes. "You wanna make something of it?" he snarled.

Arthur shook his head and lifted his own pant leg to show the brace fastened there. "So do I."

"Well, I'll be a . . ." Boyd leaned closer. "You figure out some way to straighten 'er out?"

"Kind of. The brace helps."

"Can I get one of those?" For the first time, Boyd sounded like an eager boy instead of a worn-out old man.

"We'll see what we can do first thing."

A slow smile spread across Boyd's face, and with it a surge of joy filled Arthur's chest. He wasn't curious about what happened to Gentry anymore. He didn't mind that Lorna didn't return his feelings. He wasn't sorry he'd been jilted. He wasn't even thinking about how he could grow his business. All he cared about was putting more smiles like that one on his brother's face.

"Come on then. We have a train to catch." He wrapped an arm around Boyd's thin shoulders. "Brother."

And there it was. The grin.

⸱⸱⸱⸱⸱⸱⸱⸱⸱⸱

They hadn't bothered to get a room. Once they made it back to Wheeling, it was just a few hours until their train was due. They made the best of the hard benches at the station to catch a few winks. Now they were settled on the train heading south, and as tired as he was, Arthur still couldn't sleep.

For a while, he just watched Boyd sleep. The boy was sprawled in his seat, arms and legs flung wide. It was a pose of absolute abandon and gave Arthur hope that his brother trusted him. Of course, they both still had plenty to learn about each other.

Or maybe the deep sleep had something to do with the smell of liquor that Arthur had thought they'd left behind in the shack on the far side of the Ohio River. But no. The smell was clearly part of Boyd. In his clothes, in his pores, in each peaceful exhalation. What fifteen-year-old drank enough to smell like that? He hadn't seemed drunk the night before, so maybe it was just a symptom of his circumstances. Once they got to Asheville, he'd get Boyd cleaned up and that should take care of it.

Arthur finally dozed, jerking awake as they slid into the Asheville station. He sat up to find Boyd fully awake, nose pressed to the window, trying to see everything at once.

"You live near here?" the boy asked.

"Not far."

"You got a car?"

Arthur chuckled. "No, but I might one day. Once my business takes off."

Boyd turned and narrowed his eyes. "What sorta business?"

"Woodworking."

Boyd's hand shot out and snatched one of Arthur's before he could even think. The young man examined his palm like he was assessing a diamond for its cut and clarity. Finally, he pushed the hand away. "I guess you do real work. Is it timbering you mean? Woodcutting?"

"No, more like crafting and carving. I make furniture—bowls, frames, even some toys. That sort of thing."

"No lie?"

"No lie. We're headed to my shop. I'll be glad to show you." Arthur breathed in and breathed out. "I could even teach you a few things if you want to learn."

Boyd looked at him sideways but didn't say anything.

"Come on. It's less than a mile. Think you can walk that?" Arthur had agonized over hiring a cart to take them. He wanted to help his brother, but he didn't want to insult him. He figured if the boy could make it out to the place where he'd found him, he could do some traveling on that bum foot of his.

"I can walk it."

Arthur wanted to ask Boyd a hundred questions as they walked out of Biltmore Village and headed south. But he pressed his lips together. He needed to let his brother settle in and get his bearings. There'd be time enough for questions later.

# 24

# LORNA

**BILTMORE VILLAGE**
**OCTOBER 1923**

Lorna extracted the drafts from beneath the riser on the third stair. She carried them to the dining table and spread them out on the oilcloth. She'd used all but one of them. Well, two if she counted the one Olive had given her.

Placing that draft next to the others erased any doubt she'd harbored that the same person had drawn them all. Vivian was Gentry's mother. Lorna remembered how the girl longed for the mother who had died when she was so young. For a fleeting moment she wished she knew where Gentry was so she could connect her with Olive. Surely talking to someone who'd known Vivian would be some consolation. And she felt as though she owed Gentry something.

The drafts had saved her career, had helped make Biltmore Industries' homespun a household name. Mrs. Vanderbilt and her high society friends had worn this cloth. Lorna wondered if Gentry had continued weaving. She'd learned the basics, and if she'd ever settled down and applied herself, she could have become quite skilled. Skilled enough to be the weaver of the shawl Lorna had carried to West Virginia and back. The thought was like a finger of ice to her heart. If Gentry had continued her education, she'd know enough to read these drafts and recognize the patterns Lorna wove.

She swept up the pages, rolled them into a tight cylinder, and tied them with thread. She hurried to the staircase and stowed them away, then went to the kitchen and found the hammer and nails she remembered seeing in a drawer. Each thwack of the hammer sounded like a promise. Or a pledge perhaps.

She would not use the new draft. She would not try to find the elusive weaver. She would accept failure and take her medicine. In the morning, she would go to see Mr. Tompkins and would tell him that she could not complete her commission. He'd already fired her, what more could he do?

She shuddered to think.

⋯⋯⋯⋯

Lorna dressed carefully. She wore her Sunday hat and her best gloves. She might be shaking in her shoes, but at least she'd look nice doing it. She knew the best thing to do was to simply get this over with. She marched to Mr. Tompkins's office, head held high. Gloria, his secretary, was not at her desk, so she boldly rapped on the door.

No answer.

She lifted her hand to knock again when Gloria returned from whatever errand she'd be on. "Miss Blankenship, did you have an appointment this morning?"

"No, but there's a matter I need to discuss—"

"He's not here at the moment," she interrupted. She sat at her desk, flipped open a calendar, and looked pointedly at Lorna. "I can add you to his schedule at ten tomorrow morning."

Lorna's shoulders slumped, but she quickly straightened them. Perhaps it was just as well. She'd have another night to think and maybe even to pray for guidance—something she hadn't done in far too long. "That will suit," she said. "Thank you."

Lorna was still deep in thought as she disembarked from the streetcar back in Biltmore Village. She nearly jumped out of her skin when she heard someone call her name.

"Lorna!"

She whirled at the sound to see Arthur hurrying—as best he could with his bad foot—toward her.

"I'm so glad you're here. I've found her," he crowed. "Well, at least I think I have."

Lorna's heart stopped for a beat. Gentry? No. Of course not. "Who have you found?" she managed to ask.

"Our weaver." He finally caught up to her and held out a piece of paper. "I've got the directions right here. We'll have to travel for some distance on foot, but Basil tracked her down."

Lorna realized she was clutching the collar of her shirt-waist. She released it and made sure it was straight. "You're certain it's her?"

"Not a hundred percent, although I sure think it's likely." He held his arms out. "So? Shall we go find her, then?"

Lorna glanced at the watch pinned to her blouse. As if she had anywhere else to be just then. "Yes. Let's go."

Lorna felt as though her world were spinning completely out of control, and at this point all she could think to do was to ride along wherever it carried her and hope that she survived the crash she felt certain was coming.

.· ˙ ˙ ˙ •. . . . .·˙

Sweat trickled between her shoulder blades and made her grateful she'd worn her hair up off her neck. Whatever happened to cool September breezes? She was also thankful that while seemingly tireless, Arthur could only move so fast. Feeling as though she had nothing to lose, Lorna decided to ask him about it. "Your foot," she said, "has it always been that way?"

Arthur paused ever so briefly before taking the next step. "Yes. I was born with it. A clubfoot. Thankfully, it could have been much worse. Reverend Swope saw that I was fitted with proper footwear to support it and to ensure that I could walk as well as possible." He gave his speech without turning to look at her.

Lorna discreetly wiped her neck and forehead with a handkerchief. "It doesn't seem to hinder you much."

Now he did turn as though to see if she were mocking him. She took advantage of the movement by stopping and fanning herself with the damp handkerchief. "I can hardly keep up."

Arthur came to her side immediately, waving her to a fallen log and handing her a jar of water he'd been carrying. "Is this too much for you?" Those hazel eyes of his were so filled with concern, she wanted nothing more than to ease his worry.

"No, I'm fine. It's just steeper going than I'm used to. I climb stairs when needed, but rarely do I climb a mountain."

He smiled and loosened his shirt collar. "Plus, summer seems to be holding on."

They sat in companionable silence, passing the cool water back and forth between them. Finally, Arthur broke the silence. "My foot," he said, rubbing that leg. "I figured it was at least part of the reason you never did warm up to my overtures toward you."

Though he didn't look at her, she could see him swallow as though something were stuck in his throat. "No," she said softly. "I hardly gave it a second thought."

"Then what held you back? Am I foolish to hope that you might have changed your mind about me?"

She closed her eyes and tried to think. What could she say? What would she not regret later? "I was afraid," she said at last.

"Of what?" Arthur cupped her hand in his surprisingly cool palm.

Tears slipped from the corners of her eyes. "Of yet another loss. Like Mama. Like Papa. It seemed safer to feel as little as possible." She glanced at him and then away again. "Even now I think you deserve so much more than I have to give."

His fingers tightened around hers, and although warm now, the heat was oddly welcome. "I'm content with whatever that is," he said. She felt his gaze on her and turned to look into his eyes. He was going to kiss her, and she was going to let him. Even though she felt certain the memory of it would be a sweet agony of loss before too much longer.

"Who's sparkin' in my woods?"

Lorna screeched and leapt to her feet. She whirled around but couldn't see where the voice had come from.

Arthur pulled her shawl from his sack and held it high. "We're looking for the weaver who made this. Basil Howes said we'd find her on top of this mountain."

A slight figure in britches, a glorious homespun shirt, and a beat-up straw hat stepped out from behind a tree up the trail. "You'uns got a path to trod yet. Come on." The young man waved them on and then led the way forward like a mountain goat.

They looked at each other, hope and fear mingling in their eyes, and started after the man as fast as either of them could go.

# 25

# ARTHUR

**ASHEVILLE**
**FEBRUARY 1922**

Boyd slept for most of two days, and Arthur let him. He also fed him every time he woke up. Arthur remembered going hungry many a day before Reverend Swope took him in. He supposed things hadn't gotten much better over the years. Boyd's manners weren't much to start with, but by the third day he seemed to realize that Arthur would keep feeding him, so he stopped shoving food in his mouth as fast as he could.

"What say we get you fitted with a brace today?" Arthur asked on the fourth morning after Boyd had put away four eggs and as many strips of bacon.

"Fitted with a *what*?"

Arthur lifted his pant leg and tapped the metal. "A brace. It can help straighten your foot over time and makes it easier to wear a shoe."

Boyd frowned. The swelling in his eye had gone down but it was still bruised. It made Arthur sick to think about how he must've gotten it. "Will it hurt?"

"It'll be uncomfortable for a while, but you'll get used

to it. Dr. Howard has helped refit mine over the years, and that's been a big help. He'll give you exercises to do, too."

Boyd made a face. "Sounds like a lot of trouble. I get along okay as it is."

Arthur hadn't expected to have to talk his brother into getting a brace. He shrugged. "Up to you."

Boyd drummed his fingers on the table. "Okay. I guess I'll give it a try."

Arthur smiled. "You won't be sorry."

But it was Arthur who was sorry by the time they got back from seeing Dr. Howard. He'd found a brace that fit Boyd, forcing his foot into a slightly more natural position. He advised them to plan on a series of braces that would gradually move the foot. And he warned them that it would hurt. He also gave Boyd the promised exercises. Now Arthur was trying to wait out his brother's stony silence while they worked in his shop.

He gave in first. "It's for your own good, you know."

Boyd shot him a dark look. "Hurts like the dickens."

"It'll be worth it in the end." Arthur tried to sound more certain of this than he was.

"Is this what you had to do?"

"I guess. I was a lot younger, so I don't remember it all that well. I think my foot was more flexible then."

"That would be a *no*." Boyd kicked at the brace. "I did just fine on this foot."

Arthur thought to try another tack. "Look. I know better than most how hard it is to be different. To have something that makes you stand out in a crowd. Do this for a couple of months and you'll fit in wherever you go."

That dark look again. "You know that's not true. My foot might make people take the first look, and when they do, all they see is hillbilly trash. I don't guess straightening my foot will fix that."

190

Arthur flinched. Boyd was right. "It's the first step."

Boyd stilled, a smile flickering. "First step," he said, the grin breaking through. "Guess you think you're funny."

Arthur chuckled. "Not on purpose," he said. Then he laughed. And Boyd laughed with him, and something opened up between them. The tension eased as he saw his brother relax.

"Alright, I'll keep the brace on. Pap would say it's a waste of time and money, but I guess that ought to recommend it." He pulled up his pant leg and ran a finger under the upper part of the brace where it was leaving a red mark on his calf. "It'd better be worth it."

"It will be," Arthur promised.

. . . . . . . . .

Two days later, Gladys Finegold breezed into the shop and peered around as though looking for something specific.

"May I help you?" Arthur asked with a small bow. Gladys was a regular customer who often commissioned items. She was well worth catering to.

Gladys's hand fluttered to her throat. "Is Mr. McTeague not working today?"

Arthur suppressed a smile. He'd suspected his widowed customer might have ulterior motives for her frequent visits. "He and my brother stepped out to fetch us a bite of lunch. I expect he'll be back in short order." Arthur got a kick out of casually mentioning Boyd like that. Not that Mrs. Finegold noticed. He decided he might as well take advantage of the situation. He wasn't a mercenary. He was a businessman trying to make a go of it with a brother to support. "Would you like to see my latest pieces?"

Gladys brightened, clearly pleased for the excuse to linger. "I would indeed!"

Arthur guided her to a table in the front window. "With Christmas soon upon us, I've agreed to carry some items from Miss Vance and Miss Yale's Tryon Toy Shop."

"How nice." Gladys reached for a carved figure of Little Red Riding Hood. "How are Eleanor and Charlotte?"

"Quite well, although I think their success is proving a hardship for the neighbors, who aren't used to so much traffic in their neighborhood. They hope to build a store soon, but funding is always the sticking point."

"As in so many things," Gladys agreed. "I do like this charming Goldilocks set. I think it would be just the thing for my grandniece." She picked up each piece, examining them minutely. Arthur suspected she was less concerned with quality than she was with the passage of time, yet he could help there if it meant a sale.

"Take a look at Mama Bear," he encouraged. "See the handbag she's carrying on the front?"

"Charming," Gladys said.

"Now look at the back."

She flipped the piece over. "Why, she's knitting a sock— how clever! Yes, Gloria must have this for Christmas." She handed Mama Bear to Arthur. "Can you wrap them up for me? Perhaps you could wrap each one individually, so she'll have the pleasure of discovering them one by one?"

"Certainly." Arthur understood that he should take his time with the process. He carried the figures into his workroom just in time to see Angus and Boyd come through the back door with something wrapped in butcher paper that smelled delicious. "We have a customer," he said to Angus. "She's made her selections, but perhaps you could keep her company while I wrap them up?"

Angus frowned, then peeked into the shop and brightened. "Aye, I can do that."

"Madam Finegold," Angus said as he strolled into the

showroom. "Aren't you looking ever so fine on this golden autumn day."

"And aren't you clever, Mr. McTeague. It *is* a glorious day."

Arthur beckoned Boyd over to show him how to wrap the toy set, all the while keeping one ear tuned to the pair in the shop. Boyd gamely pitched in, although Arthur was pretty sure he'd rather just eat. His brother was walking more smoothly with the brace, and Arthur was optimistic that eventually it would set Boyd to rights.

"Is that a new frock?" he heard Angus ask. *The old so-and-so*, thought Arthur. Angus couldn't care less about a lady's dress.

"Why, yes, this is the latest fabric from Biltmore Industries. Edith Vanderbilt herself has been wearing it. I don't pay all that much attention to fashion, but I do like to support our local entrepreneurs whether they work in cloth or in wood."

Arthur surreptitiously peeked into the shop. Was this one of Lorna's fabrics? He eyed the golden tones of Gladys's dress. His artist's eye appreciated the skill it must have taken. It was exceptional.

He pulled his gaze away from the cloth and the conversation and frowned as he turned back to Boyd. His brother had finished his work in a hurry and was eating bent over his food like he thought someone might snatch it from him. Arthur didn't comment, knowing what it was like to fear each meal might be your last.

Now, what was it about that fabric? He tried to shift his focus. As he pondered, a tune came to mind. One that he hadn't thought of in years. An old-time mountain tune. Gentry. That was it. The fabric made him think of Gentry, sitting in the sun playing her dulcimer, lost in the music.

Arthur tucked the wrapped toys in a pasteboard box, added some twine, tied a big bow, and carried it out to Gladys. "Your package wrapped and ready to delight young Gloria."

"Thank you ever so much. Will you add this to my bill?"

"Gladly," Arthur said. He tilted his head. "And if you don't mind my asking, do you know who designed the fabric you're wearing?"

"Lorna Blankenship," she said with obvious pride. "She's come out with what they're calling the 'Nature Series' of fabrics." She swished her skirt from side to side. "Isn't it gorgeous? They call this one 'Sunflower.'"

"It is lovely. Lorna's a friend," he added.

"Oh?" Gladys gave him a coy look and lightly elbowed Angus, who was standing very close beside her. "A friend, is she?"

"Yes. We've known each other for years."

"Well, she's quite talented. I only hope she continues to produce such lovely cloth. This trend toward ready-made items is all well and good, but I prefer to begin by choosing the best fabrics and then to have things tailored just so."

Angus waggled his brows. "And aren't you fetching in your just-so dress."

Gladys flushed like a girl and waved Angus off in a way that made it clear he could go on in that vein if he liked. "Well, I suppose I ought to be going," she said, looking at Angus with eyes that somehow seemed larger than normal.

"Allow me to accompany you," Angus said, and she flushed more deeply. "To carry your package," he added.

"Aren't you the gentleman." She gave him a smile that might have made another lady suggest that she was being less than genteel. "I'd be delighted to have your company."

Angus took the package from Arthur, winked, and escorted Gladys out into the street.

"My driver should be around somewhere," Arthur heard her say. "Perhaps if we start walking in this direction, he'll be along."

Arthur chuckled and shook his head. He never would

have thought to put Angus McTeague next to Gladys Finegold, but he supposed there had been stranger pairings. He thought of Lorna and her fabric that reminded him so strongly of Gentry. Those two had certainly been a strange pairing. One serious and meticulous, the other flighty and exuberant. He pictured the fabric of Gladys's dress. Then again, maybe Gentry had rubbed off on Lorna at least a little. He wondered what had become of Gentry and hoped that some of Lorna's good sense had rubbed off on her apprentice before she disappeared.

# 26

# ARTHUR

**South Asheville**
**March 1922**

Boyd was sleeping late on a Sunday morning. Arthur had gone to church only a few times since his brother's arrival, and he had yet to take Boyd with him. He was grateful for the chance to be in attendance today. Church had always been a still point for him, no matter what else was happening in his life.

The day, caught between winter and spring, was gray, threatening rain. Arthur tucked his large umbrella under his arm as he left All Souls Cathedral. He saw Lorna nearing the exit and slowed so their paths would intersect. He hadn't done more than nod and say hello to her since Cornelia's birthday party back in August.

"Did you enjoy the sermon?" he asked as she approached, tugging at her gloves and peering at the sky with an expression of concern.

"It was excellent," she said but in a distracted way, which made him think she hadn't necessarily paid attention. Well, that was all right. He'd been distracted himself—trying to think what all he needed to do now that he was responsible for his brother.

"Shall I walk with you?" he asked and held up the umbrella. "I'm prepared should the sky open up."

"I wouldn't want you to go out of your way."

"I won't be," he assured her. "And it would be my pleasure. I haven't had a chance to talk to you in far too long." He decided not to bring up the note she'd never answered.

"We've been busy in the weaving room, preparing for the summer rush." Arthur offered his elbow, and Lorna slid her gloved hand into the crook. "Thank you." She sighed, then looked embarrassed. "I should be grateful for all the orders, but it's been so hectic lately, all I do is process paperwork. I've hardly woven a thing in months."

"I saw one of your new patterns not long ago." Arthur felt her fingers tighten on his arm. "Gladys Finegold was wearing a remarkable yellow fabric. It made me think of sunshine."

"Oh? That's nice." The noncommittal response didn't match the increasing pressure from her fingers. He suspected she wasn't aware she was clenching his arm.

He laughed so as to put her at ease. "You know what else it reminded me of?" He didn't wait for a response. "Gentry. Goodness, how long has she been gone?"

Lorna's fingers dug deep before she apparently caught herself and tugged her arm free. "I can't remember."

He wasn't sure how to gauge her reaction, so he plowed ahead for lack of anything else to say. "Let's see, it was the year of the flood. So that would make it—" he paused, counting with his fingers—"almost six years ago. I wonder whatever happened to her?"

"I wouldn't know. She was always a flighty thing." Lorna crossed her arms, cradling her elbows tight against her chest as they walked.

"Didn't she show you one of her mother's designs? Did you ever get around to weaving it?"

Lorna licked her lips. Arthur could tell this conversation was unsettling her, and he was afraid of the reason why. "That yellow fabric isn't one of them, is it?"

"Of course not," Lorna snapped. "It's my own design." She flicked a look at him, then away. "Inspiration comes from so many sources."

"Yes, it does," Arthur said as a fat rain drop plopped onto his hat, followed quickly by others. He raised his umbrella and stepped closer to Lorna. She shied away. Then when raindrops hit her face, she ducked closer. He took her arm again and found that she was shaking. "Lorna, are you alright?"

"I'm just cold," she mumbled. "I'll be fine once I get inside."

They scurried to her porch, and Arthur led her under its roof as the rat-a-tat of the rain filled their ears. She was shaking hard now and spoke through chattering teeth. "Thank you so much, Arthur. This was very kind of you. But I think I'd better get inside before I catch a chill." She was at the door before he could respond. She fumbled with the knob and then disappeared inside.

He stood on the porch for a moment, listening to the drum of the rain. He gazed out across the green toward the Swannanoa River. *The year of the flood.* It had been more than five years now since that terrible day. He glanced back at the door Lorna had closed firmly with a click. Just how much had that day changed her?

. . . . . . . . .

All thoughts of Lorna and her designs were soon driven from Arthur's mind. He'd known he was taking on a lot of responsibility with Boyd, but he felt as though he'd entered a foreign country without an interpreter. They were a couple of months into their new arrangement and yet he still felt like he was starting over every day. On this day, though, he was determined to make some headway.

"Boyd, you up?" he called. He'd set up a space he'd been using as a storeroom for his brother. The apartment over his shop was small with a tiny kitchen in one corner of his sitting room, a bedroom, a bath, and the storeroom. He'd apologized to Boyd for the tight quarters, but his brother didn't seem to care one way or the other.

He heard some rustling. The storeroom door creaked open, and Boyd came out fastening his shirt. He yawned. "This durn brace is giving me fits, but yeah, I'm up."

"But are you up and *ready*?" Arthur asked, ignoring the complaint.

Boyd frowned. "What's that supposed to mean?"

"Are you ready for some excitement?"

Now his brother looked suspicious. "I'm not sure you and me would agree on what's exciting. Especially this early in the day."

Arthur chuckled. While his brother was rough, he was no fool. "Here, catch," he said, tossing the boy a rucksack. "We'll eat what's inside once we get where we're going."

Boyd made a face. "And where would that be?"

"Follow me." Arthur led the way down the back stairs to where two bicycles waited. "You know how to ride one of these?" This was the moment he was most worried about. His plan would go up in smoke if Boyd couldn't manage a bicycle.

Boyd's eyes lit up. "Pap got me one when I was eight or nine, but then it disappeared after a few months. I reckon he sold it." He slung a leg over the seat. "Always did wish I could have another one."

"These are for us to use for the day," Arthur said. "But maybe we can look into getting you one of your own." And he would, too. No matter what. Seeing the smile on Boyd's face guaranteed that.

"Where are we going?" Boyd asked.

"You'll see," Arthur answered with a grin of his own.

They pedaled the mile to the entrance of Biltmore Estate. Arthur let Boyd come up even with him as they approached the Lodge Gate. He wanted to see the boy's expression, but Boyd tore past him, shooting through the open gate, and pedaled hard until he disappeared behind a stand of bamboo. Arthur waved at the gatekeeper and caught up.

Boyd had pulled his bicycle off the side of the road. He stood panting and wide-eyed. "Are they comin' after us?"

"What? Who?"

"We're not supposed to be up in here, are we? Fancy entrance like that. I figure there must be a big house or something up ahead."

Arthur struggled not to burst into laughter. "Or something—yes. There's a house I want to show you, but we're allowed to be here. I used to work here. Still help out now and again."

He thought Boyd might collapse right then and there. "Whew. That's a relief. I'm better at runnin' and hidin' after dark."

Arthur balanced his clubfoot on the pedal. "You ready for some heavy pedaling? It's a long way up to the house."

Boyd grinned. "Race ya," he said and shot off down the road as if his own brace didn't bother him a bit.

Arthur filled his lungs with the brisk winter air and followed at a more leisurely pace. Boyd would find out soon enough.

．・＊＊＊．．．・＊

While the ride up Approach Road required three miles of pedaling, Arthur never found it toilsome whether he was in a cart, on a bicycle, or even on foot. He didn't know much about landscape design, but he did know Frederick Law Olmsted—the same fellow who'd designed Central Park in New York City—had created this winding road very intentionally. And Arthur was glad he got to enjoy it.

Boyd seemed to be having a fine time, as well. They stopped now and again to admire the newly leafed maples and birches rising from behind mountain laurel and rhododendron with their dark green leaves. There were also streams and pools where they could stop to scoop up a drink of icy, clear water. In the spot where the road diverted to the side to allow horses to stop and drink, they left their bicycles and skipped stones in the clear mountain stream.

Boyd flopped onto the bank, pushing a mass of curls so like Arthur's own off his face. "Seems like there'd be some good spots for a still on up this creek," he said.

Arthur laughed. "I doubt the Vanderbilts would want anyone making corn liquor on their property. But you're probably right. Who knows, maybe there were stills before they came and bought up all this land."

"Say, how much land do they have here?" Boyd asked. "Seems like a pretty good-sized piece of property."

Arthur choked on a laugh. "I don't know exactly, but it was originally something like one hundred and twenty thousand acres. I heard Mrs. Vanderbilt sold off nearly ninety thousand acres to the National Forest folks back in 1914 after her husband died, but it's not like they'll do much with it."

Boyd blinked. "No. Really?"

"Really. Nothing but trees and rivers and mountains as far as the eye can see."

Boyd shook his head and furrowed his brow. "I thought it'd be fine to have twenty acres or so. Enough to run a few cattle and maybe have a tobacco bottom." He looked all around as if he could see the breadth of the property from this secluded spot. "What do they *do* with it?"

Arthur blew out a breath. "Well, they have a dairy. And there used to be a plant nursery, but that got wiped out in a flood. They farm some. Do some timbering too, although the land's pretty poor yet. It'll take more than twenty years to make it fertile again after the mountain farmers wore it out." He scratched his head. "I guess, in a way, you could say they're mostly saving it."

Boyd nodded as though he liked that notion. "Yeah. The only thing better than farming a little piece of land would be just enjoying it." He stood and picked up his bicycle. "Let's get on up the road and see this house. I'm thinking it's going to be something special."

Arthur chuckled. "Yeah, it is."

⋯⋯⋯

Arthur managed to get far enough ahead of his brother to watch his expression as he passed through the gates at the top of Approach Road and looked to his right.

"Holy smokes." Boyd hit his brakes hard. He dropped his feet to the ground and stared. "Is that it?"

"No. The real house is back behind that one."

Boyd rolled his eyes. "Are you telling me people *live* there?" He made it sound like it was the most preposterous thing he'd ever considered.

"They do. Although I don't think the family's at home right now. It's just staff in the house."

"And you worked there? Why'd you leave?"

"That's a long story," Arthur said.

Boyd turned expectant eyes on him.

Arthur braced himself on his handlebars and stared at the château. "The man who built the house died unexpectedly. Money got tight." He laughed. "Well, probably not like you and I would think of it. But things weren't as easy as they had been, and Mrs. Vanderbilt, the wife, decided to sell off the weaving and woodworking businesses." He shrugged. "They needed someone to run the woodworking shop. I'd practically grown up in it and so I agreed to do it."

Boyd narrowed his eyes. "That's not such a long story. Is there something more to it you ain't saying?"

Arthur straightened. "Isn't there always? I'll tell you the rest another day." He pushed off his bicycle and cruised along the rows of tulip poplars leading up to the house. There was a huge fountain in the middle of the flat lawn. He kept one eye on where he was going and the other on his brother, who nearly crashed twice as he gawked at the house. They looped back to the main drive and headed through a second set of gates down toward the walled garden and the conservatory. Arthur didn't stop, knowing they could easily spend all day admiring the gardens of Biltmore Estate, even before spring had fully arrived. Yet he had another destination in mind.

They passed through the last of the formal gardens, cruised by the bass pond with its bridge and waterfall, and came into the bottomland along the French Broad River. The going was easy now, and they rode along side by side.

"Are we still on their land?" Boyd asked.

"Yeah," Arthur said, "and we're just about to our destination."

He took a left onto a gravel path that looped around another pond. They called it a lagoon, but really it was just a big pond. They circled to the back, then stopped and leaned the bicycles against a couple of trees. Arthur led his brother to a spot with an open view across the water.

Boyd gasped. The view of the west side of Biltmore House had that effect on people. Especially on a day like this with a brilliant blue sky, the leaves beginning to bud, and the house reflected in the still waters of the lagoon.

Boyd's voice dropped low, almost reverent. "I didn't know there was such a thing in the whole world. Mam would have loved to see this."

The comment was like a blow to Arthur's chest. He'd long ago put his parents out of his mind. They gave him away. And while it had been to his benefit, it wasn't something he'd ever been able to forgive. "What was she like?" he asked his brother. "I guess I've tried to forget her."

Boyd made a face. "Mean when she was sober. Happy when she was drinking. And sad in between." He stared at the water. "But she sure did like pretty things. I could bring her flowers, and she'd act happy, drunk or sober. Pap brought her a necklace one time. It had a little gold heart on it. She wore that necklace all the time."

"What happened to it after she died?"

Boyd shrugged. "She'd stopped wearing it a while before that. Probably sold it. Or lost it." He sighed. "She was mostly mean toward the end."

"Do you miss them?" Arthur asked, surprised to realize that he did. Or maybe what he missed was the idea of them suddenly brought back to him after all these years.

Boyd looked up at the house again. "Not much." He turned dark, sad eyes on Arthur. "I kind of wish I did, though."

Arthur swallowed hard. "Yeah. I know what you mean."

# 27

# LORNA

**MADISON COUNTY, NORTH CAROLINA**
**OCTOBER 1923**

Lorna had thought herself reasonably fit, but the mountain man leading them on put that notion to shame. She wanted to ask questions but didn't have the wind to do it. Her legs burned, her lungs throbbed, and she'd sweated through her shirtwaist. She felt certain her hair was a horror by now, but she didn't have the energy to care.

They finally crested a long slope, popping out onto a mountain bald. A cabin was tucked off to the side, smoke curling from its chimney, with ample firewood stacked neatly under a lean-to. The view of fold upon fold of mountains bathed in the colors of autumn was breathtaking. Not that Lorna had any breath left to take.

She braced her hands on her knees and panted, no longer trying to pretend she wasn't as winded as she'd ever been. Her only consolation was that Arthur was almost as bad off. He stood in the shade fanning himself with his hat. His brown hair was wet and curling around his ears, and he carried his rumpled jacket.

"You'uns ain't cut out for the mountains," their guide said matter-of-factly.

"Does the weaver live in that cabin?" Lorna asked, even as she puzzled over that husky voice of his. There was something about it . . .

"Yup. That'd be my cabin."

Lorna's head came up, and she eyed this mountain man more closely. "You're a woman."

"Last I checked."

Lorna stared. Was this Gentry? She had the same wiry build, the same chin, and the same stubborn look in her eyes—although Lorna could have sworn Gentry's were green, while this woman had brown eyes. Gathering her wits, she stood upright, tugged her sleeves into place, and stuck out her hand. "I'm Lorna. You remind me of someone I used to know."

"Well, I don't much know anybody, so must not be me."

Lorna worried her lower lip. "What's your name?"

The woman narrowed her eyes. "Let me see that shawl you brought."

Arthur stepped forward and handed it over. The woman examined it. Her face softened, and her back straightened. She nodded once. "I made this. Hope you paid what it's worth. Me, I trade my stuff for what I need, which ain't much." She handed the shawl back and opened her arms to the sky. "So long as I have all of this, what more could there be?"

"But what about having nice things or being entertained?" Lorna asked. "And what happens when you need cash money?" If this weaver didn't want anything she could offer, what chance did she have of persuading her to part with a special design?

"Money." The woman made a curse of the word. "And I have nice things." She held out her arm so Lorna could admire the fabric of her shirt. "Bet you don't have clothes as pretty as a redbird sitting on a holly bush in the snow."

Lorna pinched the cloth between her fingers and had the sense that she'd just stroked the cool, sleek feathers of a bird. She snatched her hand back, and the woman laughed. "Come on in a minute. I'll show you some more, but don't go thinking any of it is for sale. Only way you'll get somethin' from me is if I think of somethin' I want from you."

Lorna darted a look at Arthur, who shrugged and followed their hostess. The front room of her cabin was spotless and sparsely furnished with a table, one chair, and a cookstove. A massive loom took up the rest of the space. A half-finished piece of fabric sat waiting. Lorna was drawn to it as surely as a moth to flame.

"This is exceptional," she breathed. Her eyes darted to the window and back to the loom. "It's your view." She laid a gentle hand on the cloth woven in curling shades of rust, burgundy, gold, and deep moss green. A cool breeze caressed her cheek with the promise of a crisp night and the smell of moldering leaves. "How do you do this?"

The woman shrugged, yet the gleam in her eyes told Lorna she enjoyed the appreciation. "It just comes to me." She nodded toward the window. "I go out there, and when I come back in here, whatever I've seen, smelled, heard, felt, and tasted finds its way to the loom." A luminous smile spread across her face. "It's a wonder, and I just thank God for it." The smile dimmed. "And it's a comfort when I remember hard days."

Arthur, who had been standing in a corner taking everything in, stepped forward. "Are you Vivian Cutshall?"

Lorna jerked her head toward Arthur. The woman's face went ashen. "Who are you?" she rasped.

"I knew your daughter." Vivian staggered and collapsed onto the chair. "Gentry. I knew Gentry."

"That's not possible."

Lorna shook her head, confused. "Arthur, what are you talking about? Gentry said her mother was dead."

"Maybe that's what Gentry thought." Arthur stepped forward and took the woman's shaking hand. "Is it true? Are you her mother?"

"I was, but Gentry died." The woman's eyes darted like a bird trapped inside a house. "My father-in-law said she died. That's why I left. There was no reason to stay without her."

Arthur knelt in front of Vivian and clasped both of her hands as though providing an anchor. "I think your father-in-law may have lied to you. When she was thirteen, he sent Gentry to learn to weave with Lorna."

"Where is she now?" Vivian's cry sent crows cawing from a tree outside the door.

"We don't know. She left in the fall of 1916—seven years ago now. No one's heard from her since."

Vivian's head fell forward, sobs shaking her whole body. "My baby. My child. My heart." She fell forward. Arthur caught her and held her tight.

Lorna thought the woman might literally shatter if he let go. She stared at Vivian's shirt. What reminded her of the wings of a cardinal moments ago now looked like slashes of blood. And she could almost smell the sharp, coppery aroma she remembered from a hog killing. She ran outside, unable to bear witness to such raw emotion any longer.

⁘⸱⸱⸱⸱⸱⸱⸱⸱⸱⸳⸳

Arthur joined Lorna where she'd come to rest on the rough-cut stones of a root cellar behind the cabin. "She's sleeping," he said. "I've never seen someone break like that."

"Haven't you?" Lorna snapped.

Arthur reared back like she'd swung at him. "No, I don't guess I have."

Lorna bit the inside of her cheek until she tasted blood. She'd broken like that, only she'd had the grace to do it quietly. Silently. Which meant no one noticed that she was nothing more than thin skin stretched over jagged pieces about to poke through.

"You know, I started out looking for Gentry once. Then . . ." He wrestled with his words for a minute. "Then I got distracted." He rubbed his hands against his britches legs as though trying to clean something off. "Vivian wants us to find Gentry. Guess we can start where I left off." He squinted at the sky. "That was just two years ago. Who knows?"

"What if she really is dead?" Lorna didn't recognize her own voice or the hard words. They lay like stones between them.

"I guess Vivian would want to know that, too." Arthur reached for her but then drew his hand back. "Are you alright, Lorna? I know that was an emotional scene, but you've found your weaver. She says she'll weave anything you want if you promise to help her find Gentry."

Lorna's head jerked around, and she stared at him. "You told her I need a design."

"Well, yes. That's why we came here, isn't it?"

Lorna looked away and wrapped her arms around herself. "Yes," she answered, her voice barely audible. "But I'm not sure I can afford her price."

"Finding Gentry? Seems like a good deal to me. And just think what it would mean to them both to be together again. Each one thinking the other is dead?" He shook his head. "My parents didn't want me. They gave me away. And then—" he cut himself off. "I'm just saying it would be awfully nice to help a family be a family again."

Lorna sat as though paralyzed. She remembered how

alone Gentry always seemed. Unable to connect with other people, always putting folks off. Lorna had been alone, too. But she sensed that where she'd decided to keep people at arm's length, Gentry had desperately wanted connection.

"She was there when you pulled me from the water."

Arthur frowned, but then his face cleared. "Oh. The day of the flood. That's right. You were so wet and cold. I asked her to put her arm around you because it didn't seem quite the thing for me to do it."

"She changed after that," Lorna said. "That was such a hard time. I guess I hadn't really thought about it before, but she was different." She swallowed hard. "She even tried harder in the weaving room."

"And then she disappeared," Arthur said. "Do you have any idea where she went?"

"No," Lorna responded absently, lost in thought. "But she was trying to raise some money."

"Really? How do you know that?"

Lorna winced. She could hardly tell Arthur it was because Gentry was selling her mother's drafts. Drafts she'd paid too little for and then claimed as her own. Her breath caught. Drafts that belonged to the woman in the house in front of her.

She let her head drop into her hands. She was in so much trouble. If Vivian saw those old patterns, she'd surely remember them and expose Lorna. If she helped her find Gentry, then Gentry would expose her. If she refused to help, Arthur would think her uncaring. Every path led to the same conclusion: She'd lose Arthur's respect, her reputation, and any hope of getting her job back. There was simply no way out.

She stood abruptly, squinting at the slanting rays of the sun. "If we're going to get down this mountain before dark, we'd best get started." She glanced at Arthur. "Leave Vivian a note letting her know we'll look for Gentry. And the sooner we go, the sooner we can get to work."

"But . . ." Arthur sputtered, "don't you want to work out the details of your design?"

"Never mind that," she said with a wave. "Right now, finding Gentry is the main thing."

Arthur scrambled to his feet and went inside, presumably to leave a note. Lorna walked to the top of a rise that offered the cabin a measure of protection. She expected there'd be a beautiful sunset this evening. Her parents had enjoyed sunsets. They used to sit snugged up tight together on the porch swing and "watch the show," as her mother put it.

Lorna supposed her life had been in ruins ever since she lost them with no hope of ever being a family again. She just hadn't known it before. And now that she did, the only thing she could think that was worth doing was to gather the threads of someone else's family so it could be woven together once again.

# 28

# LORNA

**NORTH ASHEVILLE**
**OCTOBER 1923**

The return trip to Asheville was silent. Lorna, lost deep in thought, barely noticed that Arthur was also distant. It was only when they arrived at her front door that she realized they hadn't spoken a word since leaving Vivian's cabin.

"I guess I haven't been good company today," she said.

Arthur made a face. "Nor have I. Guess all this talk about the past has got me thinking about some things." He gave his head a shake. "But what we should be focused on is finding Gentry. What say I come by after work tomorrow, and we can start making plans."

"I'm not going to work tomorrow."

Arthur's eyebrows shot up. "Why not?"

"Arthur, I . . . it's complicated."

He rubbed the back of his neck. "For me too. Can we sit a minute? I won't stay long."

She motioned toward a chair on the porch. The night was

refreshingly cool. She collapsed into a rocker, moaning a little at the pleasure of just being still.

"Feels good, doesn't it?" Arthur said. She could hear the smile in his voice.

"It does. I should offer to fetch us a drink or a plate of cookies, but I don't think I can make my feet carry me to the kitchen."

"Just sit. There's something I'd like to tell you." His voice lowered. "I'm afraid it doesn't reflect well on me."

The words both intrigued and relieved her. If Arthur had something terrible to hide, maybe he wouldn't hold her secret shame against her when the whole truth came out. A flicker of hope stirred inside her.

"I have a brother," Arthur said.

Lorna stared. This hardly seemed like a terrible secret. "That's nice. I wish I had a sibling."

"No, it's . . . I have lots of brothers and sisters. My parents were . . . prolific."

"Do they live around here?" Lorna was losing hope that Arthur's secret was a dark one. She also realized how little she knew about his family. She'd always thought he was an orphan.

"I don't know where most of them live." He rubbed his hands on his pant legs. "My parents pretty much gave me away when I was just a youngster. That's how I ended up here in Asheville with Reverend Swope. He was my caretaker— the closest thing to a parent I ever knew."

Lorna set her rocker in motion and settled in to listen.

"But then, early last year, Rodney—Reverend Swope— got word that my parents were both dead and had left a much younger brother orphaned." His hands scrubbed up and down his thighs. "So I went back to West Virginia and fetched Boyd home with me."

Lorna frowned. She'd never seen this brother, but then

she'd hardly seen Arthur in a long time. "Where is he now?" she asked. Maybe Arthur had sent him off to boarding school. That seemed like the sort of responsible thing he'd do.

Arthur hung his head. "That's just it. He's here. In Asheville."

"I'd love to meet him. Any brother of yours is bound to be a good fellow."

Arthur let out a sigh. He glanced at her, then back at the floorboards. "I hope you can one day. But right now he's . . . staying at Oak Lodge."

Lorna tried to think where Oak Lodge might be. It sounded familiar, but she couldn't place it. "I'm not sure where—"

"At Highland Hospital."

She blanched. The last time she'd heard that hospital mentioned had been soon after her near drowning in the flood of 1916. Even as her body recovered from the effects of all those hours in the water, her mind couldn't seem to catch up. She'd lain there in bed, feeling as if she were walking through deep sand every moment of every day. And some days, it just didn't seem worth the effort. It was only when she heard the nurses whispering about a transfer to Highland Hospital that she'd managed to shake the languor. She'd forced herself to smile and interact, to appear interested in what was happening around her.

Anything to avoid being relegated to a mental hospital.

And, surprisingly, acting as though she were well made her feel that perhaps she was. Or could be. And she'd come around enough to stop the talk about a transfer. Enough to go back to the weaving room and to wake up each day prepared to set one foot in front of the other.

She'd fooled them all. She had perhaps even fooled herself. Hearing the name of the hospital now brought her rocker to an abrupt stop. "You mean . . . ?"

"He was addicted to alcohol. And maybe other things, too.

I didn't know it when I brought him home with me." Arthur ran a hand through his hair. "I thought I could help—could be a family for him. But I was wrong. I tried for a year or so and then . . ." He turned anguished eyes on her. "I failed him."

Lorna wanted to comfort Arthur, to tell him that he'd done the best he could, but she wasn't sure how to do that. "I don't know what to say," she finally managed.

The look on Arthur's face told her that was the wrong thing to say. "I just wanted you to know," he mumbled. "I didn't want you to find out some other way and think . . . Well. It doesn't matter now."

She was doing this all wrong. What was he afraid she'd think? That he was a bad person for getting his brother the help he needed? "What's he like?" she asked.

Hope crept into Arthur's expression. "He's smart. And brave. Mostly because he's had to be." Arthur seemed to be thinking. "And he's pretty funny, although that might've been the liquor."

Lorna tried a small smile. "So, he's a lot like you? Except for the drinking," she added.

Arthur flushed. "I don't know about that." He looked at his feet. "He has a clubfoot, too." His eyes came slowly up to meet hers.

"Guess that's part of being brave," she said. "Living with something that makes you different."

"Yeah," he said, his eyes gone soft and wet. "Do you think I did the right thing? Putting him in the hospital when I couldn't get him sober?"

Lorna shook her head. "I don't know. But I do know that you've always put other people ahead of yourself." She took a deep breath and let it out slowly. "I feel sure that whether it was the right thing or not, you did it for the right reason."

"Thank you for that," Arthur said. "It's been hard knowing I couldn't love him enough to fix whatever made him turn to liquor."

They chatted a while longer, Arthur sharing stories of Boyd when he first arrived in Asheville, skipping over the difficult bits, she was sure. And they talked about their plans to find Gentry. But even as they talked, Lorna couldn't help but compare Arthur's secret to her own. His shame was in having to let someone else help his brother. Hers was in casting Gentry's well-being aside for her own gain. She longed to bare her soul to Arthur, to get his absolution, she supposed. But if she told him her secret, would he wish she'd kept it? Would she? Better not to find out, she decided.

She stood, her feet and back protesting silently. "So we'll begin our search for Gentry tomorrow?"

Arthur stood, as well. "I'll be by after breakfast. Angus can manage the shop tomorrow." He started down the steps. She noticed his limp was more pronounced after their long day. He turned at the road and looked back at her as though he were going to say something more. Instead, he lifted a hand in a friendly wave and walked away.

She watched him for a long time, wishing he'd look back again. He never did.

# 29

# ARTHUR

**SOUTH ASHEVILLE**
**JUNE 1922**

Boyd was late. Again.

While Arthur tried to focus on the curio cabinet on his worktable, his ears were tuned to the floorboards overhead. Was that the thump of his brother's feet hitting the floor? No. It was just wishful thinking.

Boyd said he was still getting used to being in this new place, having regular work to do. He claimed it was hard for him to adjust. He even claimed his brace was slowing him down. Said he could move faster before they started trying to straighten his foot out.

Arthur would have thought four months was plenty of time to get used to things. And his foot had improved dramatically, although he'd likely always wear the last brace to keep it that way. Even so, there was always an excuse.

Arthur was trying hard to hold Boyd accountable without scaring him off. Boyd hinted that he might head back to West Virginia if this place didn't suit him. So Arthur tried even harder to make sure it did. Good food, new clothes, easy work in the shop, a big brother to look out for him—it would have been a dream come true when Arthur was Boyd's age.

But he knew Boyd's growing-up years had been even harder than his own.

He pulled his attention back to the work at hand. He was adding leaves to dogwood blossoms when the back door thumped open and Boyd limped inside.

He slumped onto a chair and sighed deeply. "Got anything to eat?"

Arthur looked up. "I left some fruit and a loaf of bread on the table upstairs."

Boyd groaned and let his head roll back. "Didn't see it. Man, why do you have to live up all those steps? Sure is a lot of trouble."

"It's economical to live above my business." Arthur took in his brother's mussed hair and wrinkled clothing. "Did you sleep in your clothes?"

"What's it to you if I did?"

"Nothing. Just seems like you might want to look nice in case we have customers." Arthur set his tools down and gave his brother his full attention. "Nothing would please me more than for you to learn woodcarving and become a partner here with me."

Boyd snorted. "You know, Mam and Pap never mentioned you."

Arthur winced. He didn't think Boyd meant to hurt him, so he determined not to take offense. "Guess I'd been gone a while when you came along."

"Everybody was gone. Shoot, Mam and Pap were gone most days." He squinted at Arthur. "Why'd you come for me anyway? You never even met me."

Arthur crossed the room and sat beside his brother. He sniffed. Was that alcohol he smelled? Surely not. Maybe it was just a rag with turpentine on it. "Because you're family. Like you say, our parents didn't exactly make family a priority." He shrugged. "I always wished I could be part of a big family with lots of laughing and hugging and joking. So when I heard I had a brother who needed me, I decided to do something about it."

"Needed you? Who says I need you? I can take care of myself."

Arthur flushed. "Well, sure. But isn't it good to have someone you can count on?"

"I wouldn't know." Boyd crossed his arms and slumped deeper in the chair. "Can't say as I've ever known anyone like that."

"You can count on me." Arthur felt as though the words were hanging in the air between them. It was up to Boyd whether he wanted to reach out and grasp them.

"Yeah. Maybe." He crossed his legs and massaged his clubfoot where Arthur knew the brace rubbed against it. "My name's Robert."

"What?"

"Robert. That's the name they gave me when I was born. The granny woman who helped told me about it."

Arthur was confused. Boyd didn't seem to follow the usual rules of conversation. "Is Boyd your middle name?" He'd try to play along.

"Nah." He squeezed his foot and stared at the floor. "Pap couldn't remember my name, so he called me 'boy.' Folks heard it and thought he was saying Boyd." Arthur felt as though he'd been struck dumb. "It's a good name. Robert." His eyes flicked to Arthur and away again. "But I guess I'll stick with Boyd now. I'm used to it."

Arthur swallowed the knot clogging his throat. "Robert is a good name. So's Boyd. When you become a partner, just let me know which one you want on the letterhead."

Boyd's eyes came up, and this time they didn't skitter away. "You mean that?"

"I do."

Boyd nodded once. "Alright. Guess I'll go back upstairs and eat a bite. Then maybe you can show me how to do a few things."

"I'd be glad to," Arthur said.

Boyd nodded again as though confirming something to himself. Then he limped out the door and plodded up the exterior staircase to the second floor. Again, Arthur thought he caught a whiff of alcohol, but he told himself it was just his imagination. No need to look for more trouble than he already had.

Two weeks later, Arthur was convinced that God had sent Boyd to test him. And he was failing. Badly. How a fifteen-year-old, half-grown boy got ahold of alcohol nearly every day was a mystery Arthur didn't know how to solve.

For months he'd been telling himself the smell was his imagination. He wrote off the way Boyd slept late and seemed sluggish. But now he'd found an empty bottle. Apparently, his brother was getting lax about hiding his sins. Arthur figured his only choice was to confront him. He didn't wait for Boyd to drag out of bed this time. When he found a bottle stashed on the ledge outside an upstairs window, he snatched it up—only half empty—and marched into the room he'd given over to Boyd's use. He grabbed the metal bed frame and shook it as hard as he could.

Boyd grunted, groaned, and rolled over, burrowing deeper into the covers. Arthur shook the frame again. "Get up, Boyd. We need to talk."

"Leave me alone" came the muffled reply.

Arthur grabbed the blanket and flipped it off the bed. His

brother was wearing the previous day's shirt and a pair of long underwear, along with one sock. At least he'd managed to remove his pants before falling into bed this time.

Boyd raised his head and cracked his eyes open. "Whaddya want?"

Arthur held the bottle up and swirled the liquid inside. "We need to talk."

Heaving a sigh, Boyd rolled to the edge of the bed and sat up, cradling his head in his hands. "I don't feel so good."

"I guess not with the way you've been drinking."

"Ain't none of your business what I drink."

Arthur pulled a wooden chair over and sat in front of his brother. "Yeah, it is. For starters, buying alcohol is illegal." He took a deep breath. "Where are you getting the booze?"

"Around. And who says I'm buying it?"

"How often are you drinking like this?"

Boyd shrugged. "Nobody cared what I did back home."

Arthur knew the truth of that statement. "Well, I care what you do here."

"Why? 'Cause I'm an embarrassment?"

"No, because you're my brother and I care about you."

Boyd snorted. "Sure. Whatever you say. Can I go back to sleep now?"

"No. I want you to get up, wash your face, comb your hair, and come downstairs where you'll put in a good day's work."

"Good luck with all that," Boyd said and flopped back onto the bed, tugging the pillow over his face.

Arthur felt anger well up inside him. He'd been frustrated or aggravated before, disappointed even. But this feeling was new. It was jagged and raw. It had teeth and claws, and it wanted out. He stalked over to the window, lifted the sash, and threw the bottle as hard as he could. It shattered on the paved sidewalk below with a satisfying crash.

Boyd threw the pillow aside and sat up. "What'd you do?"

"Broke your bottle. And I plan to turn this place upside down so I can break any others you have stashed around here."

"Now hold on there." Boyd's eyes looked wild. Was that fear? "You don't need to do that."

"Yeah, I do. I need to do whatever it takes to dry you out."

Boyd's hands started shaking. "C'mon, brother. I'm not hurting anyone. Just let me be. I'll even go on down and do some work. Good work. But I'm gonna need a little snort now and again."

"You're hooked on the stuff," Arthur said. He knew about addiction, had seen the church try to help people who couldn't say no to alcohol or other things. "And you *are* hurting someone. You're hurting yourself."

Boyd turned sullen. "So what if I am? A man oughta be able to live however he wants."

"It'll kill you. And I won't watch you do that."

"Guess we'll be parting ways, then."

Arthur squeezed his eyes shut, trying to think. "Boyd, I care about you. I don't want to see you drink yourself to death. You've got your whole life ahead of you." He stepped closer and laid a hand on his brother's shoulder. "You have so much to live for."

Boyd shrugged the hand away. "Yeah. I'm an orphaned cripple, living with a brother I've only just met who thinks I'm useless. Who wouldn't want to live like that?"

"I don't think you're useless," Arthur said. "And that foot doesn't need to hold you back."

"Like yours hasn't held you back?"

Arthur frowned. "What do you mean?"

"How old are you?" Boyd asked.

"Thirty-seven. What's that got to do with anything?"

"Nearly forty and still single 'cause women don't want a man with a bum foot. Slaving away trying to get people to buy all that junk you make. I heard you and Angus talking. You're not exactly rolling in the dough, are you? Maybe you should play up the foot more, get people to feel sorry for you. Then maybe they'll buy something."

Arthur flushed. "It took a lot of capital to get this place set up. I'll be making a profit soon enough. And I'm single because I haven't found the right girl."

"Yeah. Right. I heard about that dame leaving you for some other fellow." Boyd sneered. "Guess she wasn't the 'right one.'"

Arthur thought he'd released his earlier anger when he threw the bottle out the window. But apparently that had just been the appetizer. He felt like a fire had been kindled in his gut. He wanted to open his mouth and let the brimstone come pouring out. Instead, he stood, kicked his chair back against the wall, and left the room.

He went outside, slamming the door behind him as hard as he could. The walls shook, and the windows rattled. He almost wished the panes had shattered, raining shards of glass down all around him. He clattered down the stairs, walked to the far end of the back garden, and roared at the sky. Somewhere in the chaos of his mind, he noted that it would be embarrassing for his neighbors to witness this behavior. But he couldn't seem to care.

What had he done to deserve such venom? All he wanted was to help. To give his brother a family. To have a family. Was he destined to fail at everything?

Arthur fell to his knees in the cold, damp grass. His club-foot throbbed. His hands shook. His heart ached. He just wanted to stay there until all his problems disappeared. But he knew from bitter experience that wasn't an option.

A hand settled on his shoulder. He could feel a tremor in the fingers. He looked up at his brother. Boyd's expression was both wary and worried. "You okay?" he asked.

Arthur rose to his feet with a grunt. "Yeah. I'm okay. Guess I let my temper get the better of me."

Boyd hung his head. "When Pap's temper got the better of him, he took it out on me instead of—" he paused, frowning—"whatever that was you just did."

Arthur half smiled. "Think the neighbors heard me?"

"Only if they aren't dead." Boyd looked like he wanted to smile but wasn't sure it was the right thing to do.

Arthur draped an arm around his brother's shoulders. "Sorry about that. I know yelling doesn't help. I just worry about you. You're my responsibility now."

Boyd dug a bare toe into the dirt. "Guess I'm not used to anybody giving a darn." He gave Arthur a side look. "But maybe I could get used to it."

Arthur chuckled. "You'd better. 'Cause I sure enough care and don't plan to stop. Ever."

"Alright then." Boyd's smile finally broke out. "I've been meaning to do better for a while. Guess the time's just about right."

"Now, that's what I like to hear." Arthur slapped him on the back, and they walked inside together.

# 30

# ARTHUR

**SOUTH ASHEVILLE**
**CHRISTMAS, 1922**

Boyd lived up to his word. Mostly. Arthur suspected he drank a little now and then, but he was being helpful around the shop, getting up on time, and taking a genuine interest in woodworking. Not to mention demonstrating a natural talent for it.

As Christmas approached, Arthur dared to believe they had turned the corner.

Now they were dressing for the Christmas Eve service at All Souls. Arthur whistled softly as he knotted his tie and tried to get his curly hair to lay down. "You about ready?" he called to Boyd. He heard a thump in the little room he'd given his brother and then Boyd appeared in the doorway.

"Why do we have to go to church at night?" he whined. He seemed to have an aversion to churchgoing, and Arthur hadn't pressed it. Until now.

Arthur paused. That was a good question. "It has something to do with keeping vigil. Or maybe it's because the shepherds were watching their flocks at night when the angels appeared to them." He laughed. "Anyway, it's a beautiful service, and I've always liked how the church looks at night with all the candles. Maybe you'll like it, too."

"I doubt it. Just hope it doesn't go on too long."

Arthur looped an arm around his brother's shoulder and squeezed. "It won't. And then we'll get some sleep, and next thing you know it'll be Christmas morning. We're invited up to Biltmore House to have breakfast with the staff. Trust me, it'll be worth it."

Boyd turned his head and ducked away. "Alright, alright. I'm game."

They walked the short distance to the church in the bracing night air. Arthur filled his lungs and took in the glimmers of candle and electric light along the way. He'd always thought Christmas Eve had a certain magic to it. And tonight, having his brother at his side made it even more luminous.

They entered the church, and Boyd immediately ducked into the back row where he slumped in a pew. Arthur preferred to sit midway up on the right side but followed his brother. Whatever made him comfortable.

The service was just as beautiful as always. It ended with the congregation holding lighted candles while they sang "Silent Night." Arthur wanted to wrap an arm around his brother again but resisted. He'd hoped Boyd would be won over by the beauty and peace of the service, but it seemed he was merely tolerating it. *Good enough*, thought Arthur. *At least he's here.*

As soon as the final notes dissipated among the sanctuary's rafters, Boyd slipped out of the pew and made a beeline for the door. Arthur sighed but didn't hurry after him. He wanted to speak to some friends and to let Rodney know they'd be around for supper on Christmas evening.

As he moved toward the center aisle, a woman in the pew

ahead of him grasped his arm. "Are you Boyd Westcott's brother?"

"Yes, ma'am." He tried to place the matron with the ridiculous hat. He knew she was a member of the church, but he couldn't think of her name.

"There's something you ought to know." His heart plummeted. "Your brother has been caught stealing from my husband's store."

Arthur placed her. She was married to the owner of the hardware store—Mrs. Gilbert. He wet his lips. "If that's so, why am I just now hearing about it?"

The lady sniffed and laid a hand across her ample bosom. "My husband is aware of the hardships the young man has faced and took pity on him. He took Boyd to Reverend Swope, and our good rector not only paid for the missing items but assured us that no such action would occur again." She glanced around and lowered her voice. "But I've seen your brother skulking about the other shops, and I will confess I'm concerned he may not have turned from his wicked ways." She closed her eyes and exhaled. "There. I hated to do it. Especially on Christmas Eve. But I just knew it was something you needed to be aware of."

Arthur's head swam. He placed a hand on the back of the pew to steady himself. "Yes. Of course. You did the right thing."

She nodded emphatically. "I'm confident you can address the situation and ensure that no one else is—" she glanced around, then dropped her voice to a whisper—"taken advantage of."

"Absolutely. You can count on me." Arthur spoke the words as though he were an actor reading a script.

He hurried into the aisle, and instead of speaking to Reverend Swope at the door where he was even now wishing his congregants a Merry Christmas, he headed to the vestry.

His mentor would return here soon to remove his vestments before heading home. Arthur didn't have long to stew before Rodney entered the room.

"Merry Christmas, my boy! Can we count on seeing you and Boyd tomorrow evening?"

"We plan to come for the evening meal," Arthur answered. "But I need to talk to you about something."

"Certainly, but let's not take too long. Mary has a glass of eggnog and a soft pillow awaiting me at home."

Arthur decided to skip the formalities. "Has Boyd been stealing from shops in the village?"

Rodney's smile slipped. He sighed. "I was planning to tell you. I just thought it would be nice to enjoy the holiday first."

"Tell me now."

Rodney took a deep breath. "It would seem your brother has a propensity toward alcohol. I believe he's been pilfering items and even cash when he can in order to trade for or purchase whiskey." He ran a hand over his face. For the first time Arthur realized his mentor was growing old. "The shopkeepers are aware and are keeping an eye out. The last I heard, Boyd hadn't been around. Yet that was more than a week ago, and I've been busy preparing for Christmas." He heaved a mighty sigh. "I realize now I should have told you immediately. I hoped . . . Well, Boyd seemed to genuinely regret his actions."

Arthur nodded slowly. "So, you think there's hope for him?"

"There's hope for everyone," Rodney said.

Arthur managed a weak laugh. "I don't know about that, but it's good to hear you say it."

"Come to supper tomorrow. Bring Boyd. We'll show him what it means to be part of a loving, forgiving family." He squeezed Arthur's shoulder. "He's got you on his side. That's half the battle right there."

Arthur blinked away moisture. What he wanted and what was good for Boyd seemed tangled now. But with Rodney's help, he'd sort it out somehow. "Thanks." His voice was hoarse, and he swallowed against a lump in his throat.

Rodney enveloped him in an incense-scented hug. It was an aroma Arthur had known since his parents gave him away to the church. And it reminded him that he'd been made welcome, taken in, cared for. He vowed he'd do no less for his own flesh and blood.

⁙

Arthur waited to confront his brother. Boyd grumbled as he rose on Christmas morning. His eyes were bloodshot, and Arthur didn't even try to pretend that Boyd didn't smell of alcohol. Where he'd gotten it between church and now was a mystery, but Arthur supposed that wasn't his main problem just then.

He handed his brother a mug of strong black coffee and gave him a moment to swallow a few mouthfuls. "Merry Christmas," he said at last.

"Yeah. Merry Christmas."

"I made you something." Arthur handed Boyd a package wrapped in brown paper and tied with twine.

His brother looked from him to the package with narrowed eyes. "Didn't get you anything."

"That's alright. I wasn't expecting a gift."

Boyd took another slug of coffee and set his mug down. He untied the twine and folded the paper back. "What is it?" he asked, then hurried to add, "I mean, it's real nice, but what do I do with it?"

"It's a toolbox." Arthur felt color seep into his cheeks. Was he making a fool of himself? Probably. "I was thinking, if you stay on here and learn the trade, you'll need your own tools and a box to keep them in."

Boyd studied the box. He ran his fingers over the simple pattern carved around the edge and then grasped the handle. "You think I could do what you do?"

Arthur tried not to sound too eager. "Sure. I've seen you helping out. I think you've got a knack for working with wood."

A look of pleasure lit Boyd's face, like the sun slowly emerging from behind a cloud. "Yeah. I like wood."

"I'm glad." Arthur took a deep breath. Now for the hard part. "But there's something we need to talk about."

And just like that, the light in Boyd's face dimmed and blinked out. "Right. There's always a catch."

"No catch. It's just that I've heard you might have forgotten to pay for some items down at the hardware store." Boyd's countenance darkened. "And I'm pretty sure you've been drinking again."

Boyd stood with a jerk and glared at Arthur. "Who's been telling tales?"

"That doesn't matter. The main thing is, I can smell liquor on you this morning."

"Yeah, well, it ain't none of your business what I do." He fisted his hands and glared.

Arthur felt his anger spike. He supposed it was their father's legacy to them both. He was determined to tamp it down. "It is my business. I'm responsible for you. And I want to help you make something of yourself."

"Right. 'Cause the poor crippled hillbilly can't do it on his own." Boyd shoved the toolbox across the table. "I've been hearing that kind of crap all my life. I sure don't need it from you. And here I thought you were gonna be different, that you were gonna give me a chance."

Arthur held up his hands. "Look, Boyd, it's just that it seems like you might not be able to stop drinking on your own. And maybe you've done some things to get the whiskey that you're not proud of—"

"Oh, here it comes. I'm a no-good thief. That old biddy down at the hardware store claimed I stole something, but I didn't. I just forgot to put it back." He leaned closer. "Who you gonna believe? Some rich old woman or your own flesh and blood?"

Arthur flexed his hands and tried to stay calm. "Boyd, the first step is to put a name to the problem—"

"Leave me alone!" Boyd whirled around, limped to the door, and slammed it hard as he left.

Arthur sat there for a long time, staring at the toolbox he'd been so excited to give his brother, wondering where he'd gone wrong and how he was going to fix things now.

# 31

# LORNA

**BILTMORE VILLAGE**
**OCTOBER 1923**

True to his word, Arthur was waiting on Lorna's front porch the next morning. "I remembered where it was Mrs. Brady thought Gentry might have gone," he said. Lorna felt her spirits lift. "But we were just there. Monroe County, West Virginia."

Lorna slumped. "Olive would have mentioned if a long-lost daughter turned up looking for her family."

"That's what I thought," Arthur said. "But what if she found out her mother wasn't there anymore, and left? She might have learned she had an aunt who moved to North Carolina and came back here looking for Sabine. And then there's the grandfather," he added. "The one who lied to her and her mother. Might she have gone to have it out with him?"

"Those are good guesses," Lorna agreed. "Let's go talk to Mrs. Brady—see if she remembers anything else."

They were silent on the short walk to the boardinghouse. Lorna could still feel the weight of Arthur's shame over institutionalizing his brother. Not to mention her own shame for what she'd done to Gentry. Their silence nipped at her heels. She did her best to ignore it.

When Arthur knocked on the door of the boardinghouse, the sound was a blessed relief. Mrs. Brady threw the door open and beamed at them. "Lorna, Arthur, it's been much too long since I've seen either one of you. Come in! I was just having my coffee now that I've gotten everyone off to the weaving room." She frowned. "Which is where I might expect you to be, Lorna. Are you unwell?"

"I'm fine, Mrs. Brady." She scrambled for an explanation for her absence from Biltmore Industries.

"Lorna was kind of enough to help me do some investigating," Arthur jumped in. "You'll find this hard to believe, but we found Gentry Cutshall's mother."

Mrs. Brady gasped. "I thought she was dead. Come, have a cup of coffee and tell me all about it."

Lorna was relieved to let Arthur take the lead in explaining their mission. Mrs. Brady was clearly savoring each morsel of information. Lorna supposed the news would be all over the village before lunch and clear across Asheville by supper. It was too late to wonder if that mattered now.

"And so we were wondering if you remember anything about Gentry's grandfather. We thought he might be able to help," Arthur concluded.

"That old cuss is long dead," Mrs. Brady said. "But he had a daughter—Gentry's aunt. Wait right here." She held up a finger and bustled off. They heard her climb the stairs, and then there was a long silence. Lorna and Arthur looked at each other in confusion.

"What do you think she went after?" Lorna asked.

Arthur shrugged. "She seems to know everyone else's business. Here's hoping—" He cut himself off as they heard their hostess clomp back down the stairs.

"Here we are," she said, dropping a dusty pasteboard box onto the table. "I thought I had some of her things yet."

"Some of Gentry's things?" Lorna was astonished.

"Never know when an item might come in handy. And these young girls with their heads in the clouds walk off and leave all sorts of plunder. One time I had a girl who left a pearl necklace her grandmother gave her. Let me tell you she was almighty glad I save everyone's bibs and bobs when she finally came back looking for it."

Lorna lifted the lid off the musty box. She sneezed twice, much to her horror. Arthur handed her a handkerchief. She sneezed into it one more time before peering into the box. There was a comb, two lengths of ribbon, an advertisement for skin cream, and a letter.

Lorna pulled out the letter and glanced at Arthur. "Do you think it's alright for us to read it?"

"I do," he said. "I don't think she would have left the letter behind if it was secret."

Lorna pulled out the single page and scanned it quickly. "It's from an aunt named Eulah. She says Gentry's grandfather is sick and her mother is from West Virginia. That's about it."

Arthur picked up the envelope. "Here's her return address. She lives in Johnson City, Tennessee."

Lorna leaned over Arthur's arm to read the crude handwriting. "Do you think she's still there?"

"It's worth finding out if she is. And more importantly if she's heard from Gentry since she wrote this letter."

"I'll write to her this very day," Lorna said.

She dashed off a short note as soon as she got back to her house. Arthur waited, and they walked to the post office together to hand the letter directly to the postmistress. Lorna watched the woman add it to the outgoing mailbag and felt something break free deep inside her. She had the oddest feeling her life was about to change, and as much as she'd been dreading it, knowing she couldn't hide any longer was freeing.

She grinned at Arthur. "And now we wait."

It didn't take long to get an answer, although the letter itself was cryptic. Eulah hinted that she knew Gentry's whereabouts but didn't reveal much else. Lorna and Arthur debated telling Vivian, then decided it would be better to wait until they were certain. No need to get her hopes up only to dash them.

They each bought yet another train ticket. Lorna's savings were dwindling with no work and all these expenses, but she couldn't give up the search now. She thought of the expenses in terms of the money she should have paid Gentry all those years ago.

Eulah lived above a bakery in the heart of Johnson City. A seamstress, her sitting room was littered with stacks of clothing and other items in various stages of construction or repair. Lorna saw Arthur flush when his eyes fell on some ladies' undergarments. She thought she'd better take the lead in this interview.

"Thank you so much for taking time to talk with us," she began.

Eulah's expression didn't change one iota. "No trouble at all. Ain't like I got somewhere else to be."

"We're looking for your niece, Gentry. I don't suppose you've heard from her recently?"

Eulah pursed her lips and looked toward the ceiling. "Guess it's been a while at that."

"But you have heard from her?" Lorna felt a ridiculous surge of hope. Why she cared so much was a mystery. Finding Gentry would ruin her.

"Let me think now. How long has it been?" Eulah moved to a cluttered desk and rummaged around until she produced a calendar. Lorna dared to hope it hadn't been more than a year. Maybe even a matter of months.

"Here we go." Eulah tapped a date. "Sunday before last she come sailing in here. Said she missed me, but I'm not so sure about that." She sighed. "Got a life of her own now. Which I'll bet is a surprise to you if you knew her back in the day."

Lorna's mouth dropped open. "You saw her just ten days ago?"

"Sure enough. Like I said, she comes round now and again. She's real busy playing music and helping out with her *girls*." The way Eulah said "girls" sounded like she didn't think much of whoever Gentry was spending her time with.

Lorna was struck dumb. Arthur came to the rescue. "Do you know how we can find her?"

"It ain't proper." Eulah crossed her arms over her chest.

"What do you mean?" Lorna asked.

"Where she stays ain't proper. The bunch of girls call themselves singers and actresses, but I know what business they're in."

Lorna felt confused. "What business is that? Entertainment?"

Eulah snorted and looked at Arthur. "You know what I mean. Entertainment is right."

This time Arthur flushed crimson. "Lorna, she means ladies who . . . who entertain men who are not their husbands."

Lorna thumped down on the closest chair but jumped back up when she landed on a pincushion. "Are you suggesting that Gentry . . . ?" She couldn't finish the sentence.

"No. I don't think so anyway. She just plays music for the visitors as far as I know. But it still ain't proper. I've tried to talk her into moving on, but she says they need her there."

Eulah heaved a big sigh. "The one time she decides to stick with something, and this is what she picks."

"We found her mother. She's anxious to be reunited with Gentry. That's why we're looking for her." Lorna's mind was reeling. Were they really so close?

"You're tellin' me you ran to ground the woman what abandoned her own child, and *now* she wants to see her daughter? I find that a tough tale to swaller."

"She thought Gentry was dead. Your father told Vivian she drowned."

Now it was Eulah's turn to thump down on a chair. "That rotten old goat." She closed her eyes. "I knew he was mean as a snake, but I never thought he'd go so far as to bust up a mother and her child. He blamed Vivian for Elias's death. That's Gentry's daddy—my brother. He went to fetch help when Vivian was birthing Gentry, got throwed from his horse, and died a week later." She pulled out a hanky and blew her nose. "Last thing he did was ask Vivian to lay that baby across his chest so he could carry the feel of her with him into heaven." Eulah blew out a breath. "My daddy had the purest mean streak a man ever carried. I'd hate him if I thought it'd do any good."

"Will you take us to see Gentry?" Lorna asked.

Eulah slapped her knees and stood. "Come on then. That child's suffered enough without dragging it out one more minute. 'Course, she ain't a child no more. Twenty-one years old with no sign of settling down and starting a family of her own like she should."

Lorna bit her lip. She'd been picturing Gentry as the girl she'd last seen seven years ago. She knew she was older now, but she couldn't quite imagine it.

"Lead the way," Arthur said. And they all trooped out together.

# 32

# GENTRY

## MONROE COUNTY, WEST VIRGINIA
## OCTOBER 1916

Nothing was going right. Gentry tried to think who she could blame it on, but there really wasn't anyone else. Though she'd arrived in Ronceverte without difficulty, everything had been a mess since the moment she set foot on the depot platform. She'd found people who'd heard of a family named Gentry, yet no one seemed to know what had become of them.

She finagled a place to stay at the Hotel Ronceverte by offering to wait on tables and wash dishes. The owner had given her the use of a narrow little room off the kitchen that had a pallet on the floor, a washstand, and little else. And he expected her to work such long hours, she didn't have time to go looking for her mother.

She finished dressing and tied a crisp white apron over her dress so she could begin her day serving breakfast in the dining room. Thank goodness for the apron since her few clothing items were wrinkled and in need of a proper wash. That was something else she'd have to figure out.

As she entered the kitchen, her stomach rumbled at the wonderful smells. She knew, however, that she wouldn't get to eat until everyone had been served. And then she'd eat whatever was left over and be glad to get it.

"Pin that loose hair up, girl," the cook barked at her.

Gentry waited until her back was turned to stick her tongue out at her, then fiddled with her hair in a mirror. She did the best she knew how and hoped it would be good enough.

"Customers are waiting. Quit your dawdling." The cook put her hands on her hips and stared a hole in Gentry. "And I'd better not hear that you've been quizzing people about whatever long-lost relative you're trying to track down."

Anger surged in Gentry. The old biddy knew she was looking for her mother. She reached for the tie on her apron to rip it off and fling it down, about to quit on the spot.

She stopped. If she quit, what then? She had no money and nowhere else to go or a way to get there if she did. No. She had no choice but to swallow down her resentment and do this terrible job. But she promised herself she'd find a way to move on from here soon.

Gentry picked up her pad of paper along with a stub of pencil and walked into the dining room. There were people seated at two tables, perusing the simple menu. And so began a long three hours of biting her tongue. She only made two mistakes with orders, which still gave the cook fits but was better than usual.

Finally, she was given two buttered biscuits and some stewed apples. She took the food outside and ate it as fast as she could to quiet the pangs in her belly. She sopped up the last of the apple with a corner of biscuit and popped it in her mouth. As she chewed, savoring the sweetness of the apple and the richness of the bread, she saw a woman come around the corner of the hotel. She was wearing a gloriously purple shawl with a silver pin holding it in place. As soon as she saw Gentry, she marched straight to her.

"Are you Gentry Cutshall?"

Gentry swallowed. "Yes, ma'am."

"I knew your family when they lived around here. Real nice folks. It was a sorrow to them when your mama married that boy and ran off to North Carolina."

Gentry stared. Had she finally found someone who could help her? "My father died right after I was born. My grandad wasn't very nice. I think he ran Mama off." She felt as though her breakfast had formed a ball of lead in her belly. "Did she ever come back here?"

"Vivian? Not that I know of. Her parents died the year influenza took so many. Child," she said and laid a hand on Gentry's knee, "there's nothing for you here. You don't need to waste your time working at this hotel. Don't you have any other family?"

Gentry hung her head. "I have an aunt in Johnson City, Tennessee."

"Well then." The woman clapped her hands. "I'm going to buy you a train ticket to Johnson City!"

Gentry jerked her head up. "Why would you do that?"

"Let's just say I owe it to your mother."

"What was she like?" Gentry asked. "Can you tell me about her?"

A dark shadow crossed the woman's face, then dissipated. "Certainly I can. Let's see. She was pretty. You look a lot like her. And she got all the attention from the boys, but she didn't give a fig about any of them until your father came along." The darkness crept back in. "Oh, all the girls fell for him, but your mother set her cap and that was that. He didn't stand a chance."

"Was he nice?"

The woman glanced at her. "That's right. You didn't know

him." She sighed. "He was. Probably too nice. He came to town to buy a ram for his herd back home. Spent a couple of weeks on Ebenezer Holly's farm, talking sheep and looking over the flock. When he left, he took Eb's best ram and my . . . and Vivian." She stood. "That's all I can tell you. Now, let's get you that ticket."

Gentry stood. "I should let Cook know. Maybe finish out the day at least."

The woman nodded. "That would be the responsible thing to do. Guess you aren't altogether like your mother. I'll pay for a ticket on the first train out in the morning and leave it at the station."

Gentry turned to go inside. She was sorry she hadn't found her mother but relieved that she didn't have to slave away at the hotel much longer. Aunt Eulah said she should come see Grandad before he died, so maybe she wouldn't be surprised to see her. Not that she wanted to see Grandad, but it was as good an excuse as any.

She stopped and called out to the woman, who was nearly at the corner of the hotel. "Wait! Tell me your name. Maybe I can pay you back one day."

The woman stood still a moment, then called back, "Let's charge it to the dust and let the rain settle it." Then she rounded the corner and was gone.

When Gentry arrived in Johnson City, she asked the stationmaster for directions to the address she had for Aunt Eulah and was relieved to learn it wasn't too far off. She slung her carpetbag of belongings over her shoulder, tucked her dulcimer under her arm, and set out.

The smell of fresh bread and cinnamon drew Gentry more surely than the address on the side of the door. She pressed her nose to the plate-glass window displaying baskets of glossy loaves, trays of pastries, and a cherry pie that left her drooling. She had a few coins in her pocket and was about to go in when the glare from an oversized woman in a floury apron made her change her mind. Looking at her as if she was a beggar. So much for that!

She spun on her heel and pressed the buzzer beside the door numbered 1008. After just a few seconds, she leaned on the buzzer again. She heard clomping on the stairs, and then the door flung wide and Aunt Eulah scowled at her like she'd as soon skin her as welcome her inside.

"What do you—?" Eulah stopped and squinted. "Gentry?"

"It's me, Aunt Eulah." She stuck her chin in the air. "I've come to pay my respects to Grandad before he's gone."

"Hunh. Too late for that. He give up the ghost week afore last. Dead and buried and won't give anyone trouble no more."

"Oh. Can I come in?"

Eulah took off her glasses and rubbed her face. "I reckon so. You've come all this way."

They climbed the stairs in silence. At the top, Gentry stopped to take in the apartment. It was small and seemed smaller with all the stacks of cloth scattered about the room. A table near a window seemed to be her aunt's workstation. There was a sewing machine, shears, spools of thread, and a man's shirt laid out.

"I'll make us a pot of coffee," Eulah said, heading for a minuscule kitchen with a two-burner stove, a sink, and a cupboard. She ground some coffee, sending the rich scent into the air. Gentry almost swallowed her pride enough to go downstairs for a cinnamon roll. But then Eulah drew out a brown loaf and some butter. "Sit, child."

Gentry dropped her sack and shoved a basket of mending to the side so she could sit on the sway-backed sofa.

"You in trouble for leaving that place in Asheville?" Eulah asked.

Gentry shrugged one shoulder. "Probably."

"You going back?"

"Not if I can help it."

Eulah heaved another of her sighs. Gentry was thinking that was her main method of expressing herself. "What will you do then?"

"I went to West Virginia to look for Mama."

Eulah shot her a sharp look. "I expect she's dead, too."

"Yeah. Maybe. Nobody seemed to know about her. It's just . . ."

Eulah crossed the room and stood looking down at Gentry. "You can stay here for a bit. I ain't got much room. You'll have to sleep on this here davenport. And I expect you to carry your weight around the place. Help with the mending so we can buy our bread."

A lump rose in Gentry's throat. It wasn't that Aunt Eulah was being especially nice; it's just that she wasn't sending her packing. Which she'd expected to be the likeliest result of her showing up. "That'd be good," she said. "They taught me weaving. I can sew a little, too." She took a shaky breath and looked into her aunt's eyes. "I guess you're all the family I've got now."

Eulah grimaced, then reached out and laid a cold, hard hand on Gentry's shoulder. "Such as it is."

# 33

# ARTHUR

**SOUTH ASHEVILLE**
**FEBRUARY 1923**

"This cannot continue!" Mrs. Gilbert clapped her gloved hands sharply with each syllable. "It must not!"

"I'm sorry, but you'll have to be more specific," Arthur said with a groan. He'd rather not know what Boyd had done now, yet it was best to hear the worst and be done with it. Boyd hadn't come home the night before, and Arthur would be worried if it hadn't become a common occurrence. His brother had been sulky and difficult in the weeks since their Christmas morning confrontation, and he had no doubt he was drinking again.

"Theft. Drunkenness. Lewd behavior in public." She flushed and held a handkerchief to her lips. "He . . . he relieved himself in front of our store."

Arthur closed his eyes. "I'm so sorry."

"You should be! Now, what do you plan to do to remedy the situation?"

"Reverend Swope and I are having a chat this afternoon

about this very thing." Arthur tried to sound as though the meeting weren't so very important, as though it might not change his life forever.

"I should hope so. I shall expect a report about what you decide to do."

Arthur failed to rein in his eyebrows before they shot up. Who was she to demand a report? "I'm not certain—"

"A report," she repeated emphatically. "I'd hate to have to turn this matter over to the authorities."

Arthur swallowed. He'd hate that, too. "Yes, ma'am," he said, ducking his chin as the matron sniffed and flounced out the door.

"She'd be a handsome woman if she'd hold her tongue." Arthur choked on a laugh at Angus's words. "I hear the way she's bent on following your brother's every move has given her husband more peace than he's known for years."

"At least someone's benefiting." Arthur rubbed his temples. "But I'm afraid it doesn't let me off the hook."

"I wish I had some proper wisdom for ye," Angus said, "but the boy's set his heart on destruction and I'm not sure there's aught to be done for it. I've seen men get like that before. Can't lash out at the one who did them harm, so instead they lash out at everyone and everything else—including themselves." He shook his grizzled head. "Only the good Lord can heal wounds that deep."

"I didn't realize you were a religious man, Angus."

"Aye. I was like young Boyd once upon a time. Devilish. The Lord knocked me upside the head three or four times, and it finally took. Guess I'd be dead otherwise."

Arthur tried a smile. "So there's hope, then?"

"Oh, aye. The only question is which side of heaven you'll find it on."

When Arthur entered Rodney's office, his mentor looked as enthusiastic about their task as Arthur felt. "That bad?" he said, trying to sound lighthearted. He pulled the carved fawn from his pocket and tumbled it between his fingers.

Rodney didn't smile. "Yes, my boy. I'm afraid it is that bad."

Arthur sank into a chair, his legs feeling like jelly. Maybe he should have worried when Boyd didn't come home. "What's happened?"

"He's in jail. Seems an officer had to knock him over the head to get him to come along, and he's been alternating between sleeping like a dead man and hollering like a banshee since they threw the bolt in the wee hours of the morning."

Arthur dropped the carving back into his pocket and cradled his throbbing head. "How much do you think it will cost to bail him out?"

"Bail's a moot point, Arthur. Your brother is safest right where he is for the moment."

Arthur stared at Rodney through eyes he knew were bloodshot. "I can't just leave him there. He's my responsibility. It's my fault he's even here—"

Rodney held up a hand. "I'd say the blame for Boyd's situation goes back quite a bit further than your short acquaintance with him."

"But I—"

"Hold that thought. I have a solution for your consideration."

Everything in Arthur strained toward the word *solution.* "Tell me. I'm fresh out of solutions."

He heard a soft rustling, and a woman he hadn't noticed rose from a chair in the shadows. A shock of recognition coursed through him. He staggered to his feet and attempted a sort of half bow. "Mrs. Vanderbilt. I didn't realize you were here."

246

"Please resume your seat, Mr. Wescott. Reverend Swope invited me here this afternoon in hopes that I might be able to assist in your situation."

Arthur felt his cheeks flush hot. Rodney had shared his brother's sordid history with Mrs. Vanderbilt. He supposed the shame was his just punishment. "I'm grateful, Mrs. Vanderbilt, but I don't see how—"

Rodney interrupted him. "Mrs. Vanderbilt is personal friends with Dr. Carroll. He's the medical director at the . . . well, at Highland Hospital." Arthur blanched. "She's willing to have a word with him about accepting your brother's case."

"Do you mean"—Arthur lowered his voice—"the nervous hospital?"

Mrs. Vanderbilt sank into the chair beside Arthur's. "They do excellent work with those suffering from addiction. Dr. Carroll emphasizes the more natural cures such as rest, healthful food, and fresh air. Once patients are able, he even encourages playful physical exercise and employment. He's worked wonders with those entrusted to him."

"But Boyd won't want to go there. I'm sure of it."

Mrs. Vanderbilt looked to Rodney, who cleared his throat. "We would need to commit him, at least initially."

Arthur felt as though the room were swaying. "I can't do that to him," he whispered. Then, more strongly, "There's also the matter of affording such care. I'm certain it's not inexpensive, and I simply don't have the means."

Rodney cleared his throat. "Mrs. Vanderbilt subsidizes several openings at the hospital, and there is currently one available."

Arthur felt as though he were the one whose arms were about to be slipped into a straitjacket. Although he had no notion whether they used such things. But he couldn't imagine how Boyd would be compelled to stay otherwise.

"It seems cruel," he protested weakly.

Mrs. Vanderbilt laid a gloved hand on his arm. Her grip was surprisingly strong—like someone who worked and led an active life. "The cruelty would be leaving him in an addiction he is powerless to break."

Arthur hung his head. She was right. If he loved his brother, he would do this for him. No matter how painful it was to each of them in its own way. "You're right." He lifted his head. "What do I need to do?"

Rodney let out a breath and nodded once. "Bring him from the jail to the hospital tomorrow at ten in the morning. Dr. Carroll and his team will be ready to receive him."

"Very well." Arthur stood. He turned to the regal woman, who watched him with the kindest eyes he'd ever seen. "Thank you."

"You are most welcome, Mr. Wescott." She smiled. "I remember the good work you did for us while you were in the cabinet shop at the house. It's my privilege to be able to assist you during this challenging time."

A lump in his throat made it impossible for Arthur to speak. He nodded, gave another little bow, and went home to stew until it was time to hand his brother over to his fate.

.·˙˙˙·.....·˙

Arthur had been surprised to learn Angus had an automobile, but apparently he was a genius with engines. He'd gotten ahold of a broken down 1918 Model T and claimed he'd built it back "good as new." Of course, having to hand-crank the beast was a bit of an inconvenience, but Arthur wasn't complaining. And it was no trouble at all to persuade Boyd to go for a ride with him after he staggered out of his jail cell. It seemed the night behind bars hadn't done him any harm and had perhaps dampened his spirit. Or maybe that was just the hangover.

When Arthur pulled the borrowed automobile up to Highland Hospital and the orderlies hurried out to take Boyd by both arms, the look on his face was worse than Arthur imagined. He'd pictured Boyd kicking and screaming, fighting to get away. Instead, he simply looked at Arthur with stricken eyes.

"So this is how it is, brother? You'd think I would have learned never to trust anyone by now."

"I'm doing this because I care about you," Arthur said. "I want you to be well."

Boyd grunted. "To be well? Or to be well away from you?"

"I'll visit you as soon as it's allowed," Arthur called out as they led Boyd away. He suddenly looked smaller than before. Beaten. Defeated.

"Don't bother. I expect only family's allowed, and I don't have any of that."

Arthur stood staring at the door his brother had disappeared through. Was he doing the right thing? Even if Boyd hated him forever, wouldn't it be better if he weren't a slave to alcohol? Arthur told himself this was for the best, yet it did little to ease the sense of utter failure dragging behind him like a cloud of exhaust smoke.

# 34

# GENTRY

"Gentry, if you're not going to do this right, I'd just as soon you didn't do it at all." Eulah ripped the seam from a skirt and threaded a needle to begin restitching it.

"I'd rather I didn't do it at all," Gentry mumbled.

Eulah's shoulders sagged. "I need your help if we're going to pay the bills. Food and coal cost money." She huffed. "You've been here five months now, and if you're not going to pull your weight around here, you're going to have to hire out."

Gentry rolled her eyes and began strumming her dulcimer. "How about I play while you work? That'll make it go faster."

Eulah shook her head and bent over the seam, the fight seemingly gone out of her.

After she played three songs, Gentry had Eulah tapping her toe and, if not smiling, at least looking a little less sour. But that was about as much sitting in the cramped apartment as Gentry had in her. She'd always liked wide open spaces, but since failing to find her mother, the urge to be unconstrained was stronger than ever.

She plucked the final notes of "I'll Fly Away" and jumped to her feet. "And that's just what I've gotta do now," she said. "I'll be back in time for supper." She darted out the door without risking a glance at Aunt Eulah, who she felt certain would be giving her the evil eye.

She'd fashioned a strap for her instrument so she could fling it over her shoulder as she rambled around Johnson City. And there were so many interesting places to go and things to see. There were shop windows to look in, restaurants sending enticing smells out to passersby, automobiles chuffing along the street, and people. Gentry had loved rambling through the hills on Grandad's farm, but this was so much better. The energy thrilled her and filled her with longing at the same time.

After an hour or so, she came to a part of town she hadn't visited before. It didn't seem quite as nice. Although there were still big houses, they had peeling paint and missing pickets in the fences. It was a warm day for March, and there were three women squeezed into a swing on a wide front porch. They were laughing and having a big time. Their liveliness tugged at Gentry. She stepped up to the gate and tried to get a better look.

"What you want there, girlie?" one of them called. "Lookin' for work?"

Gentry perked up. Wouldn't that be something? If she went back to Eulah with a job in hand?

She pushed the gate open and peered up at the women. "Doing what?"

All three cackled like it was the funniest thing they'd ever heard. "Honey, if you've gotta ask that, then this ain't the work for you."

Gentry frowned and was about to stomp away when the

plump girl on the end leaned forward and pointed to her dulcimer. "Can you play that?"

"Like angels strumming their harps in the clouds," Gentry shot back.

"Show us."

Gentry sat on the porch steps and began playing "Raven-Black Hair." The women stopped the swing and sat listening like they were under a spell. She transitioned to "The Cuckoo Is a Pretty Bird," singing along this time in her warm, clear alto. When she got to the stanza that went,

> "'O, meeting is a pleasure and parting is a grief,
> An unconstant lover is worse than a thief,
> A thief can but rob you and take all you have,
> An unconstant lover will bring you to the grave . . .'"

she noted that all three women had tears in their lashes.

As she finished the song, a fourth woman—older than the others—stepped onto the porch. "That's some pretty music you're making out here."

"Thank you, ma'am. It's my favorite thing to do."

The woman tilted her head. "Do you know what kind of business this is?"

Gentry furrowed her brow and looked around. "A boardinghouse?"

Peals of laughter burst from the women in the swing. The woman in the doorway just smiled. "Of sorts. These girls"— she waved a hand across the porch—"live here along with two others, and of an evening we often entertain guests. I think your music would be just the thing to put everyone in the right sort of mood." She tilted her head the other way. "Would you be interested in playing for pay?" She quickly added, "Not much pay, but if you like to do it so much, then maybe that wouldn't matter."

Gentry jumped up and did a little jig. "That sounds like just the ticket," she said. "My aunt wants me to help her mend other people's clothes, but I can't hardly sit still for it. Music, though, it lets me dance in my head and with my fingers."

"Mrs. Smythe, are you sure—?" one of the girls began.

The older woman cut her a sharp look. "Oh, I'm sure," she said. Then she turned to Gentry. "When can you start?"

"How about now?"

Mrs. Smythe laughed. "Tomorrow evening will be soon enough. Come around six and we'll fix you up a little." She winked. "You need to look the part of the pretty little songbird."

* * *

"Beans and corn bread again?" Gentry wrinkled her nose.

Eulah plunked down a bowl in front of her. "You start bringing in some money and we'll have all the steaks and fried chicken you want."

Gentry shoveled some food in her mouth and talked through it. "Mebbe I wull."

"What? Don't talk with your mouth full."

Gentry took a swig of buttermilk. "I said maybe I will." She grinned. "I have a job."

"Well, glory be. Miracles do happen. What's this job, and when do you start?"

Glancing at the clock on the wall, Gentry inhaled another spoonful of beans and corn bread and stood. "Guess I'd better go now if I don't want to be late."

Eulah frowned and set her spoon down. "What kind of job starts of an evening? Are you doing shift work?"

Gentry chortled and slung her dulcimer over her shoulder. "They're paying me to play music."

"You're not playing at some juke joint, are you?" Eulah's eyes were wide, and she pressed her hands against the table.

"Nope. I'm playing for a house full of ladies." Gentry shot out the door before Eulah could say anything else, but she saw the look of utter shock, her aunt's mouth hanging open, before she was down the stairs and on her way.

Even so, she was late, arriving at a quarter past six. Mrs. Smythe looked at her with narrowed eyes. "You're a flighty one, aren't you?" Gentry shrugged one shoulder. "Well, I suppose we'll have to see. Just know there's no guarantee this will be a long-term position. Now go with Julie so she can fix you up."

Gentry followed the pretty dark-haired woman wearing a silky dress into a back room, where she fiddled with her hair, put some rouge on her cheeks and lips, and gave her a frilly jacket to slip on over her shirtwaist. Julie stood back and examined her work. "It'll have to do," she said at last. "Ain't you got anything nicer to wear?"

Gentry gave her one shoulder shrug again. "Guess not." She was liking this job less and less.

"Oh well, maybe we can find you some hand-me-downs." Julie giggled. "Some of us don't hardly wear what we've got." She winked and waved for Gentry to follow her back to the sitting room. "Tuck yourself in the corner here and play real soft. Mrs. Smythe said not to play anything too lively or too sad."

Gentry settled on a cushion in a window seat with a sniff. People telling her how to dress, what music to play, she'd thought this would be more fun. Well, she could stand it for one evening anyway. If she didn't want to come back, she wouldn't.

She took a deep breath and began to play anything and everything she could think of that was soft and sweet. As she played, more women came into the room in their fancy—and not altogether proper—clothes. Gentry supposed it was a party. Did they have one every night?

Before long she heard the bell ring, and two gentlemen came in. They sat on the sofas and chatted with the women for a little while, then disappeared up the stairs. Gentry was beginning to get the feeling she might know what was going on, but she couldn't be sure. She'd heard stories about women who *entertained* men they weren't married to, but she'd never thought to meet one. She played without thinking as she watched the evening unfold around her.

Around eight, Mrs. Smythe motioned for Gentry to follow her. She led her to a kitchen where a cup of cider and a slice of cake waited. "Time for you to rest those fingers," she said. "Think you can keep going for another hour or two? The ones who come after ten generally aren't as interested in a soothing atmosphere. They're just here for—" she stopped and pursed her lips—"well, what they're here for."

"I can play some more," Gentry said. "And I think I know what those men are here for."

Mrs. Smythe chuckled. "Do you now? And what would that be?"

"The companionship of a lady to whom they are not married."

Mrs. Smythe laughed harder. "Well now. That's one way to put it. And what would you know about such things?"

Gentry swallowed some cider and broke off a bite of cake. "Not much, and I guess I don't need to know much just to play."

The older woman tucked one of the curls Julie had so carefully shaped behind Gentry's ear. "Right you are, my dear. And now that we understand one another, what say you lay off playing those hymns? They're pretty enough, but maybe our guests don't want to be reminded of Sunday morning on Saturday night."

Gentry grinned and finished her cake. "Yes, ma'am." She decided she was going to like working here after all. She got to do something she loved. She didn't have to do it for hours on end all day long. And watching each little drama unfold in the sitting room was sure enough entertaining.

·˙˙˙˙˙·.·˙·

Gentry eased open the apartment door and slipped through. Aunt Eulah would surely be sleeping by now, and while she normally didn't worry too much about such things, it seemed like trying not to wake her would be a good idea.

A lamp clicked on, and Gentry froze. Eulah sat on one end of the sofa, the quilt Gentry slept under tucked over her knees. "What are you doing up?"

"Waiting for you to come home. I figured if you weren't back by midnight, I'd need to go out and try to find you."

"But I told you I was working."

"At night? For a group of ladies? I wasn't born yesterday. What have you gotten yourself into?" Eulah squinted at her. "Is that rouge on your cheeks?"

Gentry reached into her pocket and pulled out some coins, which she stacked on the table. "I'm not giving you all I earned, but I figure I owe you some of it."

Eulah stared at the coins, and it was like watching a war go on behind her eyes. "Are you working in a brothel?"

"I think so."

Eulah seized the quilt in both hands, crushing it against her bosom. "You *think* so?"

"Yeah, I'm pretty sure that's what it is. But I'm just playing music, and they pay me for it." She nodded toward the money.

"You cannot stay here if you're going back there."

Gentry furrowed her brow. "What do you mean?"

"I mean I've done all I can to try and give you a decent home and provide for you. Took you in when you left that job in Asheville. But this is more than I can put up with. If you're grown up enough to decide something like this, then you're grown up enough to be on your own. Sleep here tonight, but tomorrow you'll need to find someplace else to stay."

Gentry felt fire rise in her and was about to turn on her heel and stomp out when she thought better of it. "Alright," she said. "You're not the first to toss me out like last week's biscuits, and I guess you won't be the last." She set her dulcimer on the table and kicked off her shoes. "Now get off my bed so I can sleep before I'm out on my ear. Again."

Eulah huffed a great breath, shoved the quilt aside, and stalked off to her bedroom. Gentry collapsed on the sofa and burrowed under the quilt. Being sent packing was nothing new, she told herself. At least this time she was choosing where she'd go. Straight to Mrs. Smythe who, Gentry trusted, would either take her in or help her find a place to stay.

# 35

# LORNA

**Johnson City, Tennessee**
**October 1923**

Eulah led them through winding backstreets that left Lorna grateful to have Arthur with his height and broad shoulders keeping pace, if haltingly, with them. The farther they went, the more concerned she grew—especially as dusk fell around them. Was this what Gentry had been reduced to?

"What if she's not there?" Lorna wondered aloud.

"Might not be. But it's getting on toward evening, and that's when she plays her music for the so-called guests." Eulah wrinkled her nose.

They approached a two-story house, set a little apart from its neighbors. While the house had probably been grand once, now it looked like an old woman wearing too much makeup and shabby clothes. Heavy curtains covered the windows with just a narrow crack of light shining onto the porch downstairs, while the upstairs windows had tightly pulled blinds. Coarse voices burst forth when the door opened to disgorge a rough-looking man with a heavy scowl.

"Don't know when you'uns got so picky," he hollered over his shoulder. "I were good enough last week."

A woman's voice pierced the air. "You were richer and better-looking last week." Her comment was met with raucous laughter.

Lorna eased closer to Arthur, tucking her arm through his. He covered her hand and gave it a squeeze.

"This is the place," Eulah said. "Guess you can see what I mean."

Lorna was almost ready to turn back—to come again another time—when she heard the unmistakable lilt of someone playing "Redwing" on a dulcimer. She'd heard that tune before, only last time she'd been annoyed that Gentry was spending more time playing music than perfecting her weaving.

"Come on," Eulah said. "That'll be her."

Lorna felt as though her shoes had turned to lead. The time had come. She was about to confront the person she'd tricked—cheated even. Soon everyone would know the truth about her. She glanced at Arthur, and a wave of shame washed over her. He'd regretted institutionalizing his brother. But she'd done worse. Much worse. Arthur made his decision out of love and desperation. Hers had been made out of selfishness and pride.

They stepped through the door, and a woman with an abundance of crepey bosom showing greeted them. "Well now, this doesn't look like our usual party. I'm going to need to know what's brought you to my door."

Arthur cleared his throat, but before he could speak, Eulah elbowed her way to the front and stood nose to nose with their hostess. "I'm Gentry Cutshall's aunt, and we're here to see her. Nothing else."

The woman pursed her lips. "She's occupied at the moment. You'll have to come another time."

Lorna struggled to process the people, the music, the room draped in soft fabrics, and the aroma of perfume with an undercurrent of sweat. She peered over Eulah's shoulder, trying to get a glimpse of Gentry.

The music stopped. Everything stood still. Then there was a flurry of movement and a scream of recognition. "Arthur? What in tarnation are you doing here?"

And a tall, slender woman was upon them. She laughed and talked a mile a minute, asking a stream of questions and never stopping to hear an answer. She was both Gentry and not Gentry. Lorna couldn't quite grasp that she was there, a grown woman, different and yet the same.

Finally, the woman who seemed to be acting as hostess herded them all to the back of the house, where a cramped kitchen offered a small table and a pitcher of apple cider. Eulah poured them each a drink, which Lorna was pretty sure she'd seen Arthur pay for. She felt the smooth glass pressed into her hand and tasted the tang of the fruity beverage.

Silence fell then, and she looked Gentry in the eye. "We've been looking for you," she said, trying not to stare. Gentry looked good. Surprisingly good. Her eyes were bright, her cheeks rosy. Although her attire wasn't altogether proper. "We went all the way to West Virginia looking for you."

"Why?" Gentry asked. She laughed—a musical sound that pierced Lorna's breast. "You can't want me back in that weaving room. Goodness knows I wasn't much good to you." She smiled. "I've got a life here." She laid a hand on Eulah's arm. "Family. It's more than I ever had in Asheville."

Eulah covered Gentry's hand with her own. "Child. They've brought some news that's good, but I think it might be hard for you to hear."

Lorna opened her mouth to tell Gentry about her mother, but no sound came out. She wasn't sure they had the right person. Couldn't believe this was the flighty, irresponsible Gentry she'd known.

Arthur saw her distress and cleared his throat. "We found your mother, Gentry."

Gentry stared at him, then blinked slowly. "Surely not. I looked and looked for her and finally gave her up for dead." She turned to Eulah. "She's dead, right?"

Eulah sighed. "Your grandad had a mean streak a mile wide. I guess he might've let your ma think you were dead so she'd never come looking for you. And as for you thinking she was dead, well, that was just easier, wasn't it?"

Tears sprang to Gentry's eyes. "Where is she? Why did she take his word for it when he told her I was dead?"

At last Lorna's tongue sprang free. "She's in North Carolina, not far from Asheville. She's a weaver and makes the most amazing fabrics. She was in West Virginia, married your father when she was young, and then after he died I guess she just wanted to get away from your grandfather. He told her you drowned, and she gave up hope. She's been living all alone back in the mountains, making the kind of cloth I could only ever dream of." She took a breath. "And she wants to see you. She sent us to find you."

Gentry stared at Lorna for a minute. Then she busted out laughing. "Well, you've changed some since I last saw you." She wiped away a tear—of sorrow or laughter, Lorna didn't know. "I don't think you ever said as much to me in all the days we knew each other."

"I'm sorry," Lorna blurted. She buried her face in her hands and cried, "I'm so, so sorry."

"I don't know what you've got to be sorry for," Gentry said. "But whatever it is, if you'll fetch me to my mother, I guess I can let it go."

Lorna cried harder knowing she would not be getting off that easy. Arthur pressed a solid hand between her shoulder blades and rubbed a little circle. She gentled under his touch. She'd made this mess, and there was nothing to do but see it through. She accepted the handkerchief Arthur offered, blew her nose, wiped her eyes and forced a smile. "Alright. Let's all get a good night's sleep and head for Asheville in the morning."

Eulah chimed in. "Come stay with me tonight, Gentry. It's time you left this place behind." She turned to Lorna and Arthur. "I don't have much room, but if you're willing to bed down on the floor, I reckon we can all make the best of it for one night."

Lorna nodded her thanks, unable to find any more words. She doubted she'd get much sleep no matter where she laid her head. Tomorrow would be her reckoning day.

# 36

# LORNA

**NORTH ASHEVILLE, NORTH CAROLINA**
**OCTOBER 1923**

Lorna marveled at the changes in Gentry. Not to mention the things that had stayed the same. While the younger woman had an unexpected air of peace that made Lorna question if she really was the same quicksilver girl, she had retained her passionate spirit and tendency to jump from thing to thing.

As the train made its way toward Asheville, Gentry rarely stayed in her seat for more than five minutes together. She gazed out the windows on each side of the train, exclaiming over everything she saw. She'd been out on the platform between cars six times. And now she was itching to go to the dining car "just to look."

Lorna caught Gentry's wrist as she stood to see something on the other side of the car. "Sit a minute and talk to me."

Gentry plopped down beside Lorna and smoothed the simple skirt she was wearing. At the house of ill repute, she'd worn a camisole with a silky jacket open over it. Now, though, she looked demure in her shirtwaist, which was buttoned to her throat. While Eulah had insisted Gentry didn't participate in the "goings-on" at her place of employment, Lorna had to wonder.

"Tell me about your work," Lorna said. "Have you given up weaving altogether?"

The intensity of Gentry's focus on Lorna took her by surprise. She almost wished she'd let the younger woman flit away. It was as though Gentry could see inside her. "Do you mean my playing music at the brothel?"

Lorna flushed, keenly aware of Arthur listening in. "Yes. Unless you had other employment?" My, she sounded prim.

"It was the only work I could find." Gentry laughed. "At least the only work I could find that I wanted to do. I suppose Aunt Eulah would have let me sit and sew buttons on old shirts forever."

"But four and a half years? That's a long time to . . . to just play music." Lorna felt her cheeks heat again. She longed to understand this woman she'd so completely failed to understand the first time they met.

"Oh, it was more than the music." Gentry's answer was blithe, as though it were only natural that she'd been doing more than play music.

Arthur stood. "I'm just going to step out for a breath of air." Then he fled.

Gentry watched him go with mild interest. "Arthur's the best, isn't he?"

"Why, yes, he is." Lorna tried to compose her thoughts. "But what do you mean, it was more than music?"

"It was the girls," Gentry said, leaving Lorna even more confused. "I stayed there for the other girls." She leaned back and tilted her head to one side. "They were a lot like me, only they didn't have music to fall back on. They had it rough and usually ended up there because they didn't have anywhere else to go." She looked down. "I know what that feels like."

"I'm not sure I understand . . ."

"They needed me," Gentry said, moisture coming to her eyes. She turned toward the window. "I don't think anyone had ever needed me before. But they said that when I played, it was a comfort. And maybe my music even made the men—" she hesitated, then shrugged—"gentler, I guess. Anyway, going to see Mama is about the only reason I'd leave them. There are only two girls still there from when I started, and they said I should go." Tears flowed freely now. "They said they'd carry my songs in their hearts, and that would be enough."

Lorna saw that Arthur had slipped back inside and had heard Gentry's last words. He sat beside the younger woman. "It's good when we can help each other," he said. "Even in ways we don't understand."

Gentry nodded, took a deep breath and scrubbed the tears away, brightening in that lightning quick way of hers. "I'm going to the dining car. I've never seen a restaurant on wheels!" And then she rabbited off down the aisle.

Arthur watched her go. "She's the same old Gentry we knew and loved."

Lorna looked at him blankly. The same? Loved? She tried to consider Gentry through his eyes. Had she ever loved Gentry Cutshall? Unfortunately, she could answer that question quite easily. No. She had not. Of course, she couldn't claim to have loved any of the girls she trained or worked with. She tried to remember the last time she'd felt love for anyone. Instantly, the memory of the day she lost her father washed over her. She stood abruptly. "I need some air," she said, then darted for the door Gentry had just passed through. She stood on the rocking platform, gripping the rail as though she might be swept away. And so she might, she thought. Swept away by the memory of all that water.

"Are you alright?" Arthur appeared behind her and placed a gentle hand on her shoulder.

"I'm fine," she whispered. She wanted to accept his comfort, to turn into his arms and let him kiss her like he had on that other train. To feel something that felt like love, even if it wasn't. But goodness, look at all that had happened since then. They'd found Vivian, he'd told her about his brother, they'd found Gentry, and now they were barreling toward her own comeuppance.

"I need to tell you something." She turned to Arthur and grasped the lapel of his coat. She looked into his eyes and saw such compassion there, it took her breath away.

"Yes?"

His eyelashes were so long and soft, framing eyes that said he thought she was wonderful. Amazing. Perhaps even worth loving. A tiny flame lit in the center of her chest at that look, and when she spoke it wasn't what she'd meant to say at all.

"I think you did the right thing for Boyd. He's lucky to have you for a brother."

Arthur took her hand and curled it against his chest. "Thank you. It broke my heart to send him away. Still breaks my heart. But I have reason to hope he'll soon be able to leave the hospital, healthy and whole."

Lorna rested her cheek against his rough jacket. She could almost wish to go to Highland Hospital herself. It would be lovely to be told what to do. Given what to eat. Told when to get up and when to lie down. And perhaps they would let her weave simply for the pleasure of it. She sighed deeply.

Arthur reached down and tilted her chin up so he could see her face. "Thank you for being so understanding."

Lorna pulled back. "Understanding? Who am I to judge anyone for anything? I have no right." She flung her free hand into the air. "I may as well throw stones in a glass house."

Arthur chuckled. "I suppose that's true of all of us. But I can't imagine your sins are *too* severe." His voice was playful, but the words struck at her heart.

She tugged her hand loose. "Arthur, you need to know that I—"

"We're almost there!" The shout reached them even as Gentry barreled onto the platform, nearly knocking them to the rails below. "Come on, you two. I'm finally going to see my mama!" She laughed and clapped her hands. She might be a young woman in her twenties, but the impulsive child was still inside.

Arthur threw his head back and joined in the revelry. "I'd forgotten how you could spout joy when something tickled you," he said and wrapped an arm around Gentry's shoulders. "And you're right. We don't want to waste another moment."

He reached out and grabbed Lorna's hand, pulling her into the celebration on the small platform. For just a moment she thought things would be simpler if she did stumble and disappear under the wheels of the train. The horror of that image shook her, and she forced a smile. Very well then. She'd face the music as it came. There was nothing else to do anymore.

"How much farther?" Gentry strode along, doing little to hide her impatience.

Lorna laughed, remembering she'd had the very same thought the day Vivian first led them up this mountain.

"We're almost there," Arthur said with a grin.

Lorna marveled at the way he never let his twisted foot keep him from doing anything he wanted to do. The thought hit her like a gust of wind. What difficulties had she allowed to alter her course? Before she could ponder that too deeply, they topped out on the bald. Gentry squealed at the view awash in the colors of autumn. The late morning sun played with scudding clouds, so that the russets, golds, and oranges glowed and dimmed like turning a kaleidoscope.

"Have you ever seen the like?" she chortled.

Lorna braced her hands in the small of her back and took it all in. She had seen many a view like this before, but this morning it felt like something entirely new.

Her focus was tugged from Gentry taking in the view to the cabin off to their right. Vivian stood as still as a shadow at the corner of the porch, one hand over her mouth. Even though she couldn't make out the other woman's expression, Lorna could feel love rolling across the field. Then, as though she felt it too, Gentry turned slowly toward the cabin. She stood perfectly still for just a moment.

Then she was all movement. Arms and legs pumped wildly, hair flew, and a wild keening sound sent a chill down Lorna's spine.

Vivian stepped out into the sunlight just as Gentry crashed into her. The two fell to the ground in a tangle of laughter, tears, and words.

Lorna watched, feeling as though she should turn away. Should give them privacy. She felt a hand on her shoulder, and Arthur's solid presence blocked the sun, cooling her skin heated from the climb.

"This might be the most wonderful moment of my life." His voice rasped, and he cleared his throat. "I'm glad we did this."

Lorna reached up and twined her fingers with his. "So am I," she said. And she was surprised to realize it was true.

.·**···.·.·**·

Lorna and Arthur sat on the porch steps, watching Vivian and Gentry approach them arm in arm across the bald. They held on to each other as though someone might try to pry them apart. Lorna had never seen anything more beautiful in her life.

"They love each other," she said.

"Of course they do," Arthur agreed.

"But they haven't seen each other in seventeen years. They don't even know each other anymore."

"I think they do. I think they know each other as only a mother and daughter can."

Lorna felt the air leave her lungs. Had she experienced such a connection with her own mother? She couldn't remember. It was as if the sorrow of losing her mother so unexpectedly had wiped any earlier memories from her mind. "I felt that way about my father," she said without realizing she was speaking aloud.

"Did you? I remember him. He was a good man."

"He was," Lorna said, "but I think I lost him after Mother died. Or maybe he lost himself. It was only when he—" she choked, pain gripping her chest—"tried to save me during the flood that I remembered how he'd been before. And then he was gone."

Arthur shifted closer and wrapped an arm around her shoulders. She leaned into him, remembering the feel of her father's arms that endless day when the water tried to take them all. A memory bobbed to the surface like a cork. When the waters finally took him, he'd held out a hand to her and came as close to cursing as he'd ever done. "Shucks," he cried. "Shucks, shucks" was the last thing she'd heard him say. He'd been sorry to leave her.

She held her breath as Vivian and Gentry drew near. She knew what she needed to do.

"I stole Gentry's designs." The words burst from her as though they could drown out the memories trying to find purchase in her mind. She felt Arthur stiffen, then relax. Vivian just smiled and shook her head.

Gentry, though, could be trusted to speak. "What designs?"

"I didn't steal them exactly. If you remember, I gave you

some money. Not enough." She was babbling but couldn't stop now that she'd started. "The thing is, I claimed them as my own. All those wonderful designs that ensured my place at Biltmore Industries—that helped grow the business. They were yours. Well, your mother's, but I got them from you."

"What are you talking about?" Gentry asked.

Lorna felt Arthur release his hold, but he didn't break contact completely, and she took courage from that.

"When you were trying to raise money to go look for your mother, and I had a little—not as much as you deserved—but I gave you that, and you gave me the designs and . . ." She took a shuddering breath. "And now we're here." She swiped at tears she hadn't realized were falling.

Vivian stepped forward. "Feels good to get it off your chest, doesn't it?"

Lorna nodded, suddenly out of words. She felt Arthur rubbing her back and wished he'd go on forever while also wishing he'd stop because she didn't deserve to be comforted.

"Wait a minute," Gentry said. "You told people those designs were yours?" Again, Lorna nodded mutely. "How could you?" Gentry turned to Vivian. "She stole your designs—can you believe she'd do such a thing?"

Vivian waved her hand as though shooing away a fly. "Oh, I've known about it for years. I saw my work in the catalogs and the ads. I supposed your grandfather Floyd found them and sold them."

Lorna gripped the rough wood underneath her. "You knew?"

Vivian snorted. "You're a weaver. Wouldn't you recognize your own designs? I may choose to live away from the world, but that doesn't mean I never come in contact with it."

"Why didn't you—?"

"Call you out? It didn't matter." She laughed. "In a way, it was nice to see my patterns getting their due. I like the idea of fine ladies wearing my homespun cloth to their fancy soirees." She tilted her head. "And they are my patterns. Doesn't matter if you put your name on them or not. I know the truth."

Gentry's mouth dropped open. "But that's wrong." She stomped her foot at Lorna. "You should be ashamed of yourself."

Vivian laid a gentle hand on her daughter's arm. "And you? Are you a little bit sorry that you let them go so easily?"

Gentry flushed and ducked her head. "I needed to find you."

"And now you have." Vivian wrapped an arm around Gentry's waist, holding her close. "And you and I are going to create more designs together. Patterns like no one's ever seen before."

Gentry's shoulders sagged. "But I hate weaving."

"No," Vivian said. "You hate *having* to weave, just like you hate being made to do anything. I'm going to teach you to weave for the pure pleasure of it." She winked. "And the first thing we're going to do is design a pattern for Lorna that will steal the show."

# 37

# ARTHUR

**HIGHLAND HOSPITAL**
**APRIL 1923**

Arthur flexed his fingers and sharpened the crease in his slacks. He knew he was fidgeting, yet he simply couldn't help it. It had been a little over two months, and he'd finally been given permission to visit Boyd.

He'd been worried about what he'd find, picturing dingy and sterile hospital corridors, barred windows, and other horrors. But when he was directed to Oak Lodge, the residence for male patients, he found a grand shingled building with a wide front porch and sunny verandas, where patients could take in the spectacular view. Inside was equally pleasant with comfortable chairs, low tables, and reading materials ready at hand.

Arthur picked up a book and then set it down again. What was taking so long? Maybe Boyd had refused to see him.

A nurse approached, smiling. Probably to try to soften the blow she was about to deliver. "Boyd's in the games room. Please follow me." She turned and headed down a hallway.

Arthur lurched to his feet and hurried after her, nearly tripping over a fancy rug. She indicated a doorway with a wave. "Right through there, Mr. Westcott."

He had to take a moment to get ahold of himself. Squaring his shoulders, Arthur marched through the door and stared at the spacious sunlit room that looked more like a gentlemen's club than a hospital. He heard the crack of a pool ball finding its target. There. His brother hunched over a table with a cue stick in hand and sank the seven ball in a corner pocket. He glanced up and gave Arthur a nod. Arthur had no idea if it was merely an acknowledgment or an invitation.

"I'll reset the table if you want to play," Boyd said.

Arthur couldn't think of how to respond. Then his words came rushing out. "That'd be great. Yes. Reset the table. I'm a terrible player, but I guess you won't mind that." He pressed his lips together and shoved his hands in his pockets. He denied himself the comfort of stroking the fawn.

Boyd laughed and shook his head. "Glad to see you feel guilty for sticking me here." He gathered and grouped the balls. "You wanna break?"

"Sure." Arthur selected a cue from the rack, took aim, and muffed the shot completely. The cue ball hopped and nearly left the table before rebounding and bumping into the other balls just enough to stir them.

"Man. You aren't any good." Boyd reset the balls, placed the cue, took careful aim, and sent balls flying, including two that went into pockets. He grinned. "I was aiming to show off, but that was mostly luck."

Arthur laughed, and it felt like someone had released a valve somewhere in his chest. "What do you say we go sit on that big ole porch out there?"

"Can't."

"Why?" Arthur was confused.

"I'm not allowed outside on my own." His lip curled. "I still need to be *accompanied*." He said the word like it was dirty.

"Oh. I . . ."

"Yeah. You didn't know. It's a nice cage, but it's still a cage." Boyd shrugged. "We can sit over there by the window. There's a deck of cards if we run out of *conversation*." Again, the last word held a sneer. "Unless you're bad at cards, too."

Arthur took the chair Boyd pointed to, and his brother slouched opposite him. Arthur rubbed damp palms on his pants. "Are they treating you well? How's the food?"

"The food is surprisingly good. And they give you all you want. As for how they're treating me, they treat me like a dog that has to be brought to heel."

Arthur flinched. "But . . . they aren't mistreating you, are they?"

Boyd barked a laugh. "They probably don't think so." He ran both hands back and forth over his short-cropped curls. "You probably wouldn't think so either. But when a man's been used to doing as he pleases, this place is pure torture."

It was on the tip of Arthur's tongue to point out that Boyd wasn't quite a man yet, but he held the words back. "I'm sorry." He reached for the deck of cards on the table and began shuffling them. "But are you . . . better?"

"Better than what?" Boyd bounced right back at him.

"Than before. Than when you were drinking all the time."

"Well, I'm sure as shooting not drinking now if that's what you mean."

Arthur cut the cards and began dealing. "So do you feel better, then?"

"No, Arthur. I do not feel better. I feel rotten. I feel like a bottle of whiskey would fix every problem I've got and set the world to rights." Boyd picked up his cards and began arranging them in his hand.

Arthur stared blankly at his own cards. "Do you want to get off alcohol?"

"Not really. Guess that's why I'm not allowed to go out on my own."

"But wouldn't your life be better if—"

Boyd flung his cards down. "Do you know how I got started drinking?" Arthur shook his head mutely. "Pap gave me my first drink when I was six. By the time I was ten, we drank together most nights. Sometimes there was nothing in the house to eat or drink but booze. When your belly's emptier than a pauper's purse, whiskey will fix you up right quick. You're still hungry, but you don't care so much about it." Boyd stared out the window. "You were the lucky one."

Arthur had to take a moment to compose himself before he could trust his voice. "How's that?"

"They gave you away to somebody who treated you right. Brought you up proper." He turned glistening eyes on Arthur. "Made sure you could get on in the world. Me? I'm no good to anybody."

Arthur wet his lips, trying to think what to say. "I guess you're right about me being lucky. Although it didn't much feel like it when I was just a kid, sent off by myself."

Boyd's laugh was dry and rusty. "Guess they didn't do right by any of us." He shook his head. "I'll tell you one thing. I don't miss either one of them, not even a little bit." He turned his gaze back to the window and repeated himself, more softly this time. "Nope, not at all."

After Boyd returned to his room, Arthur met with Dr. Carroll. "How did you find your brother?" he asked.

"Sober. Angry. Sad. Is he alright?"

Dr. Carroll's smile bordered on patronizing. "Those words describe what he's experiencing well. He doesn't want to be here, so he's angry about that. He's been ill-used by your parents, so he's angry about that. And underneath it all is a depth of sorrow he's not been willing to plumb yet."

"That all sounds terrible," Arthur said. "I thought you were supposed to be helping him."

"And so we are. Addiction is not an easy situation to overcome. It takes time, persistence, and the desire to get better." He frowned. "Your brother has yet to embrace that desire. That's why we recommend a minimum treatment period of eight weeks." He smiled again. "And in some instances— like your brother's—a period of six months or more may be required to restore the body and mind."

Arthur felt his heart tumble. Even with help he didn't see how he could afford to keep Boyd here that long.

"Fortunately, Mrs. Vanderbilt has left instructions for all his needs to be met for however long his rehabilitation requires. Our ultimate goal, of course, is complete abstinence." The smile grew wider. "And we have been quite successful with that in many cases."

Arthur wanted to protest. Wanted to say that he would pay his brother's bills and would ensure that he had the best care possible. But that simply wasn't possible. He would have to swallow his pride and accept this gift. "I'm grateful for all that you and Mrs. Vanderbilt are doing," he said at last.

"Excellent," Dr. Carroll said and stood, clearly indicating that the meeting was over. "I recommend that you visit no more than once every other week. Boyd needs to build trusting, strong relationships with the staff here."

"Yes, sir," Arthur mumbled. As he shuffled out of the office, he thought he might have some inkling about what Boyd meant when he described himself as a dog being brought to heel.

# 38

# GENTRY

**NORTH ASHEVILLE**
**NOVEMBER 1923**

Gentry stood facing the window in her mother's cabin. She wrapped her arms around herself as she watched a chill wind dash across the bald, trying to tear the last of the season's leaves from the trees out back. She could hardly believe she was here. Could hardly believe the years of frustration were at an end. She'd given up not so long ago. Had adopted that houseful of scarlet women as her own and convinced herself she had no need of a mother.

But she did need her mother. That had been clear the moment they saw each other right here outside this window. She'd felt music and color gush over and through her like stepping under a waterfall on a hot day. She'd been drinking Mama in since and couldn't get enough. She doubted she'd ever get enough.

She saw movement and watched Lorna approach from the trail below. She was wearing a striped orange shawl snugged around her neck to keep the cold out. Gentry noted, with pride, that it wasn't so fine or fancy as the ones her mother made.

Mama had asked her former teacher to come see the draft they were working on. She said they might even begin the weaving itself today. Gentry wasn't altogether certain she wanted Lorna's help. This time belonged to her. Her mother belonged to her. And she hated to share, especially since Lorna had stolen from Mama. From them both.

She puffed a breath on the glass so all she saw was a blur of orange as Lorna approached. She thought about how Lorna's mother died, and how her father was swept away in that awful flood. She thought about how Lorna didn't have her gift for music or her mother's gift for design. Gentry had spent the last seven years with women who lost—or who never had—the joy she was blessed with now.

She guessed maybe she could share just a little.

Lorna knocked and slipped inside out of the harsh wind. Mama bent over the crackling fire, scooping fresh embers onto the top of a cast-iron spider perched on its three legs. The rich smell of beef and baking bread filled the air. "Come on in the house," she called. She wiped her hands on her britches and ambled over to the table.

Gentry joined them, although she didn't quite smile in welcome. Mama had forgiven Lorna. It was going to take her some time to catch up. She almost smiled thinking about how the tables had turned. Once upon a time, Lorna was the one holding Gentry accountable for her mistakes, and now . . .

"Come see the draft we've designed." Vivian interrupted Gentry's thoughts. "We're almost ready to start setting the loom."

Lorna bent over the paper, squinting at it, frowning with intensity.

"You can't quite see it, can you?" Mama almost whispered

the words. Lorna bit her lip and shook her head. "Will you trust me?"

Lorna looked into Mama's warm brown eyes as though fighting some sort of battle inside. Gentry wanted to poke her, to wake her up from whatever silly struggle she was going through. Who wouldn't trust Mama?

"I will," she finally said, and it sounded oddly like a wedding promise.

Mama nodded once and moved to the loom. She picked up a cross of turquoise-blue thread. "There's just one problem."

"What's that?" Lorna asked, accepting the hank of thread Mama held out.

"I need you to do the bulk of the work."

Lorna frowned, as did Gentry. "What do you mean?"

Mama held up her hands. "I can hardly hold a thread anymore. I saw a doctor a while back, and he said all my years of working at the loom have damaged the nerves in my hands and wrists. My fingers are numb, and sometimes they tingle like they do when your hand falls asleep." She shook her hands, rubbing one with the other back and forth. "And I drop things. Fine work like threading heddles is just about impossible for me."

Lorna just stood there gaping. Gentry sprang forward, glaring at Lorna. "I'll do it for you, Mama. My hands work just fine."

Mama gave her a ferocious hug that melted any resentment she harbored toward Lorna. "My darling, I love you for offering, and I have hopes that you can be my hands as you become more skilled. But for this design, we need a master weaver." She smiled at Lorna. "And luckily, we have one." She released Gentry and gave her a sly look. "And who knows, maybe you'll learn a thing or two from her while she works."

Gentry sighed. "For you, Mama. I'll try to learn for you."

Lorna set to work right away, soon falling into the rhythm Gentry remembered all too well from her time at Biltmore Estate Industries. And while she didn't remember everything about the actual weaving process, she remembered enough to be a help. She was surprised to find herself enjoying work she had once considered pure torture. Lorna even complimented her on how patient and careful she'd become. She blushed and glanced at Mama to see if she heard.

Vivian interrupted them before long. "C'mon, you two. Let's eat a bite and then we can hit another lick."

They both stretched and moved to the table, where steaming bowls of stew and golden biscuits sat before them. There was also a dish of fresh butter and a jar of apple jelly.

Lorna grabbed her spoon, but Gentry held up a hand. "Mama always blesses the food," she said, bowing her head.

Lorna looked at her like she'd just sprouted horns or maybe a halo, but she put her spoon back down and bowed her head. Mama said the simplest of prayers and then they dug in. The food was every bit as good as it smelled.

"Venison," Vivian said. "Got the deer myself. It's amazing what a woman can do when she puts her mind to it."

Gentry glowed with pride in her independent mother. She knew she was going to learn more than weaving from this amazing woman. And now she could take her time doing it. The thought quieted that place deep in her belly that still spilled over with frustration and hurry on occasion. Maybe one day, Mama would bring stillness to that place altogether.

"I'd love to hear your story," Lorna said. "How you came to be here on this mountain. How you and Gentry got . . . separated." She glanced between them. "Of course, if it's too personal, I understand."

"Oh, Gentry and I have talked through the hard parts," Mama said. "And I do enjoy telling a story." She buttered a biscuit and took a bite as though she needed a moment to think where to begin. Gentry almost expected her to say *Once upon a time.*

"As soon as I saw Elias Cutshall, I was done for. He was looking for new breeding stock for his sheep and ended up with me." She laughed lightly. "Plus some sheep. All the girls were smitten with him, and when he asked me to come with him, I thought I'd won the prize." She glanced at Gentry. "I loved Elias, and he loved me, but life was harder than I expected. His father, Floyd, was a difficult man who didn't take kindly to my unexpected arrival—not to mention that we were soon expecting another mouth to feed."

Gentry sat perfectly still, hanging on her mother's every word. She loved to hear about her father.

"I cooked and kept the house. I helped with the sheep and spun yarn. And finally I persuaded Elias to buy me a loom. Floyd didn't speak to him for a week or more, livid about what he said was a waste of money. But then I began to weave fabric and sell it. That changed the old man's tune. Or rather, he still had little to say, but his eyes lit up every time Elias added some coins to the family purse."

She paused as a shadow crossed her face. "And then Elias died. It was an accident. He was going for help for me—for Gentry, who had a hard time coming into this world." She took Gentry's hand and gave it a squeeze. "I think Floyd blamed us for the loss of his son, and his anger was like another person in that little house. I couldn't bear it and began scheming how I'd take Gentry and run away." She blinked back tears.

"The details are tedious, but after a few years of torture, I devised a plan to slip away while Floyd was driving that year's lambs to market. Only he must have learned what I intended. And when the day came, Gentry was gone. I had our belongings packed and waiting. I had a little money hidden away. All that was left was to wake my girl, wrap her up warm, and hurry down the mountain to the train." She cleared her throat and wiped her eyes. "But Gentry wasn't in her bed. I panicked and searched the house. Then I went outside to search every nook and cranny of the farm. Floyd found me outside the smokehouse. His britches were wet to the knee, and he was shivering." She closed her eyes and took a deep breath. "He told me Gentry drowned in the river. He said she'd been washed away before he could pull her out. Then his eyes turned to ice, and he told me he knew I was planning to run off. He said if I couldn't keep my own child safe, then he wanted me gone."

Silence freighted the room. Gentry twined her fingers through her mother's, tightening the grip. She swallowed hard, a memory rising to the surface of her mind. "I think I told him," she whispered.

Mama stared. "What?"

"That's how he knew. I remember being excited. Going somewhere, riding on a train. I think I told him." Tears tracked her cheeks. "It's my fault he hid me and lied to you."

"Oh, Gentry, you were so little." Mama wrapped her in a hug. She ran her hand over her hair again and again. "I should never have told you. I should have just taken you and left."

Gentry melted under her mother's touch and cried harder. It was almost as if she were that frightened child again, not understanding why her mother had left her. She didn't try to make sense of the pain, just let it run out of her one tear at a time.

"I'm going to step outside for a minute," Lorna mumbled, but Gentry ignored her as she soaked up her mother's love like the dried-out husk that she was. A husk that was slowly coming back to life.

# 39

# LORNA

**ASHEVILLE**
**DECEMBER 1923**

Lorna spent much of her time at Vivian's cabin, weaving the magical fabric her friend had designed. She was also teaching Gentry, who proved to be a much more apt pupil as an adult. They'd found peace together, the three of them, on top of a mountain transforming thread and mountain air into something miraculous. But after Thanksgiving, Vivian had insisted that Lorna take a few days off.

She paced her bedroom from window to door, seeing neither. She felt oddly unsettled. She still wasn't sure of what Arthur thought about her pawning Vivian's patterns off as her own. They had so much history together. She'd scorned him once, and yet he'd been there for her the moment she'd needed him. And the many moments she'd needed him since. And that kiss on the train . . .

She felt as though she'd been asleep for years and was finally waking up. Finally feeling something again. And those tangled, muddled feelings were making her head hurt. She supposed she'd shut herself off from people in some ways. This business of letting people in—Arthur, Vivian, Gentry—it left her exhausted and confused.

She'd begun this journey to save her job and her reputation. To help Biltmore Industries. Now she was without future employment, and the people who had come to matter most to her knew that her reputation as a designer was based on lies. She could still help Biltmore Industries by following through on this commission, but then the business would succeed or fail without her. So, what was left to save?

Which meant she didn't have to pretend anymore. Lorna gasped. The truth was out. Biltmore Industries didn't want her. Once she delivered Vivian's fabric, her commitments would all be met. And at that point no one would have any further expectations of her.

Lorna felt something shake loose deep inside her. She would be free. Free to do anything. She could become a secretary. Or an administrator. Those skills had been thrust upon her at Biltmore Industries. She could write to Eleanor Vance and Charlotte Yale, who had opened the Tryon Toy Makers about forty miles south of Asheville. Perhaps they could use her skills. She laughed. Or perhaps they could teach her to make wooden toys. Wouldn't Arthur get a kick out of that?

Arthur.

Lorna decided it was high time she had a proper conversation with Arthur.

· · · · · · · · · · ·

Angus McTeague greeted Lorna at Arthur's shop. "Are ye here for a hearth brush, or would ye be looking for Arthur?" he asked with a twinkle in his blue eyes.

"The latter, if you please," Lorna answered, surprised to hear how lighthearted she sounded. She ought to be terrified of what the future might bring, and perhaps she would be later, but right now she simply felt light.

"He's in the back fussin' and cussin' over some new project."

"May I?" Lorna asked, moving toward the curtained door at the rear of the salesroom.

"Yes indeed. And see if you can distract him from whatever gloomy thoughts have been eating at him the last day or two."

Lorna paused. "He's worried?"

"Seems to be, and over what I have no notion."

She pushed through the curtain, wishing she'd caught Arthur feeling more upbeat. She wanted to have a serious conversation with him and feared it would be more difficult if he were in low spirits.

"Arthur? Are you busy?"

Arthur pushed something away with a growl. "I am, but I'm only too glad to set this aside. I simply can't get it to look the way I picture it in my mind's eye."

"I know how that is," she said. He gave her a blank look. "My designs. I was never successful on my own because what I could see up here"—she tapped her forehead—"refused to be translated to the loom."

"Ah." Arthur was noncommittal. As well he might be, knowing she'd stolen patterns because of her inability to be original.

"Arthur, I have some things I'd like to say to you." She ducked her head. "Some things I'd like to clear up between us. Do you have time to talk?"

"I'll make time," he said, and she realized the patient, thoughtful man she cared about was back. He smiled. "I'll also make coffee. Would you like a cup?"

"I would."

"I'll just run up to my living quarters and be back in a jiff."

"I'll come with you," Lorna offered.

He looked surprised and hesitated. "I don't suppose it's quite proper . . ."

"Pishposh. What do I care for proper?" Lorna nearly burst out laughing at the look of shock on his face. "Alright, I do care. But I trust you, and I'm not sure I have enough reputation left to bother about it. Especially since no one need know."

"Alright then," Arthur agreed. "Come on up."

In the small apartment above the shop—which was clearly the abode of a bachelor—Lorna sat primly on a settee and watched Arthur make coffee.

"I drink it black, and I'm afraid I don't have any milk. There should be some sugar around here, though . . ." He opened cupboards and drawers, clearly not finding any sugar.

"Black is fine." Lorna preferred quite a lot of milk and sugar, but what she mostly wanted was something to hold while they talked.

Arthur handed her a thick mug of coffee that she cradled between her hands. She inhaled the rich aroma and took a sip of the bitter liquid to demonstrate that she was indeed content with black coffee. Arthur settled into a nearby armchair with worn upholstery and drank from his own cup.

"What would you—?"

"Arthur, I need to—"

They spoke on top of each other. Lorna bit back a nervous titter and smiled. "Let me speak." She smoothed her skirt and sipped the coffee again for something to do. "Arthur, I need to apologize to you."

"For what?"

"First, for the night you took me to dinner at Grove Park Inn." Arthur looked utterly confused. "I know. I'm about two and half years late with this apology. But you were so kind and gracious, so caring, and I . . . I was focused on my own problems. Plus, I accused you of reading a note from Mr. Seely, chastising me." She looked down and peeked at him through her lashes. "I held you at arm's length for a very long time. And then when I did reach out to you, it was only because I needed your help."

"Lorna, I don't mind—"

She held up her hand. "I know. And that makes it worse. I've taken advantage of you." She felt emotion thicken her voice. "In so many ways."

"I don't understand."

"That's what's so wonderful about you, Arthur. You're so purehearted it doesn't occur to you that anyone else's motives might be less honorable than yours." She huffed a breath. "Even when I welcomed"—she felt her cheeks flush—"your affections, I knew your feelings would change once you learned that I am a . . . a liar and a thief." She gripped the mug with both hands and looked out the window so she wouldn't have to see his face. "I am a fool and a hypocrite, and I thought it was high time you knew that I know it."

She felt the settee cushions shift beside her. She turned, her heart thrumming in her chest. Arthur had set his mug down somewhere and was looking at her intently with those warm, caring eyes of his. He reached out and took her mug, setting it on a side table that she realized, fleetingly, he must have made.

She held her breath, waiting for him to speak.

"I don't care."

"What?" She gaped at him.

"I don't care that you've made some mistakes. I don't care that you spurned my advances. And I really don't care what your motive was for letting me kiss you." One side of his mouth curled up. "What I care about is *you*."

Tears began to fall. She sniffled. "Why?"

"Oh, Lorna. Because you are smart and lovely and talented. Because you have a gift for weaving and teaching. Because you have lost so much and yet you carry on doing the best you can." His eyes glistened. "Because you fall down but you get back up." He sighed. "Because I can't help it." He leaned in and kissed her so softly and so tenderly that she couldn't breathe. "Lorna?" He looked alarmed.

She gasped and pressed a hand to her chest. "Arthur, I don't deserve any of this."

He smiled and took her in his arms. "No one does," he said, and this time his kiss told her exactly how forgiven she was.

Back downstairs in the workshop, Lorna tucked a stray lock of hair under her hat. She hadn't dared linger too long upstairs with Arthur, although she would have been content never to leave the nest of his arms again.

Arthur reached out and toyed with a button on her sleeve. "I have a favor to ask," he said, not making eye contact.

"Anything," she breathed.

"Don't be too quick now. Let me tell you what it is." Lorna folded her hands, in part to keep them from reaching for Arthur, and waited. He cleared his throat. "Boyd is being released. I spent Thanksgiving with him at the hospital, and we all agreed he's ready to leave." He flicked a glance at her. "Will you come with me to bring him home?"

Lorna felt her mouth go dry. She'd never even met Boyd. Was he safe? Was he balanced? She gave herself a mental shake. She would not let fear rule her anymore. "Of course I'll come." She smiled. "I'm eager to meet your brother."

Relief washed over Arthur's face. His shoulders relaxed, and he took a deep breath. "Excellent. I've borrowed an automobile. I'll come for you at two tomorrow afternoon."

"I'm looking forward to it," Lorna said. "Now, I'd better leave you to your work."

"Are you sure I can't walk you home?"

"Yes," she giggled and blushed. "I could use some fresh air to clear my head."

He glanced around the room and then took her hand and demurely kissed it. "Until tomorrow then."

She laughed and boldly leaned in to give him a peck on the cheek just as Angus poked his head through the curtain. He looked pleased with what he saw. "Customer out front, Arthur. Interested in a commission."

"Go." Lorna waved him on. "I'll bake a cake to welcome Boyd home."

Arthur grinned and disappeared into the showroom. Angus sauntered over to Lorna. "He's a good 'un. You could do a lot worse."

Lorna laughed, her heart lighter than it had been in years. "And so I have. I suppose it's high time I started making better choices."

# 40

# ARTHUR

**ASHEVILLE**
**DECEMBER 1923**

Angus's borrowed car sputtered to a stop in front of Lorna's house. Arthur sat for a moment, wondering if he was a fool. Taking his dream girl to pick up the brother who probably still thought he'd been betrayed might not have been his best idea. But having Lorna along felt like such a comfort. And surely Boyd would behave himself in front of her, even if he was still angry.

Arthur let his head fall forward onto the steering wheel. Why did he keep trying to manage people? It seemed like he'd been doing it his whole life. Trying to sense what others were thinking or feeling. Trying to stay at least one step ahead so he could meet expectations and avoid problems. The only time he'd risked himself was that dinner with Lorna at Grove Park Inn. And now, with Lorna's apology fresh in his mind—not to mention her lips—he wondered if maybe he should spend more time simply letting life happen.

He straightened in time to see Lorna come out and skip

down the steps, carrying a cake box tied with twine. He smiled, his fretting and worrying dissipating in the light of her presence. He jumped out and helped her into the motorcar, stowing the box in the back seat.

"Where in the world did you get this automobile?" she asked. "It's ever so much better than the one we used in West Virginia."

"Would you believe it belongs to Angus? He's a dab-hand with automobiles and was happy to give us the use of this one today." Arthur hurried around to the front to crank the engine, then hopped in behind the steering wheel. Soon they were chug-chug-chugging off in the direction of Highland Hospital.

They didn't try to speak above the noise of the Model T, but once Arthur parked it below Oak Lodge, he cleared his throat and said, "I'm awfully glad you're here, but I'm having second thoughts about asking you." He reached over and took her gloved hand. "What if Boyd hasn't forgiven me? What if he's rude to you? He's certainly better, or healthier, yet he's still giving me the cold shoulder. I'm afraid I was thinking of myself more than you or Boyd."

Lorna squeezed his hand. "Oh, Arthur. It's high time you considered yourself. I think you're the most selfless person I've ever met. You're always looking out for everyone else. I'm glad you asked me along today. Goodness knows you've been doing favors for me for months now, and this is little enough to repay you." She leaned in and gave him a quick kiss on the corner of his mouth. "And don't forget I used to manage Gentry when she didn't want to learn how to weave. I've seen sulky, sullen behavior before. I think I can handle it."

Arthur smiled. "Thank you." His voice was husky. "Having you here is more comfort than you know."

Lorna blushed and withdrew her hand. "Right then. Let's get on with it."

Once inside the hospital, Arthur had to leave Lorna in the expansive hall with its leather chairs and mission-style side tables. He hesitated, but she made a shooing motion as she settled near a sunny window. He gulped back his worries and followed an orderly to his brother's room.

Boyd was sitting on the edge of a bare mattress when Arthur entered the room. He sprang to his feet and then stood, shifting from foot to foot. He looked from the orderly to Arthur and back again. "What's the play?" he asked.

Arthur tried not to let his brother's nerves affect him. "I've already signed the paperwork. Grab your stuff—I have an automobile waiting outside."

"That's it? No big rigamarole?"

Arthur glanced at the orderly, who nodded. "Yup. That's it."

Boyd wiped his hands on his britches and grabbed a carpetbag Arthur had brought on his last visit. He barreled out the door like he thought someone might try to stop him. Arthur jogged—as best he could—to keep up. "Hey there, Boyd, slow down. I wanted to tell you that I brought—"

Boyd burst into the entry hall and came up short. Lorna stood and smiled. "Boyd, it's so good to meet you."

"You brought a dame?" Boyd asked.

"She came along to keep me company." Arthur felt uneasy. "And she baked a cake to welcome you home."

"Home." Boyd said the single word like he wasn't sure what it meant. "Where's that?"

Arthur reached out a tentative hand to clasp his brother's shoulder. Boyd flinched but didn't pull away. "Home is my place for now. If you think home's somewhere else, we can talk about it."

He felt Boyd's knotted shoulder sag. "Okay. I guess that's alright." He put on a smile for Lorna, and it reminded Arthur of a kid trying on his father's shoes. It was too big and plenty awkward, but at least he was trying.

·····

Lorna cut immense slices of her lemon pound cake while Arthur finished brewing coffee. This time he had plenty of milk and sugar on hand. They sat at the tiny kitchen table in Arthur's apartment. The space was tight, and he wished he'd thought of using the worktable downstairs. It wasn't ideal, but at least there was more room. He squeezed the sugar bowl and creamer next to the cake and distributed mugs. Then he looked for a place to settle the coffeepot and failed to find one. Lorna chuckled and moved the cake to his one section of kitchen counter. He plunked down the pot in its place with relief.

They took turns pouring coffee and adding what they liked to their cups. Then it was just the clink of forks against plates and the sounds of chewing. Arthur racked his brain for something to say. He felt sweat pop out on his upper lip. He sipped his coffee and dabbed his lip with his napkin. He flicked a look at Lorna, who seemed vaguely amused.

Boyd set his fork down. "Thanks for the cake, Lorna. It's real good."

"I'm glad you like it. I don't take time to bake very often."

Arthur's relief at hearing them speak dissolved as silence returned.

Boyd stirred his coffee and took a sip. "Coffee's okay too," he said. He looked Arthur in the eye. "But don't you have anything stronger?"

Arthur felt his eyes bug out. He sputtered, "Are you asking me for . . . I mean, surely you don't mean—"

He stopped short when he saw Boyd's barely contained mirth. Then his brother burst into guffaws. "Had you goin' there, didn't I?" He elbowed Lorna. "Did you see the look on his face? Thought he was going to have to start all over with me."

Lorna laughed so hard, tears leaked from the corners of her eyes. Arthur stared at them both blankly, then began to chuckle. "You scallywag. You had me going!"

Once the laughter died down, Lorna leaned in and addressed Boyd directly. "Honestly, how are you doing?" Arthur could have kissed her for dealing with the elephant in the room. Of course, he wouldn't mind kissing her anyway.

Boyd stared into his coffee cup and spun it around. He huffed out a breath of air. "Honestly, I feel better than I have in a long time. Maybe ever. They fed us real good and kept us busy with plenty of stuff to do. I got to work in the gardens and"—he flicked a look at Arthur—"I liked it. It was good to see something I planted in the spring grow all the way to harvest. Even if it meant I was in that place an awful long time."

"What did you grow?" Lorna asked.

"Flowers mostly, but we had some vegetables, too. Beans, tomatoes, stuff like that."

"Grandma had a garden." Arthur felt lost in another time and place. "She used to send me home with whatever was ripe. Guess she knew Mam and Pap weren't feeding us good."

The brothers glanced at each other and then away again. "That must've been before I came along," Boyd said. "Guess she was dead by then."

"Yeah, she would've been. She died right before I went to stay with Rodney."

"You were lucky," Boyd mumbled. "Getting out of that mess."

Arthur rubbed a thumb along the lip of his cup. "I sure didn't feel lucky. I felt like no one wanted me."

"That preacher wanted you."

"Not really. It was just something he felt like he had to do. He warmed up to me I guess, but I always felt like my place was . . . temporary."

Boyd frowned. "I still think you had it better than me."

"Probably," Arthur said. "I guess you just always wish you could go home again—even when home isn't all that great."

Boyd slumped in his chair. "I miss it. As bad as it was, I still miss the view off the back porch and the way Pap would throw an arm around my shoulder and call me his best drinkin' buddy." Boyd's eyes glistened. Arthur swiped at his own eyes.

Lorna reached out and took each of them by the hand. "Sounds to me like you both had difficulties in your own way. And it seems to me neither one of you could find a better person to listen to you talk about those difficulties." She squeezed their hands. "Maybe that's the trick. You have to let all that bad stuff out before you can turn loose of it."

"They told me something like that back at the hospital," Boyd said. "Called it a talking cure." He chuckled. "I've never been much for talking."

"Me neither," Arthur agreed. "But I'm willing to give it a go if you are."

Boyd sighed. "Guess I need to find something to do other than chase after liquor. Talking to you might be alright."

They sat in silence, only this time it felt comfortable. Arthur had hoped to get his brother back. He hadn't counted on getting a confidant who really and truly understood what he'd been through back in West Virginia.

"Say, how about we put some open shelves in front of that window in the back of the shop? Maybe you can grow things there all year round." He spoke without giving it too much thought, and then he worried he was pushing too hard. He didn't want Boyd to think he was trying to keep him occupied lest he start drinking again. "I mean, only if you want to."

Boyd released Lorna's hand and cradled his coffee cup. "You know, I think I'd like that. And I guess I can still help you around the shop." He hesitated. "If you want me to."

"More than anything," Arthur said. "I've just about got your toolbox filled up if you want it." Boyd didn't speak, but his smile was exactly the response Arthur had been hoping for.

# 41

# LORNA

And still there wasn't any word about a wedding. If the whole business turned out to be a figment of Mrs. Harshaw's imagination, Lorna didn't know what she'd do. Would the society matron still want the cloth? Would it do Biltmore Industries any good if it wasn't a gift for a Vanderbilt? The notion that all of this might be for nothing was a crushing weight.

And yet what else was there to do but finish the commission? Lorna practically moved in with Vivian and Gentry to work on it. As she watched the pattern come to life beneath their fingers, Lorna almost wished she could work on it all day and all night. It was like uncovering treasure, and she was addicted to the slow progression of colors and patterns unfurling across the loom.

Initially, she'd been worried about Gentry helping, remembering the girl as prone to missing heddles when setting the warp and bungling designs when she got distracted. But this new Gentry was calm and steady. At first, Lorna thought it was simply that she was older, but the more her story spilled out, the more she realized Gentry had been transformed. She'd chosen to stay at the brothel playing music because she'd finally felt needed. Instead of being stuck with a cold and angry grandfather or shipped off to learn to weave, her natural gift of music had blessed people whose lives were impossibly hard. Gentry told about girls her own age who'd been neglected, mistreated, and forced into letting their bodies be used in the meanest of ways.

"I guess it made me grow up—seeing that," Gentry said. "I thought I'd had a hard life, but at least I had a way to make a living without having to . . ." She sighed and shook her head. "The least I could do was stick it out with them. To be there with them when they cried and when they thought they couldn't stand it another minute."

Despite Gentry's trials, it was hard not to be envious. She had been reunited with her mother. Her childhood sorrow had been redeemed. Lorna would never be able to fill the hole her parents had left in her life. There was no mistake about them being gone. No chance of a miraculous reunion.

So, as she worked the treadles and sent her shuttle flying, she allowed herself to daydream. It wasn't something she'd done much of in the past. She supposed with all the losses she'd experienced, dreaming of what might be felt too risky. But the mother-daughter reunion unfolding before her eyes each day gave her unexpected hope. And Arthur gave her fodder for dreaming. What if they were to wed? They could have a family of their own. She could work in his shop. Or she might even acquire a tabletop loom to make smaller items like scarves and table runners that could be sold alongside Arthur's pieces.

She imagined working at a loom in Arthur's workshop. He'd lay down the piece of wood he was carving so he could lean over her shoulder. He'd sweep the hair from the nape of her neck and—

"Lorna!" She felt a hand on her shoulder and blinked her eyes. "Goodness, I called your name three times." Vivian stood laughing at her elbow. "Woolgathering while working with wool. That's a good one."

Lorna flushed and stilled the loom. "Sorry. I was a bit lost in thought there."

"It's remarkable to me that you can be a million miles away and never miss a change in the pattern." Vivian admired the rows Lorna had added to their fabric. "I may have a gift for design, but you have a gift for bringing designs to life."

Lorna grimaced. "I suppose, but your gift is so much more impressive."

Vivian frowned. "I don't see that. You weave faster and more accurately than I ever have." She laughed. "Than Gentry can ever hope to. It seems to me our gifts work together to get the job done, and that's what matters. In a hive the drones are just as important as the queen. There wouldn't be honey without all of them working together."

Lorna stood and stretched. "Are you calling me a drone?"

"Perhaps I'm calling you a queen bee. Now, come eat before the food gets cold."

They joined Gentry at the table for a simple lunch of vegetable soup and hot bread. Lorna ate with relish, finding the work, the mountain air, and the company all working to increase her appetite. A thought struck her. "Gentry, what happened that time you went to West Virginia to look for your mother? I haven't heard that part of your story yet."

Gentry slurped her soup and nodded. "I worked in a hotel there for a while. But I didn't find Mama, and nobody seemed to know anything about her."

Vivian frowned. "When was this?"

Gentry waved her spoon in the air. "I don't remember. It was whenever I left Asheville."

Lorna puckered her lips. "That would have been . . . October 1916. Yes, that's when you gave me your mother's drafts for train fare." She shifted uncomfortably and darted a look from mother to daughter. "Can I tell you again how sorry I am about that?"

"It's forgiven." Vivian waved a hand. "Are you sure it was October of that year?"

"Quite sure. I was still reeling from the flood and losing my father."

Gentry snapped her fingers. "That's right. It wasn't long after the big flood."

Vivian shook her head. "But Sabine was still there in October. She didn't leave until February of the following year."

Gentry's spoon clattered in her bowl. "No one knew anything about you. I asked everybody."

"What hotel?" Vivian asked.

Gentry thought for a moment. "Let's see . . . it had a funny name. The same as the town. It was hard to say until you'd heard it a few times."

"The Hotel Ronceverte?"

Gentry smiled. "That's it!"

Vivian paled. "Sabine sold butter to that hotel. We wrote to each other now and again, though not as often as I would've liked. She had a hard time forgiving me for marrying your father. It was only after we both became widows that we reconnected."

"I asked everyone while I was there." Gentry shrugged one shoulder. "I wasn't there all that long. Maybe I missed her."

"I suppose, yet it's just hard to believe word wouldn't have gotten to her that you were asking around. The people at the hotel wouldn't have remembered me, but they would have talked about a girl asking questions."

"There was one woman who said she knew the Cutshall family. She told me they were long gone, and then she bought me a ticket for Johnson City. That's why I left."

"What was her name?" Vivian asked.

Gentry furrowed her brow. "I don't think she ever said."

"What did she look like?"

"She had hair about the color of mine and was kind of pretty. I don't remember much else. Oh! She wore the prettiest purple shawl with a silver pin like a little sword. I really liked the pin."

Vivian pushed her bowl away and braced her hands on the edge of the table. "I can't believe she would . . . that she would intentionally . . ." She couldn't seem to get any more words out.

Lorna reached for her friend. "Vivian, what's the matter?"

"That was Sabine. That pin—I know precisely the one. Not to mention the purple cloth. It had to be her. And she . . . she kept us apart. I knew she was angry, but . . ." Vivian stood abruptly. "I need to go for a walk. I'll . . ." She turned and went out the door like a sleepwalker.

Gentry turned confused eyes on Lorna. "I don't understand."

"Neither do I," Lorna said, "but it sounds like that might have been your aunt Sabine at the hotel. And for some reason, she didn't help you find your mother."

"But that was—" Gentry counted on her fingers—"more than seven years ago. Do you mean she could have told me where Mama was that long ago?"

"I think so."

"What a horrible thing to do! I wish I could tell her what I think of her." Gentry scowled and thumped the table.

"She's dead now," Lorna said. "She died of cancer a few years ago."

"Oh." Gentry's face clouded. "I don't know how to feel

303

about that." She looked out the window, where they could see Vivian walking along the crest of the bald, head down, hands clasped behind her back. "I'll try not to be glad that she can't make Mama mad ever again."

.·⁺¨˙˙·…·˙

Lorna had an idea. On her next trip home, she gathered all the scraps of Sabine's fabric that Virgie had given her. She took them to Vivian's cabin and spilled them out on the table. "There's a woman in Weaverville who befriended your sister. Sabine gave her a trunkful of fabric, and these are the leftover scraps."

Vivian sifted through them mechanically. She smoothed each piece and stacked them together. Tears welled in her eyes.

"I hope this isn't too painful," Lorna said. Had this been a mistake?

"We wrote to each other now and again. And I thought when she came here, we might become true friends again. But it was obvious something was eating at her. The few times we visited she was so stiff, so uncomfortable." Vivian flicked a look at Lorna. "Now I suppose it was guilt. She knew my daughter was in Johnson City and yet she never told me." Tears began to streak her cheeks. "How could she?"

"I suppose she was angry and hurt," Lorna said. "Pain can make us do inexplicable things. I suppose it would have been awfully hard to confess what she'd done. I certainly know the truth of that."

"These are mine," Vivian said, laying a hand on the smaller of the two stacks she'd made. "The rest must be Sabine's." She flipped through them and tugged out the sunrise fabric. "This one is particularly lovely. Sabine had a real gift."

"Virgie made a skirt out of that and took it to show Sabine. She told me what your sister said when she saw it. I was so struck by it that I went home and wrote it down." Lorna pulled out a small notebook. "She said the fabric reminded her that 'weeping may endure for a night, but joy comes in the morning.'"

Vivian pressed a hand to her lips. "Oh my. That's what we used to say when we were angry with each other. Being angry was like the sun setting in our hearts, but then . . ." She choked on a sob. "But then love would win. It would always win—like the sun rising again in the morning." She crumpled into a chair, pressing the fabric to her face.

Gentry came into the room and rushed to her mother's side. "What is it, Mama?" She glared at Lorna. "What did you do?"

Vivian looped an arm around her daughter's waist. "It's alright, dear heart Lorna has done the most wonderful thing. She's brought me a scrap of forgiveness." She held up the fabric. "And I expect we can fashion it into something that will keep us warm for a long time to come."

Gentry shook her head. "I don't know what you mean when you talk like that."

Vivian laughed through her tears. "No, I expect not, but I plan to teach you. Your heart is wild and a little skittish yet. But we have time. Thanks to Lorna and Arthur, we now have time."

# 42

# GENTRY

Gentry watched as Lorna freed the fabric from the loom. She had to confess, she'd come to enjoy working on this project with her former teacher. Now Lorna moved with something like reverence, as if she were in a church.

"This is my absolute favorite moment in handweaving," Lorna said in a hushed voice. "Up until this point, the cloth is stationary, bound by the rollers. But with the snip of my shears"—she demonstrated, snick-snicking the air—"the cloth becomes pliable, ready to be shaped into something wonderful."

*Something fit for a bride*, Gentry thought.

"Is Mrs. Harshaw planning to have it made into something, or will she just give Cornelia the whole cloth?" Vivian appeared at Lorna's elbow.

"I don't know," Lorna answered as she freed the cloth with a flourish. "Frankly, I wonder if she might have been mistaken about a wedding. The Vanderbilts haven't even announced an engagement. Surely if Cornelia was getting married in a few months, the whole world would know."

"Well, I'm certainly not one for listening to gossip, so I wouldn't know anything about it."

Lorna puddled the yards and yards of fabric on the table, and they all admired the play of color. Gentry reached out to touch it, then froze. "Oh! It reminds me of a tune!" She darted into the bedroom she shared with her mother and reappeared with her dulcimer. She sat and began playing the music conjured by the cloth.

Lorna cocked her head as if trying to place the song. Then in a clear, warm alto, Mama began to sing:

> "'Walking in sunlight all of my journey,
> Over the mountains, through the deep vale,
> Jesus has said, I'll never forsake thee.
> Promise divine that never can fail.'"

Tears spilled from Lorna's eyes. She pressed a hand to her mouth as Gentry joined in, singing harmony to her mother's melody:

> "'In the bright sunlight, ever rejoicing,
> Pressing my way to mansions above.
> Singing His praises, gladly I'm walking,
> Walking in sunlight, sunlight of love.'"

Yes, the song did echo the fabric. Mama had designed it so that the colors shifted and changed as they wove. It started with deep moody blues—the French Broad River. Then it shifted to warm greens with a hint of brown wreathed in wisps of bluish-gray—the Blue Ridge Mountains. Finally, it ended in oranges, reds, and pinks—the sunset view from the back of Biltmore House. Mama had captured the thing folks said

George Vanderbilt loved most about his North Carolina castle, the setting and the view he'd been so intent on capturing.

When she first arrived at Biltmore Estate Industries, Gentry had heard a story about how Mr. Vanderbilt first built a tower where he hoped to build his château. He climbed it to make sure his castle would capture the view he wanted of the mountains unfolding all the way to Mount Pisgah.

*Sunlight of love.* Gentry gazed at the fabric and thought she could see the shifting light as clouds moved across the landscape, highlighting now this rise, now that hollow. It was breathtaking.

She suspected Lorna could see it too when she looked up at Mama and asked, "How did you know to do this?"

Mama shook her head. "I couldn't say. The notion came and I let it." She shrugged. "I wish I could teach you both how to do it. But I think I'm simply the vessel for something passing through." She settled a hand on Gentry's shoulder. "And often the colors are accompanied by music in my mind. This one seems able to hear the music, as well."

"It's perfect," Lorna breathed.

"Not quite," Mama said with a smirk. She dug through the cloth until she came to a section where the mountains turned to sky. "Here. I added a flaw." She smiled. "My particular flaw. The design is yours to claim, but I'll always know where it came from by this."

"I can't claim this as mine," Lorna said.

Gentry set down the dulcimer. "Why not?"

Lorna shook her head. "Because it's not."

"Those others you claimed weren't yours." Lorna was being silly. Why lie then but not now?

"That was different."

"How?"

Lorna huffed a breath. "It just was. I was desperate then. I had to claim them if I wanted to get ahead."

Gentry did her one-shouldered shrug. "And now you can get ahead again. And this time you have Mama's permission." This seemed so simple. Why was Lorna making such a fuss about it?

Lorna looked like she might burst into tears. "I don't deserve your kindness and generosity. And I certainly don't deserve to claim anything as fine as this."

Gentry burst out laughing. That was rich. "My whole life I've been a pain and a bother to just about everyone." She waggled a finger at Lorna. "You would have gladly tossed me into a dye vat when I couldn't get anything right. Then I ran off, and poor Aunt Eulah probably wanted to murder me more than once." She spread her arms wide and wrapped them around her beautiful mother. "And now look at me. I've got Mama, a place to live, work I don't mind, and music to play. I guess if I'd waited to deserve all this, I'd still be waiting." Why couldn't Lorna accept the good being poured out in front of her?

Lorna just stared at Gentry like she'd never seen her before.

Mama hugged her back. "I could tell a similar story about what I don't deserve." She gave Lorna a watery smile. "Don't look a gift horse in the mouth, my dear. Just take the fabric and see what happens."

Silently, Lorna nodded and gathered up the cloth, carefully rolling it and wrapping it in brown paper. "Thank you," she said at last.

A stab of sympathy pierced Gentry. When she'd been given this gift of reuniting with her mother, she'd grabbed it with both hands and held on for all she was worth. Even now she didn't want to loosen her grip even a little for fear it might slip away again. Lorna, on the other hand, didn't seem to know a good thing when it landed in her lap. Maybe she'd seen too many good things slip away—her mother, her father,

her reputation. Gentry supposed she could see how it might be hard to trust anything anymore.

"Lorna," she said, "thanks for not drowning me in a dye vat when you had the chance. If you had, I would have missed this." She nestled against her mother's side. "Maybe it's your turn for something good to happen." She held out her free arm, motioning for Lorna to join them.

With a sob, the older girl rushed to them and fell into their mutual embrace.

# 43

# ARTHUR

ASHEVILLE, NORTH CAROLINA
FEBRUARY 1924

Arthur watched Lorna arrange the fabric across the table one more time. She'd asked if she could invite Mrs. Harshaw to his shop to collect her commission. He wasn't sure why she wasn't handing off the fabric at Biltmore Industries. Then again, he considered that Lorna hadn't gone to the weaving room for quite some time. She'd mentioned to him that she was taking a sabbatical, but now he wondered if perhaps she and Mr. Tompkins had parted ways. He wanted to ask but told himself it wasn't really any of his business.

The finished cloth was stunning. He'd never seen anything like it before. And yet Lorna seemed nervous.

"Mrs. Harshaw is going to be thrilled when she sees this," he said, touching a fold of the undulating fabric. "It's incredible."

Lorna bit her thumbnail. Something he'd never seen her do before. "Yes. It is exceptional. I'm sure she'll be delighted."

Arthur tilted his head. "Then why do you seem uneasy?"

"Do I?" Lorna pressed her hands to her stomach. "I suppose it's been such a long journey, and I can hardly believe we're finally at the end."

Arthur smiled and took one of her hands. It was cold and clammy. He gently rubbed her fingers. "You've worked so very hard, and you've accomplished what you set out to do. I wish I could be there when Cornelia sees this for the first time."

Lorna tugged her hand away and fiddled with the cloth some more. "Yes, well, there hasn't even been an engagement announced. I'm not altogether certain Cornelia is getting married."

"Rumors suggest she is." Arthur flushed at Lorna's look of surprise. "I don't mean to listen to gossip, but the ladies who come to shop often chatter on and, well"—he shrugged—"one can't help but overhear. They say he's British royalty."

Lorna raised her eyebrows. "Wouldn't that be something. A prince come to live in the North Carolina castle."

"I don't think he's a prince, but you never know."

Lorna knotted her hands together as though to stop them from fussing with the cloth again. "I doubt a royal will appreciate our mountain homespun." She frowned. "What if Mrs. Harshaw changes her mind? What if this isn't the right sort of gift after all?"

This time Arthur captured both her hands and tugged her closer. "Then Mrs. Harshaw is a fool." He pressed a quick kiss to her mouth and saw a smile bloom, then just as quickly fade away. He released her before she could pull away again.

The bell jangled above the door, and Lorna turned with a smile he could tell she had pasted across her face. Mrs. Harshaw swept into the room wearing a broad hat with an oversized bow that Arthur wasn't sure was her wisest fashion decision.

"Mrs. Harshaw, it's lovely to see you," Lorna said. "And thank you for meeting me here."

The matron waved a dismissive hand. "It's closer to my home, so really it was quite convenient." She bore down on the table covered in fabric. "Is this it? Is this what I have waited for so long to see?"

Arthur saw Lorna go pale and stiffen her spine. Was Mrs. Harshaw not pleased?

"Yes, ma'am. It's intended to be representative—"

"Of the estate's Blue Ridge Mountain view," Mrs. Harshaw inserted. She tugged off her gloves and ran her fingers over the fabric. "Oh, my dear, it's absolutely exquisite."

Lorna exhaled and sagged against the edge of the table. Then she recovered herself and smiled, more genuinely this time. "Thank you. I'd hoped it was what you had in mind."

Mrs. Harshaw got a glint in her eye. "And it will most certainly be the only gift of its kind." She looked around the room as though someone might be spying. "The engagement is to be announced within the month." She lowered her voice another notch. "I understand the wedding will be soon thereafter."

"Shall I wrap this for you?" Arthur asked.

"That would be lovely. We don't want anyone to see it before it's time." She turned to Lorna. "I'll deliver the payment to Mr. Tompkins, but here's a little something for your trouble, my dear." She slid an envelope across the table to Lorna. "Your design is exceptional. I'll be sure to tell Mr. Tompkins what a treasure he has in you." She tapped the envelope. "And I'll be certain to send my friends to you for future commissions."

Arthur watched emotions play across Lorna's face, but he couldn't pin down exactly what she was feeling. Elation? Pride? No, it was a look of . . . determination.

Lorna pushed the envelope back toward Mrs. Harshaw. "I appreciate the gesture, ma'am, but I can't accept this."

The matron frowned, clearly unaccustomed to being thwarted in any way. "Whyever not?"

"It's not my design."

Now Arthur could clearly read the look on Lorna's face. Fear.

"What do you mean? Didn't you weave this fabric?"

Lorna swallowed, and for a moment Arthur didn't think she'd get any more words out. "I helped, yes, but a dear friend designed the fabric, and it was woven on her loom. All of my best patterns are actually hers."

Mrs. Harshaw huffed a breath. "I don't understand you, and I don't have time for this kind of nonsense. Is this person going to come forward and claim the fabric? Is my gift for Cornelia somehow in jeopardy?"

Lorna blinked. "No, ma'am, the fabric is yours, and there's not another like it anywhere. She was happy to let me have it. It's just that I thought she should get the credit. Not me."

"Oh, for goodness' sake, what do I care who came up with the design? Just so long as it's exclusive to my purpose."

Arthur finished wrapping the cloth as the two women spoke. Mrs. Harshaw scooped up the oversized package and nodded toward the envelope still lying on the table. "Do with that what you will. Give it to this other weaver. Keep it for yourself. It matters not to me." She spun toward the door and was about to exit when she turned. "Although perhaps I won't be sending you additional commissions. This has all been a bit too dramatic for my taste."

The bell jangled, and she was gone. Lorna sagged against the table.

"Why did you tell her?" Arthur asked.

Lorna buried her face in her hands and spoke through her fingers. "I don't know. I just couldn't stand pretending anymore."

Arthur eased to her side and placed a tentative arm around her shoulders. "If it matters, I think you did the right thing."

Her hands fell away. "Do you really?" She turned her face up to him.

He reached over and caressed her cheek. "I do," he said, his voice husky. "I'm proud of you." He was about to kiss her when she turned away.

"I don't see how you can be. All I did was confess that I lied. That's hardly admirable."

Arthur turned her face back to him. "I think it's often harder to confess something than it would have been to do the right thing to begin with. What you did was brave." He smiled. "And right. It's never too late to do what's right."

Her eyes shone with such hope that he couldn't help himself, and this time he did kiss her. He felt the tension drain away as she relaxed in his arms. "I don't deserve you," he whispered.

Lorna stiffened and pulled free. The tears he suspected had been close all afternoon spilled over. "No," she said. "I don't deserve you." She turned, ran through the workshop, and disappeared out the back door.

Arthur stood there in shock. What had he done wrong? Then he charged toward the door, determined to go after her and correct his mistake.

Angus entered as he was reaching for the knob. He laid a restraining hand on Arthur's arm. "Let her go, my friend. She needs to sort this out for herself." He chuckled. "Not that I've had much luck with women, but most of my bad luck has come from pushing in where I wasn't wanted. Give her some time, then go after her." He patted Arthur's arm. "She's still got some sorting to do on her own."

.· ˙ ˙ ˙ ·..... ·˙

"What's the deal with you and Lorna?" Boyd liked to talk as he painted the wooden toys they sold in the shop. "You know, the girl who came with you to get me." Boyd slid his brother a cagey look. "Because you were afraid to come on your own."

"How did you guess?" Arthur said with a chuckle. "But as to 'what the deal is,' I don't know."

"She likes you, but she's afraid." Boyd spoke as if his observation should be obvious to anyone.

"Afraid of what?"

"Probably that you'll die or run off on her or something like that."

Arthur set his carving tools down. "What in the world makes you say that?"

"I've been talking to her—she's nice. Anyway, her mother died real sudden. Then her dad died in that big flood. Man, that's a heckuva story. And since then, it sounds like she hasn't had anyone she could lean on." He dabbed some more paint. "Guess I know what that's like."

Arthur felt like he'd been delivered a blow. "And now I think her job's in danger."

"Oh, she doesn't have a job. That Mr. Tompkins told her to hit the road a while back."

Arthur slumped onto a stool. "That's why she had Mrs. Harshaw come here. How do you know all of this?"

Boyd set down his brush and eyed his brother. "For somebody who's sweet on Lorna, you don't seem to talk to her much."

Arthur hung his head. Boyd was right. He'd been so busy trying to wrangle the lives of the people he cared about that he hadn't stopped to find out what *they* cared about.

"Boyd," he said, raising his head, "how's it going for you now that you're not—"

"In the loony bin?" Boyd finished for him. He pulled another toy close and dipped his brush again. "Mostly good," he said, then focused on his work. "I guess there's a time now and again when I get kind of thirsty for something more than water to drink."

Arthur wet his lips. He'd opened this can of worms. He'd better be willing to sift through it. "You haven't, uh, acted on that, have you?"

Boyd frowned. "Of course not."

Arthur took a breath. He wasn't doing this right. If he wasn't careful, he was going to make things worse. "I didn't think you had." He cracked his knuckles, drawing a narrow-eyed look from his brother. "I just want you to know that you can . . . well, if you're ever having a hard time, you can talk to me. Like Lorna said that day we picked you up."

Those eyes like slits again. "Can I? You won't get mad and stick me in that place again?"

Arthur blew out a breath. "No. I'd like to think you and I could work it out without needing the doctors at Highland Hospital."

Boyd nodded slowly. "That'd be good. We could just take care of each other."

A lump rose in Arthur's throat. "Yeah." He laughed, and the tension began to slide away. "After what you just told me about Lorna, guess maybe I need some taking care of."

Boyd chuckled. "Women. They sure do cause a lot of trouble."

"That they do," Arthur said with a wink. "The very best kind."

# 44

# LORNA

**ASHEVILLE, NORTH CAROLINA
MARCH 9, 1924**

WASHINGTON, MARCH 5

*The rumored engagement of Miss Cornelia Vanderbilt, daughter of the late George W. Vanderbilt, to the Hon. John F. A. Cecil, first secretary of the British Embassy, which has occupied the attention of society for several weeks now, still lacks official confirmation by reason of Mrs. Vanderbilt's absence from town but is accepted as fact by friends of the young people.*

Lorna lowered her borrowed copy of the *New York Times*. There it was. Cornelia was indeed planning to wed. The article went on to note that the engagement was expected to be short, with the wedding taking place in the early summer. Well then. She'd completed her commission with little time to spare.

She skimmed the article again. It seemed this John Cecil fellow was royalty of a sort. Apparently, he was in line for a barony and a marquisate. Not a prince certainly, but as close as they were ever likely to get here in the mountains of North Carolina.

"Whatcha reading?" Boyd called from the front door. He and Arthur had gotten in the habit of stopping by on Sunday afternoons for a visit. Lorna found she enjoyed the routine, not to mention the company.

"I'm reading about Cornelia Vanderbilt being engaged. Of course, this is Wednesday's paper, so I suppose I'm the last to know."

"I heard the official announcement was made at a fancy dinner up at the big house the other night," Boyd chimed in. "Having money sure does make your life complicated."

Arthur burst into laughter. "That's one way to look at it." He settled into a wing-back chair in Lorna's front room. It was where he always sat, and Lorna had begun to think of it as *Arthur's chair*. Dangerous thinking, she told herself.

"Anyone want to take a guess as to the wedding date?" he asked.

"The article says early summer, so I'm guessing June fifth," Lorna said.

"I sure hope you don't expect me to play along with a stupid game like this," Boyd grumbled.

"The wedding will take place at All Souls Cathedral at noon on Tuesday, April 29." Arthur made the announcement as though trumpets had preceded it.

"And how in the world do you know that?" Lorna wondered. "That's not even a two-month engagement."

"I've been asked to do some work on the estate in preparation for the big day." He grinned. "I can't tell you all the details—I've been sworn to secrecy—but they need a special curved table for the reception, which for some reason they call a 'wedding breakfast.' And I'm proud to be the man for the job."

"I think that's a British tradition—to call the reception

a wedding breakfast, even though it's later in the day. Will Reverend Swope perform the ceremony?" Lorna asked.

"He will. I expect there will be a great deal of fuss, which Mary is excited about as the rector's wife, but I suspect Rodney could do without all the hubbub. He said that in all his twenty-five years of service at All Souls, he's never had an order quite this tall."

Boyd tilted his head. "Is that how long you've been in Asheville? As long as Reverend Swope's been with the church?"

Arthur nodded. "I remember the day Mr. Vanderbilt came to offer Rodney the job." He fished the carved fawn out of his pocket. "I was carving this."

Boyd held out his hand, and Arthur handed over the figure. "It's pretty good, but I've seen you do better, brother."

"I should hope so—I was only nine when I carved that. Well, almost nine." Arthur chuckled. "Mr. Vanderbilt admired the doe I'd already finished, and I haven't seen it since."

Lorna frowned. "Are you saying he took it?"

"He did. I suppose he might have given it to Rodney. I never thought to ask."

"That's funny," Boyd said. "A rich man like that taking a carved deer. Guess he owes you one."

"He probably just forgot he had it," Arthur said with a shrug. "It surely doesn't matter now." He took the fawn back from Boyd and repocketed it.

Lorna watched him, feeling pensive. "Have you ever thought about going back to West Virginia?"

Arthur ran a hand through his curls. "I have thought about it a few times over the years. Thought about going back and trying to run down some of my brothers or sisters. I remember some of them better than others. But it never seemed like the right time." He looked at Boyd. "And now I have my brother here. Maybe when I thought about going back, what I really was after was having a family." He grasped Boyd's shoulder. "And now I've got that." He turned his gaze on Lorna. "In more ways than one."

She flushed, afraid to hope he meant her. "I've run out of family," she said. She aimed to sound lighthearted, but the words were pitiful. She wished she could take them back.

Arthur reached out a hand, and she hesitated before taking it. "I hope you'll count us as your family," he said. "I've spent too many years thinking I needed blood relatives to be part of a true family." He winked at Boyd. "And while blood kin is great, it turns out my family's been right here with me the whole time." He turned soft hazel eyes on Lorna. "It's been Rodney and Mary, Angus, Gentry, and you."

Lorna saw love in his expression and felt the warmth of his caring heart. And while the notion of Arthur as family was appealing, she knew it wasn't brotherly affection she longed for. Oh, she might like that from Boyd, but what she wanted from Arthur was so much more. She wanted to be chosen, to be his, to be bound together with him as one flesh forever.

The surge of emotion was more than she could manage. She broke his gaze and tugged her hand free. She felt relief and disappointment in equal measure. "Thank you, Arthur. You are like family to me, as well."

Lorna struggled to sleep that night. She couldn't stop thinking about Arthur and weddings and what it meant to be family. She finally fell asleep in the small hours of the morning, waking late to the sound of something dropping through the mail slot in her door. She dressed and stumbled downstairs, grateful Arthur couldn't see her just then.

A cream-colored envelope lay inside the door. She stooped to pick it up, feeling stiff from her restless night. It was from Biltmore Industries. Her breath caught. While she had not dared to think that completing Mrs. Harshaw's commission would win her job back, the thought wasn't unwelcome. Could this be a letter inviting her to return?

She tore the letter open and read,

*Dear Lorna,*

*I am writing to request your presence in my office at 10 a.m. on Monday, March 17. I trust that this time will be convenient for you. If not, please let me know at your earliest convenience.*

*Sincerely,*
*Douglas Tompkins*

She lowered the page with shaking hands. There was little to go on here, but she hoped the brief note pointed to good news. But would resuming her job be good news? She'd confessed the truth about her designs to Mrs. Harshaw. Arthur, Boyd, Vivian, and Gentry all knew that the designs she'd presented as her own were created by another. She no longer desired to live the lie she'd committed to when she'd given Gentry train fare and left her to find her own way in the world.

She was a different person now.

Lorna reread the note, finding it no more illuminating. She sighed. It looked like she'd have all weekend to ponder what she would do if Mr. Tompkins did indeed want her back.

# 45

# LORNA

ASHEVILLE, NORTH CAROLINA
MARCH 17, 1924

Entering the weaving cottage behind Grove Park Inn felt strange after being away so long. Lorna held her head high and smiled without meeting anyone's eyes. She realized she owed her coworkers an explanation, but what would she say? She supposed that would depend on what Mr. Tompkins had to say.

Gloria sat at her desk, pecking away at a typewriter. Lorna squared her shoulders and approached. "Good morning. Mr. Tompkins is expecting me."

The secretary kept typing until she came to the end of the line of text and hit the return lever with a ding. For a moment, Lorna thought she would continue. Her mouth went dry at the notion that she was being given the cold shoulder.

But then Gloria looked up and smiled. And while it was a cool smile that didn't reach her eyes, Lorna was grateful for it. "He said that I should send you in as soon as you arrived."

"Thank you." Gloria didn't rise to escort her but looked at the closed door behind her pointedly. Lorna took the hint and opened it herself.

Mr. Tompkins was seated behind his desk, hands folded in front of him. A man she didn't recognize sat in one of two chairs facing the desk. "Come in, Lorna. Please be seated." His words sounded formal. Were they also welcoming? She couldn't tell.

Once she was seated, Mr. Tompkins pressed his hands flat against the desktop. "Thank you for agreeing to come in today. Since you are no longer an employee, it's much appreciated."

Lorna's heart sank. It didn't sound as though she was getting her job back. Of course, she was still on the fence about whether she even wanted it back.

"Our business today is of a rather delicate nature," Mr. Tompkins continued. He darted a look at the stranger, who gave a small nod. "Mrs. Harshaw has informed us that you completed your commission most satisfactorily." Lorna smiled. "However . . ." He paused, allowing tension to build. Was he doing this intentionally? Mr. Tompkins cleared his throat. "She also informed us that you told her the design was not your own." Now he looked uncomfortable. Lorna half expected him to stick a finger behind his collar to loosen it. "And if she understood you correctly, several of your earlier designs were not your own, as well."

Silence filled the room. Lorna thought perhaps she was supposed to say something, but what? Of all the conversations she'd imagined having, this was not one of them.

The stranger shifted in his seat and took a breath. "We are concerned about the legalities involved," he said.

"I beg your pardon?" Lorna's head swiveled from one man to the other.

"If someone else were to claim the designs, it could make

for a sticky situation." The stranger tapped a finger on the arm of his chair. "I am an attorney for Mr. Seely. He is eager to ensure there are no claims made against Biltmore Industries."

"Hang the legalities," Mr. Tompkins said. "It's simply bad for business. If word gets out that our fabric designs are . . . are forged, our customers will be justifiably concerned. We have a spotless reputation, and you, young lady, have opened the door to sullying it."

Lorna shrank in her chair. So. Not a job offer. It almost sounded as if they were going to haul her off to jail.

She finally found her tongue. "I'm not certain what you want from me."

Mr. Tompkins slapped the desk. "I want to know from whom you got those designs."

Lorna blew out a sigh. "From a gifted weaver—who's forgiven me for claiming them as my own. She says she's just glad to see her designs being appreciated by others."

The attorney drew out a small notebook and pencil. "We'll need her name and address so we can ensure that what you say is true."

Lorna opened her mouth, then snapped it shut again. Would Vivian want that sort of attention? Would she mind having men such as these turn up on her front porch to ask about her drafts? Lorna suspected she would mind. "I'm afraid I'm not at liberty to share that information with you. She's a very private person."

"Miss Blankenship, this simply will not do." Mr. Tompkins's face had gone red. "You must tell us, otherwise what are we to believe? That you are *forgiven* for taking credit for someone else's designs, and all is well now? Nonsense! You'll have to do better than that."

Lorna's hands started trembling. Not six months earlier she'd been prepared to go to almost any length to hold on to her job, to preserve her reputation and the life she'd grown accustomed to. Now she realized none of that mattered. Well, perhaps it mattered a little, but other things mattered so much more. She'd longed for Mr. Tompkins, Mr. Seely, and everyone else at Biltmore Industries to see her as an indispensable part of the business. She'd imagined ladies like Edith Vanderbilt wearing her cloth and recommending it to their friends. She would be *known*.

Lorna rose on shaky legs and pressed her hands to her stomach. She *was* known. By Arthur and Vivian and Gentry, which was infinitely better than being known by people who didn't care about her well-being. "I'm afraid the best I can offer is to ask the weaver if she would like to be identified. If she doesn't mind, I will give you her name. Otherwise . . ." She trailed off. Otherwise what? Otherwise these two men could go jump in the French Broad River?

Mr. Tompkins stood and leaned across his desk. He stabbed at it with a finger. "You have until tomorrow. If we do not hear from you, we will have to consider what legal action we may need to take to protect Biltmore Industries."

Lorna felt a wave of nausea wash over her, but she didn't let it show. Or at least she hoped she didn't. "Very well," she said and left on legs she prayed would see her to the door.

. . . . . . . . . .

Lorna made her way to Vivian's cabin. She had a deadline to meet. Again. And this time she was hoping that Vivian would accept the credit that was due her. Which would, of course, be the final nail in Lorna's coffin. Still, it felt right. Maybe she could just stay there on the mountaintop where no one would ever see her or know her. She would become a recluse. A strange old woman living away from the eyes of the outside world.

The idea held a certain appeal.

It also terrified her. It was one thing to imagine a new life for herself, yet it was quite another to give up everything one was accustomed to in order to have that new life.

While the day had been cold and sunny when she started her walk up the mountain, clouds had since pushed their way in, with snow beginning to fall heavily as she neared the top. Gentry must have seen her approach because the young woman burst from the cabin to run and meet her.

"Isn't the snow glorious?" she crowed. She whirled through the fat flakes, her head tilted back. She stuck her tongue out and laughed when snow melted in her mouth.

Lorna, who had been eager to get inside out of the weather, slowed and tilted her own head back. With no wind, the flakes seemed to materialize from the sky above and drift down to brush, feather soft, against her cheeks. She felt Gentry take her hand and glanced at her. Her former protégé smiled and whispered, "It's so very quiet."

They both gazed skyward and let the silence, like the snow, settle over them. Lorna felt both the cold of the day and the heat of Gentry's hand. Inhaling deeply, she tried to think how best to describe it all. Clean. Pure. Fresh. She blinked snowflakes from her lashes and turned to see Vivian standing on the porch, joy dancing in her eyes.

"What in the world are the pair of you doing?" Vivian called. "Next you'll be making snow angels."

Gentry released Lorna's hand and flopped into the snow with a giggle. Lying on her back, she swung her arms and legs wide, then carefully stood and took a giant step away so as not to mar her masterpiece. She looked back at her angel. "Haven't made one of those since before Mama and I were parted." She sighed. "It's just about perfect."

"Not quite," Lorna said. She looked around and found a stick. She carefully leaned forward and drew a halo over the snow angel's head. "There. Now she's perfect."

Vivian approached and wrapped a warm arm around Lorna's waist. Gentry did the same, and they watched the angel as it began to fill with snow.

"Perfection rarely lingers," Vivian said. "But isn't it fine while it lasts?"

Tears pricked Lorna's eyes, although she couldn't say why.

"Now, come inside and get warm by the fire," Vivian urged. "I've got a pot of hot coffee ready and, if you can believe it, angel food cake."

They trooped inside, the warmth and aromas filling Lorna's senses in a completely different way. It was like the color and texture of threads changing in a piece of fabric. Contrasting. Complementary. Shifting in a pleasing way. She stood still for a moment, an idea for a pattern filling her mind. Her fingers itched for a piece of paper.

"What brings you up the mountain on such a raw day?" Vivian asked.

Lorna startled, the idea evaporating as quickly as it had come. Right. She did have a reason for being here.

"Mr. Tompkins knows all those drafts weren't mine." She tugged off her gloves and removed her scarf and coat. "He's none too happy and is demanding to know who the real designer is."

"Did you tell him?" Vivian's question sounded sharp.

"No. That's why I'm here. I wasn't sure you'd want him—or anyone else—to know."

Vivian gathered mugs and plates, the clatter of dishes filling the gap her silence left. Finally she spoke. "As it happens, I'd just as soon my name not be bandied about at Biltmore Industries." She sliced a sizable hunk of cake, set it on a plate, and handed the plate to Lorna. "I've found peace here on the mountain."

"I promise I won't tell anyone if you don't want me to."

Gentry swallowed a huge bite of cake before chiming in.

"I think you should take credit, Mama. You're a genius, and people should know."

"Why?" Vivian asked. "So they can pester me for more?" She shook her head. "I can't even weave anymore with my hands like they are. And as for my designs, I don't create them to please anyone. I just catch them as they drift through the air. The last thing I want is for people to start asking for a little more blue or something to match their hat." She laughed. "That would kill the joy of doing it."

"Mr. Tompkins would likely pay for your drafts even if you didn't want anyone else to know," Lorna said. "It would make your life easier."

"I doubt it. Ready money is convenient enough, but as soon as you start doing something for money, it gets harder, not easier." She breathed in the steam rising from her mug of coffee. "Anyway, my life currently is as complicated as I want it." She winked at Gentry. "So how about you tell Mr. Tompkins that Sabine Brooks wrote those drafts?"

"But she's . . . dead." Lorna couldn't fathom what Vivian was suggesting.

"She is. And she was a better weaver than I. Let's give her the credit, get you off the hook, and leave me out of it."

Lorna blinked. Would that work? Would that satisfy Mr. Tompkins and put his mind at ease since a dead woman couldn't come forward to cause trouble? "But she's been gone for quite some time—she couldn't have designed the fabric for Cornelia."

"Tell him you found the draft. That no one knew it was anything special, but you recognized its beauty and claimed it."

Lorna frowned. "I'm not sure that telling more lies is the right thing to do."

"I'll leave that up to you," Vivian said. "You have my permission if you need it." Her voice turned stern. "But you do *not* have my permission to give anyone my name."

329

Lorna nodded and moved to the window to watch the falling snow. No need to decide until tomorrow. For now, she would enjoy being ensconced on the mountain with good friends, a warm fire, and a sweet treat. Everything else could wait.

The morning dawned with the brightness of a million diamonds as the sun's rays struck the newly fallen snow. Gentry was halfway out the door, ready to plunge into the white wonderland, when Vivian stopped her, suggesting they wait for the sun to warm the air a bit first.

Lorna stood at the window, squinting at the brilliance of the day. "How am I going to get down the mountain?"

"Roll like a snowball," Gentry said with a laugh.

Vivian eased up beside Lorna and slipped an arm around her waist. "I think you should wait here until it melts. March is a temperamental month. It's likely to warm up enough to melt much of this snow." She chuckled. "Or it could stick around for the rest of the week, who knows? Either way, we have plenty to eat, and weaving to keep us all occupied. Gentry and I have started a new pattern."

Anxiety crept from Lorna's belly into her arms and legs. She felt twitchy all of a sudden. "Mr. Tompkins is expecting me today. He said he needed an answer about who designed the fabrics."

Vivian gave her a squeeze, then turned to tend the fire. "Like the rest of us, Mr. Tompkins will have to get used to not always getting what he wants."

"But he said there might be some sort of legal action if I don't comply."

Vivian snorted a laugh. "I doubt that."

"What? Why?" Lorna joined Vivian at the warm hearth.

"Do you think he wants to air his dirty laundry out there

330

on the hillside along with the cloth being washed and sized in the sun? Legal action would mean publicity. And the last thing Mr. Tompkins wants is for the world to learn he's been taken."

Lorna stared into the dancing flames. There was truth to what Vivian said. Mr. Tompkins wouldn't want the society ladies to know what she'd been up to. Even after she'd confessed the truth to Mrs. Harshaw, the older woman had seemed intent on pretending she didn't understand. "You're right. Tomorrow will have to be soon enough for Mr. Tompkins."

Gentry cocked her head, like a bird considering a delectable worm. "I think you should tell him you both designed them, and there's much more where that came from."

Lorna furrowed her brow. "What do you mean?"

"Mama can't weave anymore, and you're not all that good at design—why not work together and make more gorgeous fabric? It would benefit the two of you *and* Biltmore Industries. If Mr. Tompkins knows he'll have more fabric coming, all he'll see are dollar signs."

Vivian clapped her hands. "What a wonderful idea! We can go into business together. I'll design while you weave."

Lorna shook her head, trying to catch up. "But I'd still have to tell him who you are. He'll never believe I'm the designer now."

A sly smile spread over Vivian's face. "Tell him the designs are from Sunrise Homespun, a small collective of weavers in Madison County."

Lorna stared at Vivian, trying to take it all in. Then she laughed. "You know, I think that just might work. As it happens, I could use some gainful employment. And Biltmore Industries could use a fresh injection." She gave Gentry a massive hug. "You may have just saved all our skins."

"Excellent," Gentry said. "Now, let's eat up those leftover biscuits with some applesauce and then go play in the snow!"

Vivian grinned. "I suppose I'm not too old to play just yet. How about you, Lorna?"

"It seems I get younger every time I climb this mountain." She eyed the coffeepot on the hearth. "But I'm not so young that I wouldn't like a cup of hot coffee before braving the great outdoors."

They gathered around the table for a simple breakfast, then bundled up and went outside to frolic and play in the snow like the children none of them had ever had a chance to be.

# 46

# ARTHUR

ASHEVILLE, NORTH CAROLINA
MARCH 19, 1924

Arthur watched Boyd drift around the workshop. He was supposed to be sanding toys. Instead, he'd picked up and put down the same wooden giraffe three times, not touching any sandpaper. Now he was fussing with some tools he'd left lying on Arthur's workbench. It was making Arthur nervous on multiple levels. He was trying to think how to ask Boyd if anything was bothering him when his brother turned and looked straight at him.

"Can I ask you a question?"

"Sure." Arthur tried to sound casual.

"Have you ever . . . ? I mean, you're getting up there in years, and I was wondering . . . The thing is . . ."

Arthur's unease began to give way to amusement. "Spit it out, little brother."

"Are you ever gonna get married? I know about that girl who jilted you, but do you think you'd ever marry for real?"

He slumped against the workbench, looking exhausted after stating his question.

Arthur managed not to smile. "You mean the one who pretended to like me so she could elope with the guy she really liked? You mean marry a girl other than that?"

Boyd flushed scarlet. "I shouldn't have brought it up."

Arthur chuckled. "No, I want you to know you can ask me anything. And I'll give you a serious answer." He considered how to word this. "There is a girl. One I've been serious about for a long time. I think she's serious about me too, but I'm taking it slow."

Boyd nodded as if he knew just what Arthur meant. "Lorna. It's because of the being jilted business. That makes sense."

"No. Not because of that." Arthur crossed his arms over his chest. Was it so obvious that even Boyd had noticed? "Because, well . . ." What was the real reason he didn't pursue Lorna with more determination? He huffed a breath and dug deep. If Boyd could face his demons, so could Arthur. "Because I'm afraid."

Boyd frowned. "Afraid she won't want you with your bum foot? See, that's why I'm asking. I'm just not sure a girl would ever want me. I thought this brace would fix me up proper, but I guess it can only do so much."

Arthur sat down on a bench he'd been sanding and patted the seat next to him. Boyd dropped onto it. "There was a time when I was afraid of that very thing. I figured no one would want a man with a clubfoot. But that's not what I'm afraid of now. She pushed me away once, but she's warmed up considerably since then." He thought of Lorna's kisses. "I'm afraid that if I push too hard, she'll go skittering away again." He pulled the carved fawn from his pocket. "Like a startled deer. And I'm afraid if she runs this time, I won't get her back."

Boyd nodded. "Got it. So, how long will you wait?"

"What?"

"I get that you're worried, but how long do you figure it'll take to gain Lorna's trust so she doesn't go running off on you?"

Arthur blinked. "I . . . I don't know."

Boyd rolled his eyes. "How long's it been?"

Arthur flushed. It had been years since he began pursuing Lorna and months since he'd felt her thawing toward him. "A while." Boyd looked at him expectantly. "It's not that simple."

"Women never are," Boyd said. "I'm just glad it's not your foot holding you back." Seemingly satisfied, he went back to the table, picked up the toy giraffe and a piece of sandpaper, and began to smooth its rough edges.

Arthur, on the other hand, took up drifting aimlessly about the room.

⁕⁕⁕⁕⁕

Two days later, Arthur was in the shop at Biltmore Estate, putting the finishing touches on the table that would curve around the fountain in the winter garden. Cornelia, her groom, and the rest of the wedding party would gather there for the wedding breakfast on April twenty-ninth after the ceremony at All Souls.

"Did you fellers see all that plunder in the big house?" Fred, one of the estate's woodworkers, jerked a thumb toward the house.

Arthur had seen it. Wedding gifts were displayed in the entry hall for guests to admire, and he'd been allowed a look. It was a regular treasure trove.

He'd been struck by some of the more ornate items like a Cartier vanity case made of gold with enamel and jewels he couldn't name. And he was particularly taken with a brooch for a Scottish plaid shaped in silver with smoky quartz—now, that was something he could picture Lorna wearing. But the gift that served as the centerpiece for the table was a cascade of homespun reflecting the glory of the Blue Ridge Mountains. He'd heard some of the maids saying with pride that they were certain it was Nell's favorite and that there was a buzz building among the society ladies who wanted their own bit of Sunrise Homespun. He couldn't wait to tell Lorna about it.

"Can you believe Tarheel Nell invited estate workers to her wedding? I'm guessing the wife will want a new dress." Arthur only half listened to the men talking.

"Arthur—you coming to the wedding?"

He looked up to see one of the younger workers—Andrew maybe—looking at him earnestly.

"I'm not sure," he hedged.

"Really? I'll go if Miss Cornelia wants me there. Once-in-a-lifetime chance and all."

"Yes," Arthur agreed, "I suppose it would be a shame to miss it."

He went back to making sure the sections of table fit together seamlessly. He hadn't considered what it meant to be part of Cornelia's big day, but now the idea captured his imagination. It would surely be a grand event, historic even, and he'd enjoy turning up with Lorna on his arm.

His conversation with Boyd had gotten him thinking. What *was* he waiting for? The past several months had changed him. And if he wasn't mistaken, they had changed Lorna, as well. And if she didn't want him, well, that would be good to know, too. Better to break his heart now, all at once, rather than tear it slowly apart over time.

Finished with his work, he moved to put his tools away and noticed that his hands were shaking. Right. He was thinking logically, but his heart wasn't so easily fooled.

And it certainly wasn't eager to be broken. Again.

That evening Arthur combed his hair, wishing the curls would go down and stay that way. Boyd had gone to Angus's to tinker with an automobile. The boy had a notion they should buy one cheap and fix it up, so Angus was teaching him all he knew. Arthur wasn't opposed to the idea, yet he had more pressing matters on his mind at the moment.

He reached for some cologne, then set it back down. No, he was just going to be himself. It was too late to put a shine on things.

Lorna's house was dark when he arrived. A bolt of fear shot through him. It hadn't occurred to him that she'd be anywhere else. But wait, she might be up on the mountain with Vivian and Gentry. He slumped down on her porch steps, resigning himself to having to work up the nerve to approach her another time.

"Arthur?" Lorna's voice came from the street. She climbed the steps and sat down beside him. "I thought it was you."

Arthur's heart raced at the sudden change in circumstance. Was he ready after all? "I thought you might be up on the mountain," he said. "I mean, when I saw you weren't at home."

"I was yesterday. Got snowed in up there." Arthur glanced north as though he might see a snowy mountain. She sighed. "It was one of the most beautiful things I've ever seen—all that snow glittering under the sun."

Arthur nodded in the dim light, not sure how to steer this conversation in the direction he wanted it to go. "I saw your cloth with the wedding presents up at Biltmore House." It wasn't what he'd planned to say, but now that he'd started, he supposed he'd keep going. "Right in the middle, all spread out so folks could get the full effect. Cornelia must really like it."

"I'm glad."

Arthur waited. Was that all she had to say about it?

Lorna took a breath, and he waited for her to ask to hear more about Cornelia's gifts. Instead, she went on as if he hadn't mentioned the fabric that had consumed her for months. "Things seem simpler up there on the mountain."

Arthur tried to find his footing. "I suppose they are in general." He chuckled, his breath coming out in puffs. "The fewer people there are around, the less complicated things seem to be."

Lorna nodded. "I've built a new bridge with Biltmore Industries."

"What?" Arthur did a mental quickstep to catch up. He sensed this was important.

"Mr. Tompkins knows I'm a fraud and insisted that I tell him who the real designer is." She closed her eyes and tilted her head back. "Vivian doesn't want the world to know about her, so I told him the fabric came from Sunrise Homespun—a group of weavers in Madison County—and that there's more where it came from."

Arthur blinked. "Sunrise Homespun? That's what the maids were calling Cornelia's fabric. I wondered why."

A laugh burbled up and out of Lorna like a spring on a hot day. "That was certainly fast. It's just us. Vivian, Gentry, and me. But Mr. Tompkins doesn't need to know that." She shook her head in the semidarkness. "He got all cagey. Asked if I was the go-between for this 'weaving collective.' I told him I was."

Arthur took her hand. It seemed the natural thing to do. "Sounds like you have your job back. Or one much like it."

She shot him a sideways look that he couldn't make out completely. "So you know I was fired. You know I'm a failure and a fraud. That I've let everyone down and am only escaping my sins by some impossible grace."

"I'm beginning to see why staying up on the mountain with Vivian appeals to you." He smiled, hoping she could see it in the gloaming. "You haven't let everyone down. Or at least no more than the rest of us have. And you're trying hard to set things right as far as it depends on you." He squeezed her hand. "No one can ask more than that."

"Oh, they can ask," Lorna said with a little laugh.

Arthur felt his mouth go dry. He had something he wanted to ask. Was this the wrong moment? Or the perfect one? He could see it going both ways. He sent up a silent prayer for the right words and dropped to one knee in front of Lorna.

"Lorna Blankenship, I, too, often feel like a failure and a fraud, trying to put on a good face for the world. I've loved you for what seems like an awfully long time, and I've tried to honor your wishes." She had her free hand over her mouth now. "But I love you. Have for ages, it seems." He felt a little light-headed and hoped he didn't fall off the steps. "Will you . . . ?" He cleared his clogged throat and started again. "Will you consider . . . being my wife?"

The last word came out as a croak, but he'd gotten it done. He'd thrown caution to the wind and done what he'd longed to do for years. Any moment now his fate would be decided, and he would be free—either to love Lorna for the rest of his life or to begin the painful process of letting her go.

# 47

# GENTRY

**ASHEVILLE, NORTH CAROLINA**
**APRIL 1924**

Gentry slipped the new dress her mother had helped her make over her head. It flowed over her figure like warm water. Mama had made the cloth years ago and had saved it for a special occasion. It was a double-pane plaid done entirely in shades of green so that it shimmered like the new leaves of a maple in a gentle spring breeze.

Gentry had never felt prettier. She had never felt more beloved. And she'd never been prouder of anything she'd done. Thanks to Lorna, Aunt Eulah, and now Mama, she'd had the skills needed to make a dress pretty enough for the wedding of a princess. Not to mention the patience it took to finish it. And while she wouldn't be in the chapel for Cornelia's wedding, she would be waiting outside the doors with her family to see the bride.

"Aren't you a picture of perfection!" Mama exclaimed. Tears filled her eyes. "I never dared to dream of a day like this," she added in a husky voice. "Going to a wedding with my beautiful daughter." She swiped at her eyes, blinking fast.

Gentry reached in her pocket, excitement stirring in her breast. Her mother had given her so much. Now it was her turn to give her something—no matter how small it might seem. "I've been saving this for a long time now. It's just about the only thing I managed to keep up with other than my dulcimer." She pulled out a soft white handkerchief and held it out for her mother, showing off the design.

Mama gasped. "Daffodils, my favorite." She took the handkerchief and dabbed at her eyes, laughing now. "How did you know?"

"I *remembered*," Gentry said, emphasizing the word. "Cornelia gave me that when I went up to Biltmore House my first Christmas in Asheville. I told her they were your favorite." She shook her head. "There was one with lilies of the valley too, but I lost it."

"Nearly ten years ago." Mama shook her head. "We were both so very lost then."

"But now we're found," Gentry said.

"For always."

They stood in each other's embrace as if, by loving each other now, they could make up for all the years they'd missed. And as her mother's love seeped into all the dark places in Gentry's spirit, it was like a song rolling through her, spreading light and hope.

> Amazing grace! How sweet the sound
> That saved a wretch like me!
> I once was lost, but now am found;
> Was blind, but now I see.

Yes. At long last she could see past her own sorrow and pain to a future that looked not simple or easy, but bright.

And she could see that she wasn't alone in it. There was Mama and Arthur, and yes, Lorna. All of them forgiving and forgiven.

She breathed in and breathed out, her anxious heart settling into a new rhythm that she itched to play as she strummed the chords of peace, peace, peace.

# 48

# LORNA

**ASHEVILLE, NORTH CAROLINA**
**APRIL 29, 1924**

Lorna tied the sash of her dress into a smart bow. She settled the stylish cloche hat Arthur had gifted her over carefully curled hair. Although the attention wouldn't be on her today, she wanted to look her very best for Cornelia's wedding. She smiled at herself in the mirror. And for Arthur. Although they had only been invited to the reception at Biltmore House—along with 2,498 others—Arthur had arranged for them to slip into the church at the last minute to watch the ceremony from behind a curtain.

"But don't be getting any ideas about our wedding," he'd admonished. "I'm no Vanderbilt."

Lorna flushed at the memory of how she'd assured him that she'd rather have him than the richest man in the world. An embrace had ensued that made her more eager than ever for their own wedding day to arrive.

"Where's my girl?" Arthur's voice boomed from the front

porch. Lorna hurried out to greet him with a chaste kiss. "I thought Vivian and Gentry were coming?"

"They are. They'll meet us outside the church for the procession. Although it was all Vivian could do to contain Gentry once she heard we were going to be on hand to watch the ceremony. Isn't it just like our sweet Nell to save the pews in the transepts for estate staff? I heard Mrs. Vanderbilt is even sending a car for old Frank the gatekeeper." Arthur drew her into his arms. "My but that's a fetching hat. Good enough for royalty." She laughed, and this time the kiss was a bit less chaste.

Lorna dabbed at tears as she and Arthur slipped out of the church ahead of the wedding party. The service had been lovely, of course, but each moment had also been laced with the thought that soon she would say those same words, would commit her life, and would spend the rest of her days with this wonderful man by her side.

"A family," she whispered. Yes. She would be part of a family once again.

Gentry caught sight of them and waved a gorgeous shawl in the air. Lorna recognized it as one her former protégé had woven with her mother. They hurried to join the pair in the throng waiting to see Tarheel Nell emerge from the church doors a wedded woman. She was surprised to see that even Boyd had turned up for the event. He gave her a rueful smile and ducked his head. "Once-in-a-lifetime chance, they say." He mumbled the words, but his eyes were fixed on the doors just like everyone else's.

Outside All Souls Cathedral, two rows of estate workers' children in frilly white dresses held baskets and tall floral wands to form an aisle for Mr. and Mrs. John Francis Amherst Cecil to walk along. Cornelia finally appeared, a shy smile on her lips. She looked so elegant in her lacy dress, and her husband was the very picture of a proper English gentleman.

"Do you see the flowers on her veil and the toes of her slippers?" Arthur's whisper tickled Lorna's ear. "Chauncey Beadle, the old estate superintendent, sent her those from Florida. Isn't it just like our Nell to wear them?" He took her hand, and the warmth she felt had little to do with Cornelia's sentimental flowers.

As they watched the happy couple wave and accept well wishes, Vivian slipped up on Lorna's other side. She wrapped an arm around Lorna's waist and beckoned Gentry to join them. Boyd winked at Gentry, who rolled her eyes. He might be sixteen to Gentry's twenty-one, but Lorna suspected he had a bit of a crush all the same.

Lorna looked at these people who, though they couldn't take the place of her mother and father, had become her rock and her anchor. She remembered once thinking that if she found Gentry for Vivian, she could somehow put a broken family back together again. Something that could never be done for her. And while her own dear parents could never be replaced in her heart, she realized that family might not be as elusive as she once thought. She'd been hiding for such a long time, hoping no one would know her well enough to break her heart. But now she was known again, the good and the bad, and it was . . . wonderful.

Arthur squeezed her fingers, and she looked up at him, tears in her eyes. "I love you," she said.

Such a look of love washed over his face that he didn't need to speak a word to tell her exactly how he felt. Yet she was grateful just the same when he pressed his lips to her ear and whispered, "And I love you."

# *Epilogue*

# ARTHUR

The day had arrived at last. Today he would make Lorna his own. She would take his name to go with the heart she'd stolen long ago.

Arthur stilled his hands even as he reflexively reached for the carved fawn in his pocket. His breathing slowed as he thought about that week before Cornelia's wedding. She'd come to the workshop to give her approval of the table they'd built for her wedding breakfast. All smiles and joy, she'd gladdened every man's heart. After thanking them profusely, she'd paused and taken in the men, the table, and the workshop as though she planned to describe what she saw in detail later. His breath hitched when her warm gaze landed on him.

"Arthur," she said, "may I speak to you?"

"Gladly," he answered, stepping aside with her.

She reached into the pocket of her dress and withdrew something wrapped in a bit of crinkly paper. "I found this

347

not long ago, along with a note of explanation. It would seem my father tucked it away with plans to return it to you one day." Tears glistened in her eyes but did not fall. "It's my honor to do so on his behalf."

Arthur, utterly befuddled, unwrapped the small object and found himself struck dumb. There, lying in his hand, was the deer he'd carved when he was eight years old. He smiled. Or nearly nine, as he'd thought at the time.

"That was so very long ago," he said.

"My father wrote that he was quite taken with you and your skill. He hoped that you would come to Asheville and perfect your gift." Now a tear slipped free. "I can see from your skill with this table that you did. He would be so very proud." She turned and hurried away before Arthur could speak.

"Thank you," he said to the air where she'd been.

And now the fawn no longer resided in his pocket. Instead, it stood under a little glass dome in his shop beside its mother. He'd smiled to see that as a child there had still been a great deal for him to learn about carving wood. Among other things.

He clasped his empty hands behind him and looked to the rear of the church as the wedding march began to play. Lorna appeared looking a hundred times more radiant than any princess from a castle ever could. She smiled, throwing radiance off in every direction. He marveled, uncertain how the tangled threads of their lives had come together to create this gorgeous pattern.

He'd felt like the odd man out his whole life. Forever being pushed where others thought he should fit. The flaw in life's pattern. But as Lorna neared on Boyd's arm and reached out to take his hand, he felt something click into place.

Here.

Here was exactly where he belonged.

# Author's Note

In the fall of 1999, my husband and I lost our home near the coast of South Carolina in flooding caused by Hurricane Floyd. Moving to higher ground felt like a good idea. We'd visited Biltmore Estate a few years earlier, and Asheville, North Carolina, seemed a likely spot. When I learned the public relations department at Biltmore Estate had an opening, the pieces began to fall into place.

I worked at Biltmore for just over six years. It was a dream job that meant I got to go behind the scenes of America's largest privately owned home. I had a walkie-talkie and was authorized to unhook those velvet ropes, but only for a very good reason. I had the chance to walk along the balcony in the library, and peek into the yet to be restored areas of the house. I stood in the organ loft of the banquet hall as the massive Christmas tree was hoisted into place. And one magical Christmas I was allowed to decorate the tree in George Vanderbilt's gilded bedroom. It was incredible.

But my favorite thing about Biltmore wasn't the historic house, the treasures inside it, or even the spectacular gardens—it was the people. Just as in the days when the Vanderbilts were in residence, a large staff is needed to ensure everything runs smoothly. Curators get each historical detail precisely right. The floral displays staff change out the décor seasonally. (Visit the house at Christmastime!) The maintenance staff keeps everything clean and in working order. The hosts continuously learn about and share historical tidbits. The farm and gardens staff deadhead roses and mow hay. And that doesn't even begin to cover the administrative staff.

I owe a debt of gratitude to every person I worked with at Biltmore Estate. I'd especially like to thank Ellen Rickman, director of museum services, for answering obscure questions like the one about a wedding breakfast happening in the afternoon, and Cathy Barnhardt, retired floral displays manager, for being an early reader. Both know more about Biltmore than I could ever hope to.

I write stories about Appalachia. I love how the Vanderbilts, while bringing their Gilded Age influence to the mountains, were in turn influenced by Appalachia. Edith did indeed wear a homespun suit when she famously spoke to the North Carolina General Assembly. And Cornelia, or Tarheel Nell, was beloved by the estate's staff and the locals. Yes, they really did send a car for Frank the gatekeeper so he could attend Cornelia's wedding.

If you'd like to know more about Biltmore Estate and Biltmore Industries, below is a list of books to consider:

Alexander, Bill. *Image of America: The Biltmore Estate Gardens and Grounds*. Arcadia Publishing, 2015.

Bryan, John M. *Biltmore Estate: The Most Distinguished Private Place*. Rizzoli Press, 1994.

Covington, Howard E. Jr. *Lady on the Hill: How Biltmore Estate Became an American Icon*. John Wiley & Sons, 2006.

Kiernan, Denise. *The Last Castle*. Atria Books, 2017.

Rickman, Ellen Erwin. *Images of America: Biltmore Estate*. Arcadia Publishing, 2005.

Rybczynski, Witold. *A Clearing in the Distance: Frederick Law Olmsted and America in the 19th Century*. Touchstone, 2000.

Stein, Susan R., ed. *The Architecture of Richard Morris Hunt*. University of Chicago Press, 1986.

# Acknowledgments

This is my tenth published novel, including two novellas. I'm astonished and humbled to have seen my dream of being an author so roundly fulfilled. "Every good and perfect gift is from above, coming down from the Father of the heavenly lights, who does not change like shifting shadows" (James 1:17 NIV).

Who else to thank? My indefatigable agent, Wendy Lawton. My editor, Dave Long, who constantly pokes and prods me into writing better stories even when I'd be perfectly content to settle for the first version I pitched to him. He'd be annoying if he weren't so often right. Of course, this process would be utterly impossible without the talents of the entire publishing team at Bethany House, many of whom are too humble to want to see their names in print.

Thanks also go to my baby brother and best friend, Daniel, who reads my books and tells me exactly what he thinks, even if I don't like it. And to my wonderful, supportive, handsome, and funny husband, Jim Thomas. He reads my books and recognizes their genius every time.

# For more by
# Sarah Loudin Thomas,

read on
for an excerpt from

Available now
wherever books are sold.

# ONE

**KLINE, WEST VIRGINIA**
**LATE MAY 1932**

Sulley tore a rag into strips and wrapped each coin before tucking it into the bib pocket of his overalls. Wouldn't do to jingle as he made his way out of Kline after the sun went down. Was it his fault this place hadn't had a good rain since Noah started rounding up all the animals two by two? It'd take a miracle to find water around here.

But he'd made the effort. Put on a good show. The second well they'd dug had even produced a little wet down in the bottom. But it was just a seep—not enough to matter. Still, his time and effort oughta be worth what he was tucking away with such care. Of course, not everyone would see it his way. Which was why he'd promised to give dowsing one more try in the morning.

Except he wouldn't be here come morning. He'd written out instructions for them to dig a well near a snowball bush heavy with powder puff blooms. It was a long shot, but who knew? Maybe they would hit water and he'd be a hero.

A long-gone hero. He tucked the last coin away and settled back to wait for the moonless night to hide his leaving.

. . . . . . . . .

Jeremiah Weber was pretty sure Sullivan Harris couldn't find his own belly button with both hands. But his neighbors had gone and hired the self-proclaimed water witcher, believing he was going to transform Kline by finding wells up on the hills and ridges. Currently, most everyone lived within water-toting distance of Mill Run, which was the only reliable source of water. Even Jeremiah's well—one of the best around—typically ran dry a couple of times each year. But he always managed—there were springs for drinking and cooking. As for bathing, well, that could wait when necessary.

As if finding a few wells would suddenly bring folks rushing in from the cities. For pity's sake, did they even *want* that? He'd read about Hoovervilles popping up around the country, and they sounded terrible. But the deacons at church had this wild notion they could attract businessmen who'd lost almost everything in that stock market mess two years ago. They argued Kline could capitalize on a return to the land and farming—especially with the drought out west—if they could ensure a steady water supply.

Jeremiah shook his head as he stepped up onto Meredith's front porch. Why they wanted strangers and hoboes moving here and causing trouble, Jeremiah did not know. But then he'd never been one to rock the boat. As a matter of fact, he'd long been the one they looked to when the boat needed hauling to shore, so the hole in the bottom could be patched.

"Meri? You ready?" he called through the screen door. Arnold and Wendy tumbled out, each one grabbing ahold of a leg. The boy was four and the girl almost three. They giggled and grinned up at him. "Alright then," he said. "Got a good grip?"

"Yes sir," Arnold crowed, latching on like a baby possum in a storm. Wendy just giggled some more and planted her little bare feet more firmly on top of his right boot. He began to walk around the porch, stepping wide and high as the children clung and laughed so hard tears ran down their cheeks.

"Jeremiah, you don't have to do that." Meredith appeared, wrapping a shawl around her shoulders and cinching it at her waist.

He shrugged. It wasn't any trouble, and young'uns in Kline had little enough to entertain them. Of course, lately, they'd had a water dowser putting on a show. And Jeremiah had a suspicion that's all it was. "Why they're giving that man another chance, I don't know," he said.

Meredith patted his arm. "Hope springs eternal," she said. "I think today's the day!"

"Hope so," he grunted. Meredith was forever an optimist, which was a wonder when she'd married young, had two babies lickety-split, and then lost her husband to typhus. "Now if I can pry this pair of possums off my legs, we'll go see if the third time really is the charm."

They started down the road toward the church, enjoying the warmth of a bright spring day. Jeremiah was well familiar with the church building since it served as their schoolhouse during the week and he served as the teacher. It wasn't something he'd set out to do, but while he looked like a lumberman, he'd actually gone to college and studied history. He'd meant to be a professor, until his widowed father took sick and he'd come home to look after him. It'd been twenty-five years now since Dad died and the locals asked him to teach their kids so they didn't have to go so far for schooling. He always had been a soft touch when someone needed help.

Which was why he'd tried to help by suggesting they

run Sullivan Harris off. Advice that fell on deaf ears. Just the day before, Sulley said he thought there was a likely spot for water out back of the one-room church, much to the delight of the deacons. Having a good source of water there would be a boon.

The dowser had slept on the ground the night before, claiming it helped put him in "synchronicity" with the water. Jeremiah thought it was all blather and said so, but he'd been outvoted when he suggested they ask for their money back and run Sulley out of the country.

As they approached the church, Jeremiah could see a tight knot of people out front. When Joe Randolph—head deacon—looked up, he saw him blanch.

"Found water already?" he called as they drew closer.

Joe pulled away from the group, his eyes darting all around. "Well, no. It would seem Mr. Harris has left us instructions on where to dig."

"Instructions? What kind of nonsense is that? Where is he?"

Joe swallowed hard and stuttered, "I-it would s-seem he's not about."

Jeremiah knew his face had turned stormy. Joe held both hands up. "Now, the note said he'd stayed for as long as he could. Probably has family eager to see him."

"Then why in tarnation wouldn't he have mentioned that before?" Stomping around back, Jeremiah sized up the situation. There was no camp. No bedding laid out by a fire ring. No signs of someone spending the night. "Couldn't find water so he ran off with your money," he announced to the group trickling around the corner of the building. "Nothing but a swindler. I told you we needed to ask for that money back!"

Joe licked his lips and looked nervously around the group. "Let's not jump to conclusions. He left us information about where to dig." He held up a piece of paper. "It seems to me we shouldn't call the man a swindler until we're certain of the facts."

"Horsefeathers!" Jeremiah hollered. "When did you get to be so doggone trusting of strangers?"

"But what can we do?" This from another deacon who was wringing his hands. "We borrowed some of that money we gave him from the General Conference. We have to pay it back in a year. Getting a well was supposed to bring more folks in. Help fill the collection plate." His eyes were wide, and he looked like he might be sick.

"We've got our tools ready," Joe said, sounding like he was gaining confidence. "Best thing is to dig where he said, see if we hit water, and go from there."

"You're wasting your time," Jeremiah said. "Go after him is what I'd do. And quick, too, before he has a chance to get very far." As soon as he spoke, he realized his mistake. Hope dawned in several eyes, and Meredith stepped closer to curl a hand around his arm and bat her eyelashes at him. "You'd do that for us?"

"I wasn't . . . what I meant to say was . . ." He looked at the expectant faces around him. These folks scrimped and saved to be able to pay someone to find them water. Never mind that he thought they'd been taken for fools. He let his shoulders fall. "Alright then, dig your well. Here's hoping I'm wrong."

By dinnertime, Jeremiah felt pretty sure he hadn't been wrong. And by suppertime everyone else was in agreement. The well started dry and stayed that way, hope fading with the day's light. Jeremiah might have enjoyed feeling vindicated if it weren't for the hopeful looks everyone kept throwing his way. Last thing he wanted to do was light out after some charlatan with a good head start.

Joe, who had stripped to his undershirt and was now covered in grime, hoisted another bucket of dirt from the well and added it to the mound. Jeremiah had taken his turn down in the hole and was now leaning against the side of the church, watching. Joe sighed and ambled over.

"I'm afraid you might have been right about Sullivan Harris." He wiped his face with a dirty handkerchief. "Thing is, we're stuck between the devil and the deep blue sea here. Did you mean it when you said you'd go after him?"

Jeremiah felt a knot forming in the pit of his stomach. "I was just saying what I'd do if it were my money. Wasn't exactly offering."

"Even so." Several other folks gathered around, hope shining through the dirt and weariness of the day. Meri and the kids had gone home, but he could still see their woeful faces in his mind's eye.

"We'll look after your place for ye." This from Able Stevens, his eighty-two-year-old neighbor who could outwork most men half his age. "School's about done, and we'll help out with gasoline."

Jeremiah closed his eyes and inhaled deeply, then let the air out like he was rationing it. *"Thou shalt love thy neighbor as thyself."* He'd often thought that verse was extra hard. "Alright then." He let his shoulders drop low. "Too late to start today. I'll head out come morning." He was pretty sure he was going to regret this.

**SARAH LOUDIN THOMAS** is the director of Jan Karon's Mitford Museum in Hudson, North Carolina. She holds a bachelor's degree in English from Coastal Carolina University and is the author of the acclaimed novels *The Right Kind of Fool*, winner of the 2021 Selah Book of the Year Award, and *Miracle in a Dry Season*, winner of the 2015 INSPY Award. Sarah has also been a finalist for the Christy Award, the ACFW Carol Award, and the Christian Book of the Year Award. She and her husband live in western North Carolina. Learn more at www.SarahLoudinThomas.com.

# Sign Up for Sarah's Newsletter

Keep up to date with Sarah's latest news on book releases and events by signing up for her email list at the link below.

SarahLoudinThomas.com

**FOLLOW SARAH ON SOCIAL MEDIA**

Sarah Loudin Thomas            @SarahLoudinThomas

# More from Sarah Loudin Thomas

After promising a town he'd find them water and then failing, Sullivan Harris is on the run; but he grows uneasy when one success makes folks ask him to find other things—like missing items or sons. When men are killed digging the Hawks Nest Tunnel, Sully is compelled to help, and it becomes the catalyst for finding what even he has forgotten—hope.

*The Finder of Forgotten Things*

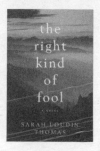

When deaf teen Loyal Raines stumbles upon a dead body in the nearby river, his absentee father, Creed, is shocked the boy runs to him first. Pulled into the investigation, Creed discovers that it is the boy's courage, not his inability to hear, that sets him apart, and he will have to do more than solve a murder if he wants to win his family's hearts again.

*The Right Kind of Fool*

After the rival McLean clan guns down his cousin, Colman Harpe chooses peace over seeking revenge with his family. But when he hears God tell him to preach to the McLeans, he attempts to run away—and fails—leaving him sick and suffering in their territory. He soon learns that appearances can be deceiving, and the face of evil doesn't look like he expected.

*When Silence Sings*

## BETHANYHOUSE

 Bethany House Fiction

 @BethanyHouseFiction

 @Bethany_House

 @BethanyHouseFiction

 Free exclusive resources for your book group at BethanyHouseOpenBook.com

 Sign up for our fiction newsletter today at BethanyHouse.com